PRESUMED GUILTY

Also by James Scott Bell

PRESUMED GUILTY

JAMES SCOTT
BELL

ZONDERVAN

ZONDERVAN.com/
AUTHORTRACKER
follow your favorite authors

ZONDERVAN®

Presumed Guilty
Copyright © 2006 by James Scott Bell

Requests for information should be addressed to:

Zondervan, *Grand Rapids, Michigan 49530*

ISBN: 0-310-28588-7
ISBN: 978-0-310-28588-5

Interior design by Beth Shagene

Printed in the United States of America

07 08 09 10 11 12 • 18 17 16 15 14 13 12 11 10 9 8 7 6 5 4 3 2 1

For E. and The Chaz Man

PRESUMED GUILTY

PROLOGUE

My life is marked by contrasts—then and now, light and darkness.

Heaven and hell.

Marked too by memory.

I remember the exact moment it started.

In fact, in a perverse recollection of detail, I even know what I was wearing—Dockers slacks and a blue golf shirt with the Wailea Emerald Course logo on it. My shoes were the brown slip-ons my wife had bought for me online a couple of months earlier. No socks.

I was in my office, looking out the window at the stunning view of the valley. The church occupied twenty of the most valuable acres in Southern California, prime property we bought when we outgrew our smaller space in Northridge ten years before.

And I can remember my thought patterns that day, leading up to the moment she walked in. I was thinking of Moses, another mountain-top man, and how his human frailty kept him from the Promised Land. He struck the rock, and water flowed, but he had disobeyed God.

As I was about to do.

And that is why I am here.

A jail cell is smaller than it looks in some old James Cagney movie. When you're in one it doesn't seem possible for life to continue, for the paper-thin fragility that is human existence to sustain itself.

But since my life has ceased to exist, I suppose nothing is lost.

Do I suppose I can regain my life by writing down these confessions? Or am I writing just so I can eventually place another volume on my shelf?

Yes, even within these walls, my ambition bares its teeth and grinds through the lining of my guilt. Maybe that's why I'm here. Maybe that's why God put me here after all.

Maybe that's why I did the unthinkable.

Unthinkable, at least, if you were to look at me ten years ago. Even five. Then you would have seen a star. Not a comet, flaming out, a fading tail of cosmic dust in its wake.

No, a real star set in the evangelical heavenlies.

Then I fell, let it all slip away, that day in my office overlooking the valley.

How did it happen? All I know is that, somehow, it began.

It began with a plea.

PART I

Other men's sins are before our eyes;
our own are behind our back.

Seneca

ONE

1.

"Help me. Please."

A note of hopelessness vibrated under the girl's voice, a soft trilling like a night bird's cry. Ron Hamilton felt it in his chest—an electric snap, a static in the heart.

"I'll do anything I can," he told the girl. She must have been around twenty, though he had long since given up guessing ages. When he turned fifty a year ago, he was certain selected segments of his brain went into meltdown, like a kid's snow cone on a hot summer day.

"I've done a terrible thing, I don't know what to do." The girl looked at the floor, and when she did, Ron couldn't help noticing her shape under the snug dress. It was a red summery thing, with thin straps over the shoulders. Before he could stop it, his gaze lingered, then he forced himself to look away. His focus landed on his seminary diploma, hanging on his office wall. Doctor of Divinity. But he couldn't keep looking at it and give her the attention she deserved.

How was he going to avert his eyes if this interview continued?

Best thing he could do was put her at ease, then ease her out of the office. The interview would be over and he'd pass her off to someone else, maybe the professional counseling team the church had an arrangement with.

"I'm sorry. Let's back up." He looked at the Post-It note on his desk, the one where he'd scribbled her name: *Melinda Perry*.

"How long have you been coming to church here, Melinda?"

"Little less than a year."

Ron didn't recognize her face. But then, with the church at roughly eight thousand members, it would have been easy for her to blend in. So many others did.

"What attracted you here?" he asked, putting his marketing hat on. He couldn't help himself sometimes. Seventeen years of good marketing sense had built up Hillside Community Church.

She looked at him. "You."

Another electrical snap went off inside him. And this time it tripped an alarm. *Danger here. Remember last year . . .*

Yet he found himself wanting to know exactly what Melinda Perry meant. What could that hurt?

"I listened to you on the radio," she said.

Made sense. His sermons were recorded and played on L.A.'s second largest Christian radio station. Three times throughout the week.

"Well, I'm glad somebody's listening." He laughed.

She didn't laugh. "You don't know what it meant. You saved my life."

Now he was hooked. "Really?"

"Oh, yes. You preach from the Bible, right?"

"Always." Well, he attached Bible verses to his favorite topics.

"You were talking about something to do with heaven. Do you remember that?"

He fought the temptation to smile. "I talk about heaven quite a bit—"

"In this one, you said heaven was going to be a place, a *real* place, where we'll live."

"Yes, what the Bible calls the new earth."

"And streets made out of gold and all that?"

"All that, yes."

"And I was thinking of snuffing my candle, Pastor Ron, I really was. You don't know what I've been through." She paused. "Anyway, I was flipping around the radio stations and I heard you. I heard your voice. I thought what a nice voice. You really have cool tones, Pastor."

"Thanks." Heat seeped into his cheeks.

"And what you said about heaven made me cry, it really hit me, and that's why I started coming to Hillside. I sit in the back mostly. I don't want people to get too close to me."

"But why not?"

"That's part of the reason I'm here. To tell you why."

Did she have a boyfriend? She looked like she could have many boyfriends.

"But I'm afraid," she said.

"Of what?"

"Talking about it."

He wanted to know. "Would it help to talk to a professional counselor? I can arrange for you to have a free session with a—"

"No. I want to talk to you. You're the only one who can help me."

"There are others who are trained—"

"No." She almost sounded angry. "You have to tell me first."

"Tell you what?"

"If God can ever forgive me."

Without so much as a beat, he ran off a familiar message. "That's what God does best. He forgives us. Anything."

"Anything? Even something so bad ..." She looked down.

There was no way he was going to let her go now. He almost got up to put a comforting hand on her shoulder, but the alarm sounded again, and he stayed in his chair.

"Go ahead and tell me. Take your time."

He watched her chest rise with breath.

"All right," she said. "It started this way."

2.

Dallas Hamilton put her hand over her left eye and said, "Whoop-de-do!"

The boy looked at her, confused, then shook his head. "That's not a pirate."

"You think all pirates have to say *argh*?"

The boy, a six-year-old named Jamaal, nodded tentatively.

"How boring! You can be any kind of pirate you want. That's the thing about the imagination. And this ship can be as big as you want it to be."

Dallas picked up the square of Styrofoam from the craft table, took a straw, and stuck it in the middle of the square. The boy and his mother watched Dallas as if she were a diamond cutter.

"See that?" Dallas said. "That's the mast."

"What's a mast?" Jamaal said.

"The place where the sail goes. We're going to put a sail on the straw, see?" Dallas held up a square of construction paper. "And that's how you get a sailing ship. And here's the best part." Dallas took a couple of thumbtacks and a rubber band from the clear plastic box on the craft table. She'd carved out a square section from the stern of the foam boat and now secured the rubber band across that span with the tacks.

"This is where we're going to put the paddle. You wind it up in the rubber band, and it'll make the boat go in the water. No batteries required."

"That's nice, huh, Jamaal?" the boy's mother said. Her name was Tiana Williams. She was twenty-three, but to Dallas she looked ten years older. The ugly puffiness around Tiana's right eye was part of the reason. It marred what was otherwise a pretty face of smooth, dusky skin.

"That's your ship," Dallas said, "and you don't have to be like any other pirate. You can say *whoop-de-do* or any other word you want."

Jamaal smiled. It was what Dallas had been looking for all along. Smiles rarely occurred inside the women's shelter on Devonshire. Six years ago, the church board at Hillside Community gave Dallas the go-ahead to start Haven House, a place where abused women could find safety. The board appointed her to oversee the daily operations and fund-raising. She also taught classes in child rearing and women's self-defense.

On a couple of occasions, she'd given a room in her own home to one of the women, for a few days anyway, when Haven House got overcrowded. Ron, good husband and Christian that he was, supported her all the way.

Her favorite place, though, was right here in the craft room, where the kids could imagine and create. So many of the women had children with them.

"Would you like to color some?" Dallas asked Jamaal. The boy looked at his mother. Tiana nodded.

Dallas got a fresh coloring book and a box of crayons from the cabinet and set Jamaal up at one end of the craft table. There was a little girl there, hunched over her own book. Jamaal grabbed a red crayon, opened his coloring book, and took to his work with an optimism that made Dallas want to weep.

"You got kids?" Tiana asked as they watched Jamaal.

"Two," Dallas said.

"How old?"

"My daughter, Cara, is twenty-seven. Jared, my son, is twenty-four."

"They turn out all right, don't they?" The anguish in Tiana's voice was familiar. Dallas had heard the same anxiety in countless voices over the years. "I want Jamaal to be all right. I don't care about anything else."

Dallas had no doubt about Tiana's sincerity. It was her choices that mattered most, and she would have to make one right here and now. "Tiana, you can't go back to where you were."

Tiana looked at Dallas with sunken eyes, cavernous with dread. "I've got nowhere else to go."

"We have a network of places, rooms. We can find something."

"Got no way to pay for it."

"We can help get you on your feet. Maybe look for a job with you."

"What do you know about it?"

Dallas put her hand on Tiana's arm. "Don't go back, Tiana. Let me help find you a place."

Tiana pulled her arm away. "Jamaal needs a father."

"He's an abuser, he—"

"I can talk to him. I know how."

"No, you can't, not someone like that."

"You don't know him."

"I know about abusers."

Tiana slapped the table with her open palm. "I can talk to him! He loves me and Jamaal, and you don't know what you're talking about." Tiana paused. "You don't know anything about me."

"Maybe I know more than you think. I was down pretty low once, had someone who took it out on me, but God was there to pull me up."

Tiana shook her head. "I used to go to church. With my mama, before she died."

"Our church isn't far from here. My husband's the pastor. We'd love to have you and Jamaal come."

"Your husband preaches?"

"He's wonderful. Has a radio program. You may have heard him sometime."

"Don't listen to the radio much."

Jamaal's voice broke in. "Look, Mama!" He was holding up the coloring book, which was now a madcap swirl of multicolored lines.

"That's good, baby," Tiana said, as if willing herself to believe it. "That's real good."

"It's a pirate ship," he said.

"A big one, huh?" said Dallas.

Jamaal nodded and said, "Whoop-de-do."

Dallas's heart melted into a mixture of hope and uncertainty. *Oh, Lord, let these two make it. Please, let them make it.*

3.

"I was just this dumb kid from North Dakota," Melinda said. "Ran away and I was gonna make it in Hollywood. You know the story."

Yes, Ron thought, like countless other teenagers who flooded into Hollywood. A lot of them did come with hopes for stardom, and every now and then one of them had what it takes. Melinda, on looks alone, could have been one of those exceptions. Her face held the mix of beauty and girlishness that Marilyn Monroe had early in her career.

Ron remembered watching *The Asphalt Jungle* with Dallas a couple of years ago, and how striking Monroe was in her brief appearance on screen. Almost as striking as Melinda was in person.

"I thought I could get a waitressing job or something to tide me over, but it's rougher than it looks out there. I ended up on the street. I didn't know what I was going to do. I thought I might have to start, you know, selling the goods."

Ron noticed his right hand trembling. He put it in his left hand and put both hands in his lap.

"I saw this ad in one of those free papers they have down in Hollywood. Open auditions. Made all these promises, like they'd get a tape to agents and producers. I figured I didn't have anything to lose, so down I go to this dumpy-looking place, and they have a camera set up, and when they told me to take off my clothes I figured that's what it takes these days. I'm going to have to show myself onscreen sometime. They kept saying all these nice things and then all of a sudden they call in this guy and ..."

Her voice trailed off in a muffled sob and it was everything Ron could do not to get up and go to her. He wanted to hold her. He wanted to hear the rest of her story. He was suddenly very afraid, but not enough to open his office door.

"They told me I could make five hundred dollars that day, right there, and all I had to do was ... Five hundred dollars. Only I didn't know it wasn't five hundred all at once, until after. They said they'd give me the rest over the next couple of weeks, but that I could make more, and if it worked out and I was good enough, a lot more."

Melinda looked at Ron, her eyes savagely probing. "I want to get out of this life. I need to get out. But I'm in so deep. I want God to save me, but I don't know how to ask."

Ron felt suddenly lacking, as if all his years of study and preaching and writing amounted to exactly nothing at this particular moment in time. But there was something more disturbing, he realized, muddying the counseling waters. No, polluting them. In his mind he kept seeing her, Melinda, in scenes his imagination was firing at him with involuntary vividness.

Call this off right now. Set her up with a counselor. Open the door. Get her out.

Suddenly she was up, turning her back on him and walking toward a bookcase. Her red dress hugged her form, and the form swayed—

Melinda put her fingers on the spine of a book, delicately. And then her head slumped forward and her shoulders began to shake.

Ron got up.

Open the door.

He went to her, her cries rising up, anguished. He touched her shoulder.

4.

The phone rang the moment Dallas stepped through the door. She took it in the kitchen.

"Hey, kiddo!" Karen, Ron's literary agent, chirped in a good-news sort of way. "You sitting down?"

"No."

"You got pillows under you?"

"What is it, Karen?"

"That book deal we've been working on? It came through. And it's a monster. A million for three books."

Dallas nearly dropped the phone. "Is this for real?"

"Honey, would I kid about this?"

Joy filled Dallas to the brim. What a confirmation from God this was. Dallas had always believed in her husband and his ministry. She had prayed long and hard for it to prosper, and now God was opening doors, windows, and floodgates.

His last book was a surprise bestseller. It tackled the dangers of pornography, a subject suggested to him by Dallas. She'd seen her share of girls trying to escape what was euphemistically called "adult entertainment." It was a hell on earth is what it was.

She also knew firsthand what a porn addict could do to a woman. It had happened to her once, long ago.

But that was in the past, God had covered it, and now Ron's new series on prayer had sold for a million dollars. More money than they'd made in the past ten years, counting all the speaking Ron was doing now, his church salary, and the book sales to that point.

"Dallas? You there?"

"Karen, I don't know what to say."

"Say praise the Lord."

"Praise the Lord."

"Is Ron at the church? I don't like to call him at work, but this—"

"Oh, Karen, let me tell him." Dallas and Ron needed something to celebrate, an excuse to put all the strains aside and laugh and be joyful. "I'll tell him when he gets home. I'll put some sparkling cider on ice, make it an event."

"Do it. I'll be getting the contract in a week or so and then we'll go over it. Don't go spending it all right away now."

"Well, there is that small island I've had my eye on."

Karen laughed.

"I don't know how to begin to thank you," Dallas said.

"Just give me one of your imitations saying it."

"Who do you want?"

"How about Katharine Hepburn?"

Dallas always thought it was God's sense of humor that gave her the ability to do impersonations. She couldn't sing, draw, or play the piano, but by golly she could do Bette Davis and a whole bunch of others.

"Here it comes," Dallas said, switching to Kate Hepburn. "I am so, so thankful. Rally I am."

Karen cracked up. "Perfect, dahling! I'll call Ron tomorrow. Enjoy."

Enjoy. Yes. *Oh, God, thank you for sending this at just the right time.*

Just the right time to beat back the fear hissing at her from an inner cave, the fear of growing older and becoming less attractive to her husband, the fear that sometimes clutched her when she'd nuzzle up to him at home and ask, "Love me?"

He always said yes. Or stroked her cheek. Or shook his head at her and said, "How can you ask me that?"

Never did he say, "I love you so much, I can't even begin to tell you."

He would never cheat on her, of course. She knew that. She trusted him completely. But she feared worse—a seepage of neglect, building up over time until it calcified into something impenetrable.

Dallas put a bottle of Martinelli's sparkling cider in the fridge. And waited. Yes, they would celebrate. It had been so long since she and Ron had actually spent time together, intimate time. Maybe the good news would be just the thing.

It was later than normal when Ron came through the front door. Darkness was already falling over their home two miles from the church.

Dallas jumped up to greet him, throwing her arms around his neck and kissing his mouth.

He sighed and said, "I'm really tired. What's to eat?"

Dallas tried to conceal the excitement in her voice. "Come in and sit down."

"Huh?" Ron was already heading toward the kitchen.

"Come into the living room and sit down."

Ron stopped, turned. "Is that an order, Captain?"

Her smile dropped. "Of course not. I just want to tell you something."

"Can it wait? I want to grab something and go for a swim."

"I think you'll want to hear it."

"Is Jared in trouble?"

"No, no. This is good news."

"Just tell me then."

"I want ... how about a glass of sparkling cider first?"

Ron frowned. "Dallas, will you just tell me what the news is?"

Not the reaction Dallas was looking for. She wanted a buildup, a production. But she'd come to the point in their marriage where she could, like a master chess player, anticipate several moves ahead. If she kept up the pretense of getting him into the living room, sipping cider, she could foresee disaster. She capitulated to reality.

"Karen called," she said. "Your deal has come through."

"When did she call?"

"Around two."

"Why didn't you call me? Why didn't she call me at the church?"

"Because I asked her not to call. I wanted to tell you myself. I wanted to make the announcement a little special. That's what the sparkling cider was for."

"Well, what is it? What are the details?"

"Ready? A million dollars!"

"For how many books?"

"Three!"

Ron looked at the ceiling. "Don't you think I would have wanted to know that?"

"I wanted to tell you—"

"You should have had her call me at the church." He looked at his watch. "It's too late to call her now. I wanted to talk to her."

"You can call her in the morning."

"Thank you. That's not the point."

Dallas bit down on the insides of her cheeks. "I thought the point was going to be that you and I could celebrate some great news together."

"When it comes to the books, let me handle the business part of it, okay?"

He turned around and started walking down the hall toward the bedroom. Dallas followed him. "Can't we just consider this a blessing from God and be happy about it? We can call Cara tonight."

Her husband did not stop. He pulled off his shirt and threw it on the floor near the bedroom door.

"Ron?"

"Let me just go for a swim."

"Did something happen today? At church?"

He spun around. There was an anger in his eyes, a cold fury that Dallas had never seen before. It froze her.

"Yeah, something happened at church. I didn't get a phone call I should've gotten."

That hurt as much as a slap in the face. "Please don't do this, Ron."

"What am I doing?"

"Being angry."

"I'm going for a swim."

He started to get out of his pants. She tried to understand. He'd been under a lot of stress lately with things going on at church, some fallout from the antiporn book. They were just a few miles away from the porn capital of the world, Chatsworth. But the book deal should have made him happy.

She sat on the bed and shook her head slowly. "Why didn't we see this coming?"

"See what coming?"

"This ... hardening."

He slipped on his swimming trunks. "Dallas, look. I know things have been stressful the last couple of months—"

"Stressful! We make coffee nervous."

"Very funny."

"Oh, Ron, can we just go away for a while and—"

"I'm going for a swim."

He turned quickly and strode out of the room.

5.

Jared Hamilton took a long hit on the glass pipe, held the smoke deep in his lungs, let the music play on. Combination was everything now. A high would calm muscles and mind, while urban bass from the radio pounded his brain and kept memories at bay.

The combo was the only ritual in his life, so he treated it with a gentle reverence. It came on Fridays around four, because on that day Scott would let his crews off a little early. Scott worked them fifty plus and paid them for it. But there was nothing like a jump start to the weekend to keep up morale.

Jared had been working for Scott almost six months now. Good, steady work. Painting houses. It was a routine, and he needed routine.

So when he finished on Fridays he said good-bye to Carlos and Guillermo, the two he usually worked with, and headed off in his beat-up but running red Chevy pickup for Bautista Market on Fourth Street. It was a small, family-run operation, and they knew him there. He liked being known by them and not too many others.

He would buy a six-pack of Dos Equis and a bag of Doritos and a small jar of salsa. It was, he would sometimes think, his communion. That thought was always accompanied by an ironic smile. If his dad were to see him now ...

He would then drive to the park on Lake Avenue. In his pickup he had a camping chair, the kind that folds into a cylindrical shape for an easy fit under the arm. He always kept a tent and bedding ready too, for he was not sure from one day to the next if he'd have a roof over his head.

He would set the chair on a nice patch of grass, in the shade of a pine tree, with the sun behind and the fields in front of him. The fields where the children played.

The games were organized, mostly. Soccer practices, baseball, volleyball. The little ones were his favorite. They still did what the adults said and were eager to please. Like he'd once been.

He would open a beer and the bag of chips. He'd set the chips on his lap and put the bottle of Dos Equis in the cup holder of the camping chair. He'd open the salsa and place the lid on the arm of the chair.

He would sip and eat until the nameless guy came with the weed. He was a friend of Guillermo's and sold him a nickel bag. Jared would pay him and the guy would sit on the ground for a minute and want to talk.

Jared never talked.

The guy would leave and Jared would fold up his camping chair and throw it into the back of the pickup and take his beer and salsa and Doritos and grass and drive to a new place each night. Listen to music, loud.

The combo.

He was convinced it kept him from blacking out, the way he had a few times since coming back from Iraq. Yeah, keep the mind lit up and the music playing.

This night he was sitting on the hood of his truck in an empty parking lot without lights and feeling it, eyes closed, the music loud in his head and—

"... down, will ya?"

Jared looked up at the sudden appearance. It was dark and cold this night, and in all of Bakersfield there had to be this one guy who looked like he wanted to make trouble and looked like he could do it too. Big and beefy, with a faded Lakers jersey over his shirt.

"Look, man," Jared started to say loudly. Yeah, the music was blaring from the stereo—the only good piece of equipment in the whole truck—but that was the right of a guy sitting in an empty parking lot off the highway.

"It's pounding through the walls. Will ya turn it down?" The guy was big, no doubt about that, about Jared's age, twenty-four. Bigger, even though Jared was six-one and not exactly flabby of muscle. The Marines didn't go in for flab.

Jared put it together that the guy had come from the AMPM across the street.

Jared made no move off the hood.

"You gonna turn that down or what?" The Laker dude was wide, yes, but his belly showed the effects of a few too many breakfast burritos.

"I'm just sittin' here, man." Jared raised his hands in protest, all the while sizing up what it would take to put the man down. One jab to the jugular would probably do it, followed by gouging the eyes.

"If you could turn it down, that'd be cool," Laker guy said.

"You know what else'd be cool?" Jared said, just loud enough to be heard. "I could take your head off and spit down your neck."

At that moment Jared had a vision of it, of ripping the fool's head right off and leaving a wound he could look into and see the lousy messed-up soul inside Laker dude.

"I'll be calling the cops now," the guy said, turning.

"Wait, wait, okay." Jared slid off the hood, feeling light, reached in through the window, and turned the key. The music stopped. The silence of the night was like a blow to the head.

"All right," the guy said. He started back toward the AMPM. Jared, without thought, went to the back of the truck and grabbed a crowbar. It was heavy and nice in his hand. It would make a major dent in the guy's head, or his kneecap.

There was nobody in the store that Jared could see. Maybe he could lay the guy out and take a few things. Sure—

Then it was like a beautiful scene in a movie playing in his mind, the guy lying on the floor with blood all around, bright red, living color. Jared Hamilton, hero, Tarantinoesque—he'd have made a difference. To himself.

The scene was vivid.

Stuff like that kept showing in his mind ever since he got back.

The crowbar heavy in his hand.

What would his father say?

No. Who cared? It was Mom. What would she think?

In his head: *Do it anyway. That's the combo. That would really put the bad thoughts away.*

TWO

1.

Resistance is futile.

Dallas smiled as she drew herself a bath, threw in some salts from the Burke Williams spa, and settled in for a good, rejuvenating, sweet-smelling soak. One thing she had not tried lately was the venerable art of marital seduction. She knew that was one thing their relationship needed, and the one thing that was almost entirely up to her.

Last night Ron had come home and avoided her, gone swimming, disappeared into his study, and slept there.

Tonight would be different. She would make him remember.

She would make him remember how they were when they first married. She was the one with experience, a remnant of her past, and he had taken her gentle guidance and been transformed by it. But the change in her was no less intense. She was in love for the first time, really in love and not just drawn physically to a man. She loved Ron's character, his faith, his authority. She trusted him completely. Giving herself to him was as pure a thing as she had ever done in her life.

Part of the reason she felt that way, she well knew, was that she was fleeing an abusive relationship with a true lowlife. Chad McKenzie was a real piece of work—the devil's work. She barely escaped him, running from L.A. to San Francisco and living the street life.

She'd met Chad when she was seventeen. He was twenty and had a nice little business selling dope to the rich kids on the west side. It enabled him to ride around in a red Corvette and convince her that if she really wanted to get somewhere, it would be with him.

And Dallas was ready to go. Life at home was intolerable, she and her mother fighting all the time. Dallas knew it wasn't her mom's fault. Dallas had bad stuff going on inside. Without a father—he left when Dallas was three—there was just no way Mom could keep Dallas in check.

Those first couple of months with Chad McKenzie were exciting. The danger was a turn-on, as good as getting high.

Then the high turned into a nightmare. Getting kicks sexually was, for Chad, a matter of pain. Hers. He was a porn addict, the S and M variety.

She had scars on her soul, carved with the harsh blade of Chad McKenzie's sadism. He managed to make her feel like all the dirt and scum and trash of the world was, if not all, at least in large part due to her pointless existence.

And she took it. She took it for weeks, because she thought she'd never be worth anything to anybody again.

She was sure that she would be dead by now had she not run away to San Francisco.

Later, when she entered that revival meeting where the young Ron Hamilton was preaching, she knew without doubt that God had brought them together. Here was the thing she wanted most in the world—something that would *last*.

Their daughter, Cara, was conceived on their honeymoon, on a cruise down the Pacific coast to Mexico, a gift from his mother.

Three years after Cara's birth, Jared came along. And the rearing of children combined with the building of a ministry sent their lives on a different course. Their love was as strong as ever, but their energy was tapped by a thousand new demands.

Ten-year-old Cara developed a neuromuscular problem that would require three solid years of mentally draining attention. At the same time, Jared was displaying signs of ADD and a certain steely rebelliousness that Dallas was sure came from her. On more than one occasion she thought of Jared's behavior as God's revenge for the pain she'd caused her mother.

Cara healed and even became a top high school tennis player. Jared also displayed some athletic ability, and that calmed his inner waters for a time. When Dallas and Ron were finally able to peer above the troubled waters, they saw they were no longer the kids who'd met at a Jesus rally in North Beach, San Francisco.

She was a mother who had poured all her creativity into her children. From would-be hippie poetess to suburban mom—and a minister's wife, with all that went with it. Not all of it to her liking.

Ron was rising in the ranks of pastors and speakers. He was on the road more, most often without Dallas and the kids. He developed a more formal bearing, perhaps as a defense to all the people who were starting to want a piece of him.

But their love and friendship was never a question in Dallas's mind. Even though physical intimacy occurred less frequently, they managed to find time to get away together. Yet even those occasions had somehow dried up over the last few years. Dallas pledged to get them back.

Most of the strain was because of Jared, of course. Their son hung between them like a veil of division, sheer and unmentioned but present in every moment. Jared, the second born, the son. Ron had been so proud when he was born. His face lit up the delivery room. A son!

Jared was this perfect thing, an innocent baby glowing with unlimited potential. Those first few years, Ron could not stop talking about what a blessing their family was. A cute and loving daughter, a smart and curious—though somewhat serious—son. "One of each!" he would often say in those days.

But then came the growing pains and the realization that Jared had in him some traits that were not in line with what Ron had envisioned. And then came the war and Jared enlisting without a word, not a word to either of them.

Then, worst of all, his returning from Iraq a different person. Dallas prayed for him daily, intensely.

But tonight, it would be Ron she would think of, Ron she would bring back to the fold.

As she soaked in the water, Dallas thanked God she was still healthy. She worked at it. She kept in shape, went to the gym. Though her body was changing, developing knocks and pings and obeying the inexorable laws of gravity, she still weighed in at only five pounds above her wedding weight. That was something to be proud of. She enjoyed going to functions with Ron, hanging on his arm, looking good for him.

When she got out of the tub she put on a little body lotion and just a touch of Ron's favorite perfume. What to wear? She had a lacy white blouse that accentuated the positive, and some tight jeans that nearly eliminated the negative. Seemingly casual, but designed for the male eye. Deadly.

Resistance is futile.

She pulled back the covers of the bed, then went to order dinner from Stonefire Grill, Ron's favorite eatery. Dallas requested whole barbecued tri-tips, slaw, and mashed potatoes.

She would be the dessert.

At five thirty, the meal came. Dallas set the table, popped a Larry Carlton CD into the Bose.

At five forty-five the call came.

2.

"Dallas, honey, something's come up. I won't be home till late probably."

Strange, but Dallas had almost sensed he would say that when she picked up the bedroom phone. It was all too perfectly dreadful. She had made all these plans, and they simply had to be dashed, didn't they? Wasn't that the trajectory of their lives? Wasn't this going to be some bad soap-opera moment?

"Is there some trouble?" she said.

"I have to talk to someone is all."

"Why so late?"

"I have to take a drive. Not too far. But I just can't predict . . ."

She waited for him to explain. He didn't.

"So I'll call you later," he said.

"What about dinner?"

"I'll grab something."

"I got Stonefire."

Pause. "Put mine in the fridge, huh?"

And then he was gone.

Dallas sat on the edge of the bed. Was that a hint of avoidance in his voice? Or was there something more, something like her husband not telling her the whole truth?

Feeling ridiculous in her sexy outfit, she kicked off her shoes and pulled off her jeans. She could breathe again. She unbuttoned her blouse and threw it against the wall. Putting on her robe, she went downstairs, grabbed the Stonefire bag, and stuck the whole thing in the refrigerator, slamming the door. The clock on top of the refrigerator fell to the floor, and a huge chunk of the face broke off.

"Perfect," she said.

The motel had a sickly sameness to it and looked like a thousand others along a thousand freeways and roads. The parking lot was about half full. A couple of Hispanic men in undershirts leaned over the rail of the second story taking in the view, which consisted of the parking lot, an Applebees restaurant, and an auto-parts store.

I drove to the end of the parking lot, as Melinda had instructed me. I pulled into one of the last spaces near a cinder-block wall. She would be in room 105. It was around on the other side of the motel, facing north. At least from there you could see some mountains.

I gave three quick knocks, as she requested. I waited a moment, heard nothing inside. Then I saw the peephole darken.

She opened the door. "Come in, quickly."

She closed the door and put her arms around me, burying her head in my chest. I very properly patted the middle of her back with one hand and said, "It's okay. I'm here, you're going to be fine."

She didn't let go of me. I could feel her chest heaving. I could smell her hair. It was vaguely scented, hinting of spice.

I guided her to the bed and sat her on it. The only other furniture in the room was a stark functional chair and a desk with a lamp. I stayed standing, and that's when I noticed she was wearing something very sheer and revealing. It did not surprise me, because that's the world she lived in. But I backed up three steps and tried not to look at her below the neck.

"Now tell me who is after you," I said.

"The people. The people I work for." She was lacing and unlacing her fingers as she spoke, looking down at them. "They beat up one of the other girls. I saw it. They were laughing about it. I couldn't stand it. I screamed and ran out. One of them ran after me, telling me to come back or I was going to be sorry, and I better not think of going to the police or I was going to be dead."

She looked at me and I fell into her eyes. She said, "I was so scared I couldn't stop running. I thought they were going to come after me in a car. I had my coat on and a few dollars and I hopped a bus and then the Metro Link, which is how I got here. I used a credit card for the room. But now I'm afraid they'll trace the transaction somehow and find me. What do I do?"

"You have got to go to the police."

She started to say something, but I cut her off. "It's the way things work. We can't do this alone. You can't deal with people like this by yourself."

"No police!"

I thought of Jared then. The way Melinda said No was a lot like the way he used to say it when we were fighting the battles at home.

I paced in front of the curtained window, thinking. "What about getting out of town?"

She looked up.

"I can give you some money," I said. "You could start all over again somewhere."

The idea seemed to strike a chord with her. "Where?"

"Almost anywhere. I know some great churches and ministers around the country. I could tell one of them about you, and he would help get you set up in a new community."

"You really think so?"

She suddenly looked so young. All that hope in her face, like a child who's just been told her lost puppy was found.

"It's perfect," I said. "It'll be a chance for a fresh start."

Tears were starting to form in her eyes. If she had not stood up and come to me, I do believe with all my heart that none of this would have happened. That was the moment, the key, the breaking point. At least that's what I tell myself on nights I can't sleep and the memories play, unbidden, in my mind.

When she put her arms around me this time it was softer. I made no move away from her.

When she put her head on my chest it was gentler, almost a caress.

I put both my hands on her back and kept them there. I don't know how long we were like that, but when she turned her head up toward mine everything exploded, and I knew things would never be right again.

THREE

1.

Dallas awoke, calling her husband's name, reaching for his body in the dark.

She realized in the blackness that her nightmare was over, chased away by her desperate waking. A shimmer of what she deemed hope flashed across her mind, like a sliver of distant lightning in a storm-swollen sky.

She reached for Ron again, felt only the cold, empty spot on the bed.

No, he would not be there. He had not shared their bed for a week. He slept in the study, wouldn't tell her why. Just holed up, mumbling excuses.

Even more troubling, Ron had asked Bob Benson to preach for him yesterday, Palm Sunday. Ron always preached both Palm Sunday and Easter. Something was terribly wrong, but Ron wouldn't say what.

She looked at the clock by the bed. Four thirty-seven. Too early to be awake.

Sleep was out of the question.

Her head was full and heavy, a bag of nails. The throbbing behind her eyes that started last night began again.

Then she saw red lights flashing. Outside the window.

It wasn't just in her dreams.

Police car, she thought. Why? Next door, the teenager, Craig. He was in with some pretty questionable people, and who knew why the cops were here? Drugs? Stolen property?

A loud knock on the door. A pounding that was not friendly.

The red lights . . .

Another knock. Full, loud, relentless.

One of the kids. Something happened to one of the kids. Accident? Death?

She got up, heart accelerating. In the dark she reached for her robe. She rushed out the bedroom door, bits of awareness popping up like the lights of a city as night falls. Halfway down the stairs she saw the front door open and a police officer standing there.

"What's going on?" she fairly screamed.

She reached the bottom of the stairs and saw, on the porch, her husband. In handcuffs, with another police officer holding his arm.

"What is this?" Dallas heard her own voice, felt herself plunge forward.

The first cop put his hand up. "Ma'am, stay where you are, please."

"Ron!"

Ron turned to her. "Call Jeff Waite," he said.

Dallas looked at the cop inside the house. "Please tell me what is going on."

"Call a lawyer, ma'am," he said.

Jefferson Waite returned her call a little before nine in the morning. She'd left two messages on his cell phone, knowing he would be asleep like the rest of the normal world. Knowing, too, he would call just as soon as he could.

"What is it, Dallas?"

"It's Ron. They arrested him."

"Arrested? What for?"

"They didn't say. They didn't tell me. Aren't they supposed to tell me?"

"When was this?"

"A few hours ago."

"Do you know where they took him?"

"No."

Dallas clutched the phone. Jeff said, "All right, don't worry, I can find him. Is there anything else you can tell me?"

"Nothing. I can't believe this, Jeff."

"I'll find out what's going on." His voice was warm and calming. "If he calls you, tell him not to talk to anyone."

"Will he?"

"Did you hear what I said?"

"Yes."

"Tell him he's not to say anything, and I mean anything, to anybody. I'll see him as soon as I can."

"But—"

He clicked off. Dallas sat back in a chair in the gray of the morning, paralyzed.

8.

"You crazy, man," Guillermo was saying. "You gonna get lightning on your head, you keep talkin' that trash."

The three of them—Jared, Guillermo, and Carlos—were working a church, a little white Catholic number northeast of Bakersfield. A new coat of white on the inside, around the stained-glass windows, patching cracks.

Guillermo and Carlos had the radio blaring that salsa crud, and at every break Jared had to listen to somebody spouting Spanish.

At least it muted the voices in his own head.

So yes, he was crazy. Jared agreed with Guillermo on that much. But not crazy for talking trash.

"That's what I said." Jared pointed with his brush at the crucifix. Jesus hanging on a cross and set on the little altar. "He's no help to anybody. He's hanging there. It's just a stupid statue."

"You're the stupid one, man." Guillermo didn't say it viciously, but Jared could sense a bubbling beneath his surface.

Didn't matter. Jared felt a compulsion to speak. The thoughts were like bile wanting to burst out of him of their own accord, and he would let them.

"What's with people looking at statues, huh? Thinking there's anything there?"

Carlos, who was forty or so and smaller than the other two, dipped his brush in a paint can and said, "Shut up and work."

"You want some?" Jared put his hands out, challenging.

"Crazy," Guillermo said. "In a church, talkin' trash about Jesus."

Jared walked a few steps on the drop cloth toward his coworkers. "Listen to what I'm saying, genius. People are better off not knowing anything, instead of coming into a church and worshiping Jesus statues."

A voice on the radio shouted something in Spanish.

"Come on," Guillermo urged. "You bring down bad stuff on everybody, you keep talking that way."

Jared let the words fly. "You afraid of God? That what you're afraid of? Because of a stupid statue?"

"Hey—" Carlos pointed at Jared.

Now it wasn't the radio noise rattling around in Jared's head but something else, voicelike, pounding. He didn't know what this was, but it was urgent and angry. Spitting angry, and something had to be done to show these stupid—

"Get back to work!" Carlos yelled, but Jared was already going down the aisle, the noise beating inside his head, and he had his brush up.

He heard Guillermo say, "What's he doin'?" but it barely registered in the chaos of his brain.

Now Jared focused in on Jesus, on his face, looking down. Jesus nailed, a statue. Was this what they were afraid of?

With one swipe of his brush, Jared covered Jesus's face in white paint.

"No!" Guillermo shouted.

And Jared thought, *I know how to bleed too, Jesus.*

When he turned around, he saw his two coworkers staring, but not at him. At the door.

Jared looked over and saw a priest standing there, shock all over his face. And next to him Scott, the boss man, about to go ballistic.

4.

"Cara, it's me."

"Hi, Mom. Guess what? I'm getting a promotion at the bank. Today I—"

"Cara, listen to me."

"What's wrong?"

Dallas tried to make her hand relax its grip on the phone but couldn't. "Your dad's in trouble."

"Trouble? What do you—"

"He was arrested."

Cara's gasp jabbed through the phone. "Why?"

"I don't know, but the police came to the house this morning. They took him away in handcuffs. They wouldn't even tell me."

"Mom, Mom, are you all right?"

Dallas swallowed hard. "Will you start praying—"

"Mom, I'm coming over."

"You don't have to—"

"I'll be right there."

Dallas felt trapped in a fog, seeing little, hearing nothing, until Cara came and threw her arms around her and held her. Dallas returned the embrace around Cara's taut body. Her daughter, at twenty-seven, still looked like the tennis player she'd been in high school. But her face, under the short blond hair, was worried.

"Mom, you have got to tell me what's going on. I can't believe Dad would be arrested for anything."

Dallas shook her head. "All I know is what I told you. They arrested your father, just took him away like a common criminal. Why would they do that?"

"Have we got a lawyer?"

"Yes. Jeff Waite. He's going to see your father this morning."

"Is he good? Because we have got to have the best."

"Oh, yes, he's good. He's done pro bono work for the church."

Out of habit, Dallas patted her daughter's shoulder. It was the calming move. Cara had always been a bit of a control freak, an imposer of order. Dallas had spent more hours than she could count settling her daughter's nerves. Now Cara was here to return the favor.

Cara said, "Have you talked to Jared?"

Dallas shook her head. "I don't know where he is."

"Does he have a cell phone?"

"The old number doesn't work. He must have let it go."

"Probably didn't pay his bill."

"Do you know any of his old friends? People who might be in touch with him? I'm afraid of how this is going to hit him."

"I can try to think of someone."

"Please do."

Cara took her mother by the arm and sat her down in her favorite chair. Dallas felt lumps in it. It was getting worn.

"How about some lunch?" Cara said.

"I can't eat."

"Yes, you can," Cara insisted, echoing the words Dallas must have said a thousand times to her daughter during her bouts with sickness or distress.

It was a disquieting juxtaposition. Cara was the mothering one now, and Dallas the little girl. But she did not want to be little, or helpless, or paralyzed. She wanted to help Ron. Now.

And couldn't.

5.

Jefferson Waite arrived just before noon. He hardly had a foot in the door when Dallas asked him what was going on.

"Let's go into the living room," Waite said.

Dallas stood still. "Tell me now. Please."

Cara, who had been making sandwiches in the kitchen, came to her mother's side.

Jeff closed the door. He wore a powder blue dress shirt, sleeves rolled halfway up his forearms, and a burgundy tie perfectly knotted. He was in his midforties with a full head of brown hair flecked by wisps of gray. He exuded confidence, which was exactly what

Dallas needed at that moment. "I don't want you to worry the first time you hear it. These things—"

"What happened?"

"They say it's murder."

Dallas felt something flow out of her head, a sucking away like the sand under a receding wave. Cara grabbed her left arm, and that's when Dallas knew she had almost fallen.

Jeff helped Cara get Dallas to the sofa. Cara sat next to her and put an arm around her shoulder.

"It's a huge mistake," Jeff said. "I saw Ron, I talked with him, he's scared but he's staying strong. It's all a major misunderstanding."

"Who was it?" Dallas said.

"The victim is a young woman named Melinda Perry. That's all I could find out."

Young woman? "Can I see him?" Dallas said. "Where is he?"

"They've got him at the men's jail, downtown."

She looked at the lawyer. "What's going to happen, Jeff?"

He sat on the coffee table so he could take her hand. He was muscular and trim, with intelligent blue eyes. "Tomorrow he goes before a judge. I'll be there with him and get the formal charge and the arrest report. Then I'll go talk to the DA and see what they've got."

Panic burst through her. "They've got to have something. They wouldn't arrest him if they didn't have anything. What could it be?"

She heard screeching outside. The sound of tires.

Jeff went to the door and pulled back the curtain.

"Man, that was fast," he said.

"What?"

"TV people."

Pinpricks stuck her skin. Publicity. She hadn't even considered that. In her singular focus she thought only of Ron, and of this problem as one they could solve together, quietly. That's the way they handled things between them, wasn't it?

But now she realized this accusation would not be kept quiet, couldn't be swept under their private rug. Ron was a big-time pastor with a national platform. He'd been on radio and TV, once on *The O'Reilly Factor* talking about the scourge of Internet porn.

He was a media darling, with his good looks and eloquence. Now he was a target for the press—a family-values pastor accused of murder.

"Stay calm," Jeff said. "I will do the talking for you. All right? Not you, not your daughter, not Ron. Is there anyone else in the family they could get to?"

Dallas shook her head. "Only our son, Jared, but he's out of the county."

"Don't sell these people short," Jeff said. "Now stay here."

He went outside, closing the door behind him. A few moments later Dallas heard his voice, firm and resolute.

"Mrs. Hamilton will not be commenting on this matter. I will be speaking for the family ... No, we have no comment at this time ... There has not even been a formal charge yet ... No, there will be no further comment ... And by the way, any entrance on this property will be treated as a trespass. So I advise you to clear out and direct all inquiries to my office."

The muffled shouts of several voices shooting questions came next. Cara squeezed Dallas's hand.

Dallas closed her eyes. She remembered someone telling her once that the most effective prayer on earth was *Help me help me help me*.

That is what Dallas prayed now. She prayed for a sign from God, something to tell her that it wasn't true, that this whole nightmare was going to go away.

At twelve forty-five a police tow truck showed up, much to the delight of the media circus, and towed Ron's car away.

6.

How do you look at your wife from the inside of a cage?

Do you fake it? Do you put on a happy face, like that old song says?

Do you do it so your wife, who loves you, who has known only your stability and strength, won't freak?

Do you smile and give a little wave through the Plexiglas barrier and make some joke through the handset about your orange jumpsuit? "Like my new style?"

Do you do everything within your power to hide the clawing, voracious fear that is working your insides?

Or do you let go of your face? Let it all hang out?

Most important of all, do you let the truth, the whole truth, and nothing but the truth flash like neon in your eyes? Do you drop all pretense and all deceit and let her read your expressions like the front page of a tabloid?

The woman who loved me with a solid, dependable love came to see me. And I could hardly look at her.

7.

The men's jail was downtown, on Bauchet Street, just east of Chinatown and Union Station. It housed the county's ever-increasing population of criminal defendants, those waiting for trial as well as cons serving less than a year.

It had been the temporary residence of several high-profile defendants the last few years.

Like Ron Hamilton.

Dallas was shaking when she got to the visitation room. It was smaller than she'd expected, with two rows of stools in front of glass partitions. A deputy sheriff told her where to sit.

The stool was hard and cold.

What was it going to be like to see Ron for the first time? In here?

Worse, what was it going to be like for him to see *her*? She knew she looked terrible. The shock was still fresh, had been pressing down on her for the last twenty-four hours. No sleep. She felt like bags of cement were under her eyes. Eyes that fell on her husband being led in on his side of the Plexiglas. Dressed in an orange jumpsuit. Not the blue of the regular jail inmate. Orange marked him as high security.

He sat opposite her, his features gnarled in confusion. She grabbed the handset, waiting for him to pick up.

"Ron," she said, then found she couldn't coax another word out of her mouth.

His voice came through the wire thin and distant. "Dallas, I'm so sorry you have to see me like this."

"Are you all right?"

His eyes were darting around, not staying on her directly. "It's jail. Not a place I ever thought I'd be."

She put her hand on the Plexiglas. She wanted to push her hand through and stroke her husband's cheek. She wanted to break through and hold him and drag him out of there and keep the world away.

"What on earth happened?" she said.

Ron pursed his lips and shook his head. "It's not true, what they're saying."

What *they* were saying was that her husband had been "involved" with an actress in what *they* referred to as "adult films." She first heard the report on the radio news as she was driving to the jail. She almost ran into another car.

But she knew it couldn't be true, couldn't be. She fought the information with all her will.

"How then?" Dallas said, needing to know.

"Listen to me, Dallas. I was stupid. I made a stupid mistake."

She waited.

He looked up toward the ceiling. "I was counseling this girl, the one they found. She was in with some pretty bad people. She was scared. I was trying to help her."

Dallas said nothing. She watched her husband's face twitch around his eyes. He was the scared one now.

"Why didn't you call the police?" Dallas said.

"She didn't want the police. She was scared if she called them these people would find out and they'd do something to her."

"Why didn't you send her to Haven House?"

"I don't know," he said. "There's just so much I don't know."

A large woman sat on the stool next to Dallas. She had on a sleeveless dress. Her arms jiggled as she adjusted herself. Dallas caught a whiff of body odor. The woman swore as she fiddled with her handset.

"What happened, exactly?" Dallas said.

"Jeff says not to talk. This could be monitored."

"But you didn't *do* anything." And then, like a cockroach in the kitchen, distrust skittered across her mind. Dallas shook. Never had she experienced anything but complete faith in her husband.

Even in their worst times, when he could put on the big freeze and not talk to her for hours, she had never questioned his integrity. He was absolutely without fault in that department.

But now ... She refused to give the thought credence. It was the stress, the surroundings, the nightmare circumstance.

"Dallas, I didn't do anything but be stupid. They got to her, the guys she was afraid of. That had to be it." He paused. "They'll use this, you know. The porn people. They'll use this to show I'm a hypocrite. All our work will be called into question."

She couldn't deny it. She and Ron were actively fighting the spread of the porn industry by pushing for new zoning restrictions in the city. Ron, as the front man, had been called many things by his enemies. *Hypocrite* would now be added to the list.

"I'll keep the pressure on Bernie," Dallas said. Bernie Halstrom was their city councilman, the one they had worked closely with on the zoning issue.

"Thank you," Ron said, with what seemed heartfelt gratitude.

"How long do you have to be in here?"

"Jeff'll move for bail, but he told me they might not give it. This is what they call a high-profile murder case. Me, imagine ..."

"Are you all right?"

"They've got me isolated. That's the way they do it. I can take it if you can ..."

She saw his hand shake and then drop the phone. Then his head was in his hands and he was sobbing. Sobbing uncontrollably.

"Oh, Ron." Dallas jumped to her feet, pressed her forehead to the window, hit it with her open hand.

A deputy sheriff was at her side instantly, pulling her away.

"No!" she shouted. "No, please!"

"Sit down, ma'am. You can't touch the glass."

She sat. Ron kept sobbing. Then he whirled away and stood.

"Ron, don't go!"

Apparently he couldn't hear her. Or chose not to.

"Ron!"

"Keep your voice down, ma'am," the deputy said. "Looks like your visit is over."

Over.

No. Dallas steeled herself against the thought that more than this visit was over, that life as they all knew it was over and would never come back together again.

She would not let that be.

§

Jared looked at himself in the mirror behind the bar and almost spat.

You have no job now, pal. Your little game with the crucifix didn't really do it in the eyes of the ol' boss. And the good Father? Well, he was about to consign you to the fires of hell right then and there.

You thought men of the cloth were supposed to be reverent in church, didn't you? At home, didn't your father wait to unload on you until after church, when Mom was making up the lunch?

So now it doesn't matter when you drink, because you've got no job, and the only question on the table is when will the money run out?

Jared listened to himself inside his head, laughing because he was having a little dialogue up there between himself and—who knew? Somebody who knew how to drink, that was for sure.

He sat at the end of the bar this time, right by the bathrooms. He came to this little place on occasion, when he wasn't out trying to dull the ache with items of illegal pedigree.

Nursing a double shot of Daniels was just as good tonight, and it was cold outside anyway.

Tomorrow. Maybe tomorrow he'd give another run at the VA hospital. They were giving him the big-time runaround on post-traumatic stress disorder. He knew why too—because there was a whole new wave of it.

What was the number he read? Like three hundred thousand homeless vets, about half from Vietnam. But it was growing, the numbers. Guys coming back from Iraq and Afghanistan. And Jared kept hearing through the grapevine that the Iraq vets had it worst of all in the head.

But not according to the VA. To them it was illness as usual. Even when some of his buddies had to take meds that could knock out a seriously ticked-off elephant.

Self-sedation with Jack Daniels was about the best he could do under the circumstances. What did that country song say? Something about when it rains, I pour? Jared smiled and shook his head. *Good one, boy, go ahead. And tomorrow you can wake up tight and early.*

There was a pool table in the center of the barroom with a couple of guys shooting, and a TV tuned to ESPN. Not as good as rap, but almost. The obnoxious sports heads who screamed clever phrases provided a little anesthesia.

Maybe I'll just buy a bottle and go back to the room at the rat hotel. He'd have to clear out of there in a week if he didn't land something to get some more money and not spend it on weed or alcohol.

He ordered another JD, worked it, looked occasionally at the TV. The images blurred into colorful splats on the screen, uniforms and graphics bleeding together, formless.

Then he saw his father's face.

What? Couldn't be. But there was no mistake.

Some words flashed below the face. *Crime of Passion.*

A squib for another cable channel, he realized.

His father was a news story.

Then, suddenly, the face was gone.

Whoa. Jared wondered for a moment if he really saw it, or if maybe it was a trick of the mind and alcohol. Maybe the voices in his head were becoming more sophisticated now, giving him altered realities, using visuals.

But then he realized he wasn't so drunk after all, especially not after the jolt of adrenaline that blasted through him the moment he recognized his father.

Crime of passion?

He called to the bartender, a woman with a look of thirty years' hard experience as a mixer.

"Can you get the news for me?" he said, pointing at the TV.

She looked at the tube. "We got people want to watch the game."

He was aware of anxiety clutching him. The weirdness of it all, having a father on the news, even if it was a father he hated. It was like the whole world had a pipeline into his life now, only he didn't know what the pipeline was connected to.

"Just change it to the news for a second, will you?"

"I got more than you in the bar," the bartender said.

"Just *do it.*"

She gave him the look she must have given a hundred thousand surly drunks over the years. "Relax. You want another drink?"

Jared stood up and raised his voice to the whole place. "Does anybody know what's going on with this crime-of-passion story on the news?"

People stared at him. The guys playing pool looked annoyed. The three other barflies looked singularly uninterested.

"Come on, anybody?"

"Settle down, will you?" the bartender said. "You talking about that preacher?"

"Yeah, that's the one."

"Why didn't you just ask me instead of making a scene? Sit down. I'll get you another drink."

"Tell me what's going on."

"Guy's some minister down in L.A. He had a porn actress on the side, then he offed her."

Flares of disbelief shot through Jared.

"Yep," the bartender said with a laugh, "you gotta love that town."

§.

Wednesday morning the Ron Hamilton "Crime of Passion" story was front page in the *Times* and *Daily News*. A small media camp was set up on the street outside the Hamilton home, waiting for Dallas to emerge.

And the phone in the house wouldn't stop ringing. There were at least twenty messages in the voice mail now. Dallas didn't bother to listen. Cara had her cell-phone number, and that's all Dallas cared about.

But life had to go on, and she was not going to let the media make a prisoner of her. There was the church to look out for.

So, dressed in business casual and with all the makeup skill she could muster showing on her face, Dallas got into her Nissan Pathfinder, locked the doors, and clicked the garage-door opener.

As soon as she made the driveway she was swarmed.

Though she'd prepared herself to ignore them, it was unsettling to see cameras aimed at her and microphones poking at the window. Behind the microphones were anxious faces shouting questions at her. She nearly ran over a woman in a blue blazer and was almost sorry she didn't.

Dallas prayed for peace and strength all the way to the Hillside parking lot, where more news vans were gathered. This was absurd. She wanted to get out and yell at these hounds to get a life and cover something newsworthy, not just some false allegation that—

False. Please oh please be false.

She was stunned that she could think such a thought. Of *course* it was false!

Dallas pulled around to a rear entrance and used her key to get in, unseen by the reporters.

She found the office in a tizzy. The first one to see her was Dave Rivas, their head of security. Dave, a former cop, volunteered his time. He and Dallas, in fact, had done the research that resulted in the church's state-of-the-art system.

"Been like this all day," Dave said. He was around fifty and always wore a black baseball cap with LAPD in white letters on the front.

"Any incidents?" Dallas asked.

"Depends what you mean. I had one guy from KTTV try to bring a camera in, but I yanked a few cords and that was that."

"Thanks, Dave. Hang in there."

"You too, Dallas. We're praying hard for you."

Dallas continued to the reception area. Three of the church secretaries were in various stages of harried activity—answering phones, peeling faxes from the machine. They didn't even look up to see Dallas.

But Lisa Benson did. She was on a phone, waved at Dallas, said something, and hung up.

She came to Dallas and gave her a hug. "Dallas, how *are* you? It's been a zoo here."

Dallas was glad Lisa was here. Though twenty years younger than Dallas, Lisa was a true friend. And a remarkable woman. Charismatic, and a perfect complement to her husband, Bob, Hillside's associate minister. This couple was going places, just like Dallas and Ron when they'd first come to Hillside.

Which was why Dallas always felt that Lisa could understand her own problems better than anyone else. Nothing like being a minister's wife to give you laser-sharp insights into life, the universe, and everything.

"My head is spinning," Dallas said. "I had to come up here to figure out what we should be doing for the church."

"Good," Lisa said. "Bob's been working on that. He'll want to see you, I'm sure. Come on."

As she walked with Dallas toward Bob Benson's office, Lisa said, "When the dust settles a little bit, let's get together and do something, huh? Just you and me."

"That sounds good."

Lisa rapped on her husband's office door, then opened it.

"Come in," Bob Benson said. Lisa kissed Dallas on the cheek and closed the door behind her.

The young associate stood and welcomed her into his extremely neat and orderly office. He was, as he had always been to her and Ron, impressive. Only twenty-seven, he was clearly a gifted minister. Educated, witty, and above all, able to communicate.

When they were settled, Bob asked how Dallas was.

"Not real good," she said. "News trucks outside my house. I'm under a microscope."

"We all are, I'm afraid." Bob wore his brown hair in an understated spiky style, just haphazard enough to give him credibility with the younger crowd. But he could preach a great sermon to all age groups.

"We've got to get a message out to our people," Dallas said.

"Already being done."

That surprised her. "How?"

"I drafted a statement for the website. And I'm working on one for the media."

"Can I see it?"

"I'm still tweaking."

"What about Sunday? Who's—"

"Dallas, don't worry. These are things you shouldn't have to stress over, okay?"

"It's Ron's church! Of course I'm going to stress."

The moment she said it she realized how desperate she must have sounded. Hillside was not *Ron's church*, even if he was the senior pastor who had overseen its growth. It was God's church.

Bob kept his voice calm. "I don't want you to worry, because things are being looked after. I've got an Easter sermon ready for Sunday, then I'll continue to preach the same sermon series Ron was on. That way there'll be a feeling, at least a little bit, of continuity. But I plan to address the issue full-on in all our services."

"Some great Easter, huh?"

"I'll be careful, Dallas. You know, 'You've all read about this tragedy in the paper, or seen it on the news—' "

"It's not a tragedy, Bob. It's a mistake."

Bob picked up a notepad and moved it to the opposite side of his desk. "Yes, of course. And I'll mention that we do still have something called the presumption of innocence. And I'll call on everyone to pray for the church."

"And Ron."

"That's a given."

"I'd like to be part of the planning too," Dallas said. "Decisions will have to be made affecting the church."

"Sure. I'll keep you in the loop."

"When can we talk?"

Bob looked at his watch. "I have to leave tonight. I'm speaking at a conference the next couple of days."

"That's right, something about reaching Gen Yers?"

"Right. But I'll be back late Saturday."

"What are we going to do about the media out there?"

Bob spun around in his chair and looked out the window. "I'm going to go out and deliver my statement."

"May I see it?"

"Like I said, I'm still working on it."

"May I see what you have so far?"

Bob hesitated just long enough to make Dallas uncomfortable. Dallas chalked it up to anxiety, hers and his. They'd all have to pull together and heap mounds of grace on each other.

Bob took a paper from the printer on his credenza and handed it to her.

> As associate minister of Hillside Community Church, I have had the privilege of work- ing alongside Ron Hamilton for three years. During that time I have come to know him as both a friend and a boss, as a brother in Christ, and as a fellow worker in this community. We are holding him up in prayer and trust that the media will remember the most impor- tant principle of our justice system: that a man is presumed innocent until proven guilty beyond a reasonable doubt. We also would ask the media to respect the privacy rights of the worshipers here at Hillside, and not to interfere with our operations. Thank you.

She set the paper on Bob's desk.

"You look disappointed," he said.

"No, Bob. It's good. It's just ..."

"You would have preferred an outright statement that we know Ron is innocent?"

She nodded, impressed by the young minister's insight.

"That was my first instinct, until I thought how that would look to the media. Naturally they've heard all that before, the protestations of innocence from family members. And we are Ron's family, right? In my mind, that would only make them dig in deeper. But by putting it out there as objectively as possible, by saying what the law says, that Ron's innocent until proven guilty, we show we're being as objective as the law. I don't know, maybe I'm wrong, but I had to consider Hillside's reputation."

Dallas sensed his defensiveness. She reached over the desk and put a hand on his arm. "Thanks, Bob. I know you have the welfare of the church, and Ron, at the top of your thoughts."

"And you, Dallas. Lisa and I want you to remember you can count on us for anything."

"I know."

"And I'd like to do something right now. I'd like to pray with you, Dallas. Will you join me in that?"

10.

Back home again, Dallas felt like her head was finally emerging above the waters of adversity. She was able to look around, think a little bit, and remember that she had duties to people that didn't go away because Ron was in jail.

She called Haven House and spoke to Danielle, her assistant there. "Have you been able to place Tiana and Jamaal yet?"

"No luck," Danielle said. "She said she's going back to her boyfriend."

"No! Don't let her do that."

"What can I do? She's getting ready to go."

"Let me talk to her."

"She hasn't come down yet."

"I'll wait."

As she did, she peeked out the front-door sidelights at the persistent news crews. There were only a couple of diehards left. They'd rushed her as she pulled into her garage. She let the door down fast hoping it would clonk one of them on the head.

This would soon be over. Jeff Waite was going to get to the bottom of things. Ron was innocent, and when they found out, there would be egg on the face of all the major news outlets. She would demand some apologies. She was starting to get really ticked off at the smug looks.

Didn't these people know about the presumption of innocence? Of course they did, but it didn't matter, because sex sells papers and advertising. Who was going to let a little thing like the truth, or legal rights, get in the way?

Tiana's voice interrupted her bitter musings. "Yeah?"

"Tiana, this is Dallas Hamilton."

"I know."

"Danielle said you're about to leave."

"Yeah."

"Don't do it. You can't. He'll only beat you up again."

"Don't worry anymore about me."

"Tiana, listen to me, Jamaal could be beaten up too. For his sake, don't go back there."

"I've got nowhere else!" Tiana's voice was rife with anger and desperation.

"You could come here."

"Huh?"

"Come stay with me. Just for a while, till we figure out what to do. You can stay in my daughter's room. Jamaal can have my son's room."

"His own room?"

"That's right."

"Why?"

"Why what, Tiana?"

"Why are you opening up your own house?"

"I do sometimes. Please let me come get you and Jamaal. At least for a couple of days. Will you do that?"

Long pause. "Okay."

"Thank you. I'll be down there by three."

She hoped Tiana would still be there. Women in Tiana's situation could change their minds on a whim, so fragile were their psyches.

Now all she had to do was get the house in order. Good. Nothing like some old-fashioned housework to get occupied with something other than the things she had no control over.

She started with the family room and was about to go upstairs when a pounding at the back door, off the kitchen, startled her. Her heart spiked. She was certain it was a reporter.

Another knock at the door.

She thought about calling 911. But then, like a convict in an old prison movie, Dallas put her back to the wall and moved to a place where she could glimpse the door.

She saw the top half of a head over the curtain on the kitchen door.

And nearly jumped out of her skin.

11.

"Jared!"

She threw open the door.

"Hey, Mom."

Dallas threw her arms around his neck, kissed his cheek, held her face against his.

Jared said nothing. He felt rigid in her arms. She stood back and looked at him.

His dusky hair was still shoulder length. What was new was the goatee and a small ring above his left eyelid. He was wearing an old leather jacket, jeans, and dirty work boots spotted with white paint.

"Why didn't you call?" Dallas shut the door behind him.

"Maybe you wouldn't have wanted me around," Jared said.

"What!" She embraced him again and held him close, as if he were eight years old again and had come home from school crying because some older kids had made fun of him.

Jared pulled away. "So they got cameras out there in the front yard."

"I guess we're the story of the month."

"That's why I came in the back. Don't think anybody saw me hop the wall."

Dallas practically pushed him into a kitchen chair.

"Where've you been?" She sat across from him.

"Bakersfield. Painting houses."

"Good work?" she asked.

"Used to be."

"What does that mean?"

He sat back in the chair. "Did he do it?"

The directness of the question and the coldness of it hit Dallas like a blow. "No, of course he didn't do it."

"How do you know?"

"How can you say that?"

He drummed the tabletop with his fingers. "Anybody's capable of anything."

"Not your father."

"Come on, Mom. Why not Dad? He's human, isn't he?" His eyes, cool and aloof, seemed to catch a vision. "We can do bad things—"

"But not what they're accusing him of. I know he couldn't have done that."

"Did you know this girl?"

"No, she was someone your father was counseling. She had a troubled background. Anybody could have killed her."

"Right. Anybody but Dad."

Dallas looked at her son and hardly knew him. She supposed she hadn't known him since he returned from Iraq, but now he seemed even farther away.

"Listen to me, Jared. Carefully. I've seen your dad, looked in his eyes. He's confused and scared. He tried to help a girl in trouble, that's all, and then he wakes up accused of a horrible crime. And now he's in a jail cell and everyone is writing about him as a criminal. He's been convicted in the papers, the tabloids, and with oh-so-much glee. Can't you give him the benefit of the doubt?"

"When did he ever do that for me?" Jared stood up, almost knocking his chair over. He turned his back on her. She felt the onrush of bad memories from the many times Jared and Ron fought and screamed at each other.

Suddenly Jared laughed. It was a short, disturbing chuckle. He faced her. "It's funny. I remember a sermon Dad did once, about going through trials. I remember he said that sometimes God hits a Christian with suffering in order to get his attention, if he's been sinning. And so that's how suffering can be a good thing, la-di-da. I remember that, Mom, because it scared the juice out of me. Because I knew what a rotten kid I was and—"

"Jared—"

"Listen! I knew what a screwed-up case I was, so I was just getting ready to get hit with it, get God's freaking wrath poured all over me. Well, I'm over that now. Whatever this world is about, it's about getting garbage all over you. So maybe Dad was off doing something he shouldn't have, and now he can say God's getting his attention."

Jared sat down again, looking halfway conciliatory. "Look, Mom. I don't know what I'm talking about. Forget it. If you saw Dad and don't think he did it, that's good enough for me. I just don't want to see you hurt, you know? That's the only reason I'm here. It's not because of him. It's because of you."

"Will you see him?" Dallas said.

"No."

"He's still your father."

"Don't remind me."

"Stop it!" Dallas stood up. "I know you're hurt, Jared, and I know you've been through an ordeal. But don't disrespect your father. He doesn't deserve that."

"Relax, Mom, I'm not going to—"

"Do you understand me?"

Jared looked away from her. "I'm not a little kid, Mom."

But he was her kid, no matter what. Dallas embraced him again.

He said nothing but at least made no move to break away from her.

"Do you have to go back to Bakersfield?" she said. "Can you stay?"

"I sort of lost my job up there," Jared said. "You know, if I ran a mortuary, nobody would die."

"Jared—"

"So if you have any painting needs, I'll swap you for a bed."

"You don't need to swap anything," Dallas said. "This is home. Remember? The peas in the pot?"

When he was little, maybe five, he heard the expression *just like two peas in a pod* and somehow got it in his mind that the four of them—him, his mom and dad and sister, Cara—were four peas in a *pot*. He kept saying it that way, until the family adopted it.

Jared closed his eyes and nodded.

"All right then," Dallas said. "Let me get you something to eat."

12.

It's the silence that kills.

The theory of the penitentiary was that it would be a place of penitence. Stick a man in a cage and make him think about his black soul.

It works.

Of course, many of those held in isolation in the old days went crazy.

It's the silence that kills.

They built this jail back in the sixties. It's a big concrete block. Inside, a labyrinth of corridors, rows of cells, and metal gates. Garbage bags and sheets hang from cell doors to keep inquiring eyes from looking in. Shouts, curses, and clanging doors echo through the facility, which is penetrated here and there by a few shafts of sunlight.

But the silence remains for the celebrity inmates, like me. And in the silence, faces haunt you.

Faces. I see the faces of those I love.

Cara. My lovely daughter. She came to see me today and cried and I couldn't hold her. So I see her face now, wet with tears even as she told me she loved me, and the vision torments me.

Jared. Wherever he is. His face is troubled, and so it troubles me.

Dallas. I see her face all the time. I can't reach out to it; it just hovers over me. Hurt look. Accusing eyes. She tries to hide them. Can't.

Yet these are not the only faces I see.

Melinda.

Even since her death, I see her face. It screams at me.

Like a demon.

FOUR

1.

At least he was doing something other than wallowing in self-disgust. Still, Jared felt stupid behind the wheel of his mother's SUV. He was not a soccer mom. But he was, for the moment, a delivery service.

Delivering people, one of them to his own bed.

His mother—cleverly now, he realized, to get him moving—had asked him to pick up this woman and her kid and bring them home.

Now this was going to be strange. Here was a woman with a face that had been through things. Her kid, only six. Jared thought of all the children he'd watched in the park. That crack in his heart that ached for them throbbed again now. What chance did a kid like this have with a father who beat up on his mom? What chance did any kid have these days?

On the way to the house, the woman named Tiana said, "Your mom's a good person."

"Yeah."

"I mean, she didn't have to do this."

"That's my mom. Always taking in stray ... looking out for people." He wondered what Tiana's boyfriend was like, and why a girl stayed with somebody who slapped her around. He'd been with women. He didn't quite get them.

"You were in the Marines?" she said.

"My mom tell you about me?"

"A little. Jamaal wants to be in the Marines."

The boy was belted in the backseat. A six-year-old wanting to be in the Marines. How quaint.

"Tell him to go into football instead," Jared said.

"Mama, is he in the Marines?" The boy's voice was tissue-paper thin.

"Yeah, baby."

"In war?"

Tiana asked Jared, "You been in war?"

"Can it, will you?" Jared snapped, though pulling the punch a little. "Tell me how come you stay with a guy who knocks you around."

"You don't know anything about it."

"I know it doesn't make sense."

"You got a woman?"

"Not at the moment."

"Then you don't know."

Jared realized he was gunning the SUV too fast down Devonshire. He let up a little. *If you're going to crash, do it when nobody's in the car with you.*

"You seen your dad?" Tiana said.

"What are you talking about?" He knew what she was talking about.

"He's in trouble."

"Yeah, well, that's what you get, isn't it? You live, you get trouble. I shouldn't have to tell you that."

"I just asked if you've seen him. A son ought to see his father."

"That's kind of weird, coming from you."

"I was talking about you."

"Yeah, well, don't talk about me."

"Real friendly."

Oh yeah, he thought, *it's going to be great having these two in the house. Mom and her charity projects.*

"I wanna be in the Marines," Jamaal yelped from the back.

"No more talking," Jared said. "Just let me drive."

"Real friendly," Tiana said.

2.

The next day, Thursday, Dallas drove to Jeff Waite's office in Encino, summoned by Jeff himself. His voice on the phone sounded troubled, which only added to her already overcharged nervous system.

She'd picked up tension between Tiana and Jared the moment he brought her and Jamaal home yesterday. And she knew why. It was becoming clear to her that Jared's ability to relate to people was wounded, a casualty of war. She had to face the fact that this was no passing phase. He was out of it. Something had happened to him in Iraq. He was nearly gone, and she had to try to get him back before it was too late.

But how could she, when God dropped Ron's arrest on her? Or allowed it to happen, or whatever the correct theology for it was. Yes, he was sovereign, she knew that. And she knew God did things that defied human explanation. That didn't quell her hunger to know. This was her family at stake, and if she had to wrestle God like Jacob did, she would.

When she finally got to Jeff's office building, Dallas realized she couldn't recall any details of her drive there. She didn't even remember what streets she'd taken.

Jeff's unsmiling face did nothing to relieve the pressure.

He closed the door to his office.

"Ron's arraignment is tomorrow morning," Jeff explained. "I just got the arrest report from the DA's office."

"And?"

"Not good. Sit down."

"I don't want to."

"It'll be better if you do."

Dallas allowed herself to sink into a chair in duet with her sinking spirit. How much worse could this news be?

Jeff sat on the edge of his desk, facing Dallas with no obstruction between them. "How you doing, Dallas?"

"You have to ask?" She held up her hands. They trembled. "Don't put me around the nuclear button."

"You're a lot steadier than you think. I know that."

"Don't fool yourself."

"Your faith is what will get you through this."

"Tell me the news."

"All right." Jeff folded his arms. "Melinda Perry, the decedent, was being counseled by Ron. She was involved in, basically, porn movies. Went under the name of Melinda Chance."

"That's been all over the news," Dallas said bitterly. "They love that angle."

"Did Ron ever tell you he was counseling this girl?"

"He hasn't been too communicative this whole year. I just chalked it up to all he had going on. So, no, he never told me about her until I saw him at the jail. But that doesn't mean he killed her. He didn't."

Did he, Jeff? Did he? Tell me flat out he didn't do it.

"Let me tell you what the sheriff has," Jeff said. "A deputy found the girl's body early on the morning of the seventeenth, a Thursday, at a place in Pico Rivera called the Star Motel. She had Ron's card in her purse. On Friday they interviewed Ron. He went in to the Pico Rivera station. Did you know about that?"

"No."

"They asked him if he knew Melinda Perry and he said he'd been counseling her. They asked when the last time he saw her was, and he said either the tenth or the eleventh. They asked him where he was the night of the sixteenth, and he said he worked late at church. No one else was there, he said."

"He sometimes worked late there." At least, that's what he told her. *Don't let it be a lie!*

"They asked him if he'd ever been to the Star Motel. He said he'd never heard of the place."

Don't be a lie.

"Dallas, hang on. They found carpet fibers in Ron's car. They match the carpet in the room where the murder took place."

Something hard and vicious scraped Dallas's insides.

"Ron lied to the police, Dallas. That's something we can't avoid."

"But *why*—"

Because he did it.

No!

"He was scared," Jeff said. "That's what he told me. He went to the motel because she had called him on his cell phone. The police have a record of that call, on the night she was murdered. But Ron insists he just talked to her and left."

"Yes. I remember something he said. This girl was scared that some bad people were going to get her. That has to be what happened. They followed her, or followed Ron, or ..." She paused, trying to think. "Maybe they set him up."

Jeff said nothing.

"Doesn't it make sense?" Dallas slid to the edge of the chair. "This girl was in porn films. Ron's a big enemy of the industry. He's been working with our councilman, he's been vocal."

"Dallas—"

"Jeff, that has to be it."

He put his hand up. "Let me tell you the way it's got to play out. We have to deal with the evidence as it is. No judge is going to let me argue a conspiracy theory unless we come up with something to show there is at least a shred of possibility."

"Then let's find it."

"Believe me, Dallas, I have one of the best investigators in the city who'll be on this. But right now you have to be prepared for some very bad days."

And what's it been until now, a cakewalk?

Jeff sighed and looked at the floor.

"Is there something else?" she asked.

"Yes. Some detectives went over to Hillside earlier today."

"Detectives?"

Jeff nodded. "And they had a search warrant. They took Ron's computer and a bunch of his papers."

"But he's got all his stuff on there, his programs, his work."

"They have to preserve it all, under the law, but they can look at whatever they want."

"Jeff, this is unbelievable. It's so wrong."

"It's the way the law operates, Dallas. Sometimes it protects us, sometimes it invades us. Right now, it's invading. It's my job to get it all straightened out."

But what if it doesn't get straightened out? What then?

"What's going to happen next?" Dallas asked.

"Ron's entitled to a prelim within ten days of arrest. I'm not going to waive time. I'll hold their feet to the fire and try to smoke out what the prosecution thinks it has. The sooner we force it the better. This is now a big, fat media case. The DA is out there on a limb claiming Ron is the murderer. They'll fight every step of the way to make this stick. I just wanted you to be prepared. Don't talk to anyone. Refer all questions to my office."

Questions? She herself had a ton of them. Like, what really happened at the motel? And if Ron lied to the police, could he be lying to them all?

⸎

My life was changed by fire.

It was like that famous account of Pascal's conversion. I mean, there he was, living a worldly life in Paris in the 1600s, confused. What was life all about? he wanted to know. Is the sensuality I experience all there is to existence?

There he was, this genius in mathematics, founder of probability theory and advanced differential calculus. (I never even took calculus, I was too afraid.) His physics experiments led to the invention of the hydraulic press.

But he couldn't figure out life.

One night he picked up his Bible and began reading the gospel of John. Suddenly, he was filled with a sense of God's presence, so extreme and rapturous that he felt as if he were on fire. He grabbed a parchment and tried to record what he was feeling. When he died at the age of thirty-nine, they found this parchment sewed up in the lining of his jacket, where he'd kept it close to his heart:

FIRE

"God of Abraham, God of Isaac, God of Jacob,"
not of philosophers and scholars.
Certainty, certainty, heartfelt, joy, peace.
God of Jesus Christ.
God of Jesus Christ.
"My God and your God."
"Thy God shall be my God."
The world forgotten, and everything except God.

It went on, but I know how he felt. I know because it happened to me.

I was seventeen, alone in the house, watching Billy Graham on TV. I'd listened to Billy Graham before. Mom and Dad, even though they weren't Christians, said he was one of the best speakers around. I was interested in acting, so I liked listening to good orators.

Billy Graham was one of the best, I agreed. But I had never responded to his message.

Until this night.

I can't remember what his subject was, but when he started speaking about death, I got attentive. Even at seventeen, I realized I would die someday. Maybe this was something I needed to hear.

Then Billy Graham said that, for Christians, there is no fear of death. He pointed to the sky. "We're going to heaven!" he said.

At that moment, instantly, my body got hot from head to foot. I knew nothing about the Holy Spirit or the call of God. All I knew was I was brimming with an inexpressible joy and longing, the fire of it, the blaze of it, and I wanted that heaven Billy Graham was talking about.

When Billy offered the invitation, I dropped to my knees and prayed to the TV.

That was the fire of my own conversion, and it burned away everything else I thought was important to me. Basketball, hot cars, cheerleaders.

I gave my life over to him that high school year, and I knew I was going to be a minister.

Mom and Dad were shocked.

So were my friends and teachers.

But there was no going back. The fire had burned it all up—my sins, my plans, my life.

I never doubted my conversion or my choice. But over time, the memory of the fire faded.

Now I want it back.

FIVE

1.

The first Monday in April was hot in L.A. The usual snarl of morning traffic choked Temple Street as Dallas, clinging to Cara and following Jefferson Waite, approached the criminal courthouse.

Immediately, the pack of waiting reporters descended on her, barking questions at the new hot story—Dallas Hamilton.

In the last several days she had become the focus, the media star, the Garbo of wronged wives. Wanting nothing more than to be left alone, her resistance excited brute passions. She knew nothing worked the media beast into a frenzy like the pursuit of one who wished to avoid them.

Especially where sex and murder were the two angles, the salacious twins of tabloid headlines.

"No comment. No comment," Jeff repeated. He did not wear dark glasses. He smiled for the cameras. Dallas was not so naïve as to believe Jefferson Waite should want to shun media scrutiny. He was a lawyer, after all, and in Southern California, one case with publicity like this could make an entire career. But she also trusted him implicitly, knew he was good, knew he would fight to the last to prove Ron's innocence.

They followed closely, this organism of publicity, like a cloud of gnats swarming on a hot morning. Dallas kept her head down all the way to the front doors, holding Cara's arm, and was thankful when she finally passed through the metal detectors. Safe at last in the place that was the most forbidding. At least the deputy sheriffs would keep order, keep nosy reporters from getting in her face.

Ron's preliminary hearing was to begin this morning in Department 27. Judge Clifford Bartells was fair but tough, Jeff had explained. And a prelim was not generally where a case was won. The prosecution had only to provide minimal evidence, just enough to convince a judge to bind a defendant over for trial. With Bartells, that would be a low threshold indeed.

"But I'll be looking for the haymaker," Jeff told her. "Every now and then the prosecution messes up. If it does, I'll be ready."

The prosecutor, one Mike Freton, was a tall, silver-haired man with narrow eyes. The sort of man, Dallas thought, who has seen his share of evil people. How could he think that of Ron? How could anyone think that of Ron?

She and Cara were given seats in the front row, near the wall. It was on the jury-box side of the courtroom, which meant she was closest to the prosecution table. Ron and Jeff Waite, and Waite's investigator, Harry Stegman, were miles away on the other side.

Ron wore one of his suits, not the orange coveralls. He gave her one look before Judge Bartells entered. It was a look of inscrutable sadness. She wanted to go to him, hold him, reassure him. At the same time, she wanted to scream, shake him, make sure all the bad stuff was out.

Cara patted Dallas's arm and whispered, "Hang in there." Dallas nodded. She wished Jared had come too, to show support for his father. But he'd refused even to talk to her about it.

After a few words with the judge, legalese Dallas couldn't quite comprehend, Deputy DA Freton called a deputy sheriff named David Barnes to the stand.

He was a clean-cut young man who might have stepped off the beach at Santa Monica, been handed a badge, and told to catch bad guys.

After the swearing in, Freton began. "Deputy Barnes, you are with the Los Angeles County Sheriff's Department?"

"Yes, sir."

"How long have you been so employed?"

"Six years, come August."

"Turning your attention to the morning of March 17, can you tell us what your assignment was?"

"I was working out of the Pico Rivera station. I was in a cruiser."

"And did you receive a dispatch at around ten o'clock that morning?"

"Yes. I got a 911 report of a possible domestic disturbance at the Star Motel in Pico Rivera."

"Who were you told placed the 911 call?"

"The day manager of the motel, a Mr. Franze."

"What did you do next?"

"I proceeded to the location. I went to the front office and talked with Mr. Franze. I asked him if he had reported a disturbance and he said—"

"Objection," Jeff said. "Hearsay."

"It's the basis of the deputy's belief," Freton said.

Judge Bartells nodded. "Overruled."

"You may answer," Freton said.

"He said there was always something disturbing going on at this place."

The spectators and reporters in the courtroom laughed. Dallas felt a warm chill, hot ice, up and down her back. Like a fever. They were laughing at this now. At Ron.

"What did you do next, Deputy?"

"I asked him why he called, and he said somebody in room 103, a man named Knudsen, said that he'd heard—"

"Same objection," Jeff said.

"Overruled."

Deputy Barnes continued. "This man Knudsen had heard an argument the night before in room 105, some screaming, and then there was nothing. Silence. He thought about leaving it alone, but the next morning he just had this concerned feeling and felt he had to tell Mr. Franze about it. Mr. Franze went to room 105 and knocked, got no answer. He thought it best to give a call to 911."

"Did he give any reason why he thought to do that?"

"Yes. He said he was afraid of being sued."

More laughter in the courtroom. Dallas gripped the arms of her seat and shook her head. Cara took her hand and squeezed it.

"What happened next, Deputy Barnes?"

"I asked Mr. Franze to look up the registration on room 105. He told me the name was Melinda Perry. I then asked Mr. Franze to accompany me to room 105. We proceeded to the room. I knocked on the door and announced that I was a Los Angeles County deputy sheriff. There was no answer. I knocked and announced again. Still no answer. So I requested Mr. Franze to unlock the door, which he did."

"Why did you request Mr. Franze to unlock the door?"

"It was my belief that there might be someone injured inside the room, based upon the 911 call."

"What did you see when you entered room 105?"

"A young woman on the bed. Not moving. I went to the bed and said, 'Ma'am?' I said it three times. When she did not respond I checked her wrist for a pulse. There was none."

"What did you do next?"

"I secured the room and contacted the sheriff's department homicide division."

"When did they arrive?"

"Approximately twenty minutes later."

"Did anyone enter or exit room 105 before the homicide division arrived?"

"No, sir."

"No further questions."

Freton was direct, confident. And from the moment he started, a blistering dread thickened inside Dallas, nearly choking off breath. It was happening. Really happening. Her husband was really a defendant in a murder trial.

2.

Jefferson Waite stood up, buttoned the coat of his dark blue pin-stripe suit, and approached Deputy Barnes.

"Just a few questions, Deputy. You say you received a dispatch about a 911 call?"

"Yes."

Dallas noted that the witness did not add *sir* when addressing the defense attorney.

"You did not hear the 911 tape, did you?"

"Nope. I merely responded to the call."

"And the call was for a possible domestic disturbance at the Star Motel, isn't that correct?"

"Some sort of disturbance, yes."

"The dispatch told you that someone had reported screaming, correct?"

"Yes."

"That person, in fact, was the manager of the motel, Mr. Franze?"

"Yes."

"But Mr. Franze was relying on the statement of a Mr. Knudsen, correct?"

"Yes."

"And you proceeded to the scene?"

"Yes."

"Did you at any time on the way to the Star Motel receive any further information on the factual basis of the 911 call?"

"Factual basis?" Barnes said this incredulously, as if everyone in the world would know that was an absurd question.

Jeff did not flinch. "Yes, Deputy. Factual basis. As opposed to mere speculation or opinion. I'm sure they cover that at the sheriff's academy."

"Objection," Freton said.

The judge half closed his eyes. "Sustained. Continue, Mr. Waite."

"So the answer is, you did not receive any further information concerning the 911 call, is that correct?"

"No, and that's the way it always is. There is no—"

"You've answered the question. Next question. When you got to the motel and contacted Mr. Franze, did you question him about who this man Knudsen was?"

"No."

"Instead, you made him walk down to room 105 and open it up."

"Objection," Freton said. "Misstates the evidence."

"Ah, yes," Jeff said. "There was the token knock on the door. By the way, when you knocked and announced, there was no answer inside, was there?"

"No."

"No sounds from inside, right?"

"That's correct."

"Then you instructed Mr. Franze to open the door."

"Yes."

"And you went in."

"Yes."

"No more questions."

Dallas could not see that the cross-examination of the deputy had made any dent in the prosecution's case. What was Jeff after? A deputy sheriff answered a distress call, went into a motel room, and found a dead body. Hard facts indeed.

The prosecutor placed some papers in front of Jefferson Waite and was saying something to him. Jeff was looking at them with a concerned expression. Dallas saw him in profile, then he gave her a quick look. The next thing she knew he was standing and saying, "Your Honor, may we take a ten-minute recess?"

"Very well," the judge said.

What was happening? Dallas looked at Jeff. His eyes practically burned with neon, a sign spelling out *disaster*.

3.

Jared found the cardboard box at the back of the hallway closet, under the Christmas wrapping paper. He'd been looking for a fresh toothbrush, and his mother usually kept such items in this closet.

At least she had five years ago.

But the box didn't contain what he needed. It held, instead, a bunch of old stuff from his room.

Weird. Like going back in a little cardboard time machine. But it wasn't a fun trip. He was tense. His jaws were locked and hurt. His insides were screaming for some combo, but he'd stayed away from weed and beer and even loud music for his mother's sake.

He wondered how long he'd last before the inevitable fall.

On his knees in the hallway, Jared picked through his past. A couple of old Chip Hilton books. Trophies from his Little League days. Pictures of his teams—the Orioles, Royals, and Cubs. One year his dad was in the picture as an assistant coach. The season with the Pirates. That was an embarrassment. He and his father did not get along one bit that year —

"What're you doing?"

Jared looked up. Tiana was standing there. "What I'm doing is my own business in my own house."

"Just asking."

He went back to rummaging through the box, fishing out a couple of old Little League mitts. Why had his mother bothered to save these?

"I don't really want to be here, you know," Tiana said.

Jared stifled the urge to say, *That makes two of us*. But a quiet nudge not to be such a jerk interrupted the insult. He sat back against the wall.

"What's going to happen to you?" he asked.

Tiana shrugged. "Jamaal and I can't stay here forever."

"But you can't go back to your boyfriend." He looked at her closely. The ugly bruise that had marred her face was mostly gone. So was the puffiness. Tiana was really very pretty, he thought. He wanted her to stay that way.

"He's Jamaal's father. He loves Jamaal. Jamaal wants him."

"Even though he hits you?"

"Not all the time."

"I say once is too much. Don't be stupid."

"I'm not stupid." She had some attitude in her voice.

Jared started to get angry. He clenched his teeth. "Stupid's putting yourself where you and your kid are gonna get hurt. So don't—"

"Who are you to give me advice?"

"What's that supposed to mean?"

"Means you got a father in trouble and you don't even go to court, don't even talk to him. You got no cred with me."

Jared got up from the floor. His head was tight. "You don't know what you're talking about."

She put her hands on her hips. "And you do? Get over yourself."

"Hey, I don't need anything from you, okay? I'm minding my own business."

"Your mom needs you to go with her to court—"

"Shut up."

"—so get off your—"

"You want to go back? Get your stuff. Get your kid. I'll drive you."

She hesitated, then a steely resolve came to her face. "That's good by me."

And she left the hall.

Jared let her go. *Good one. Mom's gonna love you for this. But that's the way it breaks.*

Fifteen minutes later, Tiana and Jamaal were in the cab of Jared's truck, heading toward Pacoima. This was one of the most run-down, gang-infested areas of the Valley. Jared almost turned around. Forget the boyfriend. What chance would Jamaal have of even making it out of his teens here?

That's the breaks.

They rode in silence. Once, Jamaal tried to ask Jared a question, but Tiana put her finger to her lips and quieted him.

The only words spoken were Tiana's directions to the apartment building. It was a prop-up job on Dorado Avenue, within shouting distance of the rail line running along San Fernando Boulevard. What little grass there was in front of the place was brown and patchy.

"Good luck," Jared said.

Tiana said nothing as she got out, unstrapped Jamaal, and fished her trash bag of clothes from the bed of the truck.

Then she stuck her head in the window. "I hope you find what you're looking for," she said.

Jared watched as she and Jamaal shuffled toward the apartments. Suddenly Jamaal stopped and turned around.

And waved.

Jared just looked at him.

Then Jamaal saluted. He stood at attention for a moment, then turned and ran toward his mother.

4.

Jefferson Waite walked Dallas to the end of the corridor. Cara was down in the coffee shop on the first floor, waiting for Dallas to join her.

"How you holding up?" Jeff asked.

"I don't know. I'll tell you at the end of the day."

He looked back down the long hallway, like he was avoiding her all of a sudden.

"What is it?" Dallas said.

He sighed. "You need to be strong. I have to tell you something."

Strong? She felt like warm Jell-O. "What is it?"

"The next witness is the deputy coroner, the one who performed the autopsy."

"And?"

"Freton just gave me a copy of his report."

"What does it say?"

"Dallas, I will always be up front with you."

"Please talk to me."

"They found seminal fluid in Melinda Perry."

The walls of the courthouse began to close in on Dallas, even before he said what she knew he'd say.

"They did a DNA analysis. It's a match with Ron."

Fireworks behind her eyes, a momentary blindness to everything around her.

"Dallas—"

"No." She put her hand up. "Just let me alone."

She turned and walked the other way, down the corridor, a long dark tunnel now. Even with the lights, the people, the elevators, the sounds—even with all that, she was alone in a blackness that went on and on.

Thought smashed against thought. She was unaware of what she was doing. She knew she was walking, then entering the restroom. There may have been another woman in there, she wasn't sure. She saw only the first stall with its door open, and that is where she fell to her knees and retched.

5.

"Mom, what on earth?" Cara took Dallas by the shoulders and sat her down on the plastic bench in the coffee shop.

"I'm sick."

"Let's get you home."

"No. I'm staying. Your father ..." How to break this to her daughter? How to soften the blow?

"What about Dad?"

"Cara, they have evidence, that your dad and the girl ..."

"Not sex."

Dallas nodded.

"Oh, Mom, no."

Dallas was still nauseated and took a long breath. "Jeff's not finished. We don't know everything."

"Let me take you home."

"I'm staying."

"Then I am too."

Dallas held Cara's hand during the entire testimony of Dr. Edward Varaki. The deputy DA put him through a clinical, step-by-step recitation of the autopsy. Asphyxiation. Suffocation. Lack of oxygen to brain. Evidence of sexual intercourse.

And the DNA match with Ron.

She could sense the reporters working overtime, scribbling notes or clacking on tiny keyboards. They had the good stuff now, the guarantor of ratings and circulation. *It used to be about the news that's fit to print*, Dallas thought. *Now it's all the sex that fits, we print.*

She had been betrayed.

Jeff cross-examined. "Dr. Varaki, the evidence of sexual inter-course and the cause of death have nothing to do with each other, do they?"

"I offer no opinion on that."

"It's entirely possible to have sexual intercourse with someone and not kill them, isn't it?"

"Objection," Freton said.

Jeff nodded and said, "No more questions."

Freton had one more witness, a sheriff's detective named Powell Dennison. He was paunchy and graying. His hairstyle was a buzz cut, like the cops in TV shows of the sixties.

"You questioned the defendant on the morning of March 18, is that correct?" Freton asked.

"Yes, sir."

"Did you record that interview?"

"I did."

"And do you have the written report in front of you?"

"Yes."

"Referring to your report, Detective, can you tell the court if Mr. Hamilton was advised of his Miranda rights?"

"He was."

"Did he request a lawyer?"

"No. He said he would like to answer questions, to clear this all up."

"Did he sign a waiver?"

"He did."

"Did you ask if Mr. Hamilton knew the deceased, Melinda Perry, also known as Melinda Chance?"

"He said that he did know her. Said he had been counseling her at his church on occasion."

"Referring to your report, at page eight, will you please read into the record lines six through sixteen?"

"Sure." Dennison flipped a couple of pages and began to read. "'QUESTION: When was the last time you saw Miss Perry?

"'ANSWER: Oh, I'm trying to think. It was probably last Thursday or Friday.

"'QUESTION: That would be the tenth or the eleventh?

"'ANSWER: Yeah, I guess.

"'QUESTION: There is no way you've seen her in the last two days?

"'ANSWER: None.

"'QUESTION: Have you ever been to Pico Rivera, Mr. Hamilton?

"'ANSWER: Pico Rivera? I don't think so.

"'QUESTION: Ever heard of the Star Motel in Pico Rivera?

"'ANSWER: No.

"'QUESTION: Did you ever have sex with Melinda Perry?

"'ANSWER: No. No way. I would never do that.'"

Mike Freton cast a quick glance at Jefferson Waite. The hint of a smirk crossed Freton's face. Dallas thought she might get sick all over again.

Freton sat down. Jeff said he had no questions for the witness.

The last witness for the prosecution was a forensic technician from the sheriff's lab. He testified to the presence of the carpet fibers from the Star Motel in Ron's car.

Jeff cross-examined with some technical questions Dallas didn't understand. But it was obvious Jeff was trying to lay a foundation for a later challenge to the gathering of this evidence.

When Jeff finished, Freton announced that the prosecution's case was over.

Judge Bartells nodded. "Mr. Waite, do you have witnesses to call?"

Jefferson Waite stood ramrod straight. The way he did it made Dallas think of a gladiator.

"No witnesses, Your Honor. But I would like to ask for a recess until Wednesday."

"The purpose being?"

"I would like to supplement my points and authorities on my motion to suppress. I believe that what we've heard today from the prosecution leads only to one conclusion, and that is all the evidence gathered from the Star Motel is inadmissible."

Dallas thought she heard a snort from the prosecutor. The judge made no sound, but his eyes lit up with surprise.

"All of it?" the judge said.

"Every last fiber," Jeff said.

The judge looked at his wall calendar. "Very well. We'll address this on Wednesday afternoon, at one thirty sharp. We're in recess until then."

Everyone stood as the judge left the bench. Then a deputy sheriff took Ron by the arm to lead him out of the courtroom.

Ron did not turn around to look at Dallas.

As Jeff gathered his notes, Dallas tried to make her way to him. She was immediately confronted by several reporters angling for a comment. She waved them off, but still they came, like sharks to chum.

Only the bailiff, a broad-shouldered deputy sheriff, restored order with a verbal threat to the press. They shrank back with sour looks all around.

Dallas got to the rail, where Jeff saw her.

"What's going on?" she asked.

"I've got some work to do on my motion to suppress. We'll be back here Wednesday afternoon."

"What if the judge doesn't go along with this motion?"

"Let's cross that bridge when we come to it."

"What do I do now?"

Jeff put a hand on her shoulder. "Just try to get some rest. This has been a traumatic day, I know."

Rest? Out of the question. Her body and mind wouldn't allow it. Not, at least, until she looked her husband in the eye again.

SIX

1.

"Look at me, Ron."

He did. Reluctantly. His forehead was furrowed and his eyes uncertain. It was nearly four thirty in the afternoon, and Ron was back at county jail. This would be his world for at least another two days, until Judge Bartells issued his ruling.

But at the moment Dallas wasn't thinking about judges or lawyers or courtrooms.

"You lied to me," she said, letting the hurt vibrate her words.

Ron nodded, looking at the scarred table in front of him.

"I said look at me." Dallas was gripping the phone so hard her forearm ached. "Have you ever lied to me about ... about women?"

"Dallas, believe me, I—"

"Why *should* I?"

"Because I'm telling you, I'm telling you the truth with every ounce of my being. Yes, I did a terrible thing. And lied to you about it. But I'm not lying now. I did not kill that girl."

She looked at him and wondered if her instinct was right. That her husband was not a killer, could never be. He could lie to her about a sordid affair. He could lie to her about loving her, about a great many things. But not about this.

"You believe me, don't you?" Ron asked.

"You've hurt me. You've hurt your family, your church."

"I know that. Don't you think it's ripping me apart?"

"Good."

"Good?"

"Because that's the only way God is going to get through to you."

His eyes cooled. "You're telling me what God is going to do?"

"Why shouldn't I? Are you going to deny that sin has consequences?"

Ron looked away, silent.

"I see you in there and I know you're not a killer, you're just a man. You're not the man I thought you were, and maybe that's my fault. Maybe I should have come out of the fog a long time ago."

"Dallas, don't." He hesitated, then spoke again. "Is Jared going to come see me?"

"I don't know."

"Will you please tell him I need to see him?"

"Yes, I'll try." She started to get up, feeling that if she stayed another moment she'd burst a blood vessel in her brain.

"Please stay for a little while," Ron said.

"I'll be in court Wednesday." Dallas put down the handset before he said another word.

2.

That was the worst part, her going away. The palpable hurt on her face. I never wanted to hurt my wife, but of course no man does when he falls to temptation. He just has part of himself take over without thought of hurt or consequence.

There is a slash in the fabric of our marriage now, a fabric I always thought would remain whole. But a lie is a razor. It cuts quick and deep.

And what of my son? The son who turned his back on me? Or was that me doing the turning?

I was so proud when he was born. The second child, a son. Something happens to a man when his son is born right before his eyes. He receives an infusion from on high, a divine current that reshapes and remolds what is inside him.

That new shape remains until something devastating warps it.

Like now.

I am misshapen.

Dallas sighed with relief as she pulled into the garage. No media at the curb today. At least they'd figured out the Hamilton house was dry ground. They'd have to suck marrow from some other set of bones.

Her marrow was seriously depleted. Confronting Ron was not a happy event. Confronting herself about how she felt was even worse. She did not take kindly to being the thing she'd never thought she'd be—the betrayed wife.

Adultery. Betrayal.

Let him sit in jail. Let him sit there a long time and feel the punishment.

She gasped at her own thoughts. But they did not stop, and she did not try to stop them. Like steam coming out of a boiler, it was keeping her from blowing.

It good to be home, a place where people were. People who were not Ron or reporters or prosecutors. She was starting to grow fond of Tiana and Jamaal. And Jared, at least for the past week, had been civil, if distant.

But the house was silent when she came through the door. And she knew something was wrong.

"Hello?" No answer. She heard a scuffing sound in the hallway and went there. Jared was leaning against the wall.

"Why didn't you answer me?" Dallas said.

He shrugged and looked at the floor. What was he up to?

"Where's Tiana?"

"Home."

"What do you mean, *home*?"

"I took her home. Drove her. And the kid."

"Jared, look at me."

He looked. Dallas saw such a faraway aspect in his eyes that she wanted to forget everything else and hold him. She was also getting ready to scream.

"You're saying you drove her back to that abuser?"

"Mom, she wanted to go home. She wasn't a prisoner here."

"She wasn't going to go!" All sorts of terrible images came to her mind now. "I almost had her convinced. What did you say to her?"

"Nothing."

"Don't lie to me, Jared! I don't want to be lied to anymore!"

"You want the truth?" The chill in his voice nearly froze her.

"Yes. I want the truth."

"Then I'll give it to you. The truth is you can't save anybody, and it's driving you crazy. Dad's up for murder, and even if he didn't do it he probably did something he ought to be in jail for. And you can't save me. So you picked some poor woman who's going to end up dead anyway, and you made her a project."

"No—"

"Another Dallas Hamilton feel-good project, because it's a sure thing her family isn't feeling good."

"Stop it!"

"This woman doesn't want your charity. She doesn't want us, doesn't need us."

"Stop, please." Dallas sank down until she sat on the floor.

"Mom, I'm sorry."

Jared got down next to her and wrapped her up in his arms. Her tears started falling.

"No, Mom, don't do that."

She shook in his arms. He kept holding her. Like she had held him when he was sick or scared or hurting. Once when he was twelve and sick with a fever, trying to be brave, saying he didn't need anything, she lay next to him on his bed. He let her, put his head on her shoulder. Just before he drifted to sleep he said, thick of voice, "I'm glad you're here."

Dallas stopped crying and sat up. Jared started to say something, but she raised her hand.

"Things have to change," she said. "You and I have to come together on this. Your dad. He's going to lose everything. He's made a horrible mistake. He didn't kill this girl, I know it. He did wrong. He knows it. He's paying for it. Don't make him pay anything more, Jared. Go see him."

"Mom—"

"Please. He needs you. Go see him."

"I'll think about it."

"He needs you to forgive him."

"I'll try, okay?"

"Just do it, Jared."

"Mom, let me do it on my own. You want something to eat? Want me to make you some eggs or something?"

"No." She couldn't eat. She'd been losing weight.

Jared leaned back against the wall and looked at the ceiling. "It's all so messed up."

She got on her knees and faced him. "Jared, you used to believe in God when you were a kid. You can again."

"It's not that simple anymore. I mean, look at the world, Mom. Look at TV. Look at the people on *Cops*. Why would a good God allow that?"

"I know it's not simple. But, Jared, I know you used to believe, and—"

Jared shook his head. "You don't really know me, Mom."

"I do!"

"Yeah?"

He stood suddenly and pulled his T-shirt off over his head. His chest was pale under a patch of dark hair. Over his heart she saw the tattoo, USMC, with the marine insignia. She'd seen it before he'd shipped over to Iraq.

Then he turned around.

And Dallas gasped.

In the middle of his back, from neck to waist, was a blue-black tattoo of a sword. On the blade was written *I Come To Bring You Hell*.

4.

Her son's body, desecrated. The same body she had birthed and nursed and held and healed. Scarred now with this image.

Jared did not move, as if he wanted her to get the full effect of the shock.

"Pretty, huh?" He finally turned around and looked down at her. "Want to hear why I got it?"

She did not. She wanted it to go away, disappear right before her eyes, restore her son's skin to its purity. But she knew she had to hear just the same. She nodded slowly.

"I'll tell you," he said, "but you must not interrupt me. Understand that? Don't interrupt me because I'm only going to say this once, and once I get started I can't stop or it won't come out again. Got it?"

With effort she said, "Yes, Jared."

He nodded once, then lay down on the floor, facing up, and closed his eyes. For several minutes he breathed, rhythmically, his chest rising and falling like a soft swell in the ocean.

When he finally spoke, his voice was calm yet distant. "It was the end of the battle for Fallujah. Our squad was mopping up. We followed a column of infantrymen heading east just below the main highway between the northern and southern sections. It was like a science-fiction movie about the end of the earth. Rubble everywhere. Every house had at least one hole through it. We went inside houses, ready to shoot if we had to. And then, from the south side of the street, fire. And grenades. There were insurgents in a house, and they were trying to kill us."

Dallas listened, her heart falling.

"I felt a sting in my arm. I got hit in the bicep. But I didn't say anything because I could keep going. I could be one-handed if I had to. A buddy of mine got hit in the back, just below his flak jacket. They hauled him off to the big bus. That's the medical vehicle. I thought that's where I was going to end up eventually, only I was sure it would be by way of a body bag."

Jared's voice was almost a monotone. This, as much as the story itself, filled Dallas with dread.

"We kept going. Every step we had to watch. There were all these improvised explosive devices rigged. It was like they were waiting for us, just waiting. And every house we went into had some sort of weapon. Grenades. Whatever. We got to one house, empty, and some of the Iraqi special-forces guys assigned to our unit found some rice and vegetables and made lunch. We had some warm chow. But halfway through there was an explosion outside and a window shattered, throwing shards of glass into the food."

He paused, his eyes still closed, his breathing rhythmic.

"When that happened, I screamed. I screamed with anger and maybe fear, I don't know what all it was, but it didn't even seem like me. But I started to have thoughts I never had before. I won't even bother telling you about those, because it's not really the thing I want to tell. We got up and kept going, house to house.

"We got to one about two blocks from a staging area. We were almost out. It had been about five hours of this. I thought we'd make it out, and I'd get my stupid arm taken care of, get out of this hell town. And then we went into this house, full of rubble, full of ..."

He stopped for a long moment. Dallas, silent, watched him. His breathing, for the first time, quickened.

"There was something about this place. It smelled more like death than any of the others we'd been in. Like it had been down the longest, like it was leading the death parade. I was the one who went around the last corner. The last look. That's when I heard something move."

Dallas watched his chest rising, falling.

"I lifted my weapon, trigger ready. I wish it had gone off. I wish it had exploded and killed me. I saw a little girl, maybe eight, nine. Dead. Spread out dead. She wasn't moving. There was a dog on her. It was chewing her body, it ..."

Dallas felt inner wiring ripping out of sockets, shutting her down. Blacking out would have been a relief.

"I shot the dog. Just blew him away. And that's sort of the last thing I remember for a long time. I did wake up in a hospital and I do remember cursing. I cursed God because he hadn't seen fit to put me in that body bag. That's when I let go of the last of whatever beliefs I had. And that is what I wanted to tell you."

He slowly opened his eyes and raised to a sitting position.

"Jared ..." Dallas leaned forward, and the moment she did, Jared put up his hand.

He pulled his shirt back on and said, "Don't say anything. Don't do anything. Just stay here."

He stood and walked away. Dallas heard the back door close.

And immediately she thought, *He's going to kill himself.*

She ran to the door and threw it open. "Jared!"

He was getting into his truck.

"Jared, wait."

He slammed his door shut. The window was rolled up.

"Jared, please!"

The truck started and burned rubber out of the driveway.

Dallas clutched her throat. *Dear God dear God don't let him do it restrain him God keep him from it dear God dear God.*

She dropped to her knees on the concrete, closed her eyes, made fists. *Dear God dear God protect him ...*

5.

Jail has its own postal system.

It's more efficient than Uncle Sam's. There's a lot prisoners get done this way. Like making a jailhouse drink called pruno. They get a plastic bag and save up all their orange rinds and fruit bits and put them in water to ferment. It's powerful, I'm told.

But mostly they talk to each other through written messages, sometimes with the consent of the jailer.

I got one such message yesterday.

When my lunch was shoved through the door at me I saw on the tray a bit of tin foil. About the size of a marble.

That was definitely out of the ordinary. I knew immediately something was inside it.

Something meant for me.

I sat on my bunk and unraveled the foil.

Inside was a wad of toilet paper.

This I unraveled as well.

Someone had written on the toilet paper, in blue ink: "So then because thou art lukewarm, and neither cold nor hot, I will spew thee out of my mouth."

At 11:42 p.m., Officer Jennica Brune of the Los Angeles Police
Department, on routine patrol in Hollywood with her partner,
spotted an illegally parked pickup on Franklin Avenue. She pulled
her black and white parallel to the truck. She heard loud music
blaring from inside. The engine appeared to be idling.

Her partner, Officer Jeffrey Benkert, got out and directed his
flashlight into the cab. A male Caucasian was sprawled on the seat.
Benkert knocked on the window. No response.

The truck was unlocked. With Officer Brune taking the sidewalk position, Benkert opened the door.

"Whoa," he shouted above the music. "We got ourselves a
dewey."

Officer Brune knew he meant DUI—driving under the
influence.

Benkert shut off the stereo and tried to rouse the occupant. He
was out.

"I'm guessing this guy's gonna be over two-point-oh," Benkert
told Brune.

"What's he been drinking?" Brune said.

"Beer. Talk about your open containers. There must be eight,
nine bottles in here. Looks like Dos Equis is his preferred label."
Benkert sighed. "Let's take him in."

SEVEN

After a fitful sleep in a holding cell, Jared was informed he was at the Hollywood station on Wilcox, that his truck was impounded, and that he would get one free call. He used it to call Cara. He wasn't ready to spring this on his mother.

When his sister came for him, he felt embarrassed and dirty, and it didn't help that Cara was silent all the way to her car and all the way out to Hollywood Boulevard.

Finally Cara said, "So what are you going to tell Mom?"

He shrugged.

"She's been sick with worry. I won't let you stab her in the heart."

"Thank you so much. You ever thought about going into psych?"

"Shut it, Jared."

"Much better."

Cara shook her head. "You think you can dance away from this?"

"Quit trying to play big sister, will you?"

"I'm just your sister then, and you know what that means? I love you, dork."

"Sounds like it."

"Why don't you listen to your family?"

"Like Dad? Great role model he is, huh?"

"That's real forgiving of you, Jared."

"Here it comes."

Cara jammed the brakes. Tires shrieked as she turned the car to the curb in front of a Chinese restaurant.

Jared lurched against the shoulder strap. "Are you nuts?"

"You're not the only one with problems, you know."

"What are you doing?"

"I want you to come back to church," Cara said.

"What's that going to do?"

"At least you won't be drinking."

"For two hours maybe."

"It's a start."

"Just drive," Jared said.

"Promise you'll come to church. You still have friends there."

He sat still, eyes directed out the window. A man in a Dodgers hat stood outside the Chinese restaurant, yelling at someone through the door. Jared couldn't tell if the guy was angry, high, or a combination of both.

"Cara, I'm messed up," he said. "I know that. The VA says it's PTSD, but I don't know. It's like my genes got messed up and I'm this totally new person, and nobody knows who I am."

"Somebody knows," Cara said.

He glared at her. "God? Is that what you're saying?"

"Yes."

"Have him send me a memo," Jared said.

"He will. In church. Say you'll come with us."

"I'm not going to—"

"Promise or I'll get out and take you down, right there on the sidewalk."

A laugh poked through Jared's anger. He remembered when Cara could actually do that to him, back when he was scrawny and she was in a tennis champ. It got him mad back then and he swore to himself he'd become a Marine someday. Just so he could wrestle his big sister to the ground.

"I'll think about it," he said. "Now drive on."

2.

Still no word from Jared.

It was past nine in the morning and Dallas paced the family room like a big cat in a cage. She prayed but kept looking at the phone. If she didn't hear anything in a few hours, she'd call the police.

That reminded her about the strange message she'd had on her cell phone last night. A male voice, a whisper. *Call me. Very important.* He gave a number with a 310 area code.

Terrific. No doubt some reporter seeking an exclusive got her number!

How?

Somebody gave it away.

No, that couldn't be. That would mean someone close to her was leaking information. Maybe someone from the church. She couldn't allow herself to think that. She had enough to deal with without cooking up conspiracy theories. *Maybe it was Oliver Stone.*

Stop it!

It was probably just some sleazy reporter who had a way of finding out these things.

But she wasn't going to call, no way. She did jot the number down on a pad just in case she had to tell the cops about this.

She had to do something besides stew. She fired up the computer in the study and went to Google. She wanted to read more about posttraumatic stress disorder, especially as it related to the soldiers coming home from Iraq. In seconds she had a slew of links and started to check them out.

She came across the account of a Marine soldier whose profile sounded eerily like Jared's. A kid raised in a Christian home in the South, who came back covered in tattoos.

> Soldiers like this signal that a crisis is unfolding, mental-health experts say. One out of six soldiers returning from Iraq suffers from a severe type of posttraumatic stress. Experts say they have not seen its like.
>
> The Pentagon, which did not anticipate the extent of the problem, is scrambling to find resources to address it.
>
> A recent study found that 15.6 percent of Marines and 17.1 percent of soldiers surveyed after they returned from Iraq suffered major depression, generalized anxiety, or posttraumatic stress disorder — a debilitating, sometimes lifelong change in the brain's chemistry that can include flashbacks, sleep disorders, panic attacks, violent outbursts, acute anxiety, and emotional numbness.
>
> Army mental-health experts say there is reason to believe the war's ultimate psychological fallout will worsen. The army survey of 6,200 soldiers and Marines included only troops willing to report their problems.

"The bad news is that the study underestimated the prevalence of what we are going to see down the road," said Dr. Frederick J. Matthews, a professor of psychiatry and pharmacology at Johns Hopkins School of Medicine. "And there is some aggravating factor underneath the surface of all this that we need to more deeply explore."

Aggravating factor.

The words stuck in her mind. What could that be? She jotted the phrase on a pad and determined to follow it up.

She switched to the Google news site to see what was being written about Ron. More sensationalized stuff with the sex angle. There wasn't going to be any getting away from that.

One squib with the term "Melinda Perry" in it caught her attention. She clicked on the link. Dallas couldn't get past the gut feel of the woman scorned. Melinda Perry, though dead, was a rival. What had drawn Ron to her? What had she done to seduce him?

She read desperately for answers.

Melinda Perry, the deceased, was also known as Melinda Chance. She was, by the account of industry insiders, a rising star in adult films. Producer/Director Vic Lu, one of the industry's top moneymakers and principal owner of LookyLu Productions, said Ms. Perry was on the verge of stardom.

"I discovered her and knew she had what it takes to be a superstar," Lu said in a phone interview. "I mean, she had it all."

She had it all. Apparently Ron thought so too.

She skipped the rest of the sex-themed stories and found some covered locally. And then, at the *Daily News* site, she found a quote that was apparently being readied for the next day's edition:

Councilman Bernie Halstrom, who was working with Hamilton on possible regulations of the adult-entertainment industry in Chatsworth, mentioned the case.

"I know Ron Hamilton to be a good, decent man. I cannot, of course, comment on a pending criminal matter."

"Why not?" Dallas whispered out loud. "What's stopping you?"

And then it hit her. There was something bigger than Ron going on here. It wasn't just about him and his ministry. The overarching issue was the one they both cared passionately about—the evil of pornography.

This case was going to be used to try to destroy that work. She was not about to let that happen. She'd promised Ron she would keep the pressure on Bernie Halstrom, and she would.

She heard a key in the front door. She jumped up from the desk and nearly ran to the foyer.

Jared was standing there, head slightly down, with a serious-looking Cara behind him.

"I'll let you take it from here, Mom," Cara said.

3.

Cara entered the sunlight of her apartment and went immediately to the window. This was her favorite place to kneel before God and pray.

Prayer, she'd come to believe, was her particular duty, a calling. She'd been called the hard way, but that was fine with her.

When she was ten, the neuromuscular disease she had trouble pronouncing threatened to take away all the things she loved most —running, playing, keeping up with the boys. She took treatments and therapy for three years before the doctors said the disorder would stay with her for life.

That's when she really started praying. Before, she prayed in obedience to her parents and Sunday school teachers. Now it was from a scared heart.

Alone in her room, she had underlined passages in her Bible about prayer. She especially loved something Jesus said in Luke. "Which of you fathers, if your son asks for a fish, will give him a snake instead? Or if he asks for an egg, will give him a scorpion? If you then, though you are evil, know how to give good gifts to your children, how much more will your Father in heaven give the Holy Spirit to those who ask him!"

She asked. For a whole year she asked, clinging to the promises. And she was healed.

Now, almost fifteen years later, she still prayed the promises, even when the answers weren't what she expected or God seemed silent.

She didn't care that some of her friends teased her about it. One, Susan Farmer, called her "praying Cara," which was a riff on the Stephen King novel *Carrie*. Cara looked it up.

> Tommy Erbter, age five, was biking up the other side of the street. He was a small, intense-looking boy on a twenty-inch Schwinn with bright red training wheels. He was humming "Scooby Doo, where are you?" under his breath. He saw Carrie, brightened, and stuck out his tongue.
>
> "Hey . . . Ol' prayin' Carrie!"

Even though Susan only meant it in fun, it did strike Cara that she must have seemed as odd as Carrie White to those who didn't believe in God.

For Carrie, of course, the ultimate answer came in the form of murderous, telekinetic powers. For Cara Hamilton, the answers came from God.

Her apartment was on the third floor of a security building in Encino. A place she could call home and feel safe in. She still displayed her love of sports in the décor. Posters of some of her favorite athletes, like Serena Williams and Annika Sorenstam, were framed on the wall. A small case held some of her tennis trophies.

She vaguely recalled that a tournament she wanted to attend was coming up, but just as quickly the thought left her.

She had Jared on her mind now.

She'd been in prayer for her father and mother, and now her burden shifted to her little brother. This was a spiritual battle for his soul.

At the window she knelt and closed her eyes. She was going to stay on the front lines for Jared until the enemy's power was broken.

4.

After getting Jared's truck from police impound, Dallas suggested they grab a Papa John's pizza. The two of them, just like old times.

Before the storm-tossed seas of his teen years, Jared had been open and demonstrative with affection for his mother. Some of the best times they had were when Ron was on the road and Cara was in her room, talking to friends on the phone.

There would be eating and talking, a giant pepperoni pizza with extra cheese between them, sometimes watching a British mystery on television. Jared especially loved Miss Marple and liked to sit on the sofa next to Dallas, watching the intrepid Jane solve the latest to-do in her village.

Here they were again, under quite different circumstances. Dallas knew beyond question now that Jared was on a dark slide that had to be stopped. She had no idea how, except by prayer and by keeping him close.

They brought the pizza to the table out back, where once upon a time the four of them dined during the summer months. When they were settled, Dallas said, "Would you say a blessing for the food?"

"You do it," he said.

She prayed out loud for the food, adding a silent prayer for Jared at the end.

"You doing okay, Mom?"

Dallas nodded. "I've got a little bit of callus developing, I think. I hope."

"We all do, maybe."

"Why don't you go see your dad? I know he'd love—"

"How is he?"

"Scared."

"They going to let him out?"

"No bail yet. Jeff's going to ask for a new hearing."

"Funny, isn't it?"

"Funny?"

"Him in there and me out here. Shouldn't be that way."

"Shouldn't be that way for either of you."

"Maybe I'll be in soon enough."

"Don't talk that way, Jared."

He took a bite of pizza but didn't look like he tasted it. They ate in silence for a while.

Jared said, "Try not to worry about me, Mom."

"How can I do that? I've always worried about you. You're my son, that's what I do for a living."

"I bet you don't worry about Cara."

"I do. Just in a different way."

"Yeah, she's normal. And she doesn't get drunk. She's the good one."

"Jared, don't say that."

"Why not? Didn't you and Dad always tell me to be honest? Isn't that what a Christian is supposed to be, totally honest? Confess the old sins. Well, I've got a trunkful."

"Good."

"What?"

"It's good that you've got a trunkful, and that you told me about it, and now you can go to church and talk to God about it."

"Why do I have to go to church to talk to God?"

"Do you talk to God?"

"No."

"Then come to church and just listen for a while."

"I've been listening all my life. Do you know I hear Dad in my sleep sometimes? I hear his voice. He's usually telling me something that I don't want to hear. So I make myself wake up. I've lost a lot of sleep that way."

Dallas looked at the pizza box, grease stains on the bottom. *God, help me reach him. Give me the words to say.*

"Got an idea," Dallas said.

"What?"

"Remember the way we used to watch mysteries on TV?"

"Sure."

"See if one's on."

Inside, Jared turned on the TV while Dallas brought in the dishes. When she got to the family room, it was no mystery on TV.

Jared was looking at the Hank Dunaway show.

Dunaway was the hottest interview show going on cable news, sometimes featuring a celebrity or newsmaker, other times a panel discussing current events.

This night, the guest host was that blond woman, the former prosecutor who always assumed the worst about any current case. Dallas always thought she was a little too zealous, a little too show biz. And truth seemed to be the real victim whenever she clamped her jaws on a case.

"Tonight," she droned, "the Ron Hamilton murder trial. Our panel of experts will analyze what will go on in court tomorrow, and what we can expect in the months ahead. All that and more on *Hank Dunaway Tonight.*"

"You want me to turn it off?" Jared said.

"No. We might as well see what everybody's saying."

The blond looked at the camera with her liquid sincerity and in her superior tone explained what "everyone" already knew. Ron was guilty. The pretrial motions were just smoke and mirrors. Then she handed it off to a guest, some lawyer in Florida, a guy with hundred-dollar hair.

"No surprises," he said. "Jefferson Waite will make a motion to suppress, and it will be denied. Then Ron Hamilton will be ordered to stand trial. Remember, the threshold at a preliminary hearing is very low, so it doesn't take much to convince a judge to bind a defendant over."

"But the evidence is overwhelming," the blond insisted. "I mean, you have the DNA, the sexual contact, the lying to police."

"We don't know that he lied," hair boy said. "We know that he didn't volunteer everything."

"That's a lie in my book, and a pretty stupid one. It was bound to be exposed."

"Turn it off," Dallas said.

Jared clicked the remote and the tube withdrew into blessed silence.

"See if you can find a DVD or something." Dallas's phone chimed. She recognized the number. Karen, Ron's agent.

"Oh, my dear sweet Dallas, how are you? I just watched the Dunaway show."

Dallas leaned against the kitchen wall. "Some fun."

"You doing okay?"

"Hanging in there. The way those circus guys used to hang by their teeth way up in the air."

Karen chuckled. "Tell me about it. I've had days where my clients were all …" There was a pause, and Karen said, "I'm sorry. There's no comparison to what you're going through."

This time there was a longer pause, and Dallas knew there was more to this call than an expression of concern.

"Dallas, I'm afraid I've got some bad news regarding the contract."

Dallas closed her eyes. Her mental wheels turned and locked in place. It made sense and seemed so inevitable. "Canceled, I suppose."

"Withdrawn, actually, since the contract never went out. I'm just sick about it."

"So the publishers have assumed his guilt, have they? What wonderful people."

"I know it doesn't help, but if you see it from their perspective, they—"

"Why should I? Are they sitting around seeing it from my perspective?"

"You have every right to be hurt."

"Thank you for that permission."

Silence. Then Dallas added, "Karen, I'm sorry. It's just that this is another—"

"You don't have to say it, Dallas. I understand completely. I'm not going to give up fighting for this project. And if there's anything I can do, anything, I want you to call me."

"Sure."

Dallas clicked off. And threw her cell phone across the room.

5.

It was nine thirty the following morning before Dallas felt sufficiently calmed down to turn up a little heat on Bernie Halstrom.

Halstrom's chief aide, Clark Thoms, tried to give Dallas the administrative runaround when she showed up at the field office.

"The councilman's schedule is just packed, Mrs. Hamilton," he said. Thoms was a bushy-haired grad-student type, with wire-rimmed glasses framing ambitious eyes. "But I know he wants to talk to you."

"No time like the present," Dallas said. "I won't be ten minutes."

"I wish I could, but—"

"Just ask him." Dallas made it sound like *tell him*. "And remind him that the reporters want to talk to me in the worst way, and I don't want to have to say anything negative about anybody."

Thoms's forehead made little rows. "Let me see what I can do."

Predictably, Thoms could do what was expedient, and a few minutes later Dallas was in the office of Councilman Bernie Halstrom.

Dallas knew his history. Bernie was elected to the city council in the late nineties after a twenty-year career with the Los Angeles County Sheriff's Department. He was fifty-two, married, with two successful sons. One of them was a Wall Street lawyer. The other was a graduate of the famous USC film school and was slowly climbing the Hollywood ladder.

Bernie greeted Dallas with his usual gregariousness. "Dallas, I'm so glad you came over." He took her hands in both of his and held them warmly. "I've been thinking about you and Ron almost nonstop."

Dallas wanted to say, *Then why aren't you supporting him?* Instead, she said, "Thanks," with little enthusiasm.

"Been meaning to come to Hillside soon for services," Bernie said. He was a true Los Angeles politician who did not practice any single religion but walked among them all. Voters, after all, were in synagogues and mosques as well as churches and cathedrals.

"I'm sure this whole thing is going to be straightened out. Jeff Waite's a great lawyer." He offered Dallas a chair, then took the one next to it.

She started to feel a little foolish. What was she to expect from a man who had more than just the Hamilton family problems to worry about?

"Bernie, I'm sorry for imposing on you like this."

"Nothing of it. I'm happy to have this chance to talk to you."

"It's just that this has become such a high-profile case now."

"Tell me about it." Bernie shook his head. "It's something you can't control. It's arbitrary what the media decides to clamp down on. If it wasn't Ron, it'd be somebody else. I've been there, believe me."

Bernie became a huge target three or four years ago when a female aide in his office accused him of sexual harassment. It was front-page news in the *Times* for about a week. As usual, the *Times* took the side of the accuser, slanting all their coverage against the councilman. They even brought up a fifteen-year-old accusation from his time on the police force, one that had been summarily dismissed by an administrative proceeding.

The *Times* never questioned the female aide's story. When a *Daily News* reporter discovered she had a lurid past and had lied on her official employment documents, the *Times* waited two days before making a tepid admission that the case against Halstrom was going nowhere.

"One of the things you have to do," Bernie said, "is hang onto your faith that the truth will come out eventually. I know Ron couldn't have done what they say. Murder, I mean."

Bernie cleared his throat. What was left unsaid, Dallas realized, was that the other part, Ron's adultery, *was* something he had done.

Quickly, Halstrom added, "Ron is as decent a guy as I know. We're all human around here. Even me." He laughed. "We make mistakes. But that's all they are, mistakes. Sins, you would say. Isn't God in the forgiving business?"

Dallas half smiled. That's exactly what Ron used to say. And then she realized why Bernie was so good at what he did. He knew, really knew, about the people he worked with. He knew enough to quote one of Ron's own expressions.

"You're right," Dallas said, even as she wondered if she could forgive Ron. That hadn't happened yet. "I was just hoping that maybe you'd keep up the pressure on the porn regulations you and Ron were working on."

Bernie's district included Chatsworth, which was by all accounts the center of the pornography business in the United States. Dallas had never understood how it could be allowed to prosper like a legitimate enterprise. Nor had Ron.

When Ron's book became so popular, it was Bernie who called on him with the idea of hammering out a new set of regulations for the city that would severely limit, if not eliminate, the manufacturing of pornography in Los Angeles.

It was admittedly an uphill battle. So little had been done over the years. Politicians had shown all the backbone of soufflé against the porn that enveloped neighborhoods and polluted souls.

"Believe me, Dallas," Bernie said, "I'm as determined as ever. This setback is not going to stop me from trying to put the brakes on the porn business."

"It's flesh trade, not business." She thought a moment. "What do you know about this guy Vic Lu?"

He blinked. "How did you come across that name?"

"I read about him on the Internet. He's apparently one of the bigwigs in pornography around here. He was the one who discovered Melinda Perry and put her in his movies."

Bernie scratched underneath his chin. "Yes. LookyLu Productions. Nice double meaning there, huh? Cute. But he's well known around here. He's one of the more successful adult-film producers."

"You mean pornography, don't you? Calling these *adult films* seems too respectable."

"Agreed."

"Let me just ask you, Bernie. Straight out. I've never really gotten a square answer on this. How can the law allow sex acts to be filmed and sold? I mean, prostitution is illegal. Why isn't this?"

With a bemused smile, Bernie said, "The courts have given this some strange thought. They have held there is a distinction between people being paid to have sex as actors, but not as individuals in a free exchange."

Incredulous, Dallas asked, "What on earth is the difference?"

"You've got me. Lawyers pretend to understand this stuff."

"Incredible."

Bernie nodded. "What it all comes down to, Dallas, is that we have the kind of society we want. If enough people want porn, they're going to get it. The courts have not been helpful. Over the years they've allowed more and more stuff to be produced, protected by the First Amendment. I doubt our founding fathers would be pleased."

"Give me a flamethrower and some addresses," Dallas said. "I'll take it out of the hands of the courts."

"I believe you would. Heck, I might even join you. Until flamethrowers become legal, though, rest assured, I'll keep pushing for tighter controls. And, Dallas, try to get some rest. You can't carry all this on your own."

6.

At one thirty, Dallas arrived back at the criminal courts building for Jeff Waite's argument to suppress evidence. There was a massive press presence outside, with news vans and camera lights and scurrying talking heads holding microphones.

Dallas got in, feeling sick. But she refused to let it show. She walked inside without a word to the screaming press or to anyone else and found refuge in the elevator.

Jeff Waite was already in the courtroom, sitting at the counsel table, going over notes. The friendly bailiff showed her to her reserved seat. As he did he wagged a finger at some reporters. The warning was clear. *Keep away from her unless she talks to you first.*

Seated, Dallas took a moment to pray. She found herself praying for wisdom, which surprised her. Why wasn't she praying for Ron's outright release?

Because I have doubts.

Before she could argue with herself, the side door opened and Ron was led in by a deputy. He looked pale. And thinner.

He gave Dallas a cursory glance before sitting down next to Jeff.

At one thirty-five, Judge Bartells entered the courtroom and called the case.

"Mr. Waite, you may address the court on your motion to suppress."

Jeff stood up and went to the lawyer's podium. Without notes. "It's really quite simple, Your Honor. Deputy Barnes testified that he arrived at the Star Motel without probable cause to search. All he had was a 911 dispatch."

"Which certainly gives a reasonable suspicion to investigate."

"Investigate, yes. Break into a motel room, no."

"But it was the motel manager who let him in."

"That is irrelevant, Your Honor. It's true that Mr. Franze is a private citizen, and normally a citizen does not trigger the Fourth Amendment. But it does trigger when the citizen is working at the behest of law enforcement. It was at the request of Deputy Barnes that Mr. Franze unlocked the motel room door. As you know, Your Honor, a motel room is as protected as any residence, which means the police must have a search warrant before they can enter. And Deputy Barnes did not have a search warrant."

"What about exigent circumstances? Didn't Deputy Barnes have reason to believe a victim of a crime might be inside room 105?"

"To qualify under the exigency exception, there must be a factual basis for that belief. Which brings us back to the uncorroborated tip of an anonymous informer."

"That would be Mr. Knudsen," Judge Bartells said. "Not anonymous."

"For the purposes of this preliminary hearing, Judge, he is. He was not called. We don't even know if he exists. All we have is Mr. Franze's testimony about him. And Mr. Franze's recollection about a hearsay statement from this Mr. Knudsen that there was trouble in room 105. Even that is not enough to establish a factual basis. All we have is a hearsay report that there was some screaming going on in room 105. But that screaming may have been in the nature of a loud argument, or it may have been in the nature of screaming in ecstasy."

"Ecstasy?"

"We don't know. All we have is an opinion that was phoned in. No case has ever allowed that to be the basis of a warrantless entry, Your Honor."

"What about the DNA evidence?" the judge asked. "That would have been discovered during the autopsy, no matter when the body was found, or by whom."

"But my client would not have been in custody as a suspect. The connection was only made because of the illegal entry and the subsequent evidence that was gathered as a result. This, Your Honor, is the fruit of the poisonous tree. It must be suppressed."

The judge paused, thinking about it, and Dallas felt a tenuous reed of hope spring up in her. Could it really be possible? Suppress the evidence? She'd seen Court TV a few times. Didn't suppressing evidence mean the case was tossed out? Over? That Ron would walk out of the courtroom a free man?

She looked at the prosecutor again and saw him sit up straight in his chair. Jeff's sword had drawn blood.

"Mr. Freton," the judge said, "do you have a response?"

Freton stood and buttoned his coat, as if formally rising to lead a flag salute at a chamber of commerce luncheon.

"I must say I admire Mr. Waite's creativity. But I must also remind the court of the notice requirements. Our office received no notice of these grounds."

"And I would remind my colleague," Jeff said, "that it was evidence adduced on the stand, from his own witness, that gives rise to these grounds. Where there is a warrantless entry, it is the burden of the prosecution to prove an exception."

The judge put up his hand, then lowered it slowly like a sage. "I believe Mr. Waite has the right to make his motion. What have you got to say on the merits?"

That seemed to throw Freton a curve. He bent down to confer with his colleague, a woman in a dark burgundy suit. She was the one doing most of the talking. She flipped through a book on the table and pointed to something.

The prosecutor addressed the judge. "Your Honor, there is the question of standing. It was not the defendant's motel room. The defendant was not present when the search occurred. The Fourth Amendment is personal, Your Honor, and the moving party must have a proprietary interest in the place searched. The defendant does not have this. No standing, no motion."

Dallas was not following all the words. It was a legal fight. But Jefferson Waite did not look fazed.

Jeff said, "Your Honor, it is the prosecution's theory that my client was having an affair with the victim. If that is so, he was in that motel room as an invited guest. The Supreme Court, in *Olson*, held that an invited guest has standing to challenge the search of a premises."

Now there was a long pause from the judge. He was thinking about it. Dallas felt her heartbeat quicken.

She also felt something strange and disturbing. It was about Ron. His betrayal was heavy upon her. She wanted to ask the judge to stop the proceedings before he granted the motion. Stop so she could go over to Ron while he was still in custody and make sure he was feeling the torment and consequences of his actions. Look in his eyes, maybe, and see if they still held love for her, any at all. Because if they didn't . . . what would she do?

The judge said, "I have considered your points and authorities, Mr. Waite. Your motion asserts that the defendant has standing because of his status as an invited guest, based on an assertion that he was having an affair with the victim. But the People have not made that essential to their case. I don't know of any case that holds the defense can base a motion on a theory yet to be made by the prosecution. In view of that, the court denies the motion to suppress."

Even though Jeff had prepared her for this, Dallas still felt the defeat personally, almost as if she herself were on trial. Maybe she was. Certainly in the court of public opinion her every move was being monitored.

"I further find that the People have presented sufficient evidence to bind the defendant, Ronald Hamilton, over for trial. Shall we set a trial date, gentlemen?"

7.

And so I go to trial, up there for the world to see and flay. Oh, Dallas. What's this going to do to her?

Got them to get me a Bible. At first my guy, my keeper, my chief jailer —Deputy Dawg, I call him; his name is Daugherty—said I couldn't have one. I reminded him of my rights under the US Constitution and that this was a very public case and it would not be good press if this ever got out.

Deputy Dawg is not a bad sort. He said he'd see what he could do.

Came back an hour later with a paperback King James. Good old King James. Hadn't cracked one of those in years.

I opened to the passage I wanted to read. Revelation 3. I scanned down until I found the key word, Laodiceans, *and read:*

> And unto the angel of the church of the Laodiceans write; These things saith the Amen, the faithful and true witness, the beginning of the creation of God; I know thy works, that thou art neither cold nor hot; I would thou wert cold or hot.
>
> So, then, because thou art lukewarm, and neither cold nor hot, I will spew thee out of my mouth.
>
> Because thou sayest, I am rich, and increased with goods, and have need of nothing, and knowest not that thou art wretched, and miserable, and poor, and blind, and naked,
>
> I counsel thee to buy of me gold tried in the fire, that thou mayest be rich; and white raiment, that thou mayest be clothed, and that the shame of thy nakedness do not appear; and anoint thine eyes with eyesalve, that thou mayest see.
>
> As many as I love, I rebuke and chasten; be zealous, therefore, and repent.
>
> Behold, I stand at the door, and knock; if any man hear my voice, and open the door, I will come in to him, and will sup with him, and he with me.

I tried to remember what my prof said about this passage in Bible college. Revelation was always a mystery to me, and I never got heavy into prophecy and end-times stuff. All I remembered was that lukewarm was something not to be. Being spewed out of Christ's mouth was not a good prospect.

I have grown lukewarm over the years of my success.

Was it even success at all?

I had a church of eight thousand. In the eyes of my peers and the church world I was a rousing success.

I.

The word that crept into the center of my unspoken vocabulary.
How did it happen? How did I drift away?
Questions. More questions.
Who was my interrogator, the toilet-paper prophet?

§.

"Dallas," Jeff Waite said, "we have a very important decision to make. Not an easy one."

Once again he had graciously come to the house to talk to her. It was the day after the decision to send Ron to trial, so there was a fresh media encampment out on the street. That was another reason she was grateful for Jeff's presence. Someone to run interference.

"It's going to be Ron's call," Jeff said, "but we're family here. I want you to know everything, because you may need to help Ron make the decision."

"What decision?"

"Whether to plead guilty."

"But he's not." Dallas searched his eyes. "Is he?"

"I can only tell you what the evidence is. You heard it. You know what we're up against. They've got Ron caught in a lie, and they've got the forensic evidence to prove he had sexual relations with the victim. It's what the prosecutors call a slam dunk."

"He didn't kill her. I know he didn't."

"All that matters is what the jury will be allowed to hear, Dallas. No one will care what we think about Ron. If I had something, anything I could put on in Ron's favor, I would. Stegman, my investigator, tracked down this guy Knudsen and interviewed him. He's not going to be of any help. He didn't see anything, only heard some voices he can't identify."

"So we're just throwing in the towel?"

Jeff shook his head. "If you and Ron want to go to trial, I will do everything in my power to create a reasonable doubt about every aspect of the prosecutor's case. That's my job. But it's also my professional obligation to inform you of what we're up against and what the options are."

"Are there any good options?"

"If Ron pleads to second-degree murder, he'll be looking at fifteen to life, but with the possibility of parole. To be quite frank, this victim does not appear likely to have anyone who will appear at a parole hearing to argue against Ron's release."

"That we know of."

"This isn't one of those cases where a nice girl from some well-to-do home in a nice neighborhood gets brutally murdered and someone from the family shows up every time there's a hearing."

"That sounds harsh."

"I'm just giving you the reality. You need that. Now, if Ron elects to go to trial and is convicted, he's going to get the max. He'll die in prison."

She tried to let that picture pass over her, but it stayed. "How long do we have to make a decision?" she asked.

"All the way up to trial. Stegman and I will keep looking around for something, but this case seems pretty straightforward."

"Except for the fact that Ron didn't do it." Her voice was louder than she'd expected.

Jeff folded his hands together as if trying to be patient. "If we could find some exculpatory evidence, pointing toward innocence, we'd have something to hang a trial on."

"Then we have to find it," Dallas said. "Oh, one other thing. Jared was picked up for drunk driving."

Jeff nodded, almost as if he'd expected the news. "Did you get an appearance date?"

"Next month."

"I'll handle it."

"Jeff, I can't ask—"

"I'll handle it, Dallas. Let's wait and see what the arrest report says. Meanwhile, is there anything else I can do for you?"

She folded her arms. "Reverse time?"

"Hey, there are some things even lawyers can't do."

Dallas tried to smile.

"One more thing," Jeff said. "Ron doesn't want bail."

"What?"

"I tried to talk him into it, but he said he absolutely doesn't want me to move for bail. That means I can't."

"Did he say why?"

Jeff shook his head. "I have a feeling he wants to punish himself. If you can talk him into reconsidering, I've got a bail motion all ready."

But Dallas wondered if she wanted to talk him out of it after all. Maybe some jail time was just what Ron needed to get his life straight.

EIGHT

Sunday morning Dallas shook Jared awake at seven-thirty.

"We're going to church," she said.

He grumbled something vaguely negative.

"Rise and shine. Cara's meeting us."

"Mom, I said—"

"I know what you said." She drew the covers halfway off him. He was facedown. She saw the vile tattoo. "We are going to the house of the Lord together, and I don't want to hear any more about it."

He turned his face toward her. "I'm not seven, Mom."

"Listen to me, Jared. I don't care how old you are or how old I am, or what's happened to you in the past. All I know is that we need to go worship God and that's what we're going to do, and I have access to ice water and I will use it. Don't think I won't, because I'm not completely rational at the moment, if you get my drift."

An hour later, Dallas and Jared were on their way to Hillside.

This was her first Sunday back since Ron's arrest.

It felt a little like coming home, and a little like stepping into the spotlight on a bare stage. There were plenty of well-wishers and hugs, and double the number of curious, probing eyes.

She didn't blame Jared for standing off to the side, leafing through the visitor pamphlets with his head down. At least Cara joined him there, looking protective.

When the worship band started in, they made it to a row in the back. A few more hellos and hugs and even a hand or two for Jared.

Who did not sing any of the worship songs.

At least he's here. At least he came. Witness to his spirit, Lord.

The order of worship was the same as always, with a beautiful solo by Priscilla Potts, who was a member of Hillside and a recording artist.

Then Bob Benson took to the pulpit.

"Welcome to Hillside," he said, his voice full and vibrant. "We hope this is a place where you can settle back and be comfortable for a while. We're glad you're here."

Behind him, on the big screen, a video appeared. A dour-looking man walked along a busy sidewalk.

"I'd like to introduce you to a guy I know. Negative Ned is a guy you've seen around. Probably pass him on the street all the time. He usually has his head down. Probably just kicked his dog too."

On the video screen, as if on cue, the man looked directly at the audience, frowning, and that's where the image froze.

Ripples of laughter around the church. Though it was harder than she'd expected to see someone besides Ron up there, Dallas had to admit Bob had *it*. The charisma, delivery, and timing that put an audience into the proverbial palm of his hand.

"What would you say to ol' Ned if you met him on the street? Go home and kick the dog again? Or would you try to tell him that God has a better way? Would you tell him we all go through tough times, but we all have a choice how to handle them?"

If only it were that easy.

The video started up again, this time with an actor smiling and practically dancing down the street. It was over the top, and the whole church laughed.

"That's my other friend, Positive Pete. He's the guy with the perpetually sunny disposition. You don't see him as much, do you?"

Jared leaned over to Dallas and whispered, "Are we in third grade here or something?"

"Shh."

"But Positive Pete has learned to trust God and make the choice to be positive about his circumstances."

"Why doesn't he crack open a Bible?" Jared said.

"Quiet."

Bob did use a few Bible verses, shot up on the screen for all to see. But mostly it was an entertaining and uplifting sermon. Dallas couldn't help feeling some tension, though. Part of her didn't want the people to be uplifted or entertained. She wanted them to be sad about Ron. Were they so quick to forget?

At the end of the sermon, as if reading her mind, Bob changed to a serious tone. "As we leave today, let's remember to keep praying for our brother Ron Hamilton. Pray for justice to be done. For his protection. For his recovery."

The last word rankled her a bit. But she couldn't argue with it. Ron did need to recover.

More well-wishers approached her after the service. Lisa Benson was last of all, with a warm embrace and an invitation to have coffee the next day.

Cara said good-bye in the parking lot and kissed her brother. "Be good."

He looked at her, plastered a huge grin on his face, and jumped up in the air. "I will! I'm Positive Pete."

"Nice sarcasm," Cara said.

"I'm trying to be good at something," Jared said.

Dallas took Jared's arm and started him toward her car at the far end of the lot. "Your sister loves you," she said.

"That makes two of you."

"And your father."

"Sure."

"Jared."

He was about to say something, then stopped. He pointed. "Look at the car."

Dallas saw that her front left headlight was smashed. "Just great! When did that happen?"

"There's a note."

A piece of paper under the driver's-side windshield wiper. Dallas removed it and read: *Why don't you return my call?*

"What's it say?" Jared said.

Dallas couldn't speak.

"Let me see." She handed it to him. "It's got to be a joke," he said.

"A sick joke, if it is. But who would do that? And who would know this is my car? Someone at church?"

Jared shrugged. "I think we should call the police on this."

"Wonderful. Just what I need to cap a fine day at church."

"Don't be a Negative Ned, Mom."

"Be quiet."

2.

All night Dallas kept jerking awake, thinking about the headlight, trying to find some way to believe the vandalism was just random. She knew it was not. Somebody was out to mess with her mind. But who?

In the morning she took a long bath. At nine o'clock she felt just human enough to meet Lisa for coffee.

Dallas wore a broad-brimmed hat and dark glasses and drove out to a Starbucks in Agoura, making sure no newshound followed her.

When she got there she found Lisa similarly attired. It was Lisa who had suggested the disguises and the location. Agoura was far enough away from the Valley that Dallas felt she could walk around without hassle.

Still, she was glad for the hat and glasses.

"This is all so cloak and dagger," Dallas said as she and Lisa took their lattes to an outside table that afforded a fair degree of anonymity.

"But fun, you have to admit." Lisa fairly giggled. "Don't you think half the fun in the world is putting the big runaround on the know-it-alls? Like the stupid media that's hounding you?"

Dallas smiled in agreement. She couldn't help feeling swept up in Lisa Benson's youthful exuberance. The girl was so full of life and energy.

Putting on her Bette Davis voice, Dallas said, "Fasten your seatbelt. It's going to be a bumpy morning."

Lisa shook her head. "You crack me up. Where did you ever learn to do that stuff?"

"It's a gift."

"You should be on Leno with that act."

"Thanks. And thanks for asking me out."

"I just wanted to spend time with you," Lisa said. "For support and prayer."

"I appreciate it."

"Bob and I are just like you and Ron, in a way. I absolutely know what you're going through."

Did she really? She and Bob were in the spring of their marriage, and it was still fresh and clean and vital. And she did not have a husband who was an admitted adulterer.

"How did you and Bob meet?"

Lisa leaned back, her flaxen hair framing her face. "Oh, wow. I was the one who pursued him."

"Really?"

"We were in the same youth group at church. He was mister big shot. All the girls had their sights set on him. It was pretty funny."

"He fought them off with a stick, huh?"

"He had a big head too. Had to be taken down a peg. That was my job."

Dallas took a sip of coffee, enjoying the tale. "How'd you do it?"

"I ignored him. Totally. Just to get his goat. I knew it'd make him crazy. I knew eventually he'd make his move. And sure enough, he did. One night after youth group I was walking slowly to my car, knowing he'd been scoping me, and he called my name. I pretended not to hear him."

"You're a stinker."

"Oh, yeah. So he calls out again, louder, and I slowly turn around. I give him a look, like, why are you bothering me? And it stops him cold. For a couple of seconds he doesn't say anything. And then, finally, he goes, 'So, how come you never talk to me?'"

"Just like that?"

"Just like that. And I say, 'Who are you again?' And his mouth just drops open. I keep a poker face as long as I can, which was about five seconds, then I just started cracking up. And he starts laughing, which is why I decided I liked him. And the rest is our little history."

"That's a cute story."

Lisa said, "How did you meet Ron?"

"It was a God thing. I was running away from a very bad situation, ran up to San Francisco. This was '77 and I thought maybe I'd try to become a hippy poet. But all the hippies were pretty much gone by then. I was a day late and a flower short."

Lisa laughed.

Dallas searched her memories. "I stayed in North Beach with a friend who had her own little marijuana operation going, which caused me to lose track of about a week of my life. But I do remember walking along Columbus Avenue this one night, in a stupor, when I heard music coming out of a place, rocking and rolling. I went inside. All these smiling faces looked at me. I thought I was tripping. Somebody showed me to a seat. It was a little theater. I thought that was cool. Or *groovy*."

"I got it."

"I was into the music, and then it stopped, and then this guy comes out and starts talking. He's got all this energy and he's good-looking too. Pretty soon it breaks through to me that he's talking about Jesus. And he's holding a Bible. And pretty soon I really *was* tripping, but it was on what he was saying. I know now that was the Holy Spirit doing his work in me. When he gave the invitation, I walked up to the front and asked for Jesus to save me. It was Ron, of course."

"Revival Ron?"

"You wouldn't have known him then. He was really into street preaching, and he was good at it." *When did he lose that zeal?* "Anyway, we were two completely different people. How we ended up together is really something God did." Dallas said it and wanted to believe it.

After a pause, Dallas said, "If you ever found out Bob had an affair, and lied to you about it, what would you do? Would you forgive him?"

The half smile that Lisa had on her face faded. "My first instinct would be to kick his loving you-know-what. My second instinct, and I'm being totally honest here, would be to divorce him."

"Wow."

"Wait a second. I said instinct. That's just a knee-jerk reaction. I think ..."

"Go ahead, Lisa, if you want to."

Lisa looked away.

"Lisa, what is it?"

Lisa looked like further words might crush her.

"Please," Dallas said. "Maybe I can help."

"It's not about me." Only then did Lisa look at Dallas again. The look was a bridge to a cold, dark place.

"What is it then?" Dallas said, wishing she hadn't been insistent.

"I didn't think I'd ever have to say."

"Say what, Lisa?"

"This is so hard." Lisa lowered her voice. "All right. I guess I have to say it, because it's something Jeff Waite needs to know about."

"Jeff? What's he got to do—"

"Because the prosecutor is probably going to find out."

"The prosecutor? How—"

"They want to interview me and Bob."

"Interview?"

"That's right," Lisa said. "They want us to come in. I told Bob to tell them to take a flying ... Well, I don't know if we're going to be able to get out of it. I think it stinks."

"What could he possibly hope to accomplish?"

Lisa took a long moment to answer. "That's what you need to tell Jeff. There's something, if they ask me, I'd have to tell them."

"Tell me now, *please*."

Lisa inhaled deeply. "This woman, this Melinda whatever-her-name-is?"

"Yes?"

"She's not the first woman Ron had an affair with."

3.

How does it begin?

In innocence, I tell myself, as if that makes a difference. In ignorance too, as if there were no danger involved, and no consequence.

You tell yourself that you can handle it, that you are an adult and therefore beyond the juvenile temptations to associate with this kind of stuff. And you tell yourself that it is merely research, as if by labeling it that way you remove the sin from it.

You also know, without admitting it to yourself, that you like the power. You like the idea that with the touch of a button, the click of a mouse, you can control a veritable universe of forbidden fruit.

I wanted to see just how easy it was to access pornographic images on the Internet. I could have answered that question quite easily one hundred miles from a computer. Everyone knows it's easy. Everyone knows the skin trade and the pedophiles and the sick and the bored control the vast majority of territory in the electronic cosmos.

But I told myself it was research as I typed the word into the search engine, a word I would never use in public or even privately. And in a microsecond I had it all before me.

I was sweating, I remember that. Sweating and trembling. I was not praying, nor was I thinking about God at all. Or if I did, I shoved those thoughts far back into the dark alleys of my mind, stuck them into abandoned warehouses with boarded-up windows and firmly locked doors.

The images literally took my breath away. My research was done. It was easier than getting a Coke at the 7-Eleven or channel surfing at home. Indeed, it was easier than almost anything, and that was the lure of it.

That, and being all alone in my office, no one to look over my shoulder, no one to call me in to dinner.

My "research" lasted almost two hours.

And when I was done I knew the images would always be there waiting for me.

Always.

And when they weren't on my screen, they would be in my mind.

Always.

4.

Jared sat in the truck across from the apartment complex and waited. What was he doing here? What possible good was going to come out of this?

He had no ready answer, but that wasn't strange. He didn't have answers to a lot of things.

But this was something to do, something besides stew in his own juices at home, feeling like a total loss.

For an hour that morning he'd tried to get to someone at the VA, a human voice. He wanted somebody to tell him what he could do to stop the bad things, what pill he could take, what injection to the brain would stop the memories.

No human voice. And his next appointment wasn't until August.

August! He wondered if he'd even be breathing in August. He wondered if he could stand it until then. There were other ways out. There were guns, and he could get one and—

He saw Jamaal run into a fenced front yard. Or what was a bad excuse for a yard in this fallen suburbia.

Jamaal was alone, holding a football that was as big as his chest. He cradled it, looking like he didn't know what to do.

Jared got out of the truck and walked to the fence.

"What's up?"

Jamaal looked at him, then smiled. "Nothin'."

"Your mom around?"

He shook his head.

"Dad?"

Shook again.

So what's he doing in a yard all alone? Jared told himself to leave. This was a stupid idea. A desperate reach. What was he looking for? He shouldn't have come.

But something about being with the kid, one of the innocents. For a moment at least it soothed the burn inside.

"Why you here?" Jamaal asked.

"Hey, came to see how you were, you know? So ... how are you?" He looked closely for any marks on Jamaal. Saw none.

"Good," the boy said.

"Cool."

An older woman shuffled down the walk and gave Jared a suspicious look. A long look. Like she was remembering his face. Then she went on.

He couldn't blame her. The way things were these days, a stranger talking to a boy was something to note. She was a one-woman Neighborhood Watch.

"You a football player?" Jared pointed at the pigskin in the boy's arms.

"You said."

It took Jared a minute to figure that one, but then he remembered. The kid wanted to be a Marine. Jared had suggested football instead.

Amazingly, the kid had apparently listened, taken it to heart. Jared could hardly believe it.

He went around to the gate and let himself into the yard. Jamaal ran up to him.

"Toss it," Jared said.

Jamaal made an attempt to throw Jared the football. The ball was so large in Jamaal's hands he had to use both for the throw. The ball went nearly ninety degrees sideways, hitting the fence.

"Oops," Jamaal said.

"Looks like we got a little learning to do." Jared picked up the football. It was all rubber. He held it up to Jamaal. "See these white things here?"

Jamaal nodded.

"Those are the laces. Let's see your hand."

Jamaal put his right hand out. Jared turned it palm up and placed the football in the middle of it. Jamaal's hand disappeared under the ball.

"No problem," Jared said. "You'll grow into it. You feel the laces on your fingers?"

Jamaal concentrated. "Uh-huh."

"Okay. What you want to do is keep your fingers on those laces when you throw. Pretty simple, huh?"

Jamaal shrugged.

"Give it a try."

The boy paused, then started to lift the ball. It teetered. He put his left hand on it.

"Hold it," Jared said. "Try it one-handed."

Jamaal took his left hand off. And then was motionless. "I can't."

"Yeah, you can. Keep your fingers where they are and just move your hand toward me. Go ahead."

The boy gave it a try. The ball went about a foot. But it went forward.

"Yeah, man," Jared said. "Good one. You see that?"

The kid blinked.

"Wanna try it again?"

"Yeah," Jamaal said.

Jared put the ball back in the kid's hand, then took two large steps backward. "Okay now, all the way to me."

With a determined look, Jamaal reared back with his arm and flung the ball. It made it all the way to Jared, who caught it over his shoes.

"Yeah, baby!" Jared put his hand up. "High five." Jamaal ran over and slapped Jared's hand.

"Let's do another," Jared said, and Jamaal nodded.

Then a voice said, "Hey."

Jared turned and saw a man walking toward them from the east side. And then he saw Tiana, right behind him, her eyes wide with surprise.

Jared knew this was the boyfriend, Jamaal's father. Jared sized him up. He was about Jared's height, but his shoulders were broader and he was older, maybe thirty. He wore a tight black T-shirt and he had packed muscles.

Jared noticed that Jamaal did not run toward him. Didn't move, in fact.

"What's goin' on?" the man said, hard and quick.

Jared looked at Tiana's face. It virtually begged him not to say a word.

"Just doing a little football," Jared said. "Kid's got quite an arm."

"Who are you?"

"Just passing by."

The guy stepped up to Jared, closer than was comfortable. "I said who are you?"

Jared felt the heat, his muscles tensing.

From behind, Tiana said, "Rafe, he's the guy brought us home."

Rafe gave her a snap look, then came back to Jared. "So what are you doin' here?"

"I was driving by and—"

"Why?"

"Why what?"

"Were you drivin' by?"

"Rafe," Tiana said, "drop it, okay?"

"I ain't droppin' nothin'." He pointed at Jared's face. "Don't come around here no more."

"Rafe, he's just—"

"Shut up."

Tiana closed her mouth.

It was all Jared could do not to grab Rafe's throat. He was conscious of Jamaal watching everything.

Jared looked at Tiana. "Is this what you want?"

Before she could say a word, Rafe was in Jared's face. "You don't be talkin' to her, you got that?"

"Go, please," Tiana said.

"Yeah," Rafe said. "Now."

There was something else here, not just the four of them. Not another person, but a presence. Jared felt it as fully as he had sometimes in Iraq. He always thought it was just the circumstances, the obvious stress, a thing stirred up by the acids in the stomach when the heat was on.

Now he wasn't so sure about that.

He gave a quick look at Jamaal before walking back to his truck.

5.

When Dallas got to Jeff's office, he did not greet her with a smile. His normally crisp white shirt was wrinkled and his desk a mess of files and papers. He looked more like a law student stressing over finals than a successful trial lawyer.

Which was only going to make it harder to trip the land mine that Lisa had revealed a couple of hours before.

"I saw Ron," Jeff said immediately. "He doesn't want to plead out. Says he did not kill the girl and that it would be a lie to plead guilty to anything."

"So what does that mean?"

"It means ..." A pained look flashed across Jeff's face. "Please sit down, Dallas."

The heavy weight of her heart forced her into a chair.

"There's no easy way to tell you this," Jeff said.

Him too? "Just tell me. Straight out."

Jeff closed his eyes. "I'm thinking of withdrawing from the case."

"What?"

"Dallas, listen carefully. I am obligated to represent a client with zeal. That's what the code of ethics says. That requires a certain trust, on both sides. When things happen that destroy trust, the zeal that's supposed to be there fizzles. I won't be doing Ron any favors by continuing to represent him."

"What happened? What did he say to you?"

"It's what he didn't say. I have the feeling he's holding back something, not being up front with me."

Dallas stared at him. *Just wait.*

"Ron originally lied to the police, and he lied to you and me about whether he had sex with Melinda Perry."

"Yes, he did, and he's sorry for that. I really believe he is and—"

"I think he's still lying."

"How?"

"I don't know. But I have a terrible feeling he's lying to you too, Dallas."

Dallas clenched her teeth. She couldn't fight it any longer. "He is holding back, Jeff."

He sat on the edge of his desk. "What do you know?"

"I had coffee with Lisa Benson today. She told me the prosecutor wants to interview her and Bob."

"Did she say why?"

"Boy, did she." Dallas rubbed her right temple, which felt like an earthquake's epicenter. "She found out that Ron had an affair."

"Someone other than the victim?"

Dallas nodded. "About a year ago. I remember the woman. Her name was Amy Shea. Does that name ring a bell?"

Jeff shook his head.

"You'd probably remember her if you saw her. She was a striking woman. I never got to know her real well. It's easy to come and get lost at Hillside. But that's that. Will this hurt the case?"

"It may. If the prosecution finds her, she could be called as a witness to establish a pattern in Ron's life. Regardless, this is another example of Ron's not being up front with us."

Dallas took a couple of deep breaths, and they felt like the last gasps of a drowning woman.

"Jeff, won't you stay on? I can't imagine getting another lawyer."

He hesitated, then said, "All right, Dallas. For you I'll do it."

She almost cried then but managed to make it out of the office with her eyes dry. And then she drove to the ocean.

She parked along Pacific Coast Highway near Point Dume, then walked down to the sand and sat and just looked.

She'd grown up in California, always lived near the coast. She couldn't imagine not having the ocean near her.

At least until now.

Now she thought what she might do. Sell the house and buy some place in the South. A place that was not California, where she could start over, out of any limelight.

She had no husband now. She was not married to Ron Hamilton after all, but a phantom, a liar, a shadow man.

He was sick in a deep, spiritual way. Well, she didn't have to share that sickness.

Divorce. Everyone would understand. No one on earth would accuse her of selfishness or abandonment. Not after this.

She thought about praying but decided not to. Right now she didn't want to hear the voice of God. That was tiring. She didn't want to pray for herself, or Ron. Let him pray for himself, if he had any faith left.

It was almost noon. She could sit here all day, watch the waves, let the world go on without her. No Jared, no Ron. Give up and not fight it anymore.

She remembered another beach, near Big Sur, where she'd stopped after thumbing out of L.A. to get away from Chad. It was twilight and she was wearing a long cotton dress and she kicked off her shoes and waded into the water, toward the gentle waves.

There'd been a split second there, as her dress got soggy with brine, that she thought she might just keep going, get beyond the waves and let the current take her out, then under. Give it all up to a beautiful cleansing and rest and absorption into peace. Chad had made ground meat of her soul, and this seemed a perfect place and time to dump the whole mess.

And then she began to weep.

She didn't know how long she wept, but suddenly a man, an older man in a bathing suit, was in the water next to her asking if she was okay. He had gray hair on his chest, a gray moustache, and a nice smile.

Stammering something, nodding, she returned to the shore and sat on the dry sand and cried some more. When she finally stopped she looked around, and was completely alone in the oncoming darkness. She ran to the road and caught another ride, this one all the way into San Francisco.

Now, looking out at her beloved ocean, hearing waves hitting sand, she wept again, and thought about the heaviness of water.

§

As I got busier, as my writing and speaking invitations grew, as Hillside began to burst and began a new building program, as I started on the radio, as I spent more time in my office than at home, how could I not have expected my spiritual life to atrophy?

I did not read the Bible much, except to find verses to pin on my sermons. My sermons were no longer about the power of God, the good news of redemption. When people came to my services—MY!!—I wanted them to feel that I—I!!—was giving them words of comfort for their "felt needs."

I was not searching the Word so it could search me, nor was I praying as I ought, with a passionate longing.

Not like when I was preaching on the streets of San Francisco, when I had no choice but to depend on the power of God, on the power of his Word.

When I first came to Hillside, the pastor I was replacing, Roger Vernon, took me aside and asked me what the most crucial thing to do was, and I said, "Pastor the people."

"More crucial," he prodded.

I said I didn't know what was more crucial than that.

And he said, "Where does the word crucial *come from?"*

I shrugged.

"It comes from the word cross. *That is what you must do. Preach the cross of Christ, make it the center of everything you do, first and foremost in your own life."*

*

"What is it, Dallas?" Ron, on the other side of the Plexiglas, frowned. He looked like he'd aged five years. "Why don't you say anything?"

"I'm trying to gather my thoughts," she said. She'd been trying to gather them for the past three days, since learning about his other affair.

"What is it? Something's wrong. Jared?"

"Jared is a topic for another time."

Ron shook his head. "You seem so distant, Dallas."

"Do I?"

"I don't understand."

"No, I don't think you do."

How like a little boy he looked now, knowing he was in trouble but not knowing the details. "Please talk to me, Dallas."

"Before I do, I want to lay down some ground rules."

"Rules? What are you—"

"Just listen. If you want me in here again, you will listen now, okay? Nod if you understand."

He nodded.

"Good. The first and most important rule is this. You will not lie to me. Ever again. And I mean ever. Do you understand that?"

"Dallas, I wish you'd tell me—"

"*Do* you understand that?"

"Of course I do. If you're still angry about what I did, I thought that—"

"Quiet. You're still listening to me. The second ground rule is that you are to speak to me directly and not try to hide behind words. I want direct answers and admissions. Is that understood?"

"I guess so." He was looking worried now, and Dallas felt a pang of sympathy for him. She had never talked to him this way. He had always been the leader, the authority in the family. He looked truly pained that she was talking like this.

Tough.

"Here it is, Ron. And I want you to think very carefully before you answer. Because if I sense any evasion whatsoever, then I am out of here. For good."

Ron blinked, then nodded his agreement.

"I know about Amy Shea," Dallas said.

For at least ten seconds, Ron did not move, didn't even twitch. Dallas kept her eyes trained on him, not giving an inch. She was not going to soften. Not this time.

Ron looked down. "She came to see me once. She was going through a divorce and said she needed spiritual counsel. I tried to give it to her. I honestly tried to tell her to keep her marriage together."

Dallas almost snapped at him but stayed quiet.

"She asked me if I'd meet with her again, and I agreed. Only she said she wanted to meet at her place of business, and could I do that. She was running a pretty successful boutique in Malibu. So I went. I thought seeing a little more of her life would give me good insight into her problem. Stupid mistake."

Dallas felt the heat of humiliation in her, pushing upward toward her tear ducts. Still, she remained silent.

"She insisted on taking me to lunch, to show her appreciation. I told her I didn't think that was a good idea. Honest, I did. I knew it wasn't. But ... I just went."

What wasn't I giving you, Ron? Why did you feel the need?

"We had lunch at this place by the beach, looking out at the ocean. She was, I guess, in her element. I was the fish out of water. But then she started talking about my preaching, about how she thought I was a natural for television, about this and that, and I just got caught up in it."

Nothing like the power of flattery from a beautiful woman. Men, in some fundamental ways, are so weak.

"We went back to her boutique. She told the other girl there that she wanted to close up early. Amy locked the place up. And that's when it happened."

"In the *boutique*?"

Ron nodded, looking down.

"How long did it go on?" Dallas said.

"A few weeks. Then I stopped it."

"Why?"

"Because"—he looked into her eyes—"I couldn't handle the guilt. And because I love you."

The words did not melt her heart, and that was surprising. For so many years Dallas had fed hungrily on those words, which came less and less frequently from Ron's lips. Now they were nearly unpalatable.

"One more question, Ron."

He waited.

"Were there any others?"

"No. I give you my absolute word."

"Was it me?" she said. "Was I lacking in some way? Did I—"

"No, Dallas, no. Please believe me."

She tried to.

"Now I have a question for you," Ron said.

"What?"

"Will you forgive me?"

She stared at him, wondering if she could.

NINE

I.

Saturday morning and her head was about to explode. *I'm a Hindenburg waiting to happen*, Dallas thought as the walls of her house crowded in around her.

She'd already turned away one reporter who'd come knocking at the door like a Jehovah's Witness with three thousand questions.

She had to get away. And in Los Angeles that always meant hopping in a car and driving as far as you wanted. Alone.

She grabbed her purse and went.

She got to the freeway and was relieved that no news vans were following her. She headed east toward Pasadena with the radio tuned to the classic-rock station. A nice blast from her past. She'd always liked the music of the seventies. She didn't want to think about anything but driving and listening and being anywhere but home.

At least the day was clear. The San Gabriel Mountains on her left were looking fine. Nothing ever bothered them, except a few brushfires now and again. Or floods sometimes, which caused the mountains to shed muddy skin, sloughing it into the yards and swimming pools of the homes foolishly packed below.

She remembered the first time she'd seen these mountains as a little girl when her mother had moved them here. They drove over the Sepulveda Pass and looked down on the Valley where the San Gabriels merged with the Santa Susanas. And it seemed like a wonderland then, a land of adventure, a place where she would meet wonderful friends and where, one day, she'd become a famous singer. All this was years before meeting Chad McKenzie and learning that dreams were kid stuff, and sometimes deadly.

She'd had a different dream when she moved back here with Ron. A dream of new beginnings and a marriage that would be a permanent and glorious thing. Moving back to Los Angeles then was a way of recapturing hopes and sharing them with a man she finally loved and trusted and would stay with forever.

Dallas merged onto the Foothill Freeway, and as she did she found she was crying. She wiped the tears with the back of her hand. The rock station was playing "Love the One You're With." She punched the *off* button. This time, the music was no help.

Maybe it's me. Maybe I wasn't a good enough wife or mother. Maybe I just blew it. And maybe all that stuff from Ron about loving me and wanting forgiveness is just the last gasp of the dying man who really doesn't care. Maybe we're better off without each other.

She drove on, through Pasadena, and then past Sierra Madre and Duarte. Towns where normal life was happening, to people who weren't her.

She saw the 605 Freeway coming up, and her inner geography kicked in. The 605 south would take her to El Monte, La Puente.

And Pico Rivera, infamous of late as the town with the Star Motel.

Don't do it. Leave it alone. Keep driving. Find a movie theater. See a comedy. But don't torture yourself by—

She took the 605 south.

When she got off in Pico Rivera she pulled into a Shell station next to a pay phone. She got out and looked in the Yellow Pages and found the address for the Star Motel, which didn't do her a lot of good, not knowing where the streets were.

But the nice young man at the counter told her, in his New Delhi accent, that the street she wanted was just two blocks away.

2.

The Star looked like it had been built in the fifties, the golden age of motels in Los Angeles County. But the years had not been kind to it. The exterior was done up in weather-beaten white with a muddy aqua trim. The letters spelling out *Motel* on the roof were red and accented with neon lights that, in the sunshine, looked superfluous and ugly.

Dallas turned into the driveway and noticed only a few cars parked in the lot. The lot itself appeared to form a horseshoe shape. She followed it to the far end and saw there was another driveway in the back.

And she saw the room. Number 105, at the very rear of the building, the dull silver numbers easily readable from the car.

She almost drove on. What good was this? What did she hope to accomplish?

To find something, anything, that would show Ron didn't kill Melinda Chance. Jeff said they needed some evidence, and it wasn't forthcoming. But maybe her eyes could see something here others had missed.

Didn't that happen on the TV shows? Some CSI person would find a shell casing or carpet fiber or ... who was she kidding? This was reality, and she was no trained forensic specialist.

But she could at least say she tried everything she could think of.

She pulled her car into the last spot in the lot, facing the street in back of the motel, and let the car idle. Finally she turned it off and got out and faced the building.

There was no car in front of the room, and no one appeared to be around. The news hounds had taken their fill of pictures. Curiosity seekers had no doubt driven by in the first few days after all the publicity.

Maybe this place would end up on a map someday, the kind sold by street hawkers in Hollywood, which showed tourists movie stars' homes or famous crime scenes. *See where Charles Manson did his thing! See the room where Ron Hamilton offed that girl!*

Dallas shivered then, even though the day was hot. There was evil here. Bad things going on behind closed doors.

She was vaguely aware of a grating sound, turned, and saw it was a boy on a skateboard, coming into the parking lot from the back street. He was Latino, around twelve. The lot was big enough that it probably made a nice track for skateboarders.

But instead of heading toward the lot, he came right up to her and stopped.

"That's where it happen," he said.

"Excuse me?"

"The killing, you know? Right there."

He pointed at room 105.

Dallas nodded. "I know."

"Lots of people come by to look."

"Sure. Do you live around here?"

He jerked his head over his shoulder. "There. So you want me to tell what happen?"

"I already know."

"She was hot."

"What? Hot?"

"Lady that got killed."

Dallas almost jumped. "Did you see her?"

He shook his head. "My friend."

"Your friend saw the lady that was killed here?"

The boy started to look a little nervous.

Easy. Back off a little. "Go ahead. What else can you tell me?"

"Nothing."

"Wait, you said you had a friend—"

"I don't know nothing."

"But you said—"

He turned and pushed off on his skateboard.

"Wait!"

He didn't wait. Dallas took two steps after him, but he was fast. The sound of skateboard wheels on pavement was all he left her.

"Please!"

She watched helplessly as he disappeared around the cinder-block wall.

Something had scared him off. She had to know what it was. She ran to her car, started it, backed out of her space. A car horn blared at her.

She slammed on the brakes. She'd almost backed into a Lexus. The driver, a man in sunglasses, yelled at her, gesticulating with one arm.

Dallas gunned her car forward, almost scraping the wall. She actually burned rubber out of the driveway. She stopped at the road and looked both ways. No sign of the boy. There was a strip mall to the left and some housing to the right.

She chose right, drove, then caught sight of the boy a fair distance down a residential street. She stopped, backed up, and turned down the street.

What on earth was she doing? Chasing a kid on a skateboard? A scared kid at that.

It didn't matter. He was a thread, a chance.

And what would she do when she caught up to him? Money. Give him a five or a ten, get him to tell her something, anything, to get her to the next step. Whatever that was.

She was only vaguely aware of the topography of the neighborhood. The homes were smallish, probably built around the same time as the Star Motel. There were manicured lawns next to fenced yards. Spare trees, testaments to faded glory, leaned against cracked curbs.

The boy disappeared up what looked to be a driveway. She followed into what turned out to be an alley. A wooden fence on one side, block walls on the other. City garbage cans lolled against the fencing.

And the kid had stopped and was talking to someone.

A group of someones.

Dallas stopped, saw the boy pointing at her. The one he was talking to was older, wore a white wifebeater and black jeans, and had a blue bandanna tied around his head.

He was about thirty feet away from her, but when he looked directly at her she saw everything she needed to know in his eyes.

It was more than enough to get her to put the car in reverse and start backing out the way she came.

Only now she couldn't. Because a car had somehow come up behind without her noticing, and it was blocking her way. Purposely, she knew.

A moment later four doors flew open and young men who might have been wearing neon GANG signs poured out.

And started slowly walking toward her.

3.

Jared stopped and looked at his reflection in the dirty window, darkened on the inside so the early drinkers could be shielded from sunlight. In the window he saw the same dumb face he'd seen for the last couple of years, staring back with eyes as dark as the pane of glass, as bereft as the hopes on the other side.

What were you thinking? You think you matter to a kid and some woman whose life is shot because that's the way she wants it? What're you after, idiot? Quit pretending that it's going to get better. Go in, have a drink, get some cheap bourbon down your throat, feel the nice warm glow that comes out your nose when you knock it back neat, and maybe later you can grab some weed and get high before you decide where you're going to head off to so you don't bring your mom down anymore and make your sister crazy.

You gave it a shot, but let's face it, boy, you are damaged goods, no use.

He turned back to the boulevard and thought maybe a fast-moving truck would be the best solution for everybody. All he'd have to do is jump in front and take a good thumping and that would be that. Unless he lived, of course, in which case things would be worse than ever and Mom would have way more to deal with than he would wish on anyone.

No solution, then, after all. Which spun him right back to the bar.

Go get that drink, fool, what're you waiting for?

He started to go in when he heard someone call his name. He turned around and saw Joe Boyle walking toward him. Joe. They'd been in youth group together at church. Jared hadn't seen him in years, hadn't kept in touch.

"Thought I recognized you!" Joe threw his arms around Jared and gave him a hug. Jared let him but didn't return the favor. "How you been, man?"

Joe looked a little more prosperous than he had in high school. He wore khaki slacks and a knit shirt and looked like he could be getting ready to go to the golf course and actually play golf, not get high like they used to, sneaking out at night.

"I'm fine," Jared said.

"You just get back? From the Marines?"

"I been back a while."

"Bummer about your dad." Joe shook his head. "I don't believe it, you know."

"Thanks."

"What are you doing now?"

Getting drunk at 11:00 a.m. How about you? "Not a whole lot. You?"

"Vista Ford. You know what? I really like selling cars. I mean, I'm good at it."

"No doubt." Joe had always been good at anything.

"Married too." He held up his left hand, showing a gold wedding band.

"Who'd you end up with?"

"You mean who took my sorry self? Remember Rona Conroy?"

"Oh, yeah." Very nice looking, as he recalled.

"Yeah, baby too. Little girl."

Was he rubbing it in or something? "Cool. Congratulations."

"Hey, I'm just stopping over at Wendy's. Can I buy you a burger?"

"No, thanks. I got some things to do."

"Well, let's get together." Joe took out a snap case and pulled out a business card. It had raised gold lettering on it. Joe was a *Sales Executive*.

Jared took it. "Sure."

"I mean it." Joe pointed his finger at him, gun style.

"Right. You bet."

Joe gave him a slap on the shoulder. "See you. Call me."

And he turned and walked back along the sidewalk, toward the Wendy's a block away. Jared watched him, waited until he was out of sight, then went into the bar, crumpling the card as he did.

4.

"What you want?"

The kid with the blue bandanna was standing at her window now, the boy on the skateboard behind him. The others were around her car, two of them directly in front. She was going to have to talk, so it might as well be now.

"I was looking for … I don't want anything, I just wanted to ask a question."

"You scared or something?"

"Yes."

"What, you think this big bad banger, he gonna mess you?"

She nodded. She could hear blood pulsating in her ears.

"I look like a banger to you?"

She nodded.

He smiled, showing perfect white teeth that fairly gleamed. On his neck were tattooed the words *Mi Vida Loca*. He slapped the top of her car, creating a popping sound that entered her ears like ice bullets.

Loca turned to the boy with the skateboard and said something in Spanish. The boy looked at Dallas and nodded. Loca turned back to Dallas. "So you come to see the place, huh, the place where the guy smoked her?"

"Yes."

"Why?"

She could fudge around it or tell him. She could try to finesse her way out or lay it on the line. Something told her fudging could only lead to worse trouble.

Dallas opened the door so she could get out and face him. He let her. He was not very tall. She was eye to eye with him.

"My husband is the one they think did it."

He gave her a long look, then said, "He musta been on something, huh?"

"He didn't do it."

"Yeah?"

"He didn't. The boy said he had a friend who saw the woman."

The gangbanger slapped the back of the boy's head. The boy yelped.

"You got money?"

"Yes."

"Give it to me."

Dallas reached into the car and got her purse. She had twenty-two dollars and some change. She handed it over.

"Okay," Loca said. "You did good. You come with me now."

5.

He led her down the alley, the others following. Was she being a complete fool to go with him?

Yes.

But two things kept her going. Instinct and faith. She had the idea that she could trust this guy, and being in the daylight helped. But she also had faith that she was protected and she had to step out in that, had to at this moment in time because she'd come this far.

Near the end of the alley was an open garage. Only this was done up like a room, with posters and shelves and secondhand carpet over the cement. At the back of the garage was a mattress, and on the mattress sat a rotund teenager. His white T-shirt was too small for his frame, and an ample portion of stomach protruded out over his jeans. He held a comic book in one hand and looked up nonchalantly as Loca entered the space.

"Hey, this lady wanna talk about the lady you saw at the motel, huh?"

The kid slowly looked at Dallas with a dark moon face.

"You don't got to be afraid, man. Talk to her."

Dallas sat on a crate, tried to speak calmly. "Will you tell me what you saw?"

Loca kicked him, half playfully, half rebukingly. "Go on, Ratón. Tell her."

"She was hot." The words came out of Ratón slow and childlike. Coupled with the detached look in his eyes, Dallas concluded that he was mentally challenged.

"Where did you see her?" Dallas probed.

Ratón was silent.

Loca said, "He hangs over there at the place. He likes to watch the people. It's like his TV. Crazy, huh?"

"He watches the motel?"

"And the 7-Eleven. That's how he changes channels." Loca laughed.

Ratón laughed, looking at Loca as if taking his cues from him.

The strangeness of the scene coalesced around her. Gangbangers, a kid on a skateboard, a handicapped kid on a mattress who may have seen something, may not have. But why stop now? "Please tell me what else you saw."

"The man." Ratón looked at Loca. "Should I say about the man?"

"What man?" Dallas said.

"Yeah," Loca said, sounding like this was news to him too.

Ratón licked his lips. "He was fast. He ran fast. Went into that place."

Dallas said, "You saw a man go into a room?"

Ratón nodded.

"What did this man look like?"

"Black."

"He was a black man?"

Ratón frowned and shook his head, then rubbed his hands on his T-shirt. "All black."

"You mean he was dressed in black clothes?"

Ratón nodded quickly.

Dallas considered the information. A fast man dressed in black. That did not sound like Ron. He wouldn't dress that way if he was just meeting with Melinda.

"Did you see this man go into the room?" Dallas asked.

Ratón squinted. "I think. And then he came out, ran away."

This was such a thin thread, even if she could believe what he said. But it was the only thread she had in hand.

"What else?"

"Huh?"

"What else did you see?" She couldn't temper the desperation in her voice.

Ratón's eyes widened, and he made a little squeaking sound in his throat. He looked at Loca.

Loca said, "He's getting a little nervous. Maybe you should go now."

"Please," she said. "I have to know everything."

"That's it."

"No, tell him to tell me. Please."

Loca shook his head, took hold of her arm, and pulled her up. "You can go now. And don't come back."

She pulled her arm away. "You don't seem to understand."

"Oh, yeah?"

"I'm not an enemy."

Loca shook his head. "You're not a friend, neither. Now get in your car."

§.

She drove immediately to Jeff Waite's office in Encino. She knew he often worked on Saturdays and took a chance. It paid off. The security guard in the building called him and then sent her up.

Jeff was in casual clothes when he met her coming off the elevator. "What brings you down here?" he said.

"Jeff, listen, where can we talk?"

"Come on." He walked her into the suite of offices on the fourteenth floor. They went into the library, which had a table in the middle of the room. Papers and open books were spread out there.

"Just doing a little research on the admissibility of a victim's past. We need to show that Melinda Perry was not exactly running with a good crowd. Meaning there were others who could have done this."

"Can you show this?"

"It's iffy. What we'd be saying is that we have an alternative theory, and the courts have held we need to provide some factual basis for it."

"Can we?"

"Not yet. We need something that connects Melinda and her background to something in this case, like the motel."

Dallas's breath accelerated. "What if you had a witness who could do that?"

"Witness?"

"That's what I came to tell you. I was just in Pico Rivera, I went to the Star Motel, a kid was skateboarding there, and I followed him"—she didn't care how wild this sounded—"and, long story short, I was talking to another kid who saw someone at the motel that night, someone who was not Ron, and when I—"

Jeff put his hands up. "Whoa, slow down. First, who is this guy?"

"His name is something Spanish, Ratón."

"Mouse?"

"That's what this other guy called him."

"What other guy?"

Dallas huffed. "It's a little involved, a gang member—"

"*Gang* member? Dallas, what the heck—"

"Listen to me. This kid I was talking to, he saw something. He's just a little ..."

"A little what?"

"Mentally slow. But he knows what he saw, he—"

"Dallas! First of all, what are you doing going around investigating things? I have people who do that for a living."

"I know. It was spontaneous. I just had to do something."

"Yeah, and if you do the wrong thing it could blow Ron's case up, did you consider that? Did you consider you might chase away information?"

"I'm sorry, Jeff."

"And this alleged witness, you're telling me he's got mental problems. You know he might not even be competent to testify."

"You should at least talk to him."

"You've got a very unreliable witness here. The DA will take him apart."

"But what about the truth?"

Jeff dropped into a chair. "Dallas, that's what I've been trying to tell you. It's not the truth that matters. It's the evidence. It's what the jury is allowed to see. If we thought trials were about the truth we'd hook everybody up to lie detectors and let the judge sort it out. But it's not. It's about who's got the best evidence and who can bluff the other side into the best deal. If the evidence is roughly equivalent, we go to trial."

"So now we have evidence."

"That doesn't make it equal. Like I said, the DA will kill this witness's credibility. And he has all the physical evidence he needs."

"Jeff, I can't give up on him. Maybe I should, but I can't. He's still my husband, and he's still not guilty of murder."

"I want to believe that."

She looked at him hard. "You don't? Jeff, you honestly don't?"

He said nothing, and that was answer enough.

"I don't know what to do," Dallas said. "But it's got to be something."

"We'll try."

"There is no try. Only do."

"Huh?"

"It's an old saying."

Jeff smiled at her, then nodded. "You're quite a doer when you put your mind to it. All right. I'll have you talk to Harry."

Late Monday morning Dallas met Harry Stegman at Jerry's Famous Deli. Jerry's was an overpriced hangout for young movie turks and the old-money crowd who lived in the hills south of Ventura Boulevard. These people had bought homes in the fifties and sixties, and were now sitting atop the mushroom cloud of the real-estate boom.

Harry was sitting in the waiting area and got up when he saw her. He was about sixty, with a laurel wreath of white hair surrounding a bald pate. His suit was beige and rumpled. Every time Dallas saw Harry, in fact, whatever suit he happened to be wearing seemed to be the final resting place of all the wrinkles in the Western world.

His lack of spit and polish was oddly comforting, though. A bit round in the middle, Harry Stegman seemed more like somebody's competent accountant brother than a criminal investigator.

"Thanks for seeing me," Dallas said as Harry pumped her hand.

"Nothing of it, we're all part of the team."

They were shown to a booth, and Harry ordered coffee for them. Then he folded his hands in front of him on the table. "You holding up okay?"

Holding up? She was just thankful she could walk around. "Every day is its own adventure, it seems."

"You have got that exactly right." Harry smiled. It was an easy smile, smooth and calming. Dallas realized he must have comforted countless people over the years in his professional capacity.

"I been doing this a long time," Harry said, "and every time I think I've seen it all, something throws me for a new loop. At least it keeps me young. You wouldn't think to look at me that I'm only twenty-five."

"Never would have guessed. You don't look a day over twenty."

"Bless you, my child."

The server brought coffee and asked if they'd like to order any food. Dallas declined. Harry ordered a "sky high" corned-beef sandwich.

"Stuff'll stop my heart," Harry said. "But I figure we ought to enjoy our stay, you know?"

"You have family, Mr. Stegman?"

"Harry. Please. I have a daughter. In Oklahoma. She works with horses. She's got a gift." He smiled and his eyes seemed to be looking at a memory. "Wish I could see her more." He came back to the present. "Now, let's see what we can do here." He put on some reading glasses and took a pad and pen from his coat pocket. "Jeff says you think somebody else killed the girl?"

"I think Ron was set up somehow. Do you think that's possible?"

"Like I said, there's always something new. But there are some things that always stay the same. Like in murder. There has to be a reason, a motive. A strong one too, if it involved a plan to frame Ron. Let's think that one through a bit. Who might possibly entertain such a motive?"

"Ron was outspoken about pornography. He was working with Bernie Halstrom on trying to crack down on the porn industry here in the Valley. The girl was a porn star." Dallas was struck with a new thought. "What if she was part of this plan to ruin Ron?"

Harry tapped his lower lip with the pen. "Why would she have to be murdered? If they were trying to ruin Ron with an affair, she could have just come out with that story and played it to the end."

"What if she got some other ideas along the way? Maybe she was playing both sides against the middle. Maybe she was trying to get more money out of whoever hired her."

"You're pretty good at this," Harry said. "I like the way you think. Still, we have a lot of maybes. Let's see if we can link them up. We'd be talking a conspiracy here."

"Does it have to be a conspiracy?"

"It only takes two people in agreement on a criminal scheme, and that's what we're supposing here. We have the girl, Melinda Perry, and a somebody else. Maybe a few somebody elses. But as for linkage, right now we only have an untested CI."

"CI?"

"Citizen informant. The other problem is he also happens to be a gang member."

"I don't think he's a member, really, he's sort of . . ."

"Mentally challenged?"

Dallas nodded, feeling her hopes starting to drain away.

Harry scribbled some notes on his pad. The server came back with one of the largest sandwiches Dallas had ever seen. Harry's face lit up. "You sure you don't want part of this?"

"I'm sure," Dallas said.

"Because I'll just have to eat the whole thing."

"You could take half of it home."

Harry shook his head. "Good corned beef never tastes the same half an hour later. I don't know why that is, but it's one of the most important things to know in this life."

Life. Would it ever be normal again? Would she ever again be able to take pleasure in simple things, like a good sandwich?

She sensed that Harry, seasoned pro that he was, immediately picked up her vibe.

"Try not to worry," he said softly. "It's Jeff's job to look at the evidence and tell you the score. It's my job to dig and dig and find everything I can that'll help. That's what I get paid the big bucks for. That's why I can afford to buy sandwiches the size of Nebraska."

A single tear coursed down Dallas's left cheek. She grabbed her napkin and dabbed her eye.

"Let me have one bite here," Harry said, "and then you give me all the names you can think of, all the people Ron may have had connections with, places he used to go, anything at all. How's that sound?"

"Thanks, Mr. Stegman."

"Harry."

She watched him savor a bite. It almost made her want to order one for herself. They spent an hour together, and Dallas gave out all the information she could think of. Just before she rose to leave, Harry extended his hand.

"Try not to worry," he said again.

She nodded. He was looking at her closely.

"You remind me a little of my daughter." He seemed sad when he said it. "You've got the same eyes. A little vulnerable, but tough."

Dallas smiled. "I think I'd like to meet her sometime."

"That," he said wistfully, "would be nice."

⸙

On her way back from Jerry's Deli, Dallas stopped off at Ralph's for some groceries. Life had to go on. No matter what she was feeling about Ron and the whole mess, she had Jared and Cara to think of.

She suddenly remembered a scene from her San Francisco days. She'd gone over to see Alcatraz and was walking up a steep ramp at the old abandoned prison. At the top, perched on a wall, she saw a large seagull. The gull had its wings spread out, resisting a stiff wind.

Dallas approached, fascinated. The gull didn't move, but watched her closely. She smiled at it and cooed a little to settle it down. But when she was about five feet away, the gull squawked threateningly, eyes riveted on her. Dallas stopped. And then she saw the reason for the bird's defiance—two small, fuzzy chicks stuck their heads out from under each of the mother gull's wings.

She was protecting her young against the elements, approaching strangers, and anything else that might do them harm.

Though she had no children of her own then, Dallas knew that's what it would be like to be a mother. Instinct would kick in, and nothing dangerous would get close to her children without a fight to the finish.

She knew this even more now as she thought of Jared and Cara and all the events swirling around them. She would keep her wings over them, defying the dread winds, and nothing would move her from her maternal duty.

In the market she selected a man-sized rib eye to cook for Jared. She hadn't fired up a steak in a long time. It would be good to do it again. A reminder of better times.

It would be a way to break through the fence he seemed to be erecting.

As she got to her Pathfinder with her cart, she heard a man's voice behind her say, "Can I help you with that?"

"No, I've got it." She didn't want to look at him. She wanted to get in the car as quickly as possible and lock the doors.

She saw him out of the corner of her eye, just standing there. That's when she knew he was trouble.

Don't panic. There are plenty of people around.

She unlocked her door, put the first bag in. Turning for the next, she noticed the man was closer.

Security guard. There's one at the store entrance. Should I call out?

"You really look like you could use some help."

No way to avoid it. Heart kicking, she looked the man in the face.

And her heart nearly stopped.

Chad McKenzie hadn't changed much in, what was it, nearly thirty years? That was scary. Age had only added to his malice. His charcoal hair was shaved down close. He wore a black knee-length coat.

"Hi, Dallas."

His voice sliced her. How easily and eerily it all came back to her, flooding her with dark memories. Her legs started shaking. She wondered if she could even move.

"You look great. Better than on TV." He made no move toward her, but she felt cornered just the same.

"I have to go," she managed to say.

"Whoa, wait. That's all you can say to me after all these years?"

This was too surreal. How did he find her? This wasn't a coincidence.

"How come you didn't return my phone call? A guy could get a real feeling of rejection from that."

Thoughts tumbled into place. The note. The smashed headlight. The strange message on her cell phone.

Chad.

Go. Now. She looked down, as if doing so would make him disappear, and reached for her last bag. Chad snatched it out of the cart.

That was it. The breach, the physical act. He'd gone too far, but he always had. Trembling, she could sit there and take it. Or do *something*. But what?

The one advantage she had was being in a public place. "I will scream my head off if you don't give me that now."

"No need, no need. I'm not out to hurt you."

"Like I believe that."

"Why would I pick a public parking lot, huh? I just want to talk to you."

She sensed the smallest hesitation in his tone of voice and told herself not to back down. "Give me the bag."

"Just talk."

"We have nothing to say to each other."

"Now I'm hurt. After all we were together?"

"Give me the bag."

"I saw your face on the tube. Isn't that a wonderful thing? You see somebody who shared her body and soul with you, right up there on the TV, and she's in trouble. How could I not come?"

"Bag."

He didn't move. "You know, I thought about you in prison. Maybe the same way good old Ron is thinking about you right now, missing your warmth, your—"

"Stop it."

"How'd you end up with a guy like that? A preacher man? You weren't exactly into being religious when we were doing our thing."

"I will scream, I swear, if you don't give me the bag right now."

He smiled. "I was just helping." He held the bag out to her. "I'm a helpful guy."

She took the bag.

"And I want to help you," he said.

Just turn and drive away. Don't listen.

"I want to keep your sad family story from getting worse."

"What are you talking about?"

"That's better. That's nicer. How *are* you, Dallas? I really missed you."

Master manipulator. All abusers were. But he knew something, had some leverage. All right, she would manipulate him right back.

"You were in prison, huh?"

"Hey, what can I say? You make a mistake, they catch you, they make you pay. Kind of like Ron."

"You don't know anything about Ron, so just drop it."

"You ever tell him about us?"

"Of course I did. I told him everything."

"Everything?"

"I told him what mattered. About the way you beat up women."

He winked at her. "I'm what they call *rehabilitated*."

"If you have something to say to me, say it now. And say it once."

"Sure, Dallas, sure. I don't want to see you hurt any more than you have been. That guy, Ron, he ought to be taught a lesson. But your whole family doesn't have to suffer."

Her hands tightened on the shopping bag.

Chad patted the pockets of his coat. "You happen to have a smoke? I'm out."

"What about my family?"

"Hey, for old times' sake, maybe you could spot me a twenty. What do you say?"

"Good-bye."

She made a half turn as Chad snapped his fingers and said, "That's right, we were talking about your family. That daughter of yours. What did the paper say the cutie's name was? Cara?"

Dallas went cold.

"And a son who served in Iraq? Jared? Must be a fine boy."

He paused, his face congealing into smugness. "Do I have your attention again?"

"Say it!"

"The way the papers have it, you're a fine, honorable wife, holding a family together in the face of this very embarrassing turn of events. Must be hard on you and the kids. I wouldn't want to see it get any worse for them."

She knew he was leading up to something, so she waited.

"The way these reporters are hanging on every shred of story, what if they got the whole story of our passion from way back? I have pictures too. You remember the pictures, don't you?"

The pictures. She'd nearly forgotten he once hid a camera and took pictures of ... them. Awful, disgusting. If her children ever saw them ...

"They wouldn't run those," she said weakly.

"You kidding me? You know how much some of those tabloids pay? Which brings me back to my little problem. Twenty bucks ought to cover it. Call it a first installment."

The scheme was now clear. "How much do you want?"

"Like I said, a twenty."

"I mean altogether. To make you go away."

"Two zero." He put his hand out. Kept it there.

She knew he had her. Well planned and played by a con without conscience.

She fished out a twenty-dollar bill from her purse and practically threw it at him. "Now will you leave us alone?"

"We'll talk again, Dallas." He put the bill in his coat pocket. "Just make sure you answer my calls, huh? I get kind of impatient with the phone-tag deal, you know? And let's just keep this between us, because if the cops come sniffing around, that would be bad." He smiled one more time. "Hey! Great to see you again, Dallas. You look prime."

❦

Dallas drove in the grip of anger to a quiet residential area, pulled over, and called Jeff Waite. She left a voice message for him to call *immediately*.

She waited.

And as she did something was illuminated in her head, like when the high beams of a car hit a road sign at night. The sign told her there were two directions she could go.

One was to continue in the way she was already headed, dragged on by a limp but real faith to which she would occasionally respond. She needed something basic right now. Something her tenuous hope could easily grip. Not changing the status quo was easy. On the other hand, one more blow might permanently cripple her trust in God. She might never respond again.

Or she could cast off everything she could—every fear, every betrayal, every unknown—and dive into God. She could go to

God with her whole self, heart and hands and head uncovered, and scream, *Is this what you want?* and then wait for the tearing away of anything that wasn't truly his.

Do it, God, tear it all away and take me and show me and do whatever you want, because it's all over if you don't.

She had her eyes closed and her hands clamped on the steering wheel when Jeff returned her call.

"Are you okay?" he said. "You sounded desperate."

"I am."

"What's the matter?"

She told him about Chad. When she finished there was a long pause.

"At this point," Jeff said, "you've got the first step toward a criminal complaint. Write down exactly what happened—date, time, location. Keep a record. At some point he's going to cross the line. Do you have any protection?"

"You mean like a gun or something?"

"That's what I mean."

"No."

"Get a stun gun. You can carry it in your purse. The guy ever comes at you physically, you can give him a jolt."

She sighed. "I don't want to have to carry a weapon around."

"Who does? But it's an evil world we live in, Dallas."

With that she couldn't argue. *Evil world.* That was it, really it. The thing she'd not fully faced.

When she clicked off with Jeff she called Danielle at Haven House, to make sure all was well there. It was. Then she called the Hillside church office and had them look up the current number for Hillside's retired pastor, Roger Vernon.

TEN

On Thursday Dallas went to see Roger.

Now eighty, Roger was living in Palm Desert. He had been the preacher at Hillside when Ron was called. At that time, in the quaint old church building, the membership was around 300, good people, examples of Christian charity and discipleship.

Roger and his wife, Betty, were mentors for Ron and Dallas. Then they moved to Palm Desert, and over the years the contacts were limited to Christmas cards and one long letter Roger wrote a few years ago informing them of Betty's passing.

Roger greeted her in the front yard of his home. "It's been so long, Dallas. I'm very happy to see you." He gave her a hug. "What do you think of the place?"

She looked around at the sandy yard, which was like the yards of the other modest homes in the neighborhood. No grass out here. "You spent your life preaching warnings against hell. Now you live there."

He laughed. "It only gets up to about 120 in the summer. Child's play. Come on inside."

His home was done in a Southwest style. Roger was originally from New Mexico, where he pastored a church before coming to Hillside. He had some iced tea ready for them in the living room, which was decorated with a collection of multifaceted rocks.

"I hope you know I've been praying for you and Ron," he said when they were settled. "I can't imagine how you feel."

"Did you ever see *Braveheart*?"

"The Mel Gibson movie? One of my favorites."

"Remember what they do to him at the end? Well, that's what it feels like. Tearing out the insides."

Roger nodded. His face was full of understanding, as she knew it would be. He got up and took a rock off a shelf. "I collect these things," he said. "This one's interesting."

He handed the dark rock to Dallas. "What is it?" she asked.

"Gneiss."

She looked at it. "Nice enough."

"Not *nice*. G-N-E-I-S-S. Pronounced the same way. It's a metamorphic rock. The minerals that compose gneiss are the same as granite, but only after intense pressure and heat." He paused. "Think you can relate to this rock?"

"You saying I'm a very gneiss girl?"

Smiling, Roger said, "You got the picture. You'll come out of this stronger. So will Ron. I'll go see him."

"Would you?"

"Certainly. What about your kids? How are they taking it?"

"Cara's managing, but Jared ... Oh, boy." She told him about Jared. Everything. And the helplessness she felt because the medical experts didn't seem able to do anything for him. When she finished her eyes were wet.

"I'm sorry," Roger said quietly. "I'm not surprised, though."

"Why not?"

"There's an angle here the VA isn't considering, because if they did the ACLU would be all over them."

"What sort of angle?"

"Spiritual. It's spiritual battle being waged, so if they don't recognize it, how can they help?"

"You mean demonic?"

Roger nodded. "We don't know how demons influence us. How they get into our thoughts, how they suggest things. We only know they do it. In Ephesians we read about the prince of the power of the air, the spirit that now works *in* people. Then there is the horrible account of the Gerasene demoniac, in whom was Legion, many demons."

"And you think that's what's happening here?"

"I have something in a file." He got up and went to a file cabinet by his bookshelf. He opened a drawer and rifled through it. "Yes, here it is. It's something that was in the *New York Times* over a year ago. A psychologist from Stanford, reflecting on what happened at Abu Ghraib. Listen. 'I believe that the prison guards at the Abu Ghraib Prison in Iraq, who worked the night shift in Tier 1A, where prisoners were physically and psychologically abused, had surrendered their free will and personal responsibility during these episodes of mayhem.'"

"No free will?"

"*Surrendered* free will. There's more. 'These eight army reservists were trapped in a unique situation in which the behavioral context came to dominate individual dispositions, values, and morality to such an extent that they were transformed into mindless actors alienated from their normal sense of personal accountability for their actions—at that time and place.'"

Dallas could only shake her head at this.

"It's our ignorance of the demonic that is at issue here," Roger explained. "Demons are territorial. They control areas. When the people in those areas worship the demon, the demon feeds. Gains power. Gains control. And there is every reason to believe that the stronghold of all demonic forces in the world resides in southern Iraq."

"Babylon," Dallas whispered.

"Precisely. Ancient Babylon. Also known as Shinar and the land of the Chaldeans. The presumed location of Eden, now Eden corrupted. In Revelation we are told that Babylon is the habitation of devils, the hold of every foul spirit. That's quite a claim."

"Still?"

"Why not? In Babylon, the chief god was Marduk, also called Bel. I firmly believe that Marduk is real, and is another name for Satan."

"This is starting to blow me away."

"It should."

"This Marduk is Satan?"

"Listen to the development: In the beginning, God creates the heavens and the earth. He creates man and places him in Eden. The serpent, Satan, begins with Eve, and the first thing he does is call into question God's Word. 'Ye shall not surely die,' he tells her. He is a corrupter of God's truth.

"The Babylonian creation myth is a corrupted version of the truth. In this story, Marduk becomes chief god by defeating the goddess of the sea, Tiamat. Marduk, Satan, rewrote the truth for his benefit, and Babylon fell to worshiping him."

"I've never heard this before."

"It's not surprising. Let me show you something." Roger went to his bookcase, which was packed, and pulled out a heavy volume. He leafed through it until he came to the page he wanted, then laid the book on Dallas's lap. She looked down at an image of some sort of monarch.

"This," said Roger, "is a drawing of Marduk, taken from a carving dating to ancient Babylon. Notice that he's wearing a crown studded with fine stones. His garment is equally resplendent, and he holds a rod and ring, symbols of authority."

"And what's the creature at the bottom?" A terrible-looking head popped out from behind Marduk's robe.

"That is a serpent, but it is not a separate entity. It is the bottom half of Marduk himself."

"This is so strange . . ."

"Now, who was the original inhabitant of Eden?"

"Adam."

"Before that."

Dallas frowned. "Satan?"

"Precisely." Roger opened his Bible, turned pages. "Listen to this, from Ezekiel chapter twenty-eight. 'Thou hast been in Eden, the garden of God; every precious stone was thy covering, the sardius, topaz, and the diamond, the beryl, the onyx, and the jasper, the sapphire, the emerald, and the carbuncle, and gold.' I'm with the scholars who say this is a description of Lucifer before his rebellion. Lucifer is Latin for *light-bearer*, which is what we find in Isaiah 14, when Satan is described as 'son of the morning' or 'morning star.' He is also equated with the king of Babylon."

"It fits, doesn't it?"

"Cut to today. Marduk, Satan, rules in the place where your son was fighting. The demons are strong. They infect, they invade. Soldiers come home affected. It's as if you were to go swimming in a polluted lake. You think you're doing fine, but all along you're being infected. Sometimes the bacteria incubates, only asserts itself later. Outside of Christ, that's what happens to us, especially when we enter strongholds of demonic presence. And no stronghold is more formidable than Babylon."

Shaking her head, Dallas said, "Are you saying that demons have followed Jared back here?"

"There is so much we don't know about demonic activity," Roger said. "Except that it's real. You've read accounts of people coming into contact with some mysterious stranger who has helped them in times of trouble and then disappears?"

"Angels."

"Right. Sometimes in a time of terrible crisis, with death imminent, an angelic presence offers deliverance. Why then would we be surprised that fallen angels, demons, don't also operate in this world?"

"It's scary."

"For those outside of Christ, certainly. But in Christ all of the power of God is on our side. Greater is he who is in us than he who is in the world."

"What do we do?"

"The Bible tells us: Put on the full armor of God. All of it. Leave out one piece and you're vulnerable. Of course, this first requires that we be in Christ. That we have the new birth. That we are a child of God. Otherwise, we're vulnerable. Your son, is he a Christian?"

"He confessed Christ and was baptized, back when he was ten."

"Then you and I, we'll pray against the powers of the air that are seeking your son's destruction."

"And for Ron." She was relieved to have said it. In that moment she made her decision. She was going to fight for Ron and for her marriage.

Roger nodded. "And for Ron. He's a target too, because he went after pornography, a powerful weapon of the enemy. But the name of Jesus is more powerful than all the host of hell. I believe that, Dallas. Do you?"

"I do."

"That's all we need."

2.

When she got back home, around four o'clock, Dallas found Jared on the sofa, his leg draped over the arm, watching TV.

"Jared, we have to talk. Now."

"What about?"

"God."

"Not now, Mom, okay?"

"When?"

He shrugged. "Look, I've been thinking of going back to Bakersfield, to—"

"You can't go anywhere. Not yet."

"Why not?"

"First of all, you have to deal with that drunk-driving arrest."

He made a James Cagney voice. "They'll never catch me."

"I'm serious. But there's something else. Jared, I know your faith isn't strong right now, but I had a long talk with Roger Vernon today. Do you remember him?"

He thought a moment. "He was the pastor before Dad took over. He taught my Sunday school a couple of times."

"Then you remember that he was always a good man of the Word."

"I guess."

"He laid something out for me, something that you need to know. It's about demonic activity."

"Mom—"

"Listen, please. You can't fight this battle on your own. You need the power of God." She told him, in abbreviated form, about Roger's Babylon theory.

When she was finished Jared thought about it for a long time. "If you were into that sort of thing, I guess it might make sense."

"Then call on God."

"What I'm saying is that I'm not into that sort of thing."

"Why not? What's changed?"

He shook his head. "We had a chaplain over there, and I went to him one day and asked him why God was allowing this to happen. He said God is just as upset as we are about it, but he's not really able to stop it. He's growing right along with us."

"That's crazy."

"Is it? I think it's a pretty good explanation."

"It's not what the Bible teaches."

"Who cares? Nobody uses the Bible anymore."

"If I believed that I'd have no hope at all."

"Welcome to my world."

"Jared, please give God another try. Put him to the test."

"It's all right, Mom."

"Don't just try to mollify me. I'm serious about this. You either believe in God or you don't. You believe in the God of the Bible or you don't."

"I don't."

Dallas flopped back in a chair.

Jared sat up straight. "Mom, you've given it your best shot. Time to cut your losses."

"Losses? What are you talking about?"

"Dad. Me."

"Stop it, Jared."

"Why?" He jumped up. "It's true, you know it. Face it! I'm gone, there's something wrong with me. It's not going to be straightened out by God or anybody else."

"Jared—"

"And Dad's been lying to you, for years probably. To both of us, to Cara too. You're too good for us, Mom. Move on with your life."

"I'm not giving up on you, Jared. Or your father. He's come clean to me, he asked me to forgive him."

"He's come clean?" Jared's voice was skeptical.

"I saw him. He told me a lot of things."

"How do you know he's not lying again?"

"I know because I was looking right at him."

"You're so naïve."

That brought Dallas to her feet, cheeks burning. "You think that? You really think that?"

"Yeah. I love you, Mom, but you're not in the real world sometimes."

"And I suppose you are? In the stinking mess you call a world, that's real to you?"

His eyes were cold. "You know it is."

"I don't know. You're the one who's naïve, Jared. You deny God. You deny the truth. You're wallowing in your misery. Well, it's time to snap out of it."

"You think I want this?"

"Maybe you do. If you don't turn it over to God, it's over."

"Then it's over. This whole idea was stupid." He turned his back on her and started toward the door.

She followed him. "What idea?"

"Coming home," he said.

"Don't go."

He faced her. "You go back to your world, Mom, if that makes you happy."

Then he opened the door and left.

Dallas didn't call after him.

3.

When you spend twenty-three hours a day in a box by yourself, you have time to think.

I was thinking about irony today.

I used to do a prison ministry when I first got to Hillside. Each Wednesday evening I'd take a little group out to Sylmar and preach to the inmates. That was before the membership at Hillside started to build, and I started putting all my efforts toward growing the church.

As I think about it now, the prison ministry, like the street preaching I used to do, made me depend on God, kept me on the edge, in a good way. The more popular I got, the less sharp the edge.

A. W. Tozer said something about preachers who seek comfort. It's easy to do in the ministry. Popularity becomes an opiate.

And that dulls the mind and even the moral sense. That helps explain Amy Shea and Melinda Perry.

Explains, doesn't excuse.

I am saying the twenty-third Psalm, over and over, out loud.

4.

That night, Dallas dreamed of something just beyond her reach. It was dark in the dream and she had to get this thing, or whatever it was, or she and her whole family would be lost or dead.

Dread, the substance of nightmares, infused her sleep. She tried to will herself to wake up, but not before transport to the edge of a cliff, looking down into dark waters. There. The thing was in there, but she was too high to reach it.

If she jumped, she might die. If she stayed, she might die. And behind her, something approached.

She woke up breathless, as if she'd fallen on her stomach. She fought for air. She was alone in the bedroom and it was still dark outside.

For a moment she sat in the silence, steadying her breathing.

And then she heard the floorboard squeak downstairs.

Jared. He'd come home.

But was he all right? She listened to the cadence of the footsteps, wondering if she could tell if he was drunk or drugged.

She couldn't. And the sounds ceased.

Which could have meant he was passed out. Or lying on the couch watching TV.

Dallas thought about going back to bed. Maybe he just wanted to be alone. But she couldn't. She had always checked on Jared, ever since he slept in a bassinette.

Throwing on a robe, she went downstairs.

It was dark. All lights out.

Then she saw the flickering glow of the TV screen.

"Jared?"

No answer. And no sound coming from the set. Just the flicker.

She went into the family room expecting Jared to be on the couch.

No one was there.

"Jared, where are you?"

The lights came on. And Dallas almost screamed.

Chad McKenzie was leaning against the far wall.

"Evening."

A hundred thoughts ripped through Dallas's mind. At the top of the heap was the one that reminded her she had not secured a stun gun as Jeff suggested.

"Get out of my house." She tried to put menace in the words, but they sounded flat.

Chad smiled. "A nice house too. You've done very well for yourself, Dallas."

"What do you think you're going to accomplish here? You've broken into my home. That'll send you back to prison."

"I didn't break anything. Did you hear anything break?"

"Then how ..."

"You invited me in, remember? Oh, you may change your story later, but since there's no evidence, there's no problem."

Had he picked the lock? No, she'd left the back door open for Jared. Stupid!

Chad took a step away from the wall. "See, what really happened was I came to see an old friend, and you let me in and we had a nice talk."

"We are not going to have a nice talk."

"Sure we are." He was still wearing the dark coat. He held his hands out in an innocent gesture. "And when it's over, you'll understand a few things."

Dallas shook her head. "I have nothing to say to you, and my son is going to be home soon and he is an ex-Marine."

The news didn't faze him a bit. "About that. I'm sure he's a good kid and all, but he won't be coming home for a while."

The horror of the unspoken filled her. "What have you done to him?"

"Maybe we should sit down like good friends and discuss this."

"Tell me you—"

"Easy there, Dallas. I wouldn't want you to fall into sin. Wouldn't that be a fine how-do-you-do?"

She could fold, do what he said. But then she wouldn't find out if he was all bluff or not.

The power is not in me. It's in the armor. She mentally stepped behind the shield of faith.

"Don't worry about the boy," Chad said. "He'll sleep it off. He's got a bit of a drinking problem, doesn't he? Too bad. Some of our boys who served never get over it."

"Wherever Jared is, God is watching him. He's watching you too, Chad."

"I'm really worried about that."

"You should be."

"Trying to rattle the old Chadster? That's not like you."

"You don't know me. You don't know anything. You're a loser, Chad. You always have been."

His left cheek twitched. Enough for Dallas to know she'd landed a blow.

In the lull she weighed her alternatives. If she could get to her cell phone, which was charging in the kitchen, she could lock herself in the bathroom and call 911.

"That's not a very Christian attitude, I must say."

Or she could grab the hammer from the tool drawer and go for the head.

Chad looked at her, long and lingeringly. "You've really kept in shape there, Dallas."

Now the serious creeps were running all over her. "Tell me why you're here," she said, "and then go."

"You work out?"

"Chad—"

"I pushed a lot of steel in the slam, kept in pretty good shape myself. And I'm still a very loving person."

He was going to attack her.

She took a step back. If she made a break, he'd be on her in a second.

The armor ...

She blurted the first thing that came to her mind. "In the beginning was the Word, and the Word was with God, and the Word was God."

Chad squinted. "What?"

What indeed. But at least she'd stopped his advance.

"Your name is Legion," Dallas said. "For you are many."

"You've gone bye-bye," Chad said.

"Every knee shall bow and every tongue confess that Jesus Christ is Lord."

"Shut up."

"Do not tempt the Lord your God."

He jumped. It was quick, hard, and he was at her before she could even think.

His hands grabbed her robe. He pushed. She slammed against the wall, her head hitting last with a jarring thud.

His face was in front of her and she could smell his breath, a noxious mix of beer and cigarettes. She fought not to gag.

She raised her arms and went for his face. He anticipated the move, locked his hands on her wrists, and pulled her arms behind her back.

Her arm sockets filled with fire.

Chad McKenzie smiled.

And then he put his face to hers.

5.

Tonight I feel the need, the urge, the call to pray as I haven't prayed in years.

I am praying now, even as I write, even as I don't know how to pray. Only that I must.

The Bible says that the Spirit intercedes for us, with groans words can't express. That's what I need right now, Lord. Intercession from the Spirit, because I don't know how to pray.

The dinner just arrived. Burrito. I find I am looking forward to burrito night. It is one of the more palatable items on the fancy menu here. They like to keep the food laden with starch and carbs, to keep the prisoners happy. The burrito is their crowning achievement, and it comes as a small oasis in this desert of a cell.

The ravens brought meat to Elijah. I am almost positive that the burrito contains meat of some sort, but I do not ask for details.

Tonight, another message in a tin foil envelope came with the burrito. It was once again in King James: "Take heed, brethren, lest there be in any of you an evil heart of unbelief, in departing from the living God."

No Scripture reference, though it sounded familiar enough. The book of Hebrews, I thought, and looked it up. Sure enough, right there in chapter three.

Someone was playing with me, someone who was following my case. Maybe it was even one of the deputies who watches this cage.

Whoever it was, he was pressing a hot iron into my soul.

Yes, I feel the need to keep in prayer. I'm stopping now and getting on my knees.

§.

"Yo!"

Jared heard the word through a thick wall of brain matter.

"Yo, you better get up and get out, now!"

A kicking in the ribs. Jared opened his eyes. It was not easy. They were heavy and tired.

Cold. It was cold and he didn't know where he was. Hard ground. The sound of cars, an echo chamber. Dark. Some time of night.

Now a string of swear words from the voice and another kick in the ribs. Jared tried to focus. He looked up and saw a face staring at him.

It was not like any face he had ever seen.

The eyes were feral and fiery. Superior. The guy's face was distorted, not by expression but by some permanent force that had twisted bone and skin.

Around his head was a dirty blue bandana, and a stained coat covered the rest of his body. Jared caught a whiff of whisky and sweat.

"Gonna stomp your head to Jell-O, you don't get out now. Anywhere you go, I'll know where you are ..." And more foul language poured out of the man's malformed lips.

Jared's head was pounding like an industrial crusher. Fear shot through his body and got him to his feet.

The face did not move. "You're dead. You don't know it. Make it real, baby."

What?

His head was mush. He had no idea where he was. But he had to move or he had the feeling his insides would be torn out.

He began to stagger down the walk. He had no idea what direction he was going.

The voice of the man echoed off the walls of the underpass. But he didn't speak words. Now the guy was howling.

And Jared tried to run. His feet were cinder blocks, his legs hot rubber.

The howling was like a mad wolf at the sight of a harvest moon.

The world vibrated around him, swirled and gyrated. What was wrong with his head? The same smell—whisky and sweat—hit him again. Was the guy behind him?

No. Jared realized the smell was coming from him.

Drunk. I got drunk and passed out here.

Headlights from oncoming cars shot beams of blinding light through his skull. He was in the street now. A horn blared and tires squealed as the lights went around him.

Another voice, another shout, another obscenity. And then the car drove on.

Why couldn't he focus his eyes? Where had he been before this?

Get out of the street!

He sucked in a huge gulp of night air and made for a streetlight. A fixed point in this sea of uncertainty. He'd grab it. He could hold on.

It became his point of reference. By concentrating, he could keep the rest of the world from spinning out of control. If he could make it to the pole, he could hold on, hold tight.

He remembered something. A story. About the Asian tsunami of '04. He'd read the accounts, one about a fisherman in a little village. His house was completely washed away; the only thing left was a pole embedded deep in the ground. The man hung on, with his three children, to the pole. He lost two of the children. But four hours later they rescued the fisherman and his daughter, then found the other two kids alive.

A miracle, the fisherman said.

This would be like that, Jared managed to think. *Don't get washed away. Get away from the guy in the underpass.*

Another car blared a horn, went around him. He kept his eyes on the light pole. Wasn't that the way they used to show drunks in newspaper cartoons? Clinging to a lamppost?

Why wasn't his head clearing?

Where had he been drinking?

At last, the pole was within reach. Jared almost fell down getting to it. But he kept enough balance to get to the standard and throw his arms around the pole.

It was rough and cold against his cheek.

No, I wasn't drinking.

The thought cleared a path in his brain. Other thoughts followed, plowing the field.

He remembered storming out of his mother's house. They'd argued. About God. Yes, and other things. He was going to move back to Bakersfield, right?

He had his truck back, and he'd driven down to the little strip mall off Rinaldi. Went in the liquor store. What did he buy?

Jim Beam. A fifth.

Where was it? Where was his truck? He couldn't remember drinking anything. But his smell.

The light pole was keeping him up, helping him clear his head. He kept one arm draped around it.

He'd bought something else.

Gum. He bought some gum at the liquor store. He checked his right front pocket then. A mashed pack of Big Red. Cinnamon gum covered the smell of alcohol best. If he drank and drove and was stopped, Big Red would help him hide the fact.

But he did not drink. He was going to the park on Reseda to do it. He remembered getting out of the truck, taking the bottle with him.

The park. Something happened to him in the park.

7.

"You're still so fine," Chad said.

Dallas could not move. Chad's arms were like steel beams.

"Your man's been messing around on the side," he said. "Don't you think you deserve a little action?"

He's just talk. He wants to see you sweat.

But she could not deny that his talk always turned into physical abuse. Just before she left it had been the worst. He used duct tape to bind her, then beat her for an hour with a wire coat hanger.

No, he was not just talk.

He brought his face to her again. She turned hers. He licked her cheek.

Her mind flashed back, her body took on the full remembrance of how she'd felt when she finally worked up the guts to leave him. She'd thought seriously of killing him in his sleep.

She felt that way now.

"Listen, suppose we start all over again," Chad whispered. "I'm going to be getting a steady job real soon. Good future. Your man'll be sitting in the joint for the rest of his life. Fine woman like you shouldn't be alone."

He smiled and, once more, leaned toward her.

This time Dallas did not turn her head. She relaxed.

Chad ran his tongue over her lips.

She let him.

His grip lessened. Slightly.

With a quick jerk she thrust upward with the heel of her hand and smashed his nose.

She felt the crunch of cartilage.

Chad shrieked and stepped back.

In another defensive move, one she'd taught many women, Dallas smacked Chad's ears with her cupped hands. He screamed again. His eardrums would be damaged and his equilibrium upset.

She pushed him hard in the chest with both hands.

He staggered back, hands on his face. She saw blood seeping through his fingers.

She ran.

An onslaught of obscenity erupted from Chad, and she knew she had to get out of the house or she'd be dead.

She was aware of her robe flapping and pulled it tight. She was barefoot. How far could she get that way? He'd catch her.

Outside, she could scream. But would anybody hear? Were all her neighbors blissfully asleep?

Chad's voice, behind her, guttural and foul, getting closer.

She knew then she wouldn't have time to unlock the front door, throw it open, get outside. She knew, too, that getting outside would not bring freedom.

I have to get to a phone. No, no time to call.

Lock myself in a room.

How long would that last?

Dear God, help.

She charged up the stairs. *Stupid.* But there was no turning back.

There was, however, a heavy table at the top of the stairs. Her grandmother's oak table, given to Dallas shortly after her marriage. Not the flimsy kind the furniture warehouses sold by the bushel. This wood had substance.

Halfway up the stairs Dallas heard Chad charging around the corner. She didn't have to turn and look.

She had to get to the table. Throw it down on top of him.

But was she strong enough to move it?

"Got you now, baby." Chad's voice mocked her. Dallas sensed that he'd stopped to gloat. She was at the top stair and looked back.

He was smiling, his hands out wide, his face grotesquely smeared with blood. "Come to papa!"

The fear and rage in her practically lifted her off her feet. She knew, simply knew, that she'd have no trouble with the table. It was squat, with a doily on top. And a drawer. In the drawer were some old pictures and papers she hadn't looked at in years.

The past surrounded her.

"Alone again ..." Chad was singing!

Her back was to the stairs, the table against the wall. *Leg muscles. Use your leg muscles to lift.*

"... naturally ..."

She lifted. And the table was slightly off the floor.

It was heavy, like holding a sack of cement. Leaning back, she let the weight of it produce momentum.

One shot at this. One.

Chad had stopped singing.

When she whirled around and let the table go, she knew she'd been perfect. It took a bounce, then hit him.

Table and man fell down the stairs, leaving a bloody streak on the beige carpeting.

And then Chad's body lay at the bottom of the stairs, motionless.

Dallas, aware of her own breathing, watched. She hoped he was dead.

Then she ran to the bedroom, locked the door, grabbed the phone, and dialed 911.

A woman's voice answered. "Dispatch, how may I help you?"

"There's someone in my house. He wants to kill me." She was sure that was his intent.

The 911 operator, calm of voice, began to ask a question. Dallas didn't wait. She gave her address. "Get someone out here right away."

"We are notifying the police right now. Can you hang on?"

"I don't know, I—"

"Are you safe, ma'am? Are you in a secure location?"

"Just hurry."

She put the phone on the bed and considered her options. Maybe she'd better get out of the house, but that would mean going past Chad's body. But what other choice was there?

She quickly threw on a workout pants and jacket, and a pair of Nikes, not bothering with socks.

She heard a siren in the distance, getting closer.

She reached under the bed for the big flashlight, the kind the police carry, which she kept there in case of earthquake.

Now she was glad she had it for another reason. It was a perfect club.

If he broke in, she'd be ready for him.

०.

Jared was finally getting his bearings. The freeway was the 405. He saw the sign for the onramp.

He was remembering what happened in the park.

Blackout.

One moment he'd been sitting on the top of a park table, feet on the bench, the bottle of Jim Beam beside him, the dark trees his only company.

The next moment he was out.

And now he was in a different location, not knowing how he got there.

But there was something strange here.

His mouth, for one thing. His tongue was not thick, nor his throat dry, the way they would be if he had too much to drink.

He looked up at the light, blurry to his eyes. He tried to focus on it.

But there was still a fuzziness in his brain.

Why was this happening? It was like a hole had opened up in his head in Iraq, and darkness poured in, something foreign and vicious. It wasn't PTSD, like the VA kept saying. It was a whole lot scarier.

But now what? He couldn't stay here all night.

His truck. Back at the park.

Could he make it? How far had he walked?

More to the point. What would he do when he got to the truck?

And then, he knew.

§.

Dallas tried not to breathe loud enough to be heard.

The sirens were close now, and she was still alone upstairs.

She hoped.

She listened at the bedroom door. If Chad was indeed out there and tried to break in, she'd have a slight advantage. She'd planned it out in her mind. She'd throw the door open, then knock a homer with the flashlight.

She was amazed at how anxious she was to do it. Chad McKenzie was back, and he'd done something to Jared. She wasn't going to turn the other cheek at that.

Threaten my family and you're toast.

No sound outside her door. The sirens stopped.

Half a minute passed.

A knock at the door.

She had to go down. The front door was locked.

Holding the flashlight at the ready, she threw open the bedroom door.

And saw pieces. Four pieces of a photograph.

It was a wedding photo, the one of her and Ron looking at each other adoringly, the one she had selected above all others to be framed and hung in the hallway.

Now it was removed, torn and quartered, and placed like a mocking curse in front of her bedroom door.

ELEVEN

1.

The police officer took a half hour to get the story from Dallas. A tech arrived, and the officer suggested Dallas find another place to stay while they finished gathering evidence.

Dallas remembered that Cara was up in Santa Barbara with two girlfriends for a couple of days. So she called the Bensons and got Lisa.

"I know it's late," Dallas said. "But something's happened."

"What is it?"

"Can I come over?"

"Of course, but—"

"I'll be right there."

Bob and Lisa Benson lived in Canoga Park, about a fifteen-minute drive from the church on a low-traffic day.

Lisa was waiting for her outside the house.

"I'm so sorry to get you up," Dallas said.

"No worries," Lisa said. "Come on in and tell us what's going on."

Bob, his eyes a little red, looked concerned. Lisa brought her into the living room of the little "starter" home. In the Valley, where the median price of a home was over half a million dollars, young couples like Lisa and Bob had to start out on the lower end of the spectrum.

That meant less house in an older neighborhood.

But for its very smallness, it was homey and put Dallas just the slightest bit more at ease as she sat.

"I was attacked tonight. In my home."

Lisa put a hand to her chest. "Attacked?"

Dallas told them the story. She found she was trembling at the end, as if Chad were right there in the room with them.

"Are the police doing anything?" Bob asked.

"They came to the house and I told them what happened. They said they'd look into it, but I know Chad. He's toyed with the law before. He knows what he's doing."

"Would you like to stay here tonight?" Lisa asked.

Gratefully, Dallas accepted. Lisa made up the bed in the small guest room of the two-bedroom house. When she was finished, she sat on the bed next to Dallas. "This is all going to pass," Lisa said. "You're one of the strongest women I know. You're holding up under a lot of strain."

"I don't have any other choice."

Dallas's cell phone beeped. She looked at the screen. A number she did not recognize. Her entire body shuddered with a deep chill.

What if it was Chad?

"You going to answer?" Lisa whispered.

"I don't know."

But then she decided to take a chance, for only one reason.

"Hello?"

"Mom?"

She'd been right. "Jared, where are you?"

"I'm somewhere in North Hills, I think. I just wanted to tell you not to worry. I'm not going to make your life any worse."

"Jared, wait—"

But he was gone.

"No, please."

Lisa put a hand on her arm. "Where is he?"

"North Hills is all he said. I'm afraid he's going to kill himself." Not just afraid. Practically certain.

"Maybe we can find him."

"How could we possibly?"

"Let me see your phone."

Dallas gave it to Lisa. She flipped it open, hit a couple of buttons. "Come on."

She bounded out of the room like an excited schoolgirl. Dallas followed to the dining room, which for the Bensons was also an office. A laptop was on the dining-room table.

Lisa sat in a chair and patted the empty one next to her. Dallas sat in it.

"I'm going to show you an awesome search site," Lisa said, her fingers already on the keyboard. Dallas watched with a feeling of admiration and unease. She was as far removed from this generation as her own mother had been from Dallas's. For her, computers were complex and barely tolerable. Oh, she could do common things and even surf the Net, but for Lisa it was like second nature. In no time she had called up a site with little phone graphics all over it.

"I'm going to type in the phone number where Jared was."

She did. Then hit *return*.

In two seconds a result came up.

"We can find out where that phone is," Lisa said. "All it'll cost is $14.95. You want to?"

"Yes! I'll pay."

"We have to put in a credit card."

"I'll get mine." Dallas retrieved her Visa card from her purse in the guest room, brought it to Lisa.

"You trust me with the number?" Lisa said. "I can order lots of cool stuff with this."

"Hurry."

Lisa typed in the card number and expiration date. Hit *return* again.

"Here it comes," she said. "It's a pay phone."

"Pay phone? Does it say where?"

"It sure does. The intersection of Lassen and Sepulveda."

"Can you drive me there?"

"Let's do it."

They drove to Lassen and Sepulveda in Lisa's Camry, but there was no sign of Jared by the battered pay phone. The sidewalks were deserted. Lisa took the car through some strip mall parking lots, past bus stops and mini-marts.

"Maybe we should call the police or something," Lisa said.

"Based on what? That I want to talk to my son? He's an adult. They wouldn't help."

"I suppose not."

"But you have," Dallas said. "Thanks anyway."

"Let's go home. Get some rest." Lisa turned the car around.

It was good to be going back with Lisa, good to have a friend taking the reins, at least for this night.

I remember vividly my first fight with Dallas.

She was mesmerizing to me. When I baptized her in the ocean, her face was the most radiant thing I'd ever seen. I kept thinking of that story where the sinful woman anoints Jesus's feet and cries over them, wiping his feet with her hair. Jesus told the Pharisee that because she had been forgiven much, she loved much.

That's what Dallas's face reflected, and I was a little jealous of her.

I admit that now. It was wrong, but I was.

Because I had never experienced what I saw reflected in her face.

Later, we fought about that. It was before we were married.

I should say, I fought about that. Dallas was doing volunteer work with our evangelism team, and she could not stop talking about Jesus. She was flush with the enthusiasm that overtook converts in those days. I don't see it happening that much anymore.

At least not at Hillside.

But one day I told her she needed to cool it a little.

"Why?" she asked.

"Because, well, you're coming off as a little bit fanatical."

"And that's bad?"

"A little."

"Why?"

"It just is."

Without any hesitation at all, without any realization that she had no training or knowledge in matters theological, she said, "That seems a little bit strange, coming from someone trying to keep people from going to hell."

Maybe it was the word strange *that got to me. But I proceeded to tell her she was making it all too simplistic, that she was missing the bigger picture.*

"What's bigger than showing people how to get to heaven?" she said.

"You're a little young in the faith yet."

"Stop trying to control me."

"I'm not—"

"You are. And don't tell me you're not, because I've been with a pro, baby, the big leagues. Don't play that game."

I unloaded on her for that. And she just looked at me with these eyes that said she understood more than I did.

Now I know she brought something of her worldliness to her new faith and was more on fire than I had ever been.

I knew I had to have her for my wife. I did not mean to put out her fire.

§

Jared's first thought was that this was not his father. It was some actor, cast in a TV movie about Ron Hamilton. A good likeness, but not the man who raised him, whom Jared had idolized, then run away from.

His eyes were not familiar. The assurance and certainty of purpose they once held was gone. He had wounded eyes now, red-rimmed with affliction.

Why had he even come? Last night, after calling his mother, he drove to the top of Chatsworth, a place he'd gone to many times to get away. He slept in his truck, trying to figure out if he wanted to see his dad one last time.

He did know he was going to get out. Leave L.A. He didn't care about the DUI or anything else. He was messed up, and hanging around here was just making life worse for his mom.

Time to cut the cord. And that, in the end, was what brought him to the jail. Two cords needed to be severed.

"Hello, Jared." His father's voice was tinny coming over the wire.

Jared nodded.

"Thank you for coming. I didn't think you would."

"So how you getting along in here?"

"Oh, not so bad, considering."

There was a taut formality between them, which Jared grasped lightly as a protective covering, like an awning against rain. Who would be the first to take it down, dare to get wet?

"I really came here to help Mom get through this thing," Jared said.

"That's good. That's really good. How are *you* getting along?"

"I been working. Up in Bakersfield." He decided not to go into any greater detail. What his father didn't know about his recent past was best left hidden.

"That's good," Ron said.

But Jared heard the subtle disheartenment in his father's voice. It stretched out in a ribbon of silence.

"Don't believe what the papers are saying," Ron said. "I did not do this."

Jared shrugged.

"You have to believe that, Jared. I couldn't stand it if I thought you didn't believe me. I couldn't do such a horrible thing. Ever."

You have no idea what horrible things you, what anybody, can do.
"Sure."

"There's just no way."

But Jared did not believe him. There was a desperation about him now. He would say anything. In a way, Jared understood. His father was a man who put great stock in appearances. How could Jared expect him to come clean in front of his son?

Lies. He'd been taught his whole life that lies were sin. Now his father used them for his own sanity. Jared couldn't really blame him for that. Sanity was something hard to keep hold of.

"I really wanted to see you again," Ron said.

"I know."

"Jared, please pray for me."

Jared said nothing.

"Will you do that for me, Jared?"

"Just don't hurt Mom anymore."

"No, I don't want to. Jared, please tell me you believe me, will you? Can you tell me that?"

Jared looked at the table.

"You do believe me, right?"

Jared started to stand.

"Don't go yet. There's so much I want to know about you."

"No. You don't want to know, Dad. I'll see you."

"Wait!"

4.

He did not wait. My son.

Why?

Why didn't it all work out as planned? My family was supposed to be my big achievement.

I remember being embarrassed about Jared. When he started to show signs of rebellion, I didn't want it known. It would have hurt my reputation.

When he got in trouble at school, I sent Dallas down to do the dirty work. I didn't want anybody to see me show up.

I wanted to sweep Jared under the rug.

He knew that. Kids always know.

I tried to reach him. But I did it with that stupid concept called "quality time." He needed time, period.

I found that out too late.

5.

Jared sat in the truck in front of his mother's house, wondering if he should continue waiting for his mom.

Maybe it would be best to forget the good-byes and just go. He could always call later and not have to face her. There would be tears and it would get all complicated.

He didn't need that.

As he gripped the steering wheel he knew he'd never be back. The last good time he could remember in his life had been in that house. It was when Cara came to his room one night and they didn't fight. Instead she'd confided in him about boyfriend troubles and asked for his advice. For once he was the one who had the wisdom, and she'd actually listened.

After, she kissed him on the cheek and hugged him, and he felt loved by his sister, and that was good. The last good time.

A tap on the window startled him.

Tiana was standing outside his truck, Jamaal behind her.

Jared got out. "What is this?"

"Hey," she said.

"What are you doing here?"

"Came to find you."

"Me? Why?"

"I wanted to tell you something."

"How'd you get here?"

"Bus."

Jamaal stuck his head out from behind his mother and smiled at Jared.

"How you doin'?" Jared said.

"Good," Jamaal said.

Tiana knelt down. "Jamaal, go over and sit on the steps there, will you, baby? I need to talk to Jared."

"I wanna stay."

"Go on."

"I wanna *stay.*"

Jared looked at him. "If you go do like your mama says, I'll toss the football with you some, huh?"

"You will?"

"Sure."

"Deal." And he ran off toward the front steps of the house.

"So what's going on?" Jared asked.

"Something's up with Rafe. Something that has to do with you."

Jared shook his head.

"After you came to see Jamaal that day, he whaled on me good. He said something was going on with you and me."

Jared put his hands on her shoulders. "You're not going back, you hear me?"

She closed her eyes. "I just came to tell you he said he's going to do something to you. Mess you up."

"I don't care about that. I don't want you and Jamaal going back."

"What have you got to say about it?"

"I don't want you back there."

"Who cares what you want? I've got nothing else."

"You've got me."

The words stunned him. But he knew he meant them.

Tiana shook her head. "What're you talking about?"

"The three of us are going to figure it out together, and you're not going back. Stay with me. I'll take care of you."

"How?"

"I'll figure it out. First thing we do is get a place. I know where we can go. You coming?"

She paused, then looked past him. Jared turned around. Jamaal was looking at him.

"Can we throw the football now?" Jamaal said.

Tiana said to Jared, "What have you got in mind?"

§.

"I've got two things to talk to you about," Jeff said as he closed his office door. He did not look pleased.

Dallas took in a labored breath. "Bad news?" Of course it was bad news. That's why he hadn't told her anything over the phone. Instead, he told her to come to his office even though it was nearly six at night.

Jeff smoothed his tie—red with understated palm trees on it, very L.A.—and sat on the corner of his desk.

"I got the arrest report on Jared's DUI," he said. "And I think I can get a dismissal."

"You mean completely gone?"

Jeff nodded. "There's a little thing called a driving requirement for a DUI. The person actually has to be driving. Even if it's only an inch. But according to the report, Jared was passed out in the car. That's not going to cut it."

"Any good news at this point is welcome," she said. "And I have something to tell you."

Jeff waited.

"Chad, the guy I told you about, he came to my house last night. He attacked me."

"What?"

"I managed to call 911. The police came, but he got away."

"This is terrible." Jeff walked to the window of his office, which looked out on Ventura Boulevard and the Valley beyond. The tone in his voice was so ominous it made Dallas think of horror movies. She was about to be lowered into some sort of pit.

"Jeff, what is it? What's the other news? Did Mr. Stegman talk to that witness I found?"

"He tried."

"Tried?"

He turned back to face her. "Dallas, I've always been up front with you about this case, and I don't want to stop now. Are you with me on that?"

Fighting back a jitter, Dallas said, "Yes. I want to know everything."

"Then I'll tell you. First of all, that witness you found, like I told you before, is not going to be very helpful. There's a gang connection, and the issue of mental competence."

"But it's *something*."

"Less than that, Dallas, believe me. I've been doing this a long time. But yes, it was the one thing that had any sort of connection."

"What do you mean *was*?"

Jeff paused as if looking for the right words.

With all the strength she had, Dallas fought against the anguish trying to open a hole inside her. "Tell me, Jeff. Tell me right now."

"It's going to hurt."

"Tell me."

"Dallas, this morning I received several reports from the prosecution. Evidence they intend to introduce in a trial."

"What sort of evidence?"

"They completed an inventory of what they found on Ron's computer."

"And?"

Very slowly and deliberately he said, "Dallas, it's loaded with pornography."

A momentary darkness hit her behind the eyes, as if someone smashed out the lights with a club. Air rushed from her lungs.

"Pornography?" She could barely say it.

"I'm afraid so."

Dallas fought to keep coherent. *This can't be happening.* "You said *loaded?*"

"According to the report, there are over seven hundred images."

Seven hundred!

Dallas conjured an image of Ron in her mind, sitting in front of his computer with a devious grin on his face. She scratched it out of her brain. That couldn't be right. The deception involved. She would have known. She would have—

"Where are they?" she said.

"Where are what?"

"The reports. I want to see them."

"Dallas, don't go there—"

"Show me!"

Jeff pursed his lips and reached for something on his desk. It was an inch-thick sheaf of papers. "Don't punish yourself," he said.

"Give it to me."

It was page after page of thumbnail pornographic images. At about the fifth page she dropped the report on the floor, fell from the chair to her knees, and sobbed uncontrollably—huge, lung-collapsing sobs.

She felt Jeff's hands lifting her like deadweight. But that was the only sensation outside of her manifest grief and shaking body that she was aware of.

The sobs melted into audible gulps, full of more despair than she could ever remember.

She had entered the office clinging to a safety line. She'd begun to think there would be a change in trajectory soon, that God would not allow more than she could bear.

Now this. No more clinging, no more line. She was falling.

Jeff handed her a tissue and she stabbed at her eyes with it.

"I'm so sorry, Dallas. We'll talk about the case later."

"What case?" she said bitterly. "He's guilty. He did it."

"Dallas—"

"He lied to my face. Again. He's never stopped lying! There's no way he's not guilty."

"He insists—"

"I don't care what he insists! I don't care what happens to him. Let him rot in prison."

"Dallas, let's give this a day or two—"

She stood up. "I don't need a day. I don't need another second. What you do with Ron is up to you. I want no part of it anymore."

Jeff looked at the floor. "I can't say that I don't understand. Listen, if there's anything you need, call me."

"There is something I need."

"What is it?"

"The name of a divorce lawyer."

PART II

Meanwhile the passions rage like tyrants,
and throw into confusion the whole soul and life of men.

Augustine

TWELVE

1.

"Tonight, an exclusive. The first interview with Dallas Hamilton, wife of Ron Hamilton, the minister accused of murdering Melinda Chance at the Star Motel. She speaks out publicly for the first time on *Hank Dunaway Tonight*."

Dunaway's trademark theme music—synthesized trumpets with a military air—played. And Dallas tried to swallow. Her throat was dead dry.

But she knew Dunaway was a master at putting people at ease. She hoped he was on his game tonight.

Dunaway looked into the camera.

"Ron Hamilton, a minister from Los Angeles, sits in jail tonight awaiting trial on a murder charge. The case has been all over the news since his arrest two months ago. But no one has heard from Ron Hamilton's wife, Dallas. Until tonight."

He looked at her now, his blue eyes crinkled at the corners. "How have you been holding up the last few weeks?"

She forced a smile. "Holding. Thanks."

"Where were you when your husband was arrested?"

"In my bedroom."

"What were you thinking when it happened?"

"That there had to be some mistake."

"And when you found out it wasn't a mistake, how did you feel?"

She thought a moment. "A two-by-four to the head."

"You hired a lawyer?"

"Jefferson Waite, yes."

"And the trial has been set for August?"

"Yes."

"You have children?"

"Two."

"How are they taking it?"

Dallas blinked. "Different reactions."

"How old are they?"

"My daughter is twenty-seven. My son is twenty-four."

Dunaway glanced at a sheet of paper in front of him. "I understand you had an incident in your home last week."

"I was attacked by a man named Chad McKenzie."

For a moment Dunaway seemed taken aback. But he kept his cool. "You knew the man?"

"He was someone I was involved with when I was a teenager. An abuser. He apparently thought he could use my trouble to his advantage. I hope the police will discuss that with him soon. He has threatened to go to the press with some sordid stories about me and claims to have photographs of me when I was with him, doing things. He wanted to extort money from me in return for his not giving the photos to the press. Well, I have a message for him. He's not going to get a thing from me, ever. What I did thirty years ago is over. I was not a Christian then. I am now, and whatever I did has been forgiven and forgotten by God."

Dunaway paused for what seemed like dramatic effect, then announced a commercial break.

"You're doing fine," he told her during the break. "You feeling all right?"

"Surprisingly, yes." And she was. It was cathartic, finally being able to talk.

When they started up again, Dunaway asked, "When was the last time you saw Ron?"

"I don't remember the date."

"You haven't been talking to the press. What prompted you to come forward now?"

This was the moment. "I wanted to talk about the bigger picture here, the bigger problem. And that is the pornography business in this city, in this country. That, I believe, is behind what's going on."

"Behind the murder of Melinda Chance?"

"She was a porn actress. She was employed by a pornographer named Vic Lu. How he and his ilk are allowed to operate I don't know. Prostitution is illegal, but this kind of filmed prostitution is not. It doesn't make sense, it's wrong, and it has to be stopped."

"Your husband wrote an antipornography book, didn't he?"

"Right."

"So you can't blame the press for picking up on that angle."

"I'm beyond blaming the press. They follow what sells. I'm more concerned about the blight of pornography in our communities, and what it does even beyond the people who make it and the people who buy it."

"What do you mean, beyond?"

"I believe there is a spiritual component to this, Hank. Evil is real, and it emanates."

"You're not calling people who buy adult videos evil, are you?"

"They're playing with a fire they don't understand."

"But evil?"

"Hank, I believe evil is real. Don't you?"

Dunaway raised his eyebrows. "Some TV critics maybe."

"I wouldn't disagree, but I also think the truth goes deeper than that."

"You said you're a Christian."

"That's right."

"What would you say to people who reject your views as merely personal and religious?"

She relaxed a little more. She and Ron had discussed this objection many times. "We're all citizens, and we can all look at our society and see if it's the kind we want to live in. And a society that condones pornography by labeling it 'adult entertainment,' that turns a blind eye to the garbage that keeps pouring out, that's not the kind of place I want to leave to our children and grandchildren."

"What can anyone do about it?"

"Get mad, for one thing. Quit sitting on the sidelines about it. And get involved. Get in line with good politicians like Bernie Halstrom, and tell them your concerns."

"Bernie Halstrom is in the studio with us tonight."

"Yes, he is. He is one of the few politicians who actually puts action behind his words. I heard someone say that evil wins when good people do nothing. Let's all do something and maybe we can start to get rid of the flesh merchants."

"We'll be right back," Dunaway said to the camera.

2.

The wind was whipping up dust in the Chatsworth hills. It was funny, pitching a tent up here. Jared had pitched camp in a lot of places, but not within a rock's throw of the 118 freeway.

Down below, the lights of the San Fernando Valley started to blink into life. In the tent, Jamaal slept soundly on top of a sleeping bag. Jared could only imagine what the kid had probably been through.

"It's kind of pretty, isn't it?" Tiana said. She and Jared sat on the dirt, looking into the Valley.

"I guess."

"Why are you doing this for Jamaal and me?"

"I don't know. I just don't want you to get hurt anymore. I don't want you going back to that guy."

"I don't know why I even went back in the first place," she said.

"Hey, we're all dumb in some way. I don't know why I do most of the things I do either."

"I'm scared though."

"What of?"

"Taking care of Jamaal. I've got no way to make money."

"Everybody can do something."

"I'm not talking about working at McDonald's. I can do that. But that's not going to be enough for Jamaal."

"You love him, right?"

"Of course I do."

"That's the most important thing." He thought of his own mother then, the way she always stood by him. Was he doing the right thing by going away now?

"What do you like to do most in the world?" Jared asked.

"I don't really know."

"Well, think about it this way: When you were twelve years old or so, what was your favorite thing?"

She grew quiet for a long time. "I guess I liked to make pretty things. Didn't have much around, but I was always trying to make things look nice. I remember once I had this dress, the one I wore to church whenever my mom took me, and I found some tinsel in a trash can, you know the kind you put on Christmas trees?"

"Yeah."

"And I took it and I took some of my mom's sewing stuff and I sewed this tinsel onto my dress. A whole bunch of it. I wanted it to look like the kind of dress I saw on TV when the movie stars'd go out and be all glamorous. When my mom saw it she about fainted. But she let me wear it to church."

Jared could hear the cars on the 118, a steady rush like a river flowing. "Maybe you can make things pretty again. I think there's got to be a place for that in this world."

Tiana said nothing.

"What happened to your mom?" Jared asked.

"Died when I was fifteen."

"How?"

"Homeboys shot up the wrong place."

Jared shook his head. "I'm sorry."

Tiana put her arms across her chest. "It's getting cold."

"We're gonna have to huddle up in there." Jared nodded toward the tent. "Hope you don't mind." Then he added, "You can trust me."

"Hope so. 'Cause I've had enough of the bad stuff."

Bad stuff. Jared closed his eyes. For this brief moment the bad seemed miles away. Down there, in the Valley. Along the freeway corridor, where angry drivers hunched over wheels. In the neighborhoods, where tempers flared and guns went off. The bad stuff was all out there in this moment, not here with the air and boulders and brush, and the three of them together.

He would not be the one to hurt them. As far as he could help it, he would not be the one.

"You were terrific," Bernie Halstrom said as they pulled out of the studio on Fairfax where the Hank Dunaway show was broadcast. Dallas had met him at his office, and Bernie had brought her to the studio in his Town Car, complete with driver. She didn't turn down the luxury. It was nice to be taken care of.

"Might have to hire you to be my personal PR maven," Bernie added.

Tired but wired from the interview, Dallas said, "Maybe I'll take you up on it."

"Anytime. I want to tell you I think you've got tremendous courage. I don't know many women as strong as you, Dallas."

"I'm running on fumes here."

"No, you did great."

"Thank you for setting it up."

"Hank's an old friend." Bernie looked at her. "And a good one to have on your side."

"I need all the help I can get."

"Have you heard from Jared?"

"One message. To tell me he's all right." But he wasn't all right. He'd skipped his DUI appearance, and Jeff said he was now subject to arrest.

She leaned back against the headrest and agonized silently. *How long, Lord, before you answer my prayers? I'm worn out.*

"How about a bite to eat?" Bernie said.

"No, thanks. Being on TV takes something out of you. How do you do it?"

"I went to Ireland last year and kissed the Blarney Stone."

"Really?"

"No. But it's a good story."

He let the ride continue in silence, which was nice. Dallas closed her eyes. She prayed for Jared then and thought of Ron and Jared together. Reconciled. No matter where they ended up individually, they were father and son after all. They needed each other.

Her thoughts drifted back to happier times, which seemed a century ago. The four of them, the whole family, at Disneyland.

Cara was healthy again and Jared had not yet lapsed into sullenness. They all got soaked on Splash Mountain, but Ron and Jared got the worst of it, and they laughed and hugged each other, a couple of soggy maniacs—

"What's the matter?" Bernie Halstrom's voice, directed to his driver, Derek, jerked Dallas to the present.

Derek had stopped short of the lot. "There's somebody standing there."

Dallas looked out the front window. Illuminated by the head-lights, a man stood in the middle of the drive. He wore a Hawaiian shirt and jeans.

"Shall I back away?" Derek said.

"Wait a second." Bernie leaned forward. "No. I know who that is." He turned to Dallas. "How would you like to meet Vic Lu?"

Have mercy upon me, O God, according to thy loving-kindness; according unto the multitude of thy tender mercies blot out my transgressions.

Wash me thoroughly from mine iniquity, and cleanse me from my sin.

For I acknowledge my transgressions, and my sin is ever before me.

Against thee, thee only, have I sinned, and done this evil in thy sight: that thou mightest be justified when thou speakest, and be clear when thou judgest.

Behold, I was shapen in iniquity, and in sin did my mother conceive me.

Behold, thou desirest truth in the inward parts, and in the hidden part thou shalt make me know wisdom.

Purge me with hyssop, and I shall be clean; wash me, and I shall be whiter than snow.

Make me hear joy and gladness, that the bones which thou hast broken may rejoice.

Hide thy face from my sins, and blot out all mine iniquities.

Create in me a clean heart, O God, and renew a right spirit within me.

Cast me not away from thy presence, and take not thy holy Spirit from me.

Restore unto me the joy of thy salvation, and uphold me with a free spirit.

Then will I teach transgressors thy ways, and sinners shall be converted unto thee.

Amen.

§.

Vic Lu had an exotic look, what Dallas thought used to be called Eurasian. His black hair was nearly shoulder length and slicked back. His casual clothes could have been worn by any number of beach-loving, laid-back Angelenos.

In his midthirties, he didn't look like the multimillionaire the reports said he was.

"I caught the show tonight," Lu said. "Man, I'm being hammered here." He smiled. His teeth were white, perfect.

The three of them were in Bernie Halstrom's office and, for all Dallas knew, alone in the government building.

"Is that what you came to tell me?" Bernie said. "That you're a Hank Dunaway fan?"

"Bernie, I'm right up the street here. We're neighbors. We never talk. I heard Mrs. Hamilton say you were at the studio with her. I figured you'd come back here. I didn't know Mrs. Hamilton would be with you. That's what you call a bonus."

"What is it you have to say?" Bernie said.

"That I'm not the bad guy here, all right?" He looked at Dallas. "Mrs. Hamilton, all I'm doing is making a living, okay? Just like anybody else."

"The flesh trade is not a living, is it?" she said.

"I'm in business. I'm a working man, all right? I came over here fifteen years ago, no money, no nothing. I used to clean up the bathrooms at the bus station downtown. You know what that's like? You have no idea. But I did it because I needed a job, and you know what? That's the best I could do at the time. I don't even have a high school diploma. I read books alone at night, trying to figure out how to better myself."

Bernie said, "Lots of people work their way up and don't go into your business."

"My business is legal, Bernie. I want to remind you of that. LookyLu may not be MGM, but it's legit. I know you're trying to do your thing, your political thing, and I accept that. But right now I'm as legal as the Ford dealer on Topanga. And I treat my actors like royalty. They get the best pay in the business, the best medical, the best HIV tests. I'm not twisting any arms to get them to be in my movies. And if I didn't hire them, they'd be working for some other dude who doesn't care half as much as I do."

"But it's what they *do*," Dallas blurted, unable to stop herself. "It's ..."

"Indecent?"

"That's a nice word for it."

"Sinful?"

"Yes."

"I know you've got religious beliefs, and I respect them. I really do. I believe in America. I believe in freedom of religion. And if a guy doesn't have religion, he's free too. And as long as he obeys the law, he's allowed to run a business. Bernie, tell her I'm legitimate, will you?"

Bernie allowed his desk chair to swivel. "That's not a word I prefer to use."

"Then at least stop the personal stuff," Lu said, looking at Dallas.

"I have the right to speak, just as you have the right to make pornography."

"Come on, Mrs. Hamilton," Lu said, spreading his hands wide. "What I'm doing is legal. What you're doing is a personal attack. Is that what Jesus would do, Mrs. Hamilton?"

"Let's not bring Jesus into this," Bernie said.

"Why not? She has."

He was right, of course. "All right," she said. "But that doesn't mean I'm going to stop trying to change the laws."

"Fair enough," Vic Lu said. "That's America too." He stood up. "I know you don't approve of me, Mrs. Hamilton, and I respect that. I respect the right of people to disagree. I also have feelings involved in this."

"Feelings?" Bernie said. He remained seated.

"Melinda Chance, she was one of my girls. Now she's dead. I've had a death in the family. Can you understand that, Mrs. Hamilton?"

She hadn't thought of it that way before, that he could in any way be running anything even remotely like a family. But in his world, maybe that's all the family he had.

"I'm sorry for what happened to her," Dallas said. "That shouldn't happen to anybody."

"I'm sorry it was your husband who did it," Lu said. "I know that must be very hard to take."

"Let me remind you," said Bernie, "that another one of America's better assets is the presumption of innocence. We have a trial to determine guilt."

Lu nodded almost imperceptibly. "Point taken. And I've taken up too much of your time. I'm glad we had this little chat."

§.

At Cara's apartment, Dallas almost fell asleep sitting on the sofa. But thoughts of meeting Vic Lu face-to-face kept her awake. There was something about him, beyond his slick persona and filthy industry, that needled her.

Yeah, a needle in a haystack.

"You looked good on TV, Mom," Cara said, coming in with hot tea. She set the tray on the coffee table. "Very cool and collected."

"Thanks. My nerves were like a cat after an earthquake."

"You came across fine."

"Thanks for the tea." Dallas picked her cup up and waited for Cara to do the same.

Instead, Cara slipped her hands into the pockets of her jeans. It was a gesture from her childhood. The preparation for uncomfortable words.

"What is it, Cara?"

"Are you really going to divorce Dad?"

So there it was. The elephant in the room, the thing Dallas had tried to ignore.

Cara kept her hands in her pockets. Her arms looked rigid. "It's kind of harsh, don't you think?"

Dallas sat back on the sofa. "Divorce is always harsh."

"Then why are you doing it?"

"You know why."

"Just because some other stuff has turned up?"

"Other *stuff*? Cara, I don't know if you realize what's been coming out, things your father ..." She paused. "I don't want to say things that will hurt you."

"What things?"

"About your father."

"What about him? Aren't you hurting him?"

"He's brought this on himself."

Cara took her hands from her pockets dramatically and slapped her sides, just like she used to do when she was little. "Oh, that's a fine thing to say."

"You don't think it's true?" Dallas tried to keep her voice low, but it rose anyway.

"Can't you just forget about what's in the past and go on?"

"Maybe once I thought I could do that. But the lies—"

"Now he's a liar?"

Yes, Cara, he is. "I know it's hard on you, really."

"No, you don't. What makes you think you really know what's going on, anyway?"

"Cara—"

Her daughter shook her head and, without another word, left the room. Dallas didn't have the energy to pursue her. Spent, she put her head back on the sofa and closed her eyes. *God, what is it you want me to do? Keep me from sinning against you—*

Her phone chimed. She didn't recognize the number. Maybe it was Jared again.

"Hello?"

"I'm real disappointed in you, Dallas."

Chad.

She couldn't speak.

"You know what my nose looks like now? I'm not going to be pretty for a long time. We're going to have to get together soon and—"

She clapped the phone closed, trembling. It was as if Chad were in the room. Had he found out where Cara lived? Followed her? Could he circumvent the security?

What could she do? Take Cara and run? No. If she did, she'd never stop, because Chad wouldn't.

"Cara!"

A moment later her daughter appeared in the doorway. "What's wrong?"

Dallas stood up. "Help me use the Internet. I want to find somebody."

"Who?"

"Chad McKenzie. The guy who attacked me."

"Mom, don't get yourself into—"

"Cara, please. He's out there. I ..." She hesitated, studying the concern on Cara's face. "I never told you about my involvement with him, did I?"

"Only that you did some things in your past that you really regretted."

"I felt so ashamed, and I didn't want you and Jared to know."

"Does Dad know?"

"Yes. I told him everything before we were married. And now I better tell you."

She did, holding nothing back. The confessions felt like scabs flaking off her soul. But once gone, there was a warm relief.

When she was finished, Cara said nothing.

"You don't think less of me, do you?" Dallas asked.

Cara took her hand. "No, Mom. No way."

Through sudden tears, Dallas enfolded Cara in her arms and held her.

"Now," Dallas said, "help me."

She had Cara use her laptop to connect to the Internet. Using the same website Lisa had shown her, Dallas typed in the number Chad McKenzie had used to call. She paid for the search and got an address on Cherokee in Hollywood.

Just like that.

"Now what?" Cara said.

"Now I give the address to the police."

"This better work."

"You're oh so right."

THIRTEEN

1.

"I'm hungry," Jamaal said.

"I figured," Jared said. "I got it covered."

It was a cool, crisp morning up in the hills. Jared already had the little Coleman going. Tiana was still asleep in the tent.

Jamaal sat down next to the little blue flame.

"Time you learned about Spam," Jared said.

"Spam?"

"I'm not talking computers, either. I'm talking this." He held up the can so Jamaal could look at it.

"What is it?" Jamaal said.

"People been trying to figure that one out for years. But let me tell you, on a cold morning, when you fry it up ... baby!" Jared popped open the can, then slopped the brick onto the cold pan. Using his buck knife, Jared sliced up the army delicacy, thick and nice, then set the pan over the flame.

"You're gonna love this," Jared said.

"Love what?" Tiana was out of the tent, rubbing her eyes.

"Breakfast," Jared said.

Tiana gazed at the pan. "What is it?"

"Sam!" Jamaal said.

"Spam," Jared corrected.

"Spam! You can eat it."

"I never had it," Tiana said.

"Hey, I'm no famous chef from Paris and all," Jared said, "but I know my Spam. We'll eat and then hit the road."

"Where to?"

"I don't know. Anywhere. Camping here is technically illegal. The sooner we get out the better."

And then they were sitting, the three of them, eating Spam slices on crackers and sharing water from a gallon container Jared kept behind the driver's seat.

That's when a strange feeling hit him. Jared nearly shook his head at it, as if to rid himself of the unfamiliar. Was it happiness? No, that was a little too much. More a cessation of pain. A lifting, momentarily, of all the dark weight he'd been carrying around.

He wondered, too, for the briefest moment—wondered and even found himself hoping—that they, the three of them, would remain together, somehow, some way.

And then, as quickly as it had come, the thought was gone, chased out by his inner voice.

Stop it. You can't be with people anymore, you jerk. This is stupid. Get away from them before you hurt somebody.

"It's good," Jamaal said. "Spam is good."

"Yeah, real good," Jared said. "Now finish up and let's get out of here."

2.

Los Angeles Times

Preacher's Computer Had Pornographic Images

A computer seized from the office of accused murderer Ron Hamilton contains several hundred pornographic images, sources close to the case revealed.

Police took possession of the computer, found in Hamilton's office at Hillside Community Church, pursuant to a search warrant. Hamilton is awaiting trial for the murder of adult-entertainment star Melinda Perry, aka Melinda Chance.

Legal experts were divided on the significance of the evidence.

"It's highly prejudicial," said Los Angeles criminal defense lawyer Dave Danilov. "There's no way a judge is going to allow it in. If he does, he risks a reversal on appeal."

But Loyola Law School professor Levi Josephson disagreed. "If it's possible to show a connection between the images and anything having to do with the victim, then the evidence could come in. And that would be devastating to the defense."

Calls to Hamilton's attorney, Jefferson Waite, were not returned.

Trial is set to begin August 1.

Dallas put the morning paper down and closed her eyes, her insides twisted like spaghetti on a fork. Here was another level of distress. What would this publicity do to the witness of Hillside Community Church? The church at large? Every time an evangelical leader fell to scandal, the papers were all over it.

They hardly ever reported the good stuff. The daily sacrifices Christians made every day to help *the least of these* went unnoticed.

Cara came in, startling her. "Sorry, Mom."

"I'm a little jumpy, huh?" Dallas put the paper down, hiding the story.

"Coffee?"

"Thanks."

Her daughter paused. "Mom, I'm sorry about last night. I think I was kind of out of line."

"No, you weren't." Dallas took her hand. "You spoke up for your family, which includes all of us. You want it back the way it was."

"I want it even better. I want Jared back too. I can't stop thinking about him."

"I know."

"I pray for him, but sometimes it feels useless."

"Cara, remember the parable Jesus told about the unjust judge?"

Cara nodded. "The persistent widow."

"We think about how worn out the judge got. But what about that widow? She must have been worn out too, without even a hint of hope. Yet she kept coming back. That's how it is sometimes, isn't it? We just have to keep coming back. We have to storm the throne."

"Storm the throne. I like that."

The phone on the kitchen wall rang. Cara answered, then turned to her mother. "It's for you."

"Who?"

"Police, he said."

Jared. Dallas practically jumped to get it.

"Mrs. Hamilton?"

"Yes?"

"This is detective William Lacy of the LAPD. You called in an address on Cherokee last night and left this number."

"I did, yes."

"I'm at the location now. I wonder if you'd mind coming down here. I'd like to ask you some questions."

"About what?"

"About the guy we found at this address."

"Is he in custody?"

"No, ma'am. He's dead."

A rush of disbelief coursed through her. "Dead?"

"If you could come down, I'd really appreciate it."

§

Detective Lacy was in his forties and lanky. Dallas met him outside the beat-up clapboard house on Cherokee. The house, maybe twenty years ago, was once sharp and homey. Time and the city had worn it down. A couple of uniformed policemen stood just outside the open front door, which had yellow police tape across it.

"Thanks for coming down," Detective Lacy said.

"What is this place?"

"Halfway house. Place for guys on diversion drug programs or parole."

She noticed a few men sitting off to the side, smoking and looking lost.

"I know this is a tough time for you," Lacy said. "Your husband's case is all over the place."

Dallas nodded. "Part of the deal these days, I guess."

"Right. I'm just old enough to remember when you had to go to the *Times* or the *Examiner* to get your news about a high-profile case. Now you can't turn on the radio or TV without something being piped in."

He reached to his inside coat pocket and pulled out a small tape recorder. "I need to ask you some questions about the deceased. We found a couple of items in his possession that you might be able to explain."

"That's fine."

"First, what was your connection to Mr. Bryan?"

"Excuse me?"

"The deceased."

She shook her head. "No, I called in about a man named McKenzie, Chad McKenzie. I thought that's who—"

"Mr. McKenzie isn't here, although he was. No, the deceased is a man named Raphael Bryan."

"But I'm afraid I don't know anyone by that name."

"He seems to have known you."

"I'm sorry, Detective, but I'm really confused."

He nodded as if this news did not surprise him. "Apparently he was also known as Rafe."

4.

"You're not ever going to think of going back to him, got it?" Jared said. The three were heading up the 5, past Sylmar now, heading for an undetermined destination.

"I don't want to," Tiana said.

"What about him?" Jared looked at Jamaal, who was sleeping on Tiana's lap.

"Never."

"Good."

"But now what?"

Jared thought about it. "You find another place to live. You get a job and you raise your boy. Simple as that."

"What're you going to do?"

"I don't know," Jared said. "I've gotta find a place too."

"You going back to L.A.?"

"People are better off if I don't. I'm pretty screwed up. Who needs it?"

"Maybe we could work together."

He looked at her. "What's that mean?"

"You know, figure things out together. Jamaal likes you. So do I."

"That's a mistake," Jared said, looking at the highway construction, at the attempt to put a new surface on a worn-out road.

"I don't think so," she said.

"Then don't think." Sensing his words had stung more than he intended, Jared said, "I'm not one to get involved with. I'm not anybody who can have anything permanent, okay? I might end up doing the same thing to you as Rafe."

"You won't."

"How do you know that?"

"I just do."

"You don't know anything. Your choice in men, that proves it."

"I think you're just feeling sorry for yourself."

"Maybe I am. I don't really care."

"That's your problem."

"No, it isn't."

"What is then?"

"Just let me drive," he said.

5.

Alarms went off in Dallas's head. "I know of a Rafe, an abusive boyfriend of a woman I was counseling."

"Tell me more," Lacy said.

"I never met him. I just remember the name. But what's he doing here?"

"That's what we're hoping to find out. There seems to be a connection that runs through you."

"How?"

"You filed a complaint about this guy McKenzie, who attacked you in your home."

"Yes."

"Then you phone in an address where you think he is. Turns out you were right. The pay phone is the one right over there." He pointed to a unit affixed to the house, near the northeast corner.

"But what does Rafe have to do with it?"

"He turns up dead in the backyard, and our boy McKenzie is gone. We found an item in the victim's wallet, has your name on it, and the name of a Jared Hamilton."

Fear gripped her. "That's my son. Where is he?"

"I don't know anything about that. Just want to know why your names should be in his possession."

"I can't tell you that. I have no idea. Unless Chad had something to do with it."

"What might he have had tó do with it?"

"I don't know, except that he was out to get me and my family. Could he have given our names to Rafe?"

"That's what we want to find out," Lacy said.

"But that doesn't make sense."

"Things usually don't at the beginning." He paused and looked briefly at the notebook in his hand. "Does Gentri Land mean anything to you?"

Dallas shook her head. "What is it?"

"Something written on the back of the same paper that had you and your son's names on it. Just thought I'd throw that out."

"Do you have any idea what it means?"

"Not right now. If anything occurs to you, I want you to give me a call." He handed Dallas his card. "Now what can you tell me about this guy's girlfriend, the one you were counseling?"

"Tiana Williams. I didn't know her real well, even though she stayed in my house for a few days."

"When was that?"

"The end of March. Right after Ron was arrested."

"You brought her to your house to stay?"

"Her and her little boy, Jamaal. We do that once in a while."

"And the reason for that was?"

"I didn't want her to go back to her boyfriend, and she had nowhere else to go. I thought she could stay with me and sort things out."

"So you brought her home with you?"

"Actually, Jared picked them up."

Lacy registered a look, the kind that shows the gears meshing. "So there's a connection here to Jared, through this woman."

"Connection?"

"This work is all about connections, and you just hope some of them make sense."

Another alarm, this one intensely personal, sounded in the back of her brain. "You don't think Jared had anything to do with this." She tried not to sound too adamant, but her voice was firm.

"We have this guy, McKenzie, and the vic, Bryan, and you and your son, all coming together here. I don't know what it means, but I have a feeling it's going to mean a lot of shoe leather and coffee."

"I should tell you," Dallas said, "that my son is an ex-Marine and was in Iraq and has had some troubles back here. But he is not capable of killing ..."

She stopped, suddenly aware of the harsh, unremitting pattern. The words were the same she used about Ron at one time, words she was less sure she could use about him now.

Lacy said, "Do you happen to know where he was last night?"

"No, he's not been at home."

"Know where I can reach him?"

"I can't reach him either."

Why did this sound so sinister all of a sudden? *Don't be Jared. Please, don't be Jared.*

As if reading her every thought, Lacy put a hand on her arm. "Well, if you think of anything, you have my card. I appreciate your coming down here. I'll be in touch."

As she walked back to her car, in the grasp of new uncertainties, she was aware that the men of the halfway house were watching her go and making some comments. One of them laughed, clearly at her.

It felt like the mockery of demons.

§

Roger Vernon came to see me. Imagine that.

Here I am, sitting alone, not knowing whether I have a family anymore, not knowing if I have a life anymore, and I get the word that I have a visitor.

Roger looks younger than I do, even though he's thirty years older.
I know what I look like. The slam, as they say, has not been great for
my skin.

But Roger, there's a light in his eyes and a vibrancy in his voice.
Even though he only had a church of two hundred, and I one of eight
thousand, I know that it is his voice God honored.

When I saw him I broke down crying.

He waited patiently while I gained enough control to talk.

"It's good to see you, Ron."

"I'll bet."

"I mean it. I don't care what the circumstances. It's been too long
since we've talked."

"My fault. I could have kept in touch."

"It goes both ways."

"Mostly my way, I'm sure. And look at me now. This road wasn't
even paved with good intentions."

Roger shook his head.

I looked inside myself and determined I wasn't going to hold anything back. I wanted the whole house cleaned.

"I didn't want to hear from you," I said, "because I thought I was a
better minister. It was obvious to me, because the church was growing.
But maybe a part of me really believed that you had it right. That the
idea is not the number of people in the pews, but the power of the Spirit
in the people."

"I never thought that was your priority."

"But it was! I just didn't let it show. Now I've lost everything."

"I don't think so."

"How can you not?"

He didn't hesitate. "Because nothing is truly lost in the kingdom.
Christians are inverse paranoids."

"Inverse what?"

"We believe that there is a massive force always working to bring
about our good in the world. That's God working out his plan, his will
for his children."

"I used to believe that."

"What's stopping you from believing it now?"

"Me."

He waited for me to explain.

"Roger, I'm thinking of changing my plea to guilty."

"But why?"

"Maybe by giving up I'll get out of the way long enough for God to work on me again."

"But you can't plead for something you didn't do. That wouldn't be right."

I looked at him and shook my head. "But I did do it, Roger."

"What?"

"I killed Melinda Perry."

7.

"Hello, Mrs. Hamilton. Jeff's told me some very nice things about you."

The lawyer, Rich Pelicanos, was about Jeff's age, with thinning brown hair moussed to the max. He looked competitive, the kind of lawyer most people would want on their side in a divorce.

The very word made Dallas's heart do little trapeze tricks. She didn't want to be here. She knew she had to be.

Rich Pelicanos's office was in Santa Monica, which meant he was one of the upper crust. To afford the rent here, you had to be good. Jeff had assured her he was.

Mr. Pelicanos had his assistant bring in cappuccino. It was a comforting gesture.

For Dallas, it barely worked.

"Today's just a preliminary meeting," he explained. "Nothing to feel any pressure about. I want to answer any questions you may have, explain a few things, give you some stuff to fill out at your leisure. The main thing I want you to know is that your interests will be protected."

"I'm not really concerned about that. I don't expect there's going to be a big fight, knowing Ron."

Mr. Pelicanos nodded halfheartedly. "Would that were true. You just never know in a divorce how the other side will act."

"I thought I knew Ron."

"I understand. We'll just get prepared, and I'm sure we can deal with all contingencies. Do you have any questions for me, anything I can clear up?"

"Will I have to go to court?"

"Only if there's a contest."

"I don't want a contest. I don't want anything."

"Mrs. Hamilton, you must protect yourself. That's part of—"

"I don't want anything. I don't want to punish anybody or—" She thought for a moment she was going to be sick.

"Can I get you something? A glass of water?"

Ron's face flashed into her mind then. But not the Ron of the last few years. It was his face the first time she saw him, at the Jesus rally in San Francisco. Innocent yet full of fire. Inviting, because he had something that was so certain and seemingly pure. Part child, full of wonder; part Christian man, ready to take on the world.

"I can't do this," she said.

"Take your time, there's no rush to—"

"No. I can't do it."

Mr. Pelicanos looked at her sympathetically. "It's natural to have second thoughts. But in order to protect yourself, you ought to continue with the paperwork, just in case."

She looked at the packet on his desk. "I'm sorry for taking your time. I'll pay for it, of course. But I can't do this."

"Does it have to do with your religious convictions? Because I've had many clients where this has initially been an obstacle, but once they thought it through—"

"Maybe I'm being stupid. I'm sorry, but I—"

"No, please. Why don't you think more about it? But while you're doing that, let's think about setting up a separate bank account for you, getting some ducks in a row—"

"No ducks," she said. "I just need more time."

"Of course you do," the attorney said. "Feel free to call me anytime. I'm here for you."

§.

Here for you.

The words of a divorce lawyer.

They should have been the words of God.

But back at Cara's, alone in the apartment, Dallas found it difficult to believe God was really *there*. Oh, she knew it was true, the way she knew four plus four was eight. But the certainty of it, the kind of assurance that permeates the soul, she lacked that.

Maybe it wasn't there because of all the cul-de-sac thoughts she was thinking, questions that ran up to a curved barrier but could only turn back on themselves.

One question that kept repeating itself, over and over, had Vic Lu's name attached to it. She couldn't stop thinking about something he'd said.

I'm sorry it was your husband who did it.

There was something theatrical about his statement, as if it was delivered by a bad actor. He was selling her. Or trying to.

Why? Another question with no answer. There were only odd threads out there, dangling.

If only she could tie some together.

Like Melinda Perry. She'd worked for Lu, and now she was dead, and Ron was taking the fall for it. And Lu wanted to be very sure he expressed his condolences to her on that score.

But what if Ron didn't do it? As much as he had lied, she could not bring herself to believe he was a murderer. You don't live with a man for a quarter of a century and not know—

Then she remembered that case, where was it? Kansas? The serial killer who had lived an outwardly normal life for decades. He even had his wife fooled.

I'm sorry it was your husband who did it.

Why was Vic Lu emphasizing this? Control? Spite? Or was there something else going on, something connected to Melinda Perry's murder?

Using Cara's laptop on the kitchen table, Dallas ran a Google search on Melinda Chance. Scrolling through the hits, she saw a link with the term "Escort" in it. She clicked on that and was taken to a magenta screen with the words "Valley Night Escorts" on the top of the page, and an *Enter* button in the middle. Below the button was text in a large font: "Warning. You must be 18 years of age or older to enter this site. Contains adult content. By clicking the enter button you acknowledge that you are 18 years of age or older. Valley Night Escorts assumes no liability for misuse."

Dallas wasn't sure what to do. It was scary in a way. She had never been on any website like this before. It was so easy. And that was scary too. How easy it must be for kids to do this. The little warning was a joke.

Pulse quickening, Dallas hit *Enter*.

Almost immediately the screen was filled with a series of thumbnail photographs, all of beautiful women in various stages of undress. The images hit Dallas like flung garbage. A deep despair washed over her. Each one of those girls had a life, a life being wasted for this. Multiply these girls by a million, maybe more, and sadness could not be avoided.

Below each image was a small description. There were so many of them, all sexual in tone and distinguished by race, sexual orientation, particular fetish—just reading them made Dallas sick. But she went on.

Near the bottom she saw a description of private parties with film stars. The girl in the thumbnail looked like she was kissing the camera.

Dallas clicked on the kissing girl.

Another screen came up with yet another set of images. Below these images were names. Dallas scrolled down the names, looking for Melinda Chance. Then she realized that the site would have taken her off. Men don't usually pay for escorts who are dead.

Dallas sat back and just looked at the screen for a moment, silently praying, asking God over and over to do battle.

Just before leaving the site, Dallas stopped when she saw the name Gilda. That was all, just Gilda. Next to her name it said, "If you like Melinda Chance . . ."

Dallas clicked on Gilda.

Half the screen was taken up with the photograph of a pretty woman with oddly colored hair—was it purple?—and her mouth pouty in a provocative, come-hither way. The other side of the screen was a text message. "Hi! My name's Gilda, and you may have seen me on some of the hotter selling DVDs over the last year. Acting is not all I'm into. I love to party! Are you into fun? Then give me a call! If you like Melinda Chance, you can double your pleasure, because we work as a team. VIPs only."

There was a phone number. Dallas jotted it down, wondering why the text hadn't been changed in light of Melinda's death.

Cara's phone rang and Dallas picked up.

"I'm glad I got you," Jeff Waite said. "Have you seen the paper?"

"Yes."

"I'm absolutely outraged the pornography stuff was leaked to the press." His voice was hard. "It had to come from the police or the prosecution. Either way, it's unethical. It could poison the jury pool. I'm not going to be quiet about this."

"Maybe the truth is supposed to come out," Dallas said. "Did you ever think of that?"

"I don't know what you mean."

"Trials these days seem to be about gamesmanship. Each side trying to keep the other from finding things out or letting the jury hear about it. What if a trial was actually about truth for a change?"

Jeff said, "Then you'd have to change the whole system. The one we've got works pretty well."

"But that doesn't change the fact. The fact is that Ron sinned." She paused. "Funny to hear myself use that word about Ron. But that's what it is. He sinned, and he hid it, lied about it, and now it's coming out. If that leads to his facing up to what he did, not lying anymore, then maybe God can do something with him."

"Well, I'm not God. I'm only a lawyer, and I don't like what's going on."

"Neither do I. Especially now. Something bizarre's happened."

"Like what?"

"Relating to Chad McKenzie." She told him about the call from Detective Lacy and the revelation that Rafe Bryan was found shot to death at the place where Chad was recently holed up.

"What does the detective say about it?" Jeff asked.

"Nothing yet. He's still making the connections, like Colombo."

"Good old Colombo."

Dallas put on her Peter Falk voice. "Just one more question, sir."

"That's pretty good."

"Maybe I should do voices permanently, keep myself occupied."

"They might put you in the mental ward."

"That's probably where I'll end up anyway," Dallas said.

"No, you won't."

"This guy Rafe had a piece of paper with my name on it, and Jared's. And also the words Gentri Land."

"What's that?"

"I don't know. But I'm hoping this Detective Lacy finds out before we get to the trial."

"That would be nice. Because we don't have anything else."

"What about the witness, the one I told you about?"

"Dallas, he's not going to help. Harry interviewed him."

"And?"

"At the kid's mother's house. First of all, he won't even be allowed to testify."

"Why not?"

"Competence. Every witness has to have a level of competence under the Evidence Code. From what Harry tells me, this kid's mental capacity is just one problem."

"There's another?"

"I don't know what you were told, Dallas, but this kid doesn't recall seeing anybody at the Star that night. Harry asked him six ways from Sunday, trying to figure out what he may or may not have seen, but got nothing." He paused. "Dallas, I wish I could give you better news."

Dallas looked at the ceiling, wishing it would open up and send down a message from heaven.

It didn't.

§

Guillermo Padilla's mouth hung open.

"Hey, man," Jared said. "Need a favor."

His old painting partner stood in the doorway of the little house outside Bakersfield. He shared it with his mother, and it had a small shack out back where Jared had stayed a few weeks when he didn't have another place.

"What you doing up here?" Guillermo said, looking over his shoulder.

"This is Tiana and Jamaal."

Guillermo said, "This ain't no hotel."

"Look, we just need a place for a night or two, okay? Getting away from a bad situation."

"Guillermo?" a woman's voice from inside. Jared knew it was his mother.

Guillermo said something in Spanish and the woman said something back. Then she appeared at the door.

"Jared! ¿Cómo estás?"

"Bien."

"You come to stay?"

"Mama," Guillermo said in a stern voice.

His mother slapped his shoulder, then looked at Jared. "You are welcome. Come, I have food."

They all ate hot home cooking, then Señora Padilla made up a bed and two cots in the shack. She yelled at Guillermo to stop complaining, then left the three alone.

"I don't like it here," Jamaal said.

"What's not to like?" Jared said. The place was one room, small, with a water closet. Not exactly the Ritz.

"How long we got to stay here?" Jamaal said.

Tiana looked at Jared for the answer.

"This'd be a good place for you to get your bearings," Jared said. "Señora Padilla, she'll let you do some work around the place and you can stay, until you can get a job."

"Like where?"

"I don't know." Jared threw his hands up, then slapped his sides. "Go bang on some doors. Read the want ads. Do what you have to do."

"You're not staying?"

"Why should I?"

"Where you goin'?" Jamaal said.

"I don't know."

"Whyn't you stay with us?" The boy took Jared's hand. Jared pulled it away.

"Get in bed," Jared said.

"I don't wanna."

"Tough."

10.

Dallas had done nothing so strange since her days wandering North Beach.

But these were strange times, and something had to happen.

It was late afternoon, and she used her cell phone to call the number for the escort named Gilda.

She almost clicked off. But a recorded voice stopped her. It was melodramatically sultry. "Hi there. This is Gilda. I'm soooo glad you called. If you'll leave me a number, I'll get right back to you. I'm anxious to meet you, you know."

And then there was a beep.

Dallas had at least thought it through to this point. She put on a deep voice, her best one—Mel Gibson-ish—and threw in a Southern drawl to boot. "Howdy there. I saw yer picture and I'd sure like to see you. Call me back and tell me what to do." She left her cell number and closed her phone.

Are you completely nuts?

Yes.

Her call was returned in half an hour. Dallas saw Gilda's number on the LCD.

She answered in her deep Southern accent. "Howdy."

"Well, hi there." It was the same throaty voice as on the recording. "Is this the nice man who just called?"

"Shore is." Dallas's hands were shaking, but the deep voice was working on Gilda. So far.

"Well now, you sound like somebody I've just got to meet. What say you and me get together?"

"Yep."

"All you have to do is name the place."

Place! She'd forgotten about that. What was she expecting, that she'd ask a call girl to come to Cara's house?

"I'm, uh, a little nervous about this."

"Your first time?"

"Oh, yeah."

"That's so special! Oh, you sound sweet. And just because of that, I'm going to make you a special deal. I don't always do this. But for you, I will. I'll meet you for a drink at a place I know, and we'll talk a little. If you like me, I know a nice, quiet place we can go for a while. Sound like a plan?"

"Shore."

"Way cool! There's a bar called the Laurel, it's on Ventura. You just go on in and tell them you're meeting Gilda. Say eight o'clock tonight?"

"Okay."

"Don't sound so nervous, honey. We're just going to relax and have ourselves a great time. I guarantee it. Oh, and just so there's no surprises, the drink'll cost you fifty dollars."

"Huh?"

"You know, I love my work, but it is a job! I'm trying to save up for a Mercedes. Think of the drink like an initial consultation. And if you like me, we'll deduct the fifty from the rest of the evening's tab. See? Usually the first drink is a hundred, but like I said, you're special. I love showing first-timers around. What do you say?"

She could barely speak. "Eight o'clock then."

"Super trooper! I'll see you there."

ii.

The Laurel was stuck on a strip of Ventura Boulevard in the run-down section between Laurel Canyon and Lankershim. It was next to an auto-parts store, not exactly the upscale draw the boulevard was desperately seeking a couple of miles east.

The last time Dallas had been in a place like this was back in San Francisco. The bad days. She almost turned around and forgot the whole thing.

But she was close to something. No, she *had* to be close to something that would explain what had happened to her husband. Willing it to be so, she entered the Laurel. It was dark inside, and she was immediately greeted by a man with a barrel chest in a blue T-shirt stretched to the max. A silver necklace the size of a bike chain hung from his neck.

"Help you?" He seemed suspicious, as if a normal person walking into his dive was cause for alarm. No doubt it was. The place had a criminal ambience.

"I'm here to meet Gilda."

The man looked her up and down, then shrugged. "Business is business, am I right? Come on this way."

He showed her to a table in the corner, by the window. "What can I bring you?"

"Oh. Just water."

"Hey, not here. You got to order something."

Was he joking? She decided not to ask. "All right. A diet Coke."

"That's it?"

"Is that all right?"

He shrugged. "To each his—I mean her own."

Dallas watched him go and say something to the young bartender, who had dark curly hair and a jaded face. Working in a place like this, how could he not be?

The man returned with a modest-size glass of diet Coke that he placed in front of Dallas. It didn't even have a lemon slice with it.

"That'll be fifty dollars," he said.

"What?"

"Expensive Coke. Bottled in Saudi Arabia."

A criminal comedian? But he didn't smile or walk away. He was serious.

"It's for Gilda," he said.

Of course. Dallas felt a blush rushing in and was glad the place was dark. She was so unsophisticated about these things. This was the way it was done, she supposed. She fished in her purse for cash and put two twenties and a ten on the table. The man snatched it up.

"No tip?" he said.

Dallas looked at him.

"Kidding. Enjoy. I'll let Gilda know you're here."

The Coke was watery. This whole thing was watery—unsolid, unpredictable. She looked around the place. It was empty except for an older woman at the edge of the bar, looking into a martini glass. The young bartender looked at Dallas as if she were a curio.

Dallas took a small New Testament out of her purse, one she'd carried around for years. She'd read it in many a circumstance, but never one like this.

Her ribbon bookmark was in the twelfth chapter of John's gospel, and she read to the end:

> Then Jesus cried out, "When a man believes in me, he does not believe in me only, but in the one who sent me. When he looks at me, he sees the one who sent me. I have come into the world as a light, so that no one who believes in me should stay in darkness.
>
> "As for the person who hears my words but does not keep them, I do not judge him. For I did not come to judge the world, but to save it. There is a judge for the one who rejects me and does not accept my words; that very word which I spoke will condemn him at the last day. For I did not speak of my own accord, but the Father who sent me commanded me what to say and how to say it. I know that his command leads to eternal life. So whatever I say is just what the Father has told me to say."

Jesus came so that no one should *stay in darkness*. But to those who reject his words, only judgment and condemnation.

Oh, the stakes were high! For Ron and Jared especially. Would they reject Jesus after all? Jared was far away. Where was Ron? *Do not let them remain in darkness, Lord!*

She looked up and saw a woman in a red jacket with fur collar and cuffs talking to the man at the front. The woman also wore a black miniskirt from which two long dark-nyloned legs shot downward, coming to rest in black shoes with stiletto heels. Her hair was a blazing shade of purple.

And then she was walking toward Dallas with a face that did not look pleased.

"What is this?" she said.

"Gilda?"

Her face, registering annoyance, was heavily made up, especially around the eyes. They were cat eyes, and Dallas figured they must drive some men to certain distraction. Or should she say, destruction?

"I was supposed to meet a guy named Dallas."

"I'm Dallas."

"You're not a guy."

Dallas did Mel. "Thanks fer comin', ma'am."

Gilda's mouth made a little O. "Well now, that's very clever." She slid out the opposite chair out and sat down. "What's your real name?"

"It's really Dallas."

"How'd you get it?"

"My dad. He was from Texas and he loved the Cowboys."

"Oh."

"What's *your* real name?"

Gilda said, "You don't think it's real?"

"Just asking."

"Clever again. You ever see that old movie with Rita Hayworth?"

"*Gilda*. I think Glenn Ford was in it too."

"I always wanted to look like her. But you play the cards you're dealt." A distant, mournful tune seemed to play in her head. Then she snapped back. "You didn't need to do all that posing. I go both ways, I just don't advertise it. You do voice-overs or something?"

"Or something. Only for fun."

"Fun's my middle name, girl. Like what you see so far?"

What did she see? A woman of about twenty-eight or nine, on the cusp of getting too old for what she did. And then what? *Damaged goods*.

"I'd like to talk to you," Dallas said.

"Sure. We got a few minutes here."

"Fifty dollars' worth."

"That's right."

"Can I make it a hundred, and get more time?"

Gilda narrowed her eyes, now looked even more feline. "More time here?"

"Right."

"We won't need it."

"Maybe we will."

"Why?"

"Because I just want to talk. Nothing else. Should be the easiest hundred you've ever made."

"You a cop?"

"No."

"Good. Because I've got a tape going in my coat. It's just a formality in case you pull a badge."

"No badge."

"And no tape." She reached into her coat pocket and pulled out a tape recorder. Ironically, it looked identical to the one Detective Lacy used. Maybe the cops and hookers in L.A. shopped at the same store.

Gilda clicked it off. "So what do you want to talk about?"

"Melinda Chance."

Gilda's hand, holding the recorder, froze. "You *are* a cop, and I'm walking out right—"

"I'm the wife of the man accused of murdering her."

Now Gilda's body froze. For a moment Dallas thought she was going to walk out without another word. But then Gilda thawed enough to put the recorder back in her coat pocket and say, "I got nothing to tell you."

"I haven't asked anything yet."

"You don't have to."

"How well did you know her?"

"That's my business."

"I need to know."

"You don't need to know anything." Gilda took a long breath. "Look, I'll give you a word here, since you paid. Don't go anywhere with this. Forget about Melinda. She's dead. She's probably happier too."

"But I don't think my husband killed her."

"That's not my deal. I'm just telling you, don't go any further with Melinda, you understand what I'm saying?" She leaned over the table and whispered, "It wouldn't be good for you."

"Why not?"

"Trust me."

"Why should I?" Dallas surprised herself with that one, but she was not in a mood to back down.

"Look, you seem like a nice lady. Nice, respectable. And if your man did it, you won't be the first wife whose husband lied to her. Believe me, ninty eight percent of the guys I see have a little wifey at home. But the circles I run in, me and Melinda, it's not for you."

"Bad guys involved?"

"They can be."

"Like Vic Lu?"

She looked startled. "You are on thin ice, lady."

"Is that who you work for?"

"I got nothing else to say." Gilda stood up, almost knocking over the contents of the table.

"Please," Dallas said. "I need help."

"You need to keep your nose where it belongs. And do not call my number again. Stay away from this." She turned quickly and walked to the front, pausing for a word with the big man, then was out the door.

Well, that worked like a charm. A real detective she was. She took one more sip of her diet Coke, the most expensive drink she'd ever bought, and it was even more watery now. Like her prospects of helping Ron.

She felt the perfect fool too, as she started out. She could feel the bartender's eyes on her, and goodness only knew what he was thinking. *Never again, girl. Leave the cloak-and-dagger stuff to Harry Stegman.*

She didn't even want to look at the big guy with the bike chain necklace, but she couldn't avoid it with him standing right in front of the door.

"So soon?" he said.

What should she say to him? *Thank you for your hospitality?* He was creeping her out and she just wanted to get to Cara's and take a shower. She felt dirty.

"Excuse me," she said.

"You're not mad about the fifty bucks, I hope."

"Excuse me."

He didn't move.

The creepy feeling inside her grew stronger.

"May I leave?" she asked firmly.

"Sure. In a couple of minutes."

"Now."

"No can do."

She realized again that she was alone in this place, except for Necklace and the bartender. And Necklace wasn't budging.

"Move," she said.

Necklace smiled. "I need to ask you a few questions."

"Absolutely not. I'm leaving."

She took one step to try to get by him. His hand whipped in front of her and snatched her purse right out of her hands. Quick as a blink he tossed the purse over her shoulder. The bartender, now five feet away, caught it.

"Find out who this chick is," Necklace said.

Dallas tensed and considered her options. They were all bad.

As if he could hear her inner gears grinding, Necklace said, "Don't make me hurt you."

12.

Jamaal was asleep on a cot.

Tiana lay on the bed. Jared sat on the other cot, nowhere close to being able to sleep.

Back in the Padilla shack. It was like a bad dream. He'd once heard that life was just a series of recurrences. You never really got anywhere. You always ended up just going over the same ground, arriving at the same place. You died and came back and lived through it all again. Like that movie *Groundhog Day*, only it wasn't funny and you didn't remember anything.

Around and around and that was it, forever and ever amen.

"Can't sleep?" Tiana whispered.

"No."

"How come?"

"Why don't you sleep?"

"I've been thinking."

"Great. Now go to sleep."

Instead, she sat up. "Your mom's right."

"What's my mom got to do with it?"

"You got stuff going on you can't handle by yourself."

"I do all right. Go to—"

"Doesn't look to me like you do all right."

"I don't really give a flying rip what it looks like to you."

"I want to take Jamaal to church."

"He's your kid."

"Come with us."

"You do sound like my mom."

"I've been thinking this all through. You're right about me needing to get some work, and starting over again. I want to start *all* over again. Because of Jamaal. I want to give him the best life I can."

"There you go."

"You got us out of L.A., so why don't you stay with us?"

"And do what?"

She didn't answer immediately.

"You think I'm money?" he said.

"Huh?"

"You think I'm a guy you can palm off of?"

"No."

"Yeah, you do. You got that look."

What am I saying? He was starting to see pain in her eyes. The room started to go dark on him. He closed his eyes, opened them, hoping to bring in more light.

He saw Tiana staring at him.

"Cut it out!" he screamed.

"What's wrong?"

"Shut up!"

"Don't talk that way."

"Shut up I said!" Without a thought, operating on something like instinct, but from a source outside himself, Jared made a fist and raised it.

The moment he did, the moment he saw her eyes widen with shock and fear, in that moment he knew he was no better than Rafe.

He ran out of the house, jumped into his truck, and burned rubber.

He welcomed night. He could drive into it, get lost in it, stay there. Maybe if he drove fast enough, outran the demons, he could drive over a cliff or into a wall. Then there wouldn't be a blot of Jared Hamilton on the earth anymore.

He'd fought and bled in Iraq. He believed in the cause he was fighting for. He got to know enough of the Iraqi people to know how much they craved true freedom. But there was a kind of freedom some people would never know. Freedom from fear and memories and events that haunted.

He would never have that freedom.

Somewhere outside the city limits, on one of the darker roads, flashing lights came into the rearview mirror.

Cops or highway patrol. Maybe a sheriff. Anyway, they had him in their sights.

Keep going.

He pushed the pedal to the metal.

The siren split the night silence.

Now it was a high-speed chase.

Maybe end up on the evening news.

That'd thrill his mother.

Or he could charge into a tree right now, get it over with.

End it. End it now.

Yeah, right now.

He considered the trees, eucalyptus lining the road, standing and waiting, illuminated by his headlights.

Would have to be a strong one.

End it.

His mom. He saw his mom. How would she handle it?

It doesn't matter.

Yes, it does. It does matter. He couldn't do this to her now.

He braked, letting the truck come to a stop on the soft shoulder.

The car pulled up behind him.

It was a chippie. He came up on the passenger side, knocked on the window. Did not look happy.

"You miss me back there?" the chippie said. He was of the ex-linebacker style of highway patrolman.

"I stopped, didn't I?" Jared said.

"License, registration, proof of insurance."

Jared reached toward the glove compartment.

"Slowly," the chippie said.

Jared opened the compartment slowly, slid out the registration, and remembered he didn't have insurance. He took his license out and handed it to the patrolman.

Then waited as the officer went back to his vehicle. No doubt to write him up.

So what? What's a ticket gonna do? Keep going. Drive north tonight. You can figure out a way to die later, and write a note to Mom explaining it all. She'll have to make do with that.

The patrolman came back on the driver's side. And he was holding his weapon.

"Out of the truck," he said.

"What?"

"Get out, sir."

Jared opened the door. "What is all this?"

"Hands behind your back."

"Hey—"

"Do it *now*."

Jared complied. The officer slipped plastic restraints around his wrists, pulled them tight.

"What am I being arrested for?" he said.

"They want you down in L.A.," the patrolman said. "You skipped out on a DUI. They don't like that, you know."

13.

"That's better," Necklace said. He had Dallas sitting in a metal folding chair in a room behind the bar. She complied without resistance. He was going to get his way, and there was little she could do about it.

The bartender came in holding her purse and wallet. "Her driver's license says her name is Dallas Hamilton. How come that sounds familiar?"

Necklace shot him a glare. "Stupid, don't you watch television?"

The bartender looked hurt. "She on TV?"

"This is the babe whose husband offed Melinda."

A small light went off in the bartender's head. "Oh, right, right. Now what's she doing here with Gilda?"

"That's my question," Necklace said. He looked at Dallas. "You kind of pulled a fast one on my friend Gilda. Nobody would ever accuse her of being the brightest bulb on the shelf, but one thing she's got is instinct. You're in her line of work, you develop that. So I kind of agree with Gilda that you could cause a lot of trouble if you got it in your head to do that. So why don't you just tell me what you're doing here, what your business with Gilda was, and we'll figure the best way to consummate our little relationship."

"What you're doing is illegal," Dallas said. "You can't keep me here."

"That wasn't the answer I was looking for."

"Why don't you just let me go now, and there won't be any backlash."

Necklace folded his arms across his chest and looked at the bartender. "Did she just threaten us?"

The bartender shrugged.

"Did you just say *backlash*?"

"I have nothing to say to you."

"That's not good." Necklace shook his head. He had a prominent vein that ran from the top of his nose up his forehead, and split into two directions at his hairline.

She hadn't noticed it before. Maybe because it was only now throbbing.

"Now let's be up front with each other, huh?" He pulled out a metal chair for himself and sat on it backward, facing her. "You see what happens here. I provide a nice, safe place for people like Gilda to come and do a little business. It's not strictly legal, but I'm sure you didn't have to pay us a visit to deduce that."

Dallas didn't move.

"Vice knows about us, and a hundred other guys who do the same, and they let things go. It's always been that way, right? The world's oldest profession? But when somebody from the community gets upset about it, starts reporting things, then the cops, well, they think they gotta turn up the heat for a while. And that just gets to be a hassle."

Necklace ran his hand though his hair.

"So what I gotta decide here is if you're gonna go out and start making a big deal. Because that would just be bad for business, and I got a mother to support."

"Not to mention a girlfriend," the bartender said.

"Shut up." Another sharp look at the bartender.

"I'm not going to make any trouble," Dallas said, "if that's what you're worried about."

"I gotta have some sort of guarantee."

"What could I possibly do?"

"Just give me your word."

Now that was a strange thing to ask for. Why would a guy like this think anyone's word meant anything when it came down to protecting his business?

"All right," Dallas said. "You have my word."

"On what?"

"That I won't talk about you to anybody."

Necklace heaved a labored breath. "Now give me your undivided attention here, 'cause I have a guarantee for you. This is what it is: If I ever find out that you talked about me to anybody, I will not be the gracious host who sits before you now, huh?"

She believed him. The guy may have been a Tony Soprano wannabe, but he sure did a good job of convincing her he was qualified.

"Then you have no worries," Dallas said. "May I go now?"

Necklace held her gaze for another moment, then looked at the bartender. "Hey, what are you doing with the lady's purse? Give it back and escort her out."

FOURTEEN

1.

When she finally got to sleep at Cara's, Dallas fell into a dark dream. She saw Jared standing on a lake. Standing, as if he could walk on water. She was on the shore without a light, yet she could see him out there, alone.

She tried to scream at him to come in, but in the dream she couldn't make a sound. Her mouth opened, her throat clenched, but there was only horrifying silence.

Jared started sinking, slowly.

She wanted to swim out to him. Her feet were stuck in muddy sand.

Jared did not resist his own drowning.

He called, "It's better, Mom ..."

His head was about to disappear.

Dallas could not move. In her dream she prayed for God to save him. *Now.*

A boat appeared, churning toward Jared, sounding a strange little alarm, tinny and weak. What sort of alarm was it? It—

Dallas awakened to her cell phone chiming. What time was it? Her blurred vision caught the digital clock: 8:32 a.m.

The phone persisted. She glanced at the LCD. Jeff.

"Did I wake you?" he said.

"Yes, but I'm glad."

"Glad?"

"Dreaming. What is it?" She pulled herself to a sitting position. Her head buzzed with a shot of mental adrenaline.

"Ron wants to see you."

The thought of seeing Ron again triggered a dull ache in her mind. "Why?"

"I had a long talk with him yesterday. He asked me if he could plead out."

"You mean plead guilty?"

"It's actually nolo contendere, no contest. Means he's not admitting to guilt, but he's not going to contest the charge. It has the same effect as a guilty plea, but he'll get a reduced sentence."

"How long?"

"I discussed it with the DA early on. He'd agree to fifteen years to life. But that means Ron will be eligible for parole. He can, with a good record, get out."

"But there's no guarantee."

Jeff paused. "No. But like I've said, there shouldn't be any opposition to parole."

"Not even from the district attorney?"

"I don't think so."

Dallas thought about it, the awful finality. Prison. For real.

"I spoke to him a long time about this," Jeff said. "He told me he just wants it all to end, to take away the pain he's caused everyone. Especially you."

She closed her eyes and tried to imagine what it would feel like to have all this ended.

"He wants to see you, Dallas. To talk about it. I'll do whatever you two decide."

"I know you will, Jeff. Let me just ask you, straight up. Is this the best we can hope for?"

"I've looked at every angle," Jeff said. "I've considered all the options. None of them is very good. In my professional opinion, this is the best."

There is no best. "All right. I'll see him."

2.

She did, the next morning at ten. Ron was skinny, much too skinny, but there was finally some resolution behind his eyes.

"Jeff told you?"

"Yes. Why are you doing this?"

"Roger came to see me again."

"He said he would."

"I told him what I'm going to tell you. I am responsible for the death of that girl."

Dallas's chest tightened. Did this mean that—

"No, I didn't do it," he added. "Maybe you don't believe me. I guess I can't blame you if you don't. But I'm responsible. If I hadn't let her get involved with me, she wouldn't be dead."

"But you can't—"

"Jeff says that if I plead I could eventually get parole. Maybe this is due penance for my sins, Dallas. I'm tired of fighting. I want to give up."

"Is that what Roger told you to do? Give up?"

"To God, yes. He didn't tell me to plead guilty. Or no contest. That's my own decision. And that will free you too."

"Me?"

"You can go ahead with the divorce."

The cool and calm way he said it indicated long deliberation. He was like a judge passing down a sentence. His words were the gavel.

"Is that what you want?" she asked.

"I can't ask you to stay tied to me."

She closed her eyes a moment. "That's the one thing I always wanted, more than anything. To be tied to you, to be married to you, to go on with you 'til death do us part." She paused. "I wanted our marriage to be the one thing in my life that would last. Maybe I wanted that too much."

When she opened her eyes she saw Ron's were filling with tears. She could not stop her own. How many tears had been spilled through the years in the visitors' room at the jailhouse? What was the sum total of misery?

"I hurt you, I know," he said.

"It was the lying, Ron. I think I could have taken anything else. How could you have kept so much from me. The pornography on your computer, the—"

"I don't know how that happened, Dallas."

"How what happened?"

"All those images." He took a breath. "What I mean is, I don't remember that many. I was doing research one night, and—I don't know how to describe it—I was caught up. I was looking and down-loading. It was so easy. Scary easy. I lost track of time. I was ... crazy. When I came to my senses I felt so much guilt. I just couldn't tell you. But I deleted that whole file of images without looking at them again."

"Deleted them? Then how—"

"They have ways of recovering things on your hard drive, I guess, even when you think they're gone. Dallas, if there was any way I could go back and not have this happen to you ..."

And he wept again.

After a long moment of silence, Dallas said, "I don't think you should plead, Ron. No matter what you've done, the lies you've told, I don't think you're a murderer."

"I'm not admitting I did it. It's a no contest plea. A deal. People make deals. Why should I be any different than any other con?"

"Something may turn up. Jeff and Harry may find evidence that clears you."

Ron shook his head. "They're not miracle workers. Believe me when I say I'm at peace with this, Dallas. You have your freedom. You have the right to divorce me, and I am at peace with that too."

She gripped the phone hard. "If things were different, if none of this had happened, if we could go back to after Amy Shea and before Melinda Perry, would you have wanted to stay married to me?"

"Of course."

"No, I don't mean because of the Bible or your reputation or the church or anything else. I mean would you have wanted to stay married because you loved me?"

He thought a long time, then said, "Maybe it took all this for me to realize how much I did—do—love you. I do. I know that. But it's too late. I will pay for my sins, but I can't ask you to do the same. You're free, Dallas."

A deputy indicated that time for the visit was up. Ron hung up his phone before Dallas could say another word to him. He turned with a finality, as if judgment was already upon him. Upon them both.

3.

After being booked into Men's Central, Jared Hamilton nursed a bitter sense of humor about the whole thing.

Famous preacher from a large church and his only son, both in the same jail at the same time.

His dad had it easy by comparison. He had a room to himself. Jared was stuffed with five others into a cell originally built for two. It was the 4000 level, and the cell looked directly across at the sheriff's station, encased in thick glass. Jared thought it looked like a submarine passing by in this ocean of lost hopes.

His other cell mates were white. The jail, he knew, was purposely segregated. Too many gang rivalries to try and make this a color-blind lockup.

If the dark blue Aryan tattoos were any indication, four of his cell mates were white supremacists. All but one of the five were in their twenties. The exception was a guy who looked about forty. His hair was longer and his eyes more experienced. He was the only one who said nothing to Jared when he joined them.

The one with the most attitude, who called himself Pal, appeared to be the bull. Each cell had an unofficial head, usually the one who could do the most physical damage to the others.

"First things first, Fish," Pal said the moment Jared stepped through the cell door and heard it slam behind him. "I tell you to do something, that's what you do."

Pal, who was slightly shorter than Jared, gave him a direct stare with dark brown eyes.

Jared sized him up. He could take him if he had to. The problem was the other guys. They were Pal's boys. The old guy would probably stay out of things. Jared wouldn't stand a chance. He just had to take it. For two days. *Just two days.*

Pal pointed to the bare aluminum toilet in the center of the back wall, and then to a sheet secured to a corner of one bunk. "Second thing is, you want to use the can, use the sheet."

Jared said nothing.

"You understanding me?" Pal said.

"I got the picture," Jared said.

"I don't think you do. Let me show you." He took one step toward the toilet and motioned to Jared with his finger.

"Try it," Pal said.

"Try what?"

"The can."

"I don't have to."

"Just to show you how the sheet works."

"I don't have to go."

"Pretend you do."

Three of the inmates, all but the old guy, huddled around Pal and Jared. The cell, small as it was, suddenly seemed a lot smaller.

Jared shrugged and moved to the toilet.

"Have a seat," Pal said.

Without undoing his coveralls, Jared sat on the toilet.

"Now it works like this," Pal said. He took the sheet that was tied to one bunk and stretched it across to the opposite bunk. The sheet had a hole in the corner. Pal placed it over the bunk post.

Now Jared was looking at a sheet. Pal and his boys squatted on either side of him. Two grabbed Jared's wrists and twisted his hands. Excruciating pain shot up his arms. He couldn't move.

"Need to listen," Pal said. "Only gonna say this once. We got a real problem with the jigs and the wets. If it comes down to it, we gotta know whose side you're on. We gotta know whose back you got. You tell us, and we'll get yours."

Jared ground his teeth against the pain. "I'm not on any side."

The others did not let up on his hands. "You got to take sides."

"I'm not here long."

"Don't matter."

"Nobody's side." Jared's eyes were starting to water.

"You want a broken wrist? That'll get you out of the cell. You want that?"

Pain beat back Jared's voice and started to darken his vision. He expected to black out.

"I asked you a question," Pal said.

Jared sensed the darkness deepen and change, become a presence. That, more than the punks, brought fear.

"So what'll it be, Fish?"

The pain was reaching the point of unbearable.

Give it up, tell him you're in, just tell him and you'll be safe.

"Stick," a voice said.

Pal snapped his fingers and the two guys let go of Jared's hands, stood up, moved to the front side of the sheet.

Jared, his wrists aflame, stood up too.

The old guy was standing with his back to the cell door, looking at them all. Jared knew he was the one who had said *stick*.

Later, he would learn that a stick was a deputy who checked cells from the secure enclosure in the middle of the block.

"Don't want no stick in here," the old guy said.

Pal looked out the cell doors, then back at Jared. "Think about it," he said. "We'll have another talk real soon."

It was Friday. No action would be taken on bail or anything regarding Jared's case until Monday. There was no way he would be able to avoid another "talk."

The presence Jared felt intensified. And he was scared. More scared than he'd ever been in his life, more even than in combat.

He fought to keep from blacking out.

Then the old guy brushed past him and whispered, "Stay off the can."

4.

"Thank you for seeing me," Dallas said.

Deputy DA Mike Freton looked much more approachable in his office than he did in court. In that venue he seemed to be a living Rushmore, formidable and unbreakable. Here he seemed human, even warm.

But he was also a prosecutor convinced that her husband was a murderer.

"I represent the people of California, Mrs. Hamilton," he said. "You are one of the people, and if you have something to say to me about a case I'm involved with, my door is open. Even if it's a case you're very much involved with."

His delivery was sincere and smooth. He would make a good run at the district attorney position if he ever chose to go for it. In fact, he looked like he'd be successful at pretty much anything he tried.

"Does Jeff Waite know you're here?" he added.

"I don't think I told him. This is rather spur-of-the-moment. And I don't want to keep you." It was late Friday afternoon, and she imagined Freton wanted to get home like everybody else.

"You're not, Mrs. Hamilton. The office gets kind of quiet about now and I usually do some late work, especially when I'm in trial. Then I head over to a place on Temple for a bite before heading home."

"Where is that?"

"Pasadena."

"Nice."

"I like it."

He waited, punctuating an end to small talk. She said, "Mr. Freton, I know that you and Jeff have talked about Ron entering into a plea."

"Yes."

"Would that satisfy you?"

"I don't think *satisfy* is the word I would use. I do think it would be a just resolution to the case."

"Even though Ron didn't kill that girl?"

"Mrs. Hamilton, I have to look at the evidence. That's all I can do. In light of the evidence, I think a plea is the best thing for your husband."

"But what's your gut feeling, Mr. Freton? Do you honestly think Ron did this?"

"I don't use gut feeling. That would be a bad habit to get into."

But if you feel something's wrong— Dejection took over, sinking her words.

Mr. Freton seemed to sense it. "If you were to come to me with exculpatory evidence—sorry, that's legalese—evidence that would tend to show innocence, I would be interested. But I know Jeff

Waite and I know Harry Stegman, and if they don't have it by this time, it probably doesn't exist."

"I believe there is someone, or maybe more than one, who set Ron up. Because of the pornography connection. Ron is an outspoken critic of it and has been working hard to get some new ordinances passed."

The deputy DA nodded without conviction.

"You don't think that's possible?" she said.

"You know about the pornography we found in his computer."

Stiffening, Dallas said, "I know what I read in the papers. I also know it shouldn't have been in the papers."

"You're right. And I want to assure you that the leak did not come from this office."

She regarded him carefully. Perhaps his smoothness hid the truth.

"Then what are you doing about it?" she said.

"Following standard protocol for getting to the bottom of it. Meantime, I have to deal with the facts as they exist. And right now, I don't see a better resolution to this matter than your husband's plea."

"Even if that means the real killer is still out there?"

"We can't look at it that way. No one who prosecutes cases can ever see everything. Neither can a jury. The standard is proof beyond a reasonable doubt, not every possible doubt. We just have to do our best and hope things work out."

"What about the truth?"

"That's what the process is all about, as imperfect as it is."

"Forget the process. I'm sick of the process. All that's happened to me in this process is bad. I've been threatened and found people who know what's going on but aren't good witnesses and—"

"Whoa, what are you talking about?"

Should she even go there? What would Jeff think if she started telling Freton all this? Maybe it would hurt Ron.

"I'm just saying that you seem to want to convict on shaky ground, when there's people out there—"

"You keep mentioning other people, witnesses. Why hasn't Jeff produced them?"

Dallas looked down. *Quiet, motormouth.*

Mr. Freton said, "I understand completely a wife's desire to see that everything possible is done on her husband's behalf."

"Then find out who leaked the pornography story. Whoever did it might know more."

He paused. "That might not even be relevant to the crime."

"But it might."

"It's a very thin string, Mrs. Hamilton."

She stood up. "Very thin is all I have right now. So find that string, and pull it for all it's worth."

5.

"Dallas, I know where Jared is."

Dallas pressed the phone to her ear, as if that action could take her to her son through some sci-fi transference. "Is he all right?"

"He's in jail."

"What?"

"They found him up in Bakersfield, pulled him over for some rinky-dink traffic thing. They ran a check on him and found out there's a bench warrant for him for missing his court date. So they brought him here to the downtown jail."

"Where Ron is?"

"Sort of a weird coincidence, isn't it?"

Was it? Why would God have the two men in her life in the same jail at the same time? There had to be a reason, there had to be meaning, and she prayed that it would reveal itself.

"He'll appear before a judge on Monday morning," Jeff said. "I'll go with him."

Dallas looked at the clock in Cara's kitchenette. Six thirty. Past visiting hours.

"At least we know where he is," Dallas said. "Jeff, will he be safe in there?"

"It's only 'til Monday morning. Then we can bail him out."

6.

The eating area was segregated too, and staggered by time. Now it was the white inmates' turn. Jared parked himself at a metal table on a metal stool at the far end of the mess hall.

The meal tonight was some sort of macaroni and cheese. Jared wasn't sure it was even macaroni. The "cheese" was most likely made from some secret industrial powder also used for caulking ships.

He would be glad to get out of this place.

He hadn't taken two bites when someone said, "You're marked."

The old guy from his cell had slipped in next to him.

"What's that?" Jared said.

"Marked. Means you got something coming at you. And you don't know when it'll happen."

Little hot needles pricked Jared's skin. The guy was serious. Jared looked at him a moment, noticing as the guy chewed his food that one of his front teeth had a gold cap. "Can I get moved?"

"Not much time."

"Well, tell somebody, tell a deputy—"

"They don't care. They hear this all the time. You gotta watch your own back, Fish. That's it, that's all, the way of the slam. You don't look like you've done time before."

Jared shook his head.

"It's all over you, man."

"Why are you telling me this?"

"I have a reason."

Jared waited. "You want to tell me?"

"Sure." The old guy took another bite.

"So?"

"They want you in hell," he said.

"Excuse me?"

"Hell. The lake of fire."

Great. A crazy man. He was in a cell with four skinheads and a loon.

"Thanks," Jared said dismissively.

"Same as they want your old man."

Jared flinched, looked at him. "What about my father?"

"I know who he is. I know who you are."

Feeling exposed before a hundred prying eyes, Jared spoke low. "How do you know?"

The guy shrugged.

"Tell me."

The man said nothing. He shoveled a piece of bread in his mouth.

No, Jared decided, this was all crazy stuff, and all he was doing was encouraging more of it by listening. It was always possible too, that the old guy just liked messing with people's heads. Something to do to kill time.

"I don't care what you know," Jared said. "Just leave me alone."

"They won't leave you alone."

"Who?"

"The minions."

"What?"

"Of Satan. They're real." When he said this he set his jaw as if to underscore how serious he was. His gold tooth flashed like a warning light.

Certifiable nut. If he could survive another day he'd be clear of him, and the others. *Hell.* The old guy'd mentioned hell.

Perfect. Hell was just what Jared deserved.

You did it, boy. You got what you wanted. What was that illusion you had about Tiana and Jamaal? What were you thinking, man? This is the place for people like you, and no doubt whatever happens on the deuce you're going to end up here again, or a place like it. What does it matter if some guy punches your ticket now?

He looked around at all the blue-clad inmates in one big sardine can. They called him Fish—jail lingo for First In, Special Handling—and that was what he was, so the sardine comparison worked. Only nobody was going to give him special handling again. Everybody was better off with him out of the picture. His mom, his dad, his sister, and certainly that woman with a kid who couldn't catch a break. He wasn't going to be anybody's break.

The fear left him. His acceptance of death gave him a perverse hope that he wouldn't have to suffer anymore and wouldn't be the cause of anyone else's suffering.

And then chow was over, and he'd only eaten a few bites. It didn't matter. It was only an imitation of food here. He didn't feel hunger at all as he was marched back to his cell along with the other sardines. Nobody spoke—no one was allowed to speak—but he heard whispers. The whispers were directed at him.

Didn't matter anymore.

He got into his bunk and looked at the ceiling for a couple of hours, narrating moments of his life. They came on the big screen, like an ESPN video replay, complete with voice-over.

Jared Hamilton breaks his nose, ladies and gentlemen, when Freddy Van Horn throws him a baseball from the next driveway and he doesn't catch it. He doesn't put the mitt up there and ohhhh, that's gotta hurt, folks!

He remembered the stunning blow and the blood pouring out of his nose and the look of shock on his mother's face and the look of disappointment on his father's face because he had a mitt and couldn't catch a stupid baseball.

Yes, sir, and there he is trying to get Lisa Larson to like him, but she just laughs when he finally works up the courage to ask her out, and her boyfriend pushes him into the lockers, and that's when he decides he's going in the Marines someday so he can come back and deal with the boyfriend. You see that, ladies and gentlemen? You see that? Kind of sad, don't you think?

He skipped over Iraq completely, knowing those memories would come back soon enough. Over them he had no control. He thought of Tiana and Jamaal.

And there he is, folks, trying to save a woman, trying to be somebody in a kid's eyes, trying to make it seem like he's got a purpose around here. Give him a hand!

At lights-out the noise started up—the inmates came alive at night, because out on the street they were night crawlers, and in here night was their time to scream obscenities.

But he wasn't going to let the noise break him. He was going to sleep. And he did start to drift off, did start to fade away from voices and memories, when he felt something hard and sharp pressed against his jugular.

7.

They told me my son was in here!

Dear God in heaven, help him. I'm a K–10 and can't get to him, can't look him in the eye and tell him how stupid I was, how wrong, how blind, how unloving, how sorry I am now.

Jared, I let you down. I let you fall, because I was all mixed-up with . . . no, because I let myself get all mixed-up and I missed what was important for you.

God, let me see him again before they take me away. Give him another chance. Illuminate his heart toward you!

Protect him. I didn't. Protect him, Lord.

8.

"Don't move," Pal whispered.

He was standing over Jared, his back to the cell door.

"You move, you lose," Pal said. He pushed his weapon—probably a sharpened piece of metal—harder against Jared's throat.

Jared didn't move. He sensed the other three moving around, forming a human screen to cloak what was happening in the cell.

Pal put his face in front of Jared's. Pal's eyes sparked with a glint of virulent menace. Crazy eyes.

"You ready to pledge now?" Pal said.

Jared was silent.

Pal jabbed Jared's throat. It felt like it broke skin.

"Do you believe in Hitler?"

Jared said nothing.

"Answer me, Fish. And be careful what you say. Do you believe in the power and glory of Adolf? Do you, Fish?"

He glared at Pal.

"You better say something right now." Pal's weapon drew a trickle of blood.

"Do it," Jared said.

"What?"

"Do it. Now. Coward."

"You crazy ..." Pal hesitated, but his eyes widened, the color of hate filling them. "I'm gonna like this."

Jared closed his eyes. Waiting.

Then he heard the old guy's voice. "Put down the shank."

Time stopped. Jared opened his eyes and saw Pal's face flash with momentary confusion. But only a flash. "Shut up, old man," Pal said, still looking at Jared. "Unless you want some of this."

"In the name of Jesus Christ, and by his blood, I command you to turn around."

The old man spoke firmly but quietly, as if he trusted the words more than the tone.

Pal bared his teeth at Jared. Then he turned toward the old man.

§

Cara jolted awake in the blackness.

It was night and she was alone in her bedroom.

But she knew she'd been summoned, without doubt.

Jared was in trouble.

She got out of bed and looked out the window. She could see the faint glow of the streetlights below. Her brother needed help.

Cara threw on a robe and opened her door. She was surprised by soft light coming from the living room. She followed it.

Her mother was on her knees at the sofa.

"Mom, what's going on?"

Dallas looked up. "I'm praying for your brother. He needs it."

"I know. I got the same message."

She took Cara's hands. "We need to cover him then."

Cara knelt by her mother's side. "Yes. Let's storm the throne together."

10.

"Told you to shut up!"

Pal approached the old guy. Jared saw the three others in the cell stepping away toward the back wall. What was happening? Did the old guy have a weapon of his own?

No. Nothing in his hands as he got to his feet. "In the name of Jesus Christ, and by his blood, I bind you."

Jared saw Pal's body go rigid.

"If you unbind me," Pal said, his voice lower now, "I will tear your eyes out."

"In the name of Christ," the old guy said, "what is your name?"

"Bel," Pal said.

Sweat burst out across Jared's palms. *Bel? What kind of name is that?*

"Will that statement stand for truth before the true and living God?" the old guy said.

"Yessss!" The voice from Pal answered, a voice unlike his own. It sounded like the answer was yanked out of him.

The other three inmates pressed themselves against the back wall as if pinned there. Freaked out, from the look of them. Just like Jared.

The old man leaned into Pal's face, and Pal just stood there, his arms at his sides. The man said, "In the name of Jesus Christ, and by his blood, you have no authority here. Jesus Christ is your Lord and conqueror. Confess it."

Jared could see Pal's back muscles flex, the skin rippling. The shank dropped out of his hand and hit the floor. That was the most amazing thing so far.

"Jesus Christ is my Lord and conqueror," the voice that was not Pal's said through Pal's mouth.

And then Pal screamed as loudly as any man Jared had ever heard. Jared practically jumped through the upper bunk.

The old man stood there, staring into Pal's screaming mouth, unflinching.

A deputy was at the cell, holding a club. "Hey hey hey! What's going on?" He pounded on the bars with his stick.

More screams rose from the cells along the module, screams of
wild fury, like a chain reaction of otherworldly shrieks. What was
happening? The evil that he'd felt earlier, the presence, he sensed
now in the fullest force, in this place, focused.

"Get me out of here," Jared said to the deputy, rolling off his
bunk. He picked up the shank and held it out. "He tried to kill me."

The deputy's eyes widened at the sight of the weapon. He drew
his own. "Nobody move," he ordered, then called for backup.

Pal, or whatever was in Pal, looked straight at the old guy, who
said, "In the name of Jesus Christ, I command you to go to Christ
right now, to be dealt with as he sees fit."

"No!" the Pal-thing screamed.

"Now!"

The deputy's eyes were crazy wide as he shouted, "Shut up!
Nobody move!"

The only one who moved then was Pal, as he fell to the floor of
the cell.

FIFTEEN

1.

Monday morning, after another night of little sleep, Dallas appeared in court with Jeff Waite. This time there was no press crowd, because this morning it was Jared Hamilton's appearance.

The judge was a woman, Maxine Novak. Grandmotherly, Dallas thought, if your grandmother packed heat.

"Mr. Hamilton, you missed your court appearance," she said. "We don't like that. We issue warrants when people do that, and we put them in jail. You don't want to go to jail again, do you, Mr. Hamilton?"

"No, ma'am."

"If it happens again, I'm going to have you put in jail and have you stay there, is that understood?"

"Yes, ma'am."

"Mr. Waite, does your client fully understand he can't do this?"

Jeff said, "He is fully informed, Your Honor. But another appearance won't be necessary."

Judge Novak put on her glasses, which hung by a beaded string from around her neck. "You have filed a demurrer."

"Yes."

The judge looked over toward the young DDA, a woman who looked to Dallas like she had just graduated from high school.

"Ms. Heilburn," Judge Novak said, "do you have a response?"

Young Heilburn cleared her throat. "We deny it."

"Deny what?"

"The demurrer?"

"Are you asking me or telling me?"

"Telling you?"

Judge Novak took her glasses off and rubbed her eyes. "Ms. Heilburn, I understand that you're new around here, but I can't make the arguments for you. The defense says that the facts as stated in

245

your accusatory pleading do not constitute a crime. Specifically, the police report taken at face value leaves out the element of driving. As this charge is driving under the influence, you have a little problem there, don't you?"

The girl looked flummoxed.

"The engine was running, Your Honor," the DDA said. "The defendant was the only occupant of the vehicle."

"Not good enough," Jeff Waite said. "Under *Mercer* and several other cases."

Ms. Heilburn almost raised her hand. "I would like the arresting officer to testify."

"And do what?" said the judge. "Contradict his own report? Ms. Heilburn, you know that your complaint must be able to stand on its own four corners. You've left out a corner."

"Then I would like to move to amend the complaint."

"You would like to?"

"Yes, Your Honor."

"Then make your motion."

Ms. Heilburn looked around as if seeking a cue card. "The People move ... to amend the complaint."

"Motion denied," Judge Novak said. "Anything else?"

"Your Honor," she mumbled, "may I have a recess to confer with the head deputy?"

"No. Anything else?"

The young DDA was now rendered speechless.

The judge said, "There being none, I am going to sustain the demurrer and dismiss the complaint. Further, I find that the defect cannot be remedied, and so sustain without leave to amend."

"Public intoxication!" Ms. Heilburn interjected.

"Too late." The judge looked at Jared. "This action is dismissed, but I don't want to see you in here again, young man. And I certainly don't want to get even a whiff that you and booze are doing anything together in a motor vehicle, is that clear?"

"Yes, Your Honor," Jared said.

"Then you are hereby released," Judge Novak said.

Out in the hallway, Jeff explained to Dallas the sudden turn of events. "We were just lucky to get this judge at this time. She loves to put baby DAs through the grinder."

"Why?" Dallas asked.

"She used to be a prosecutor herself, in charge of training. She thinks the office has gone downhill in that regard since she left. Anyway, if a deputy isn't doing the job, she trains them from the bench. She's really pro-prosecution. She just sees herself as making them tougher. The next time Ms. Heilburn comes to court, you know she's going to be ready."

"Thanks again, Jeff."

The lawyer put his hand on Jared's shoulder. "No more beer in the car, right?"

"Oh, yeah," Jared said. "Or any other time."

Dallas wasn't sure whether she was more surprised by the announcement or Jared's apparent sincerity.

"Tomorrow morning," Jeff said, "Ron changes his plea. Try to get some rest tonight."

2.

In the car, Jared seemed about to erupt. He told Dallas to pull over.

"Now?" she asked. They were just about to pull onto the freeway.

"Now," Jared said. "Please."

She passed the on-ramp and drove down Grand to Cesar Chavez, where she pulled to the curb. "What is it?"

"Mom, I have to tell you something."

"Yes?"

"Something that happened to me in jail. You're not going to believe it."

"At this point, I think I can believe just about anything." She hoped it was good news this time.

"I was put in a cell with five other guys."

"Five? In one cell?"

"Yeah, unbelievable huh? Five white guys, and four of them were supremacist types."

"Oh, Jared."

"One of 'em wanted to scare me into making a pledge to him, and when I wouldn't he tried to slit my throat."

Dallas knew about the conditions at the L.A. jail, the overcrowding, the gangs. But throat slitting? Her own son? *Thank you, God, that he's alive!*

"I don't know if he was just posing," Jared said, "but it sure seemed real to me. He was going to do it, and I dared him to."

"You did *what*?"

"That's part of it, Mom! I was ready to die, I wanted to die—"

"Jared—"

"No, listen. That's what I was thinking, you have to know that. But there was this other guy in there, an older guy, and he warned me. He said he knew Dad, or knew all about him, and that these guys wanted me in hell. It was crazy sounding."

Dallas couldn't help thinking of Roger Vernon. Talk of hell was not so crazy.

"So this one skinhead holds a shank to my throat. He had this look in his eyes that was so freaky, Mom. I think I know why."

She waited.

"I think there was a demon thing going on."

"Jared, I'm certain of it."

"He's holding the shank to my throat and then this old guy orders him to turn around. And he does, and this guy starts saying, 'In the name of Jesus and by his blood' and the other guy says his name is Bel—"

"Bel?"

"Yeah. And now I am freaking out. He tells the guy to confess that Jesus is his conqueror, and the guy does! He admits it. And then he screams, Mom. He screams so loud! And the other guys, the guys who were part of his set, they're all standing against the back wall like they want no part of this. And me, I'm ready to run right through the bars and get the—get out of there."

Dallas could not speak. The torrent of his words covered her.

"And then a guard comes, and I tell him what's going on, and now he is looking freaked out and orders that nobody move, and calls for help, but the old guy and Pal, that's the guy with the shank, which he's dropped at this point, they keep looking at each other. And then the guy commands that this demon, Bel I guess, go to Jesus to be dealt with. And the guy screams *No!* and then falls right to the floor. Boom. He's out."

Jared took a deep breath. "Mom, it was the weirdest thing I've ever seen."

"I believe that, Jared." She put her hand on his arm. "Do you have any doubt God protected you?"

"I don't know what to believe."

"Last night, Cara and I were praying for you. We both knew you were in trouble. We had no idea this was going on. We just knew you needed help, and look what happened. It's time, Jared."

"Time for what?"

"To reclaim your position in Christ."

Looking at her, eyes searching, he said, "I feel like it's too late."

"That's a lie and you know it. You know your Bible. You were raised in it. 'If we confess our sins, he is faithful and just and will forgive us.' "

" 'And purify us from all unrighteousness,' " Jared said.

She took his hand. "You do remember. That's God's Word, right?"

"I guess so."

"Don't guess. Believe it. Like you used to."

"I can't just turn it back on, Mom. Maybe in time—"

"Your time is now." She squeezed his hand. "Don't wait. Faith is a decision. Trust comes in when you're not sure. You've got something inside you that's never gone away. Now turn it back over to God, Jared."

She was shaking. Her prayers for him had been so fervent for so long she wasn't about to let him go. She'd wrestle him all day if she had to.

"What do you want me to say, Mom?"

"You know what to say. Just go to God, right now."

"Mom—"

"Try."

He sighed deeply. Then closed his eyes, still holding Dallas's hand. "Just do it, God," he said. "Just do it, okay? Whatever you know to do. I'm sorry. For everything. I really am. I been away from you so long and I want you back, I want ..."

Dallas looked at him. Tears were streaming down his face. And then he cried out, loud and mournful. She took him in her arms, held him close as he sobbed, the wetness becoming a baptism of forgiveness.

He kept his head buried on her shoulder until his crying softened and his breathing steadied. Dallas kissed his head and pressed her own wet cheeks on his hair.

They stayed like that for several minutes, Dallas stroking his back the way she used to comfort him when he was little.

Finally she said, "Through Jesus Christ our Lord."

Jared whispered, "Amen."

3.

Tomorrow, my life changes forever.

    It has already changed.

    Tomorrow, I take what is to come, whatever it may be.

    I trust in the Lord.

    I trust in the Lord for me.

    For Dallas.

    For Cara.

    And for Jared.

    Cover them all, Lord.

4.

Jared gunned his truck up Interstate 5, pushing the outer edge of the speed limit, staying within the spirit if not the letter of the law.

Spirit. That's what had changed. Maybe it wasn't too late for things to come out right.

In three hours he was knocking on Guillermo's door.

"What happened to you, dude?" Guillermo said.

"Where's Tiana?"

"She's gone, man."

"Where?"

Guillermo shrugged. "She didn't say nothin'. Took the kid and left."

"What did she leave in?"

"She walked. I don't know what she did after that."

"Why didn't you try to stop her?"

"I'm not no nanny, man. She said she was leavin'. What'm I supposed to do?"

"Did she say anything about where she might go?"

"Nothin'."

"Where's your mother, maybe she knows." Jared started to go inside.

Guillermo stopped him. "She doesn't know. She's asleep. What are you comin' around for, man? You're trouble. *Loco*. Leave us alone. Go bother somebody else."

"I got to say something, Guillermo."

Guillermo eyed him skeptically, but at least he didn't slam the door.

"I'm sorry, man," Jared said. "You're right, I was *loco*. You remember that time in the church, when I put paint on Jesus's face?"

"Oh, man, how could I forget that? I thought lightning was gonna come, man, fry all of us."

"I made peace with him," Jared said.

"Jesus?"

"Yeah."

With a narrowed gaze, Guillermo cocked his head slightly.

"I know," Jared said. "Coming from me it still sounds *loco*. But I did it, and I'm sorry for how I treated you."

"Hey, man, you were just a little whack, you know? I never thought you were a bad dude."

"I am a bad dude, but I got something working on the inside to change that. That's what I hope. I'm betting my life on it." He put out his hand. "Thanks for taking us in."

Guillermo shook it, smiled. "My mama, she woulda killed me if I didn't."

"Mama knows best."

Jared got in his truck and left.

He knew about a couple of homeless shelters in downtown Bakersfield. He checked them, but no one answering to the description of Tiana and Jamaal had been in either one.

He went to the bus station, but the cashier—who probably wasn't on duty at the time they would have purchased tickets anyway—wouldn't give out any information. Nobody gave out information anymore. It was too likely to result in a lawsuit.

Where would they have gone?

Maybe back to L.A.

He hadn't prayed in a long time, before that prayer of repentance in the car with his mother.

He sat in his truck outside the bus station, closed his eyes, and whispered, *God, help me find them.*

SIXTEEN

1.

Tuesday morning in court, with a buzzing press gathered in anticipation, Dallas watched as her husband's future was decided—where he would be housed and for how many years. Prison was a reality.

For her as well. Someone was about to get away with murder, and if that someone was never found, Ron would remain incarcerated for a crime he did not commit.

Ron was brought in, dressed in his orange jail coveralls, hands shackled. He looked at Dallas as the deputy unlocked his restraints. His face was peaceful, his body seemingly at rest.

Judge Harvey Carson entered the courtroom, and everyone stood. He looked fair but firm. He would have presided over the trial, had there been one, and Dallas thought he would have been a good choice.

"The court has considered a motion by the defendant to change his plea," Judge Carson said. "Is that still the defendant's wish, Mr. Waite?"

Jeff stood. "It is, Your Honor."

"Then I will advise your client. Mr. Hamilton, has your counsel talked to you about this change of plea?"

Ron's voice shook a little when he spoke. "Yes, he has, Your Honor."

Dallas bit down on her lip.

"You wish to withdraw your plea of not guilty?"

"Yes, Your Honor."

"And plead nolo contendere?"

"Yes, Your Honor."

"Did your counsel explain to you that a plea of nolo contendere has the exact force and effect as a plea of guilty?"

"Yes, sir."

"And that you will be waiving your constitutional right to a jury trial?"

"Yes, sir."

"And that you will also waive any evidentiary challenge to the truth of the underlying offense?"

"Yes."

"Do you also understand that a nolo plea to a felony offense *is* admissible in a civil action against you?"

"Yes, I do."

"Do you wish to waive your constitutional rights as I've described?"

"Yes, Your Honor."

"Very well. The court finds that the defendant understands the consequences of his change of plea. Withdrawal of the not-guilty plea is granted. Mr. Hamilton, to the sole count of murder in the second degree, how do you plead?"

"No contest," Ron said.

"All right. I find that the defendant has entered a plea of nolo contendere, knowingly and advisedly. Do the People wish to be heard?"

Mike Freton, the DA, said, "No, Your Honor."

"Is there any reason why sentence should not be imposed at this time?"

Jeff said, "No, Your Honor."

Mr. Freton said the same.

"Very well," Judge Carson said. "Mr. Hamilton, your plea is accepted by the court. You are hereby sentenced to state prison for the term of fifteen years to life. The facility will be decided by the sentencing authority. We are adjourned."

Judge Harvey Carson pounded his gavel on the bench. It exploded like a gunshot in the quiet courtroom.

Ron looked at Dallas one last time before he was ushered out. He mouthed the words *I love you.*

Before she could react the press was on her, several reporters seeking comment, shouting questions. This time she was ready.

Having appeared nationwide on Hank Dunaway's show, she was a public figure. God would use this moment.

"I will be happy to make a statement," she said. "I will make it outside on the street."

The press moved like a well-rehearsed army. In ten minutes she was standing in front of a knot of microphones and with the lights of several cameras directed her way.

"The decision made today by my husband is not an admission of guilt, though that is no doubt what many people will think. I can only tell you that I continue to believe my husband is innocent of murder, and that what's happening here is something far more insidious, and that the guilty party still walks the streets.

"I leave it to you to do your jobs. This story is not finished yet. But my husband and I have reached this decision together, because we believe that God is in control. I know that sounds like a cliché to many of you. Be that as it may, that is how we choose to live our lives. From this, our faith, there is no turning back. Thank you."

A flurry of shouted questions burst toward her. She shook her head and turned her back to the microphones, nearly bumping into a serious young woman.

"Mrs. Hamilton?"

"Yes?"

"I'm Tracy Harrington. I clerk for Mr. Freton. He sent me to ask if you'd like some help in getting your husband's things."

"Things?"

"I mean the evidence that was seized. Sheesh. I'm glad he didn't hear me say *things*. Usually this stuff—darn it, *evidence*—all goes back to the police station, but he has the box upstairs and wanted to save you the hassle of waiting."

"Where do I go?"

"Eighteenth floor. I'll take you."

Good. Someone else to usher her through the maze. She hoped she'd never have to be here again.

Just before entering the building, Dallas looked back at the dissolving swarm of reporters. It was like a fog clearing.

Then, through the fog, coming into clear focus across Temple Street, she saw an unmistakable face.

Chad McKenzie was looking directly at her.

He smiled. And clapped his hands.

2.

Mike Freton was already in his office when Dallas got there with Tracy. He had his coat off and was putting a file folder away in a metal drawer. Tracy left and closed the door behind her.

Mr. Freton offered her a chair. "I know that must have been hard for you, Mrs. Hamilton."

She didn't sit. "I know that my husband did not kill Melinda Perry."

The DA nodded wearily, as if he'd heard that particular line many times over the years, only with different names. "Can I offer you coffee or anything?"

"No, thanks. You ought to know that I was attacked recently by someone I knew over twenty-five years ago, a man named Chad McKenzie. And he's out on the street right now. He was looking at me just before I came up here."

Mr. Freton took a moment to process the information. "This guy is out there now?"

"Yes. Across the street."

"Did you report the attack to the police?"

"I reported it, yes. What do you suggest I do?"

The DA went to his window, which looked out on the south side of downtown. "Tell you what. I'll have courthouse security walk you to your car. If you can ID the man for the officer, he can call for LAPD. From that point on, it will be a police matter."

"Thank you."

He made a call. "It'll be just a few minutes."

"I appreciate your doing this."

He nodded. "I've seen many women in your position. None has handled herself as well as you have, especially considering all the publicity. I also want you to know that if any credible evidence is produced that would compel another look at this case, I'll take that look."

A few minutes later, a young man in a county safety police uniform entered Mike Freton's office. The DA gave the cardboard box containing Ron's computer to the officer and asked him to escort Dallas to her car.

She and the county officer took a special elevator to the ground level. That was nice. It definitely paid to know the right people around here.

3.

She called Detective Lacy from her car. After about a five-minute hold, he came on.

"Mrs. Hamilton, I was going to call—"

"I saw him. Chad McKenzie. Just now, at the courthouse—"

"Mrs. Hamilton—"

"Staring at me."

"I'm no longer on this matter."

"What?"

"I've been reassigned. The Rafe Bryan killing has been given to another team. That happens. I'll give you the contact information."

His voice trailed off in a way that indicated to Dallas he wanted to say more.

"Is there anything else you can tell me?" she asked.

There was a long pause. "There are some odd things. I really can't go into it all."

"Why not?"

"I wish I could."

Dallas pulled her car into Cara's apartment complex and parked. "Detective, please."

"I shouldn't do this, but I figure you deserve a break. I know you've been through a lot."

"What sort of break?"

"Gentri Land."

"Yes?"

"It turns out this is a corporation with quite a few real estate holdings in California, Nevada, and Arizona."

"What did Rafe Bryan have to do with any of that?"

"As far as I know, nothing. But Gentri Land owns certain commercial buildings in Chatsworth. And one of its tenants is LookyLu Productions."

Dallas tried to figure out what that all meant, but nothing clicked.

"Lu is clearly a factor here, but my money's on your guy McKenzie as the common denominator."

She shivered involuntarily. How would Chad be connected to Vic Lu? Well, other than by their salacious tastes?

"What should I do?" she asked.

"Not much you can do. Listen, if I hear anything that you need to know, I'll contact you. But for the time being ..."

"Yes?"

"Be careful."

4.

Jared turned his truck out toward Highway 99. As he drove around the perimeter of Bakersfield with country music playing on the radio—not the hard-core beat he used to play when getting high, but the twangy tunes about good-old boys in trucks like his—he felt both free and lost.

Free in the good way, the best way, the way that he'd learned as a kid from his mom and dad and the church he grew up in. But lost in another way, because he'd been getting used to the aimlessness of his old torment.

He knew that was partly an excuse, a reason he used to run away. But where would he run to now?

Just before hitting the highway he saw a billboard with a woman on it, a woman with a face and figure posed to stir the blood of any able-bodied male this side of puberty, and letters a mile high about a casino just a few miles up the road. What a great world it had become.

He'd fought for this world, this freedom, and it was worth it. Despite the naysayers and hate mongers, he would fight for freedom again. But when it was used for stuff like this, his throat ached. *Couldn't we do more with our most prized possession than this?*

He got on 99 and pointed himself back toward L.A.

5.

On Wednesday, Dallas went to the jail to see Ron for the last time before he would be remanded to the custody of the men's penal colony at Los Rios. All things considered, Jeff told her, it was a good place, not one of the harder places like San Quentin or Corcoran. Though it wouldn't be easy time, it wouldn't be hell on earth, either.

"I wish I could tell you how much I love you," he said. "I don't deserve you, but there it is. I want you to get on with your life without me, Dallas."

"Don't talk about that now. I'll be up to visit you."

"You don't have to."

"I want to. We're in this together. As strange as that may be."

"I also wish I could tell you what I've experienced in this place. Being in here has stripped away everything I was holding onto. I've been scraped. But free. Do you remember when we read the Narnia stories to the kids?"

"Of course."

"Remember that part where Eustace is being released from being a dragon? How painful yet freeing it was? Lewis had it right. That's exactly what I'm going through. And I'm grateful. I'm sure in eternity I'll look back and see this was the only way. And I'll give glory to God."

"He has worked in this, Ron. Jared has come back to the Lord."

Ron's eyes brightened. "How?"

She told him the story as Jared had given it to her, and of his prayer of repentance uttered in the car on their way back from his court appearance.

Ron broke down. Dallas couldn't keep her own tears from falling. When he was finally able to talk again, he said, "The guy who did this, who was in Jared's cell, you said he mentioned me to Jared?"

"That's right."

"Maybe he's the one."

"The one what?"

"Dallas, I kept getting messages delivered to me in here, Bible verses and the like. It was as if whoever wrote them knew me personally, knew exactly what to say."

"Ron, there's more to this. God's not finished."

He looked at her. "I have a long time to think about that."

6.

A long time to think ...

That's what both of them would have from now on. She thought about it all day and into the night.

Naturally, she couldn't sleep. She was starting to get very tired of not sleeping, of the toll it was taking on her body. She recited the twenty-third psalm in her mind, in the King James, but even that did not help.

She reached over and flicked on the light. The clock said 1:47 a.m. This was nuts. Were sleepless nights going to be her own prison sentence?

Something was bothering her. Connections needed to be made, but they were elusive, like scattering rodents.

She swung her legs over the bed and saw, sitting on the floor, the evidence box Mike Freton had given her.

She opened it.

More than Ron's laptop was in there. The box also included a sheaf of stapled papers with a series of numbers on it, and a few letters and receipts. But it was the laptop that held her attention.

The laptop that contained the images Ron had downloaded.

What to do with it? Destroy it? Take a hammer to it and reduce it to bits?

She took up the letters. Nothing of particular relevance, as far as she could see. One letter saddened her, though. It was from Karen and included a copy of the publisher's letter, outlining the terms of the deal.

The deal that was pulled when Ron was arrested.

Her mind snapped back to the laptop.

Should she boot it up? In a way, it was like having a murder weapon in the room. It was ominous and dangerous and a threat.

The stapled papers. It didn't look like something seized from Ron's office. It was a list of a series of numbers that looked like a World War II encryption. But some of the numbers appeared to be dates. Random dates, in no particular pattern. At least, not that she could see.

What was it? She leafed through all five pages, her eyes crossing. She was about to throw it back in the box when she got to the very last page. The numbers filled only half a page.

Then, at the very bottom, was a notation:

Tomassi, L. 4903940/DASR45–4/13

Tomassi, L. Obviously a name.

She knew she wasn't going to sleep, so why not spend the morning hours trying to find out who this Tomassi was?

The answer could be in Ron's contact list.

On his laptop.

But it wouldn't turn on. No battery life. Now what would she do? Wander Cara's apartment like a somnambulant ghost? Instead, she padded down to Cara's study with the laptop. Cara had a similar model, with a power cord. In two minutes Ron's laptop glowed.

Dallas shuddered at what secrets she might find there.

Turn it off and forget about it. This is the past now. Nothing good can come from pursuing this.

But she kept looking.

She found his contacts list and opened it. Looked under the *T* tab.

No Tomassi.

She went to the *search* window and searched for *Tomassi* as a file name or part of the contents. She got the same message each time: *Search is complete. There are no results to display.*

Now she was fully awake, her mind engaged. She was going to look like a wreck in the morning. Wait, it *was* the morning.

Don't go nutty.

She logged on to the Internet. When in doubt, Google. She tried Googling *Tomassi* but came up with nearly 100,000 hits. Now *that* was a cure for insomnia. She tried to add the letter *L* to the search, but that only narrowed things down to 44,800. Sure, only take half the morning with those. She looked at the notation again. What if she tried typing in the number?

She typed in *4903940/DASR45 – 4/13.*

Nothing.

She kept staring at the code. Maybe the letters meant something. Some sort of organization maybe. What did she have to lose? It was getting on toward two thirty, and she was not going to sleep.

She typed in *DASR.*

And got 19,300 results.

That seemed strange. But she scrolled through a few and found it to be an abbreviation with several possible meanings, like Digital Air Surveillance Radar and Direct Access Service Requests.

Another dead end.

She almost logged off. But then she gave it one last try. She typed in DASR45.

And got one result.

She clicked on the link.

It took her to the website of the Los Angeles County District Attorney's Office. On a page titled "Press Releases."

An old release, from last year.

Now she wasn't just awake, her body was humming. She scanned the release, which was about a conviction being upheld on appeal. Then she got to the final section.

The court found that the error was harmless, and that introduction of internal reports from the District Attorney's office, like the DASR45 that was admitted in this case, were not inherently prejudicial.

Internal report from the District Attorney's office? That's what the form was. It must be a mistake that she had it. But what did it mean?

7.

Dallas presented herself at the DA's office at ten the next morning and asked to see Mike Freton. The receptionist made a call and asked Dallas to wait. A few minutes later, Freton's clerk, Tracy Harrington, came in.

"Hello, Mrs. Hamilton. Mr. Freton's in court. Is there something I can do for you?"

"If we could find a place to talk."

"Sure."

Dallas followed Tracy down a narrow hallway lined with filing cabinets to a little cubicle.

"My domain," Tracy explained.

"Nice."

"You're being kind. Someday I hope to graduate into a real shoebox. Coffee?"

"Do you have any that's really strong?"

"Always. We use it to reroof the buildings."

Tracy got two Styrofoam cups of coffee. And she was right. Definitely heavy-duty caffeine.

Dallas put the DASR report on Tracy's small desk. "I believe this was given to me by mistake."

Tracy picked it up, flipped through it. "Oops. You're right. This is ours."

"What is it?"

"District Attorney Summary Report. Subject number 45."

"I'm not in any trouble, right?"

"Oh, no."

"Can you tell me what it was for? The only thing I could figure out was that it's a report made out by someone named Tomassi for your office."

Tracy's face broke out into a huge smile. "Now that's funny."

"What is?"

"It's Lucas. Lucas Tomassi."

"You know him then?"

"He's my boyfriend."

"You're kidding."

"Nope. We're just one big happy family around here."

"He prepared that?"

Tracy nodded. "He's one of our IT guys. Computer whiz. Except when it's my computer, then he seems to take his sweet—"

"Could I talk to him?"

"You want to talk to Lucas?"

"Please."

Tracy frowned. "About this?"

"May I?"

"I don't know, I really don't—"

"Please. I've already looked this over. I just want to ask him about it. You can be here. If he's not supposed to say something, you can stop him."

Tracy smiled again. "I love doing that. Okay, Mrs. Hamilton."

Ten minutes later, a man of about thirty with stylishly unkempt hair and black-rimmed glasses popped into the cubicle.

"You rang?" he said.

"Lucas, this is Mrs. Hamilton."

He shook her hand. "I know. I recognize you from the news."

"That's my lot now, I guess," Dallas said.

"Bites, doesn't it?" Lucas said. "I mean, people who don't want to go public are forced to, while a bunch of people we'd rather not see more of are still out there."

"Mrs. Hamilton wanted to ask you some things about your DASR."

"Which one? I only do about a hundred a week."

"This one."

Tracy handed the report to Lucas. He flipped through it quickly. "How did you get this?"

"It was in the box that Mr. Freton prepared for me."

"This is internal. You shouldn't have it."

"It was a mistake, okay?" Tracy said. "But the case is officially over now. So don't get bent."

Lucas Tomassi issued an audible sigh, his response to Tracy. He looked at Dallas. "You sure you want to know?"

"Please."

"It's a log of all those images that we found on your husband's computer, okay? Sorry."

She had suspected it. "But what do the numbers mean?"

"They're just a collection of the dates the images were made, if they were part of the original download. And a code number for each image that I put in. For indexing purposes."

"Some job," Tracy said.

"Hey, I just work here." He looked down at his report. "And some other information like individual file size, a couple things I forgot about, yada yada—"

Dallas rubbed her temples.

"—files were downloaded, March 23, yada yada, April 11th I entered some of my own personal notations, in code of course, brilliantly conceived by me—"

"You're so brilliant," Tracy said.

With her head starting to throb, Dallas said, "Anything else besides the pornography report?"

"Nope. That's really all this is. My notations, sitting all day long and entering numbers. It's what I do all day. That's why Tracy, who makes about twice as much as I do, is taking me out to dinner tonight."

"In your dreams," Tracy said. She snatched the DASR from Lucas. "Now go back to your cage."

He bobbed his eyebrows. "I'm thinking Italian. *Ciao.*"

And then he was gone.

"Thanks for bringing this back." Tracy opened a drawer and put the report inside. "I know this whole thing hasn't been easy."

"You do know that somebody leaked this information to the press."

She watched Tracy's face carefully. The young clerk seemed stunned into silence.

"It had to come from this office, or from the police," Dallas added.

"You're not suggesting that Lucas ..."

"Maybe I'm just asking you for help, if you know."

"The case is over. I don't see how it's relevant anymore. If I did know."

"I'm not sure the case *is* over. At least for me."

Tracy took a long time before answering. "At this point, Mrs. Hamilton, I think it best that I not say anything further."

A heavy curtain fell. This scene was over.

"Thanks for the coffee." Dallas stood up. "I can find my way out."

§.

Dallas did not go to her car. Instead, she walked a couple of blocks to Los Angeles Street and entered Parker Center, home base of the Los Angeles Police Department. A large square white building, it was both solid and forbidding, the hub of all force and might in L.A. Which is what Dallas needed behind her.

At the front desk, she gave her name and asked to see Detective William Lacy. The uniformed officer who manned the desk picked up a phone and punched a couple of buttons.

"Dallas Hamilton to see Lacy," the officer said. He waited a few moments, then said, "Thanks," and hung up.

"Not in," he said. "You want to leave him a message?"

"Do you know where I can reach him?"

"You can leave a message, ma'am."

"Never mind," she said. She returned to the street, back to the public parking lot behind the courthouse. Dallas felt like a cork bobbing on a human sea. People were everywhere, and their movements all seemed random. That's what life was like now. No order. Questions, and no place to go for answers. Detective Lacy was a shot in the dark anyway. He wasn't even on the Rafe Bryan case anymore, so that probably settled it. No more help from the police.

Now what?

She got back to her car and paid the ten bucks it cost every time she came down here. The parking-lot business in Los Angeles, that was the business to be in. Maybe she could open one up and sit in a kiosk for the next twenty years, raking it in.

She thought about driving to the ocean again, finding a quiet spot for prayer. Instead she got on the freeway and headed toward Hillside. She would find someone to pray with her up there. Hopefully Lisa or Bob. He was her pastor now. Odd, but why not?

She listened to smooth jazz on the radio and tried to quiet her brain. The thoughts pinging around in there were more likely to drive her crazy than to the truth. She would find the truth at Hillside, at her church. That was the place she could get centered again.

She exited the freeway and noticed a flashing red light right behind her. To her chagrin, it was her car that had been targeted.

Terrific. What had she done? Speeding? No way. Broken taillight? She hoped the cop would show mercy. The last thing she needed in her life right now was a ticket to pay.

Then she noticed that it wasn't a black and white behind her, nor a Highway Patrol car. It was an unmarked vehicle.

Containing Detective William Lacy.

"I wondered when you were going to get off the freeway," he said when he got to her window.

"You followed me?"

"I didn't want us to be seen at Parker. We need to talk."

"You want to talk to *me*?"

"Yes."

"Then let's talk."

"Not here. Is there a place we can go, out of the way?"

She thought a moment. "Yeah, a little coffee shop called Benny's. It's a couple blocks from here."

"I'll follow you."

"You do that well."

Benny's was a diner Dallas used to take the kids to when they were little. It had a truck-stop feel to it, which Dallas liked. No pretensions. And the waitresses—they still called themselves *waitresses* here—never let coffee cups stay empty.

They took an empty booth in the back and ordered coffee. Lacy took his black.

"So what's going on?" Dallas said.

Lacy took a sip, put his cup on the table, and held it with both hands. "There's something very strange about Gentri Land Corporation," he said. "I did some follow-up information on it after we talked on the phone last. We have ways of getting information, of course. But I kept running into a wall with this Gentri Land."

"You said Vic Lu is connected."

"He leases property from them. But I looked into some of the other properties connected to Gentri Land. It's all over the map, commercial real estate and the like."

"Anything else?"

"I'm not sure at the moment. But I've got a hunch that there's more going on than we know."

"That wouldn't surprise me."

"I'm glad to hear you say that."

She looked at him.

"Mrs. Hamilton, what I am about to tell you needs to remain just between us, is that understood?"

"Yes, of course."

"I may need your help."

"*My* help?"

"Let me explain. I'm investigating a missing-persons case. We suspect murder. And the possibility that Vic Lu is involved."

"But what can I do?"

"I'm not at liberty to say anything else at the moment, but at the proper time I wonder if you would consider wearing a wire."

"You mean tape somebody?"

"Exactly."

"Like on television?"

"It happens in real life too."

She considered this for a moment, seeing herself in a dark room with all sorts of equipment on her body. "I don't know if I'm cut out for that."

"Believe me, I won't let you do it if I think it would in any way be dangerous for you."

Dallas thought about it again, a sip of coffee lubricating the mental gears. Finally she looked at Lacy and said, "Will you help me if I help you?"

"How do you want me to help you?"

"I want you to help me clear my husband's name."

Lacy frowned. "Isn't it a little late for that?"

"Not if he's innocent."

"You don't think he's guilty?"

"I know he isn't."

"Mrs. Hamilton, you know that as a police officer I don't have control over the cases assigned to me, and so I—"

"You have spare time, don't you?"

Detective Lacy smiled. "Oh, yeah. Tons."

"Then hear me out."

"Go."

At least he didn't shut the door entirely. "This possible murder. Is Vic Lu himself the suspect?"

"I can't say one way or the other."

"But that's why you thought about me, isn't it?"

"Maybe."

"Listen, what if Vic Lu was the one who murdered Melinda Perry?"

Lacy's eyebrows went up, and Dallas knew she'd struck something.

She pounced. "You know something I need to know. What is it? Please."

"You're very perceptive, Mrs. Hamilton. You'd make a good cop."

"I just want to get some sleep. Can you talk to me?"

Lacy stared into his coffee for a moment. "Lu is smart. We have to proceed very carefully. It's one of his girls who's gone missing. A girl by the name of Patricia Hood."

"Who was she?"

"Another one of the countless girls who come out here for fame and money and end up with some very bad people. I'm sure she had this fantasy floating out there in front of her and tried to grab it. She even took a stage name."

"A stage name?"

"Yeah. She called herself Gilda."

SEVENTEEN

1.

My cell mate, Ernesto Ruiz, killed two men in a bar fight in San Bernardino.

In the past, they would have had us segregated. The prisons, like the jails, did that to keep order. But the California Supreme Court came down with a decision that said they couldn't do that in state prisons anymore, so I get to be part of this grand experiment here.

The two of us didn't start out with racial reconciliation at the top of the agenda.

"You got somethin' against Latinos, bro?" That was the first thing Ernesto said to me.

"No way," I said. "If it wasn't for the Latinos, there'd be no California." I tried to say it with a smile, but my lips quivered.

Ernesto was twenty-six and, while not tall, solid as a bull. "That right?"

I gave him a short history of the California missions. "That's why that stupid decision in Los Angeles a couple years ago about taking the cross off the city seal was so misguided."

"You talk like college, man."

"Sorry."

"No, it's good. I been working toward my high school equivalent."

"Great."

"Doesn't mean I won't smoke you if you tick me off."

I looked at him, not feeling scared at all. For some odd reason.

Then he smiled. "Just messin' with you, bro. Did you really kill that chiquita?"

"Would you believe me if I said no?"

"Everybody in here's innocent, man, ain't you heard?"

"The answer is no," I said.

"Why'd you plead?"

"To get it over with. To get some peace."

"In here?"

"You'd be surprised."

"You gonna need somebody to watch your back."

"I got somebody."

His look was skeptical.

"Jesus," I said.

Ernesto shook his head. "Lots of guys got Jesus, and lots of 'em end up facedown. He don't seem like enough."

"What if I told you he was?"

"I wouldn't believe it, man."

"We got lots of time to talk about it, don't we?"

He put a finger in my face. "Don't push me, man."

On Sunday they were in church together—Dallas, Jared, and Cara. Almost a complete family.

It would have to do. The rebuilding would begin here.

Here at Hillside.

Dallas allowed herself to fully engage in the worship and the singing. Quincy, the worship leader at Hillside, always did a good job with the music. What she liked particularly was that he sometimes included an old hymn. She loved the hymns, and Quincy did too. He was thirty-five, a former gang member, and everyone said he could have been a rap star. Instead, he gave his gifts to the Lord.

Today, just before the sermon, Quincy led the congregation in "It Is Well with My Soul," which had always been one of Dallas's favorites. The message of grace in it was, she thought, as deep as any. And it all came rushing over her as she sang.

> *When peace like a river, attendeth my way,*
> *When sorrows like sea billows roll;*
> *Whatever my lot, Thou hast taught me to say,*
> *"It is well, it is well with my soul."*

Dallas soared with the words. But then the most remarkable thing happened. She heard Jared's voice. Jared, who never liked to sing, who never did after age thirteen or so, was singing now.

> *And, Lord, haste the day when our faith shall be sight,*
> *The clouds be rolled back as a scroll,*
> *The trump shall resound and the Lord shall descend,*
> *Even so, it is well with my soul.*

Dallas praised God silently for the grace of the moment, the spiritual reunion that had come to her son at last.

Bob Benson came to the pulpit subdued. But his sermon seemed touched by the same Spirit that had moved the congregation. He was spot-on this day, giving a message of hope.

And he finished with words about Ron.

"As you all know," he said, "we have gone through what I would call a family crisis here. Our beloved pastor has been sent to prison. You well know the story, but we must also remember another story, the greatest story ever told, that any sin we commit can be forgiven. Ron Hamilton has been forgiven. His wife, Dallas, who is here today with us, has told me all about it.

"I remember back when Dallas came to see me at the church a couple of days after Ron was arrested ..."

Yes, Dallas remembered that day too. It was her first visit to the church after Ron was taken away by the police.

"... and we sat in my office and I remember there was a lot of media attention, and we even had some threats called in. I was glad we had Dave Rivas looking out for our security, I can tell you that ..."

Dave, who managed the security system that Dallas had helped select.

"... we sat in my office and prayed for Ron and for God to watch over this church during this troubled time and ..."

Trouble came in bunches, in search warrants and leaks to the press and—

"... we left it in his hands ..."

—Ron was arrested on Monday.

"... and that's what we're going to do here today ..."

Dallas didn't hear the rest.

Someone tapped her shoulder. Jared.

"Mom, are you all right?"

"Wait here," she managed to say. And then she got up and left the sanctuary.

§

"Dave."

Dave Rivas looked up from the Bible he was reading. On Sundays Dave went to the early morning worship service, then spent time doing his Bible reading in the security office.

He got up to greet her. As usual, he wore his LAPD cap. "Mrs. Hamilton, it's good to see—"

"Dave, I have to ask you a question."

"Sure."

"How far back do you keep security tapes and records?"

"Everything's digital. We have archives back as far as when we set up the system."

"Can we look up a certain date?"

"Of course. That's why we got this bad boy. Remember when we did the system research? You liked that aspect, even though it cost us."

"Well, now we get to see if it was worth it."

"Okay, what date?"

"March 23." That was the date that shot into her mind at church, the date Lucas Tomassi had mentioned in passing at the DA's office, talking about his report. The date the files were downloaded, he said. One problem. The 23rd was a Wednesday, two days after Ron's arrest.

Dave tapped away at a keyboard in front of a large monitor. A series of thumbnail pictures came up showing various views of the church grounds.

"You can scan these first," Dave said, "and take a look at the time markers. Any time in particular?"

"After about seven o'clock at night. Can you isolate those?"

He did it. Another series of thumbnails. One of the parking lot. Dallas pointed to it. "Can we look at this view at various times?"

"Are beans good for your heart?"

"Huh?"

"Bad joke. Of course we can."

Dave brought up shots from the parking-lot cam, the time markers broken at fifteen-minute increments. The number of cars in the lot dwindled as time passed.

"Can we skip ahead?"

"Sure. Next set."

This set began with four or five cars in the shot and ended with only one car.

Dallas realized she'd been holding her breath.

"So," Dave said jovially, "is this system worth it or what?"

"Oh, yeah," she said, her heart dropping like a brick.

4.

Dallas sat in her car outside the Bensons' house for two hours, waiting for them to get back from church. She tried to talk herself out of what she saw, create a reasonable explanation. She couldn't, because there was only one conclusion, one thing that made sense.

When the Bensons pulled into the driveway Dallas got out of her car and met them on the lawn.

"Hey, girl, what's up?" Lisa said, concern etched on her face.

"You didn't come to rebuke me about my sermon today, I hope," Bob said jokingly.

"Can we go inside?" Dallas said.

They did, and Dallas sensed their awkwardness at her unannounced visit.

They went into the living room, but before Bob sat down Dallas said, "Would you mind if I talked to Lisa privately a moment?"

"I've always thought that whole girl-talk thing was a myth," Bob said with a forced smile. "But I know the odds are against me here. I'll be in the study."

Lisa sat on the sofa and patted it for Dallas to sit next to her.

"I'm so glad you came over," Lisa said. "I've been wanting to get together with you again. It's time for us to—"

"Lisa, were you ever going to tell me about the computer?"

"Computer?"

"Ron's computer."

Lisa's face froze.

"Lisa, I know what you did. I know about the porn on Ron's computer." She watched Lisa's reaction carefully. Her hope that Lisa would crack immediately faded.

"I'm sorry, Dallas, but you're going to have to spell this out for me."

"Ron's computer was taken from the church on the twenty-fourth of March."

"I sort of remember."

"Ron was arrested on the twenty-first."

Lisa said nothing. Her face remained impassive.

"I came to the church on the twenty-third. I saw you there, and I met with Bob. We prayed in his office. He said he was going off to a speaking engagement that evening."

"Sure, I remember that."

"Do you remember staying at the church and downloading pornography onto Ron's computer?"

Lisa's noncommittal expression morphed into cold steel. "That's a horrible thing to say."

"We have the security video. Bob drove off from the parking lot at exactly 9:17 p.m. You didn't leave until 11:33. There is a very clear shot of you getting in your car. I was at the DA's office. They have a report saying downloading was done on Ron's computer on the twenty-third. That would've been very hard for Ron to do, considering he was locked up. Shall I go on?"

Lisa stared at her for a very long time. Then, almost imperceptibly, Lisa began to tremble. But she tried to speak with conviction. "Ron had an affair and he didn't tell you about it. But I knew. I knew about Amy Shea. Do you know how hard it was for me to sit in church Sunday after Sunday listening to him? Knowing what he did to you? Knowing that you wouldn't do anything even if you knew? And then ..."

"And then he was arrested, and you thought you'd take the opportunity to make sure he was ruined."

"Dallas, he was living a lie."

"Like you are now."

Lisa shifted on the sofa, her body language stiff, as if gathering her defenses. "What do you intend to do?"

"Did Bob know?"

Lisa shook her head. "Please don't say anything, he's—"

"He's got to be told."

"Dallas, please—"

"You hurt more than just my family. You hurt the church."

"We can work something out."

Dallas stood. "I'll give you until tomorrow. Tomorrow I call Bob myself."

§.

Dallas was shaking when she got back in her car. Bitterness and pain were a lethal mix. The only note of relief was finding out that all those images weren't there because of Ron. She knew now his confession of downloading then deleting pornography was sincere. It has been Lisa who was responsible, sad Lisa whose act was driven by ambition. She wanted to seal Ron's doom in the eyes of the church and the public. Leaving a wide-open door for Bob to walk through and take over as Hillside's leader.

But Dallas was also certain that Lisa's desire to ruin Ron did not mean she had anything to do with Melinda Perry's killing. Melinda's real killer was still out there, and Dallas sensed that her opportunity to uncover the truth had not expired. But there was a connection she couldn't quite make. She was certain it had something to do with what Detective Lacy had told her.

She called him from the car and, surprisingly, he picked up.

"It's Dallas Hamilton," she said. "Can you meet me?"

"When?"

"Now."

A short pause. "Name the place."

She chose an isolated corner of a park in Chatsworth, as far west as you could go in the Valley without burrowing into a mountain. She'd often come here with the kids when they were little. It was secluded and still and dotted with oak trees. A natural spot for a game of hide-and-seek.

Dallas got there first and waited by one of the gnarly trees she actually remembered hiding behind on one outing. Jared was eight or nine, and when he couldn't find her, he got scared. He said it was because he thought he was being chased by someone. She remembered that clearly.

"Don't leave me alone!" he cried, clinging to her. She vowed she never would.

Detective Lacy walked across the large grassy area before the trees twenty minutes later, looking around. No one else was visible in the park. Dallas stepped out from behind the tree and waved.

"I like this place," he said. "Beats my office."

Dallas was in no mood for small talk. "If you want me to wear this wire, I need to know who and why. I want the details."

He nodded. "Let me tell you about it in a certain way, starting with Gentri Land. Are you ready?"

"Do I need to be sitting down or something?"

"You can lean against the tree if you have to."

She did. "I'm ready."

Detective Lacy looked around once, then back at Dallas. "Gentri Land is a legitimate corporation, at least from the outside looking in."

"And Vic Lu leases property from them."

"More than that. He's an investor. He pumps a lot of money into the corporation. Legally. In return, he shares in the holdings."

"So where's the illegal part?"

"We don't know yet if there is. But we're getting closer."

"How?"

"We've managed to identify a few of the principals. I have a list of names I'd like you to take a look at." He fished a paper out of his pocket, unfolded it, and handed it to Dallas.

There were five names on the page. She didn't recognize any of them.

"There is something that all these names have in common, besides Gentri Land Corporation," he said. "Each one of them was a major contributor in the last citywide election. And each one of them gave the maximum to one candidate."

She knew who it was even before he said it. "Bernie Halstrom."

The detective nodded.

"What's it mean?" she asked.

"Nothing yet. It's all perfectly legal. On paper. But it could be pointing to a fraud underneath."

"Fraud?"

"What if Gentri Land was a front to channel political funds into a campaign? In this case, Halstrom's. The contributions come from individuals, but Gentri Land compensates them for their contributions."

"I'm not sure I follow that."

"If Gentri Land has one principal investor, he could make a way around the campaign-contributions limit. He pumps money into the corporation, the corporation pumps it out to these individuals, the individuals hand it over to Bernie Halstrom's campaign."

She tried to ignore the sinkhole opening up in her chest. Disappointment, mostly. Bernie Halstrom was just like any other politician trying to skirt the rules. Maybe she was naïve to have thought it could be any other way.

"You want me to go in to see Bernie with a wire on?"

"If you'd be willing."

"I don't think I can do that. I'm not a very good liar."

"I'm not asking you to lie."

"In a way, you are. I would be betraying a trust."

"Just as Bernie has betrayed his public trust."

"I suppose that's true, but he's also been a friend."

"Are you sure about that?"

"What's that supposed to mean?"

Detective Lacy sighed. "I guess you trust me too. I haven't been completely forthcoming with you."

How many more disclosures were there going to be? She braced herself. "You can start now if you like."

He nodded. "There is one other name associated with Gentri Land, someone who is technically the chief executive officer. His name is Walter Channing."

"I don't know that name either."

"No need for you to know. It's not his real name anyway. His real name is Cheong."

"It sounds Chinese."

"Vietnamese. And he is the cousin of Vic Lu."

It was all a little too complex, a spider's web of sticky threads. "What do you think all this means?"

The detective leaned forward as if he didn't want anyone to hear him, even though they were alone. "It means that Gentri Land may be a way for Vic Lu to pay off Bernie Halstrom, hold his public antiporn campaigns at bay."

"When this all started," she said, "you told me Vic Lu had something to do with Gilda's disappearance."

"We don't know that for certain."

"But you think so. And maybe you think Bernie might be involved."

"That's why I've asked you to wear a wire."

EIGHTEEN

1.

Dallas set up a meeting the next day.

When she called Bernie, she made it sound important, which is exactly what it was. When he offered to pick her up, she accepted with trepidation. But meeting on his terms could get him loose enough to admit something that would help Detective Lacy make his case, which might lead to the answer on what really happened to Melinda Perry.

Lacy had her come to West Valley station, where a female officer rigged her with a wire that was a marvel of modern technology. It would record five hours on a digital media the size of a penny. She only had to be within five feet of Bernie Halstrom.

He picked her up in front of Cara's apartment. Derek, his driver, smiled and nodded as he opened the door for her.

Bernie shook her hand warmly as she slid in beside him.

"To the feed store, Derek," he said.

"Where are we headed?" Dallas asked.

"You'll see. Sit back and relax. I'm glad we have this chance to talk."

Talk away, as much as you want. She had prepared as best she could for this moment. Over and over in her mind she played out the scene: How Bernie would be the same old Bernie, glad-handing her, expressing concern. How she would have to pretend to believe it and keep her face from screwing up into a resemblance of a gargoyle.

This was going to be a lot harder in actual fact.

"I've been wanting to bring something up with you," Bernie said.

"Oh?"

"Now that Ron's case is off the front page," he said, "I thought you might like to have something to help carry on his work, a project."

"What sort of project?"

"I'm organizing a new citizens' committee to inform me on matters from a grassroots level. Everything from schools and parks to the cracks in the sidewalk. I feel like I need to have this network, and I want you to head it up."

"Me?"

"You."

"That's a lot of responsibility."

"I think you can handle it. I know you can. Will you at least consider it?"

I'll consider it before I reject it. "Sure."

"Good. I was hoping you'd say that. Maybe get Hillside involved in this. Bob and Lisa Benson."

Dallas closed her eyes for a moment. "I'm sure they'll be happy to hear from you."

"Are you feeling all right?"

She looked at him. "Just tired." Through the heavily tinted windows of the limo she could see they were heading south on Topanga, toward the canyon.

"Where are we headed?" she asked.

"My surprise. A little place in Malibu overlooking the ocean. You'll love it."

"Dinner?"

"You object?"

"No, of course not." A casual social setting might also serve her cause.

"Now," Bernie said, "what was it you wanted to see me about? You sounded very concerned on the phone, like it's something I should know."

Here it was. Detective Lacy had prepped her with the questions to ask. Now she had to make it all seem natural.

"Bernie, do you know a man named Walter Channing?"

"Sure, I know Walter. He's a great supporter of mine. You know him?"

"Not personally."

"What brought him to your attention?"

"The police."

"Police? Why?"

"They wouldn't say."

Bernie paused, his mind obviously working away. Finally, he said, "What was the nature of their questions to you?"

"Apparently he has some sort of connection with Vic Lu and a corporation called Gentri Land. Do you know what that means?"

That was it. Now was the time to watch his reactions. The tape would catch his words and, the police hoped, reveal something below the surface. Not an admission, that was too much to hope for. But statements that could be contradicted by physical records—phone calls, notes of meetings, computer files.

His face was clothed with concern. He couldn't hide it. But the wire could not capture visuals.

Bernie reached for a button on the side-door console. A black glass screen whirred upward, separating them from his driver.

"I want to keep this just between us," he said. "You must tell me everything that was said to you."

Dallas tried to remain calm. "That's really all. They asked vague questions on a lot of things."

"What other things?"

"I don't know if I'm supposed to say."

"Did the police tell you not to say anything?"

"Sort of."

"What do you mean, sort of? Dallas, please try to be clear."

"I don't know anything other than that, Bernie. Is there something wrong? You seem to be upset."

"I have political enemies, Dallas. You know that. Someone could be trying to manufacture something here. And you're being used."

"I don't think so."

He shook his head and put his hand on her shoulder. "We've known each other a long time, haven't we?"

Why was he touching her? Was this the gesture of an old friend, or something more?

"Yes, we have," Dallas said.

"And we trust each other, right?"

"Of course." She tried to sound as sincere as possible. Instead, her words rang hollow.

He kept his hand on her shoulder, patting it softly. "You know, I'm having to deal with so much. I feel I'm being accused of something I did not do. Some association with Gentri Land and Vic Lu, of all people. You don't believe that, do you, Dallas?"

She didn't know what to believe. She wanted to get out of the limo and hitchhike home.

"I'll listen to anything you have to say, Bernie."

"I'm sure you will. And who else?"

"Excuse me?"

His hand slipped down her back. "Who else is listening, Dallas?"

With a violent thrust, he pressed one hand on her mouth, pushing her head back into the seat. With his other hand he ripped her blouse. It tore away like paper. She was half-exposed now, but the shock of his attack froze her.

In one more second he tore the wire from her body and dangled the apparatus from his hand.

"Dallas, Dallas." He shook his head. "I can't believe you'd do this."

She was not going to put up any pretenses now. She let her voice give vent. "What about you, Bernie? All those years lying to my face? How could you do that?"

"Because I know you, and I know you don't get it. Politics is about compromise, and sometimes you have to do things to get the power to get things done. Good things. It balances out. But you and Ron never understood compromise."

"Lies, that's what I don't understand."

"You think I'm not doing good for the community? You think my record isn't something to be proud of?" His voice was rising. "I'll stand shoulder to shoulder with anybody for the benefits I've brought my constituents."

"Like Vic Lu." She gripped her blouse and held it together across her chest.

"Yeah, believe it or not, Dallas, he's a member of the community too. Get off your high horse. He's not a lawbreaker."

"You were supposed to change that. Instead, you used Ron and me to put up a front."

"Water under the bridge at this point. What matters now is what we're going to do about you."

She shuddered, her insides tensing like a fist. It was all so surreal, looking into the face of a man she thought she knew, thought was good, now speaking in a voice that froze her to the bone.

Bernie picked up the handset. "Derek, slight change of plans. Go back. We need to see our mutual friend. And make sure no one follows us."

He put the handset down and looked at Dallas. "Needless to say, dinner is off."

2.

Night had always been Jared's favorite time for driving. Especially on the quiet ribbon of Interstate 5. It was peaceful in its way, a place to think.

And he had plenty to think about after the visit to his father up north.

The prison at Los Rios was one of the older facilities in the California system. As such it had an almost nostalgic appearance, with its four corner guard towers right out of some old Warner Bros. movie, and a large water tower overlooking the razor-wire fence.

The visitors' room was a row of hard metal stools before wire screens. This time he would hear his father's voice for real, not over a phone line. And he wondered just how he was going to react to it.

Jared was drying his palms on his shirt when his father came through an inner door. He was dressed in denim pants and blue work shirt. He looked more like a farmer than a prisoner.

He sat opposite Jared, smiling. "You look well," he said.

"You look skinny," Jared said.

"It's a new thing—the felony accusation diet."

His father's attempt at humor went past his head like a stray bullet. "Why did you do it, Dad? I mean, plead guilty?"

"No contest," Ron corrected, then sighed. "I just chose not to fight anymore. And in a way I'm responsible for what happened to that girl."

"But you're not responsible. You didn't kill her."

"The evidence was going to convince a jury that I did."

"I don't want you in here." Jared felt a sudden burning behind his eyes. He fought for control. "I spent a lot of time mad at you, Dad. I guess I want a chance to work it out. Kind of hard when you're up here."

Ron didn't say anything for a long moment. He swallowed several times, his Adam's apple rising, falling. Finally he said, "Why don't we start with one step at a time. You know how to write. So let's do it that way and see what happens. Will you do that for me? Write letters?"

"Sure, Dad. I'll write up a storm."

And he would. As he drove back toward L.A., Jared thought about all the things he'd say in those letters, how he'd write and be totally honest and ask for forgiveness. How he wouldn't stop writing until he had his father back in his life again, because when he got right down to it, family was the only thing that really mattered in this world. Physical family, church family, any family where people came together because they needed someone to hang on to when the going got tough.

That included Tiana and Jamaal. Jared had to find them, had to resume the search. He wouldn't have any peace until he did.

A pale moon was in the sky ahead of him, partially obscured by clouds. But there was enough light to make the outline of the distant mountains stand out like sentinels. They guarded the way back home and would let him through only if he believed in the promise of reconciliations, a ton of them, laying beyond.

He believed, and drove on.

3.

Vic Lu's studio was a large cement tilt-up, a commercial building somewhere in Chatsworth. To Dallas, it might as well have been Pluto—foreign, cold, and forbidding.

This couldn't be happening to her. Bernie couldn't be this bad. But he had brought her here by force and stood by quietly as Derek the driver held her down on a hard chair.

Vic Lu, wearing a blood-red Hawaiian shirt, paced in front of her.

"How much you think you know?" he barked at Dallas.

Dallas said nothing.

"I'm asking you something, dear." Lu stopped, bent over, and looked her in the face.

"I know you're dirty," Dallas said. "And so is Bernie." It hurt her to say it.

"Hey, it's a loophole," Lu said, standing upright again. "A way to get our friend Bernie what he needs. Money is the mother's milk of politics, they say. What are you all upset by this for? This kind of thing goes on all the time, all over the place. We're not bad people."

Dallas looked at the councilman. "Bernie, how can you let yourself be used by this man?"

Bernie spoke to Vic Lu. "She's a romantic. She sees things in black and white and thinks God is going to come down and set everything right."

Lu shook his head. "That's called *deus ex machina*. It's not dramatically satisfying."

"We have to think this through carefully," Bernie said. "She had a wire, which means the police are in on this. I can pull a few strings and find out what's going on. Someone's obviously targeted me and the Gentri Land connection. Dallas, you'll save everyone a lot of pain if you tell me who it is."

She had no doubt there would be pain involved if she didn't talk. These were desperate men, a pornographer and a politician in bed together. Such a pairing could never produce anything but paranoia.

She'd seen it before. In the face of Chad McKenzie when he used to beat her. Part of the game for him was getting her to wilt in shame and fear, which she had. This was the same game. She would not play it.

Bernie sighed. "Not talking? Now we have a real situation on our hands."

"No sweat," Lu said. "You ever see *Wag the Dog?*"

"The movie?" Bernie said.

"Yeah, with Dustin Hoffman and Robert De Niro. That is one of the greatest movies of all time." Lu became animated, like he'd had too many shots of espresso. "It's a movie about taking real crisis situations and spinning them into a story that will sell a presidential campaign. Dustin plays the producer, and things keep going wrong, like planes crashing and crazy murderers getting loose, and he keeps saying, 'This is nothing. This is producing. I can take care of this.' That's all that's happening here, Bernie. This is what I do. I make up fantasies. I write, produce, and direct stories that people feed on. That's what we're going to do right now."

He paused, put his two index fingers to his temples, and closed his eyes.

"Bernie," Dallas said, "don't do this."

"It's too late, Dallas. I'm sorry. I really am."

"Quiet, please," Lu said, still concentrating. Then he opened his eyes, excited. "Got it! You two went for a nice ride, heading for a nice dinner. But Mrs. H got a headache driving through the canyon. So you brought her back home, only she never made it inside. You went home, Bernie. You are sound asleep. Tomorrow, she'll be reported missing. Naturally, the cops think you might be behind this, but she'll be spotted in Barstow. I'll get another supporting player for that."

"Then what?" Bernie said.

"Leave that to me."

"I don't want to hear any more about it."

A little-boy disappointment descended on Lu. "I'm just getting to the best part!"

"Forget it. Just take care of it. I don't want to know."

Bernie walked toward the door where Derek was now standing guard.

"So that's it?" Dallas called after him.

He did not answer. Derek opened the door, let Bernie through, then closed the door, staying inside.

Insurance.

When Dallas turned back around, Vic Lu was on his cell phone. She heard him say, "Right now," and then he clicked off.

"It won't be long," he said to Dallas. "You're gonna love the ending."

4.

Jared waited in his truck outside the dark apartment building, hoping he'd see Tiana or Jamaal go in or out.

Half an hour. An hour. No Tiana.

Then he saw a woman he thought he recognized. How? It came to him. When he'd first come to this place, she was the one who gave him a suspicious glare. The one-woman Neighborhood Watch. Tonight she was with another, younger woman. They were talking, illuminated by the bright lights on the front walk.

Jared got out of the truck and walked across the street.

The two women didn't pay him any mind until he was nearly within reach.

"Excuse me," he said.

They looked at him, the older woman examining him closely.

"Remember me?"

The woman looked at him like she did, but shook her head. "No, I don't."

"I'm a friend of Tiana Williams."

She narrowed her eyes, then slowly nodded. "I remember now. What're you doing around here?"

"I'm looking for her. And Jamaal."

The other woman joined in the glare. It was obvious they didn't trust him.

"I know all about Rafe," he said. "I helped them get away from him."

"He's dead," the younger woman said.

"Dead? How—"

"And maybe they don't want to be found," the first woman said.

"Do you know where they are?"

"I wouldn't tell you if I did. I don't know what you might do to them. Can't you just leave them alone? They been through enough."

"Then can you get a message to them? Please. I know you don't know who I am. My name is Jared. That's all you have to say. I'll give you my phone number and you can have her call me."

The woman gave him another hard look, only this time it had a dose of understanding in it. "You got a notion about the two of you, I mean the three of you?"

"Maybe. Maybe that's a crazy, stupid thing to have. The only thing I know for sure now is I want to see her again and just talk things through."

After a long pause, the woman said, "All right, young man. Wait here." She quickly added, "But if you go on and hurt that girl you're gonna have to deal with me, you understand?"

§

"... think ill of me," Vic Lu was saying, still pacing and ranting. "I mean, come on. If it weren't for people like you and your ex-husband, we—"

"Not ex."

Lu shrugged. "Hey, who am I to get involved in your personal affairs, huh?"

"Holding me prisoner is pretty personal."

"You're not listening!" He stomped his foot, a petulant child. "I've got a point. Nobody gives me credit for a point, or for making art! I write my films, lady. Did you know that? I got nominated for an Eros Award last year. Does that matter? Why am I talking to you?"

He gave a wave to Derek, as if it was time for him to take over.

In two minutes he bound Dallas to the chair. She prayed. She asked God to consume Vic Lu and Derek with fire. Why not? It was a prayer for protection, and God would work out the details.

The moment she was secured, the door to the studio opened.

Chad McKenzie came in.

"I believe you two know each other," Lu said.

Chad smiled. "Hey, babe, how are you?"

She glared at Vic Lu. "Him? How low have you sunk?"

"You hear that?" Chad said. "I used to get that all the time."

Lu pointed at Chad. "Shut up." Chad did as he was told. Then Lu looked at Derek. "Better tape her mouth," he said.

"You reading that Bible again?" Ernesto's head hung down from the top bunk, looking at me.

"You know," I said, "I think I've discovered that the Bible is reading me."

"What are you talking about, man?"

"You really want to know?"

"I got nothing else goin' on."

I sat up. Ernesto dropped off his bunk and sat on mine. We had reached a point of mutual tolerance and even, on occasion, conversation. It usually happened like this, in the twilight time between chow and lights-out. Ernesto sometimes got downright chatty then.

"It's like this," I said. "I used to read the Bible just to get something out of it for me, like for my sermons or to back up something I was going to say in a book."

"Yeah."

"But the Bible is living and active, sharper than any double-edged sword."

"What's that mean?" He looked interested. But I must say he was a true example of a captive audience.

"It means it reads me. It cuts me up. But I have to let it."

"You sound a little out there, man, you want to know the truth."

"Yeah, it sounds a little nuts. But God is doing the cutting, see, inside me. He's cutting out all the stuff I don't need, that I used to let get in the way. Now I've got plenty of time to let God do his work."

Ernesto was quiet for a long time. Then he said, "My grandmother used to try to get me to go to Mass. I couldn't take it. I got bored. Guess I had some of that attention thing."

"Deficit disorder."

"You gringos are great with the labels. But I always thought when I was in church that there was something going on, something I couldn't see, but it was there. It was floating around. Think that was God?"

"Definitely. But then I'd go one step further and say there's a way to know all about that presence. And it's in this book."

Ernesto took the Bible from me and looked at it. "I never got into it. Lots of stuff I couldn't understand when I tried."

"We can talk about it if you want."

"You gonna try to convert me?"

"No. If that happens, it'll be because of the Word and the Spirit. But I'm thinking maybe there's a reason you and I were put in the same cell together."

"Yeah, so I can keep you from getting stabbed in the back. You are so white."

"Maybe I can return the favor."

"If I get bored, and I tell you to stop, you stop, got it?"

"Deal."

I took the Bible back and in that moment asked God what I should start with. The beginning. It didn't take a bright bulb to catch on to that.

So I started with, "In the beginning God . . ."

And for two straight hours Ernesto was not bored. He did not ask me to stop, and I felt for the first time in years that my preaching was anointed by God. Right there in a prison cell.

7.

Dallas lay in the backseat of the car where Chad had thrown her like a sack of laundry. The duct tape across her mouth chafed. Plastic restraints, pulled tight, held her wrists and ankles fast.

The night was black and she had no idea what direction they were going. She had a vague idea they'd hopped on the 118 Freeway, but she couldn't be sure.

About ten minutes into the ride, Chad lit a cigarette. Dallas could smell the smoke. She tried not to breathe deeply. She didn't want to cough against the tape. But he rolled the windows up, like he intended to torture her with the smell.

Then he started talking.

"Dallas, you have to know that I never wanted it to work out this way. I loved you. You think that's funny, but I really did. You think when I hit you I didn't love you? It was because I couldn't stand the thought of you walking out on me, that's why I did it. You know what I did the night you left me? I mean, the night I figured out you were gone for good? I could have come after you, but I didn't. I released you, like a butterfly. I bet you didn't know that. Instead, I went down to the beach and beat up a couple of guys, just because I needed to get it out of me, you know? That's something you never understood, that I had to get it out of me. If you really loved me you would have understood that. But you never did, so now it has to end this way. Man, this is hard for me. I mean, we had a lot of good times, didn't we?"

Dallas couldn't help answering him in her mind. *Good times? Perverse, ugly . . .*

"Just want you to know that we could have worked something out if you hadn't been so, I don't know, self-righteous. Pretty slick move, I must say, going on TV and telling about the photos and naming me right there in front of the whole world. You know that was bad for business? I couldn't even give 'em away. I tell you, you were a lot more fun back in the old days, back before you hooked up with that preacher and got all saved."

Save me now . . .

"I also want you to know you're not going to suffer. It's not going to hurt. I wouldn't do that to you. You believe that, don't you? I'll use the amyl nitrate on you, the way Rafe used it on Jared. You don't know about that, do you? They had your son marked from the start."

They. Vic Lu and Bernie Halstrom.

"When this Rafe dude found out who Jared was, he decided to get in on things. Lu hired him."

Rafe? Why would he care about Jared? And what were the chances of his random orbit intersecting with Chad's? And Vic Lu's? When had this universe she was trying to make sense of become so small?

Chad's voice dropped an octave. "Then that Rafe tried to strong-arm me. Big mistake. I'll tell you something, *he* felt it. When I did him, he felt it real bad."

He drove in semisilence for a time, humming softly, a rock medley. She recognized a couple of the tunes, then realized they were songs she had liked when they were together. Rolling Stones. Pink Floyd.

And then one tune that came to her in a flood of disgusting memories.

Meat Loaf, "Bat Out of Hell."

She remembered what they did to that song.

He was purposely taunting her.

It may have been two hours, maybe three, before the car finally pulled to a stop. Chad came around the side, opened the door, and yanked her out, pulling her by the plastic restraints. They cut into her skin.

She saw a darkened house. She smelled wet scrub and dirt and figured they were somewhere in the desert. She could not see lights anywhere else but in the sky. The night was alive with stars.

Chad put an arm around her neck and made her shuffle to the door. He unlocked it and pulled her inside, then flicked on a lamp with a yellowed lampshade. The soft orange light made only a slight dent in the darkness.

Dallas could see it was a small house, ranch style. Chad pushed her down on an old sofa. Musty, like it was from 1950.

"You believe they actually use this place?" Chad said, looking around. "They made a porno Western here. But some of the rooms are like little studios."

He appeared to be looking around for something.

And then found it.

From a table he took a large hunting knife, so large it looked like a small sword.

"After the amyl, you won't feel this, Dallas. And the good part is you'll get to be out in your God's creation. You'll just be lizard food, of course, but if it makes you feel any better, that's where you'll be."

Dallas looked at the knife and at Chad holding it, smiling. She had no doubt he was going to do it. He wanted her to suffer right now. He wanted her scared.

But she noticed, amazingly, that her heart was not beating wildly, nor was her breathing—through her nose—labored.

She was calm.

One thought raced into her mind, a confirmation of the sovereignty of God. He was ultimately in control, despite what men might do in rebellion to him. Evil men like Chad McKenzie and Vic Lu and, sadly, Bernie Halstrom, could not escape. Even if they killed her, God was ruler over all.

She would die now, but she was not afraid.

Chad was studying her face.

She looked right back at him, talking to him with her eyes. *Do this and you will be punished, and deep down you know it, you know it right now, don't you?*

Suddenly, anger seemed to engulf him. He cursed at her.

You are the dead one, Chad. You are the dupe.

"You make me sick," he spat.

You know it, you've always known it, and you're dead. Don't do this. In killing me you'll be killing yourself.

"Shut up."

His frenzy was almost comical. She hadn't said a word, couldn't through the tape. Yet he had heard everything.

He held up the knife and looked at the blade. "Maybe the amyl's a bad idea. Maybe you'd rather have the experience without drugs."

He brought the point of the knife down slowly, like he was drawing a picture in the air. With a slight flourish he stopped with the point just in front of her face.

"I can start anywhere I want." He examined her face like a butcher considering where to make the first cut.

You are the dead one, Chad.

"You want it done quickly, Dallas? Are you ready to meet your God?"

God, watch over my family always. Protect and keep them.

"If you want a chance to call God a liar, I might be able to let you go—"

Preserve Ron, bring justice, protect Jared and Cara, comfort them.

"—or I can just get started right now."

Let them live and know that I am with you.

"So if you want to curse God, just nod your head, Dallas."

She looked him in the eye, held the look, peering into his dark pupils. They were empty caves with no flicker of light inside.

He took a handful of her hair and snapped her head back. She couldn't see his eyes now, or the knife. She only smelled his breath, beer and cigarettes. He held her like that for a full minute.

Then she felt the tip of the blade on her throat. He poked her without breaking skin.

"You are so stupid," he whispered. "It's better for you to die."

Something creaked. A floorboard.

Chad released her head and whipped around to his right.

Dallas followed his look, saw a shadowy form ten feet away. A full second of time froze in the room, then came the flash of a muzzle and crack of a gunshot, and Chad fell backward. The knife fell out of his hand as he grasped his chest, already seeping red.

The form didn't move from the shadows.

Chad gurgled and thrashed. Blood smeared the floor as he struggled like a felled deer, his legs jerking outward to find traction.

Dallas expected the shadow to move forward and finish her too.

But it waited. Chad's movements slowed into an agonizing spasm of death. He turned his head toward Dallas, eyes terrified, as if he saw something horrible behind her head. His lips quivered as he opened his mouth in a long, excruciating, and silent scream.

And then he moved no more. His dead eyes stayed open, horror filled.

The shadow figure came into the light.

§

"What?"

Tiana looked out the door of the little tract house in Eagle Rock, an expression of complete surprise on her face. The woman Jared took to be her sister stood by her side. There was a striking resemblance.

"Tiana," Jared said, "I—"

He heard scuffling feet, looked down, and saw Jamaal. The boy smiled up at Jared and said, "Where you been?"

"I had a few things to take care of. How's that arm?"

"Huh?"

Jared made a passing motion.

"Good," Jamaal said.

"Hold it!" Tiana said, hands on her hips. "How'd you find us? What are you doing here?"

"The neighbor lady from your old place gave me the address. I told her I had to find you, I—"

"After you ran out on us?" Her voice betrayed hurt mixed with the anger.

"Wait—"

She slammed the door closed.

A moment later it swung open again. This time the sister was alone with Jamaal. "Mister," she said, "what are you about?"

"I didn't run out on your sister. Or Jamaal."

The boy pointed at him and said, "You better not be lyin'."

"Believe me, kid, I'm done with that."

The sister gave him a hard, examining look. "I can't let you in here unless I'm convinced you're being straight. I'm not going to let my sister get hurt anymore, you hear me?"

"Give me five minutes," Jared said. "That's it. If you want me gone after that, I'm gone."

She considered it a moment, then stepped aside so he could come in. "My name's Lavonne," she said.

"He's Jared," Jamaal said.

Jared followed Lavonne inside. Tiana was on a blue sofa, her head in her hands. She looked up. When she saw Jared she started shaking her head.

"We can at least listen," Lavonne said.

"Five minutes," Jared said.

"I can't take any more of you," Tiana said. "You've got to leave us alone now."

"Three minutes, then I'm gone." Jared didn't wait for permission. "The night we argued up in Bakersfield, I went out and I was going to drive away, for good—you're right about that—but I got picked up by the highway patrol. They found my bench warrant on the DUI I skipped, and back I came, and I was in jail and a guy wanted to kill me, only this other guy in my cell talked Jesus to the guy and he stopped, and it freaked me out, but it woke me up and turned me around. I don't want to go back to the way I was again, no more booze, no more drugs, I'm gonna stay clean, but mostly I don't want to be away from you and Jamaal. And that's it, that's the whole thing."

The others looked at him as if he was slightly nuts.

Then Jamaal said, "Cool."

"That's a good one, all right," Lavonne said.

"All true," Jared said. "And that's why I'm here. And I want to know if you'll forgive me."

Tiana looked at him, thinking.

"Forgive him, Mom!" Jamaal said.

Slowly, a smile broke out on her face. "I do."

§.

If duct tape had not covered her mouth, Dallas would have gasped. The shadow was in full light now, and there was no mistaking who it was, though the face was terribly puffed up and discolored.

Gilda was shaking, gun in hand. Her eyes widened through the black and blue rings that were not makeup. The loud purple hair was unkempt. It looked like a handful had been torn out of one side.

She looked down at Chad and pointed the gun at him. Dallas thought she'd fire again, but instead, she kicked his side with full force. Chad McKenzie was very clearly dead.

Gilda turned her attention to Dallas, looking as if she didn't know what to do next.

Dallas tried to talk comfortingly with her eyes, but Gilda wasn't listening. She didn't look like *comfort* was in her vocabulary.

Still holding the handgun, Gilda examined Dallas's restraints, then slowly pulled the duct tape off her mouth. Dallas suspected a layer of skin came off with it.

"Why are you here?" Gilda said.

"He was going to kill me."

Gilda shook her head slowly. "Then we're both dead."

"Cut me loose," Dallas said.

Eyes wide, body still shaking, Gilda used the gun to point to her face. "Look at me! He did this to me!"

"I know."

"*What?*"

"He used to beat me up too."

"What are you *talking* about?"

"Cut me loose, Gilda, so we can talk."

"Talk now."

"All right. He was my boyfriend once. A long time ago. He tracked me down when my husband and I made the news. He somehow got hooked up with Vic Lu."

"You got that much right. I was a present. Vic gave me to him. Now look ..." Gilda's words stuck in a short sob.

Vic gave me to him. The thought jarred Dallas, but it made perverse sense. Men like Lu and Chad were into total control.

"Gilda, I can help you."

"No way. It's over. Vic is going to kill me, and he'll get you too."

"How much do you know about Lu's dealings?"

Gilda gave a weak smile. "I've been here two days. Vic and Chad and a crew were coming up tomorrow for a shoot. Guess what? I shot first."

"You were going to kill Lu?"

"I messed that up, didn't I? The luck I have."

"Why, Gilda? It's because Vic Lu had something to do with Melinda's murder, isn't it?"

Gilda said nothing.

"You knew her. You were friends, you—"

"You don't make friends in this business," Gilda spat. "You do and you only get hurt."

"You know something. Tell me. We can stop Lu."

Turning her back, Gilda muttered something that sounded like *no way.*

"Cut me loose, Gilda. Then I can take you where it's safe. It's a place where women like you come to get away from the bad guys."

"No place is safe."

"Let me prove it to you."

Gilda seemed to be retreating into herself. In a few minutes, she might walk out. Or kill herself. Or both of them.

"Trust me, Gilda."

"Why should I?"

"Because I'm not like them. And neither are you."

For an extended moment Gilda just stared at her. Then she looked to the floor, bent over, and picked up Chad's knife.

"You better be right," Gilda said. And then she cut Dallas loose.

"How'd you get here?" Dallas said.

"My car's a half mile up the road."

"Let me get my purse. It's in Chad's car. Then we'll—"

"Do we have to call the cops?"

Dallas touched Gilda's arm. "I want to talk to my lawyer first. In the morning."

Gilda seemed relieved. "Where'll we go?"

"I have a place where we'll both be safe."

"But will you drive?" Gilda said. "I'm shaking all over."

NINETEEN

1.

Dallas drove Gilda's car back toward the Valley. On the way she called Cara, told her not to worry, that she'd explain everything later. She faked enough calm to get Cara to agree to wait.

Dallas got Gilda settled into Haven House around 2:30 a.m., then crashed in the office, on the sofa. She woke up, body buzzing with adrenaline, at eight.

She cleaned up in the small bathroom and then called Jeff. He was just arriving at the office. Dallas got there at 8:45.

She told him everything she knew about Vic Lu and Bernie Halstrom, the wire she wore, the Gentri Land setup, Gilda. And Chad's body in a house in the desert. When she finished she was exhausted but managed to conclude, "That'll mean Ron will get out of prison, won't it?"

Jeff's face was impassive. Not a good sign.

"What's the problem?" she asked.

"We would have to petition the court to allow Ron to withdraw his plea. And to do that, we have to have a factual basis for allowing it, like a clear indication of another's guilt or complicity."

"We have it."

"We have Chad's and Bernie's connection to Vic Lu, yes. What we don't have is the connection to the murder of Melinda Perry."

"We have Gilda. She knows things. She thinks Melinda was used by Lu as bait to catch Ron, that the murder was set up—"

"Thinks?" Jeff pursed his lips. Another bad sign. "Dallas, remember when we discussed that gang kid you found? The problems that a questionable witness presents? The DA is going to fight this, and we'd have to convince a court this witness really knows what she's talking about, can corroborate it."

"But I know she can."

"Do you really?"

She stopped. What did Gilda really know after all? And would it withstand scrutiny?

Softly, Jeff said, "As always, Dallas, I want you to be fully informed of what's going on. When Ron entered his plea, he waived his right to challenge the truth of the underlying offense. We would have to show the court good cause to lift this waiver. We would—"

"We have to go through with this, Jeff, we have to. Even though I don't have the wire on Halstrom, we have me. I can swear to what happened. Maybe that would force him to turn on Lu—"

"It's your word against his."

"Jeff! We have Detective Lacy working on this, we have—"

"There's a bigger problem, Dallas."

"What?"

"Ron."

She looked at him, wondering what he meant.

"He would have to consent to withdrawing his plea," Jeff said. "You remember, it was his idea to plead out in the first place."

"But the truth," she said. "Doesn't that matter to anybody anymore?"

"To us it does. It always will. And that's going to have to be enough."

With resignation rising like cold water inside her, Dallas heard her cell phone chime. She looked at the number. It was Cara.

"May I take this?" she asked.

"Go right ahead," Jeff said.

She spoke into the phone. "Cara, what's up?"

"It's Lacy. I'm at your daughter's apartment."

Something was wrong with Cara. "What is it?"

"Can you talk?"

She thought maybe she should call him back, but was too anxious to hear his report. "Yes."

"It's about Gentri Land. It's owned by a shell company. Called DatJam. Gentri Land is the only thing this shell company owns, as far as I can tell."

All very interesting, but it could wait, couldn't it?

"I looked deeper, and found out who the agent for service of process is."

"What's that?"

"A corporation has to have someone who can be served papers, in case they're sued, whatever. Dallas, the agent for DatJam is Jefferson Waite."

Every muscle in her body clenched.

Jeff.

Who had denied knowing anything about Gentri Land.

She tried to keep her face from blazing a neon sign of trouble.

"Mrs. Hamilton?"

"I'm here, dear."

"Excuse me?"

She looked at Jeff. He was scribbling something on a legal pad.

"I'm with your father's lawyer at the moment," Dallas said in a light tone.

"You're at Waite's office?" Lacy said.

"We're trying to see what we can do for Dad. I'll fill you in when I get home."

"Get out of there, Dallas."

"See you soon."

She put the phone in her pocket.

"Any trouble?" Jeff asked.

"No, no. Cara's such a worrywart. I guess I'd better go reassure her."

She stood up.

So did Jeff. He walked around his desk toward her. She watched his eyes, looked at his face for clues of his intentions.

Stay calm.

"Thanks for everything you've done, Jeff. Really. You gave it your best."

She looked at the office door.

"Something wrong, Dallas?"

She fought hard to keep her hands steady as she reached for the door. "Let's not give up."

"You look worried all of a sudden."

"All of a sudden? I've been in knots for months." She clasped the door handle.

Jeff moved close to her, smiling. "You know, a lawyer goes to court, argues cases to juries, looks witnesses in the eye. He does that enough, and he develops a sense of something going on. Is there anything wrong, Dallas? Anything you're not sharing?"

She pushed down on the handle. "I know how busy you are. Let's meet later this week."

"You sure?"

"I'll call you. Thanks for everything."

"Let me walk you to—"

"I'm a big girl, Jeff," she said with a lilt. "I'll find my way out."

She passed the receptionist, who gave her a nice smile. *Just how much does she know?* The woman was probably as deceived as everyone else in Jeff's orbit.

Dallas kept her pace slow and steady to the elevator. It felt like an hour before it came. She got on alone, punched the key for the parking garage, and only then began to breathe easier.

The elevator let her out in the deserted garage. She'd parked Gilda's car in the far corner. She'd feel completely safe only when she got out of there and connected with Lacy again. Fumbling for the keys, she realized how badly she was shaking. She was just about to press *unlock* on the key fob when she heard a voice.

"Don't move, Dallas."

2.

The look on the deputy sheriff's face was almost comical. "I didn't expect to see you walk in without cuffs," he said.

Jared smiled. "What can I say? It's not that I missed the place."

"You came to see somebody?"

"Yeah. I want to visit one of my old cell mates."

"What is this, old home week?"

"In a way."

"You're entitled to visit like anyone else. Let's get you a pass. Who was it you wanted to see?"

"That's just it. I never got his name. I thought maybe you could look him up for me."

The deputy thought a moment. "Let's go ask."

Jared followed him through a door on the right into an office where three other deputies sat at desks.

"This is Jared Hamilton, one of our recent guests," the deputy said.

The others gave him the same look as the first deputy had. Jared felt a little like a walking carnival exhibit. He nodded.

"He wants to say hello to one of his cell mates, if you can believe it, but he doesn't have a name."

One deputy, a woman with a nameplate that said *Sanchez*, motioned Jared over. She had a computer on her desk and tapped something on the keyboard.

"Okay," she said. "Hamilton, right? Jared?"

"Yes," Jared said.

"Yeah, here's your module and your cell number. Let's see, you only spent a weekend here."

"Quite a weekend."

"Looks like"—she peered at the screen—"you had four able-bodied companions. Pal Ingram isn't with us anymore. He was shipped off for trial in San Mateo. Good riddance to bad garbage. He wasn't the one you wanted to see, I hope."

"No. It was an older guy."

"Older?"

"Maybe in his forties."

One of the other deputies, a man in his forties, piped, "Way over the hill."

The other deputies, including Sanchez, laughed.

"And there were five other guys in there with me," Jared said.

Sanchez looked at the screen. "I only see four names here, and they're all in their twenties."

Jared leaned over and looked at the screen. He couldn't make out the codes. Sanchez pointed at a couple of numbers. "Only four assigned to that cell, until you came in. That makes five."

"But I know there were six of us. I can count."

"All I can do is tell you what's here."

"What if your records are wrong? Does that ever happen?"

"Never!" another deputy said. "Don't tell him any different, either."

More laughter.

"Sorry," Sanchez said. "You know, you come in a place like this, it's a little stressful. Maybe you don't remember."

"No, it's clear! He saved my life."

Sanchez looked at her fellows. "Haven't heard that one in a while."

"Call Oprah," another said.

And they laughed again, having a good old time.

No amount of cajoling could get Sanchez to search any further. Jared had come in hopeful and walked out mystified. Yet most of the recent events of his life were beyond his comprehension.

Like connecting with Tiana and Jamaal the way he did.

Like knowing God had watched over him all this time because his mother and sister and father all prayed for him.

Maybe that's all the comprehension he needed.

3.

"Harry, don't."

Dallas looked the investigator in the eye, willing him to relent, to move his hand from the door of the car.

"I'm sorry, Dallas. I can't let you go."

"You going to kill me?"

Harry's face twitched slightly, like he'd taken offense. "I don't want to."

"Kill for Jeff?" She put her hand on his arm. "I can't believe you'd do that."

Harry said nothing.

"Stop now. You can still do what's right."

"And what? Go to prison?"

"You only work for Jeff, you—" She stopped. "Did you kill Melinda Perry? Was it you?"

Harry's eyes showed strain and just plain exhaustion. "Just come with me," he said.

"I'm not going to," she said. "And you won't kill me." Why she said it just that way, she wasn't sure. But she was not scared.

"Dallas, please."

"Your life is at stake."

He shook his head.

"Do the right thing," she said. "For your daughter. For yourself. Don't—"

"Is there a problem?" Jeff Waite had come up behind Harry.

Harry looked at Dallas.

"Get her out of here, Harry."

Harry didn't move.

"Harry!"

The investigator whirled around. "Do it yourself," he said.

Jeff's face went cold. Seeing his expression, Dallas thought she saw the real Jeff Waite for the first time in her life.

"Harry, you're starting to make me nervous."

Harry Stegman didn't move. He was a human shield between Dallas and Jeff Waite.

Then a sound in the distance. Sirens.

Jeff's head cocked a little, and his eyes burned into Harry. "Get out of the way!"

Harry said, "Don't do it, Jeff."

"Move!"

Dallas couldn't see the lower half of Jeff's body but got the distinct impression he was holding something.

Harry's arm moved, as if he was reaching under his coat. It moved out again.

She heard three cracks, one after another. Harry's body fell back against her, pinning her to the car. And then he went down.

Jeff Waite looked at her, shock all over his face. Red wetness spreading on his white shirt, just below the left shoulder.

He opened his mouth, looking like he wanted to curse her, but no sound came out.

And then he dropped straight down, thudding on the concrete.

The sirens grew louder.

Harry's body was on her feet. But he was moving.

He rolled left, onto his side.

"Dallas ...," he said.

"Hold on, Harry. Hold on."

4.

Detective Lacy called Dallas the next day. "Stegman's going to be okay," he said. "Waite died early this morning. I'm at the hospital now to get a statement from Stegman, but he says he wants you here."

"Does he have a lawyer?" Dallas said.

"Waived the right. But he won't talk without you. Are you up for it?"

"I'll be right there," she said.

They had Harry Stegman in post-op at the Reseda Medical Center. A uniformed officer stood outside his room on the third floor.

The detective motioned Dallas to come in.

Harry Stegman lay in a bed by the window, the only patient in the room. A tube dripped fluid into one of his arms. His other arm was shackled to the bed by handcuffs. He looked pitiful, and even though he'd been two-faced to her, Dallas couldn't help feeling sorry for him. That he should have come to this.

"Hello, Dallas," he said, weak but determined. "Thank you for coming."

She nodded.

"I'm ready," Harry told Lacy.

Lacy took out a notebook and pen.

"It started out innocently enough," Harry said. "Vic Lu came to Jeff and told him about this idea he had for boosting campaign contributions. He wanted to know if it was legal. What he was really doing was setting himself up to grease the palm of whoever the city councilman happened to be. He wanted his life in the porn business to be as hassle free as possible, and buying politicians has been the best guarantee.

"He also promised Jeff considerable legal fees for his trouble in heading up the DatJam/Gentri Land scheme. So he was buying Jeff too. Once he got Jeff to be the front man, Lu had him hooked. Not that Jeff resisted him. It was Lu who suggested Jeff get involved in your church. A perfect cover for someone involved in, shall we say, less than upright dealings."

Dallas shook her head. "It's hard to believe."

"People do strange things when they get paid for it. Lu gave Jeff more than money. He also gave him Melinda Perry."

"Jeff was having an affair with her?"

"That's a nice way of putting it. Jeff was using her. Well, there came a time when she decided she wasn't willing to be used anymore. She wanted Jeff to get her out of the business and make her Mrs. Waite. When he said no, she threatened to go to the police and spill her guts about Gentri Land."

"She knew about it?"

"She was a very clever little girl. She knew how to get information from people in return for her favors. That's why she was perfect for the little plan to stop your husband. When Jeff told Vic Lu about Melinda's threats, Lu saw a great opportunity to use her seductive power. One thing about Lu, he casts himself as a visionary. Well, he is. And he can see some pretty grand things for himself."

Detective Lacy grunted and continued to take notes.

"What he wanted to do was kill two birds, so to speak. You and your husband were making trouble with Halstrom. Your husband was becoming too popular a voice for cleaning up the community, shutting down people like Vic Lu. So Lu came up with an idea to trap your husband in a sleazy murder situation."

"Why didn't he just kill Ron and be done with it?"

"Number one, that would have been too obvious. He didn't want people asking questions about who Ron's enemies might be. But the more important reason was Lu's ego. He saw this as an elaborate screenplay, a testimony to his genius. The guy is nuts."

"Did Jeff kill Melinda?" Dallas asked.

Harry nodded. "That was all part of it. Vic Lu wasn't about to get his own hands dirty. He had Jeff and Halstrom both across a barrel. He played his hand perfectly. That's how he got McKenzie involved. McKenzie shows up at Jeff's office, says he has some information he ought to know about. About you, Dallas. He wanted money to keep it quiet. The sap didn't know Jeff couldn't have cared less. So instead of kicking him out, Jeff recruited him. One thing Jeff could do was size people up. That's why he was so good in court."

"Unbelievable," Dallas muttered.

"Jeff was into control, so how convenient was it for him to be handling Ron's defense? He wasn't interested in getting Ron off. He wanted the whole thing disposed of as quickly as possible, and so he leaked the evidence about the porn on Ron's computer to the press to help things along."

Now Dallas couldn't even mutter. The depth of betrayal was fathomless. But wasn't that the way of the ancient enemy of God? Go after the families. Well, this time the plan hadn't succeeded. Her family was not what it once was, but God would knit it together again. She had to hang onto that.

"McKenzie killed a guy named Rafe Bryan," Lacy said to Harry. "Now that they're both dead, it's a little hard to figure. You know anything?"

"Not much, except that this guy Bryan may have been looking for your son, Dallas."

"I think he was," Dallas said. "My son and Bryan's girlfriend started seeing each other."

"When two sweeties like McKenzie and Bryan get together, something's going to pop. Bryan probably wanted in on McKenzie's cut."

"There's someone who can confirm," Dallas said.

Harry waited.

"Gilda."

"You know where she is?" Detective Lacy said, his eyes virtually lighting up.

"I know. And she can give you a bunch on Vic Lu."

"When we catch up with him," he said. "He has taken what they used to call a powder."

"Maybe Bernie Halstrom knows where he is."

The detective nodded, looked at his watch. "And right about now Deputy DA Freton is paying Halstrom a little call."

Harry seemed to relax a little, like he was finally glad to get all this off his chest. Then he said, "I'm sorry, Dallas. I really am."

"I know, Harry."

"I'm not a bad man. I just ... forgot."

"Has anyone called your daughter?"

"No."

"You want me to?"

"I don't know." He looked nervous.

Dallas put her hand on his arm. "Now's the time for family, Harry. Let me make the call."

After a pause, Harry nodded.

"I guess that's it for now," Lacy said. "Your cooperation will be duly noted, Mr. Stegman."

TWENTY

"Watch the paint there," Jared said.

Jamaal looked up at him, the roller in his hand almost as big as he was. White spots dotted his face, and his T-shirt and overalls were spattered as well. The roller was dripping with paint.

"Hold it over the pan." Jared pointed.

Jamaal complied. The wet roller almost pulled him over.

"Let me show you how to smooth it out," Jared said. "If you're gonna work for me you got to do it right."

"Okay." Jamaal was nothing if not excited about his new position in Jared's business.

They were in a house, a fixer on Plummer that was the first contract job for Jared and the fledgling house-painting business he'd started four months ago, a business consisting of himself and two employees—Jamaal, who was quite affordable, and Tiana, who was the head of the design team. She would make everything pretty. She'd started attending night classes in design at Valley Community College.

Jared got Jamaal squared away on the paint, then showed him how to make an X on the wall and roll the rest of the paint across the surface with easy strokes. Jared put on the finishing touches so Jamaal could watch. This process would take a little more time, but time was something Jared had a whole lot of.

Time with people he loved.

Jared handed the roller back to Jamaal. "Okay, now do it again."

Jamaal didn't move.

"What's wrong?"

"You gonna be my dad?"

"You want me to?"

Jamaal nodded.

"I have to talk to your mom about it."

"She wants you to be."

"Oh, yeah?"

"Then we could even live in the same house!"

"That sounds good to me."

Jamaal smiled like the morning sun. Jared knelt and put his hands on the boy's shoulders. He still couldn't believe how such a great kid could have had such a lowlife father, nor how Jamaal could have come out so fresh despite what he'd been through.

What a world it was. What a place Jamaal was being handed. That's why Jared wanted to be part of it with Jamaal. Help him make it through.

He looked the boy in the eye and said, "You can always trust your mom and me, okay?"

Jamaal looked totally serious as he nodded.

"Trust me about what?" Tiana had come in through the front door. She held a plastic bag from Subway in her hand.

Jamaal ran to her. "He said yes!"

The confusion on Tiana's face gave way to realization. She looked at Jared and smiled.

She was beautiful.

2.

The Wednesday night chapel service at the minimum-security men's colony just north of Lancaster always starts at seven o'clock sharp. That's one thing I make sure of. I know from my stint on the inside that these guys calibrate their lives by the minute. They look forward to any break from routine. I'm going to give them that break, and do it on time.

About twenty came tonight, almost double the number from last week. I've been coming each Wednesday for two months now. It's volunteer work, but it's the work God has called me to. Talking to the guys in the prisons.

Just before they bounced me from Los Rios, after the DA petitioned to have my plea withdrawn and charges dropped, Ernesto told me he wanted to keep in touch, said I had a way of talking about God that interested him.

And if I could interest Ernesto, I figured God had arranged it so I could interest others.

That's the way it's going to be.

The big news this past month is that Vic Lu has been arrested for conspiracy to commit murder, and Bernie Halstrom has been indicted on that and several other counts. The two of them are now blaming each other through their lawyers.

But it is a stake through the heart of porn and corruption in Los Angeles, and it's nationwide news. That's why I got a call from my former agent, saying I was "hot" again, and how about a new book?

I politely said no.

I will not go back to celebrity, or the paid ministry, unless God picks me up and literally throws me there.

Until that time, I will go into the prisons.

※

After church, Ron and Dallas drove down to the pier at Santa Monica, just to be together and look at the ocean. They spoke very little on the way. For some reason, a reason Dallas couldn't quite fathom, words would have diluted the moment. It had something to do with the church service that morning. They'd sung one of Dallas's favorite old hymns, *Blessed Assurance*. When they got to *glory divine* Dallas thought that described perfectly the congregation, this body of Christ she and Ron called home.

After all the scandal, after Ron's fall and the resignation of Bob Benson over Lisa's duplicity—even after all that, Hillside had hung together. Sure, there was fallout. Several people left in disillusionment. But in the last few weeks others had come, filling the seats to hear the "new" preacher, the one unanimously called until a permanent pastor could be found.

Roger Vernon looked great up there, eighty years young and full of life, the kind that could only come from believing in the Word of God with every fiber of his being, and preaching it with utter conviction.

There was not one trace of discomfort for Ron in Roger's presence. Shortly after his release from prison, Ron had come forward to ask the congregation for forgiveness. It was given in an overwhelming wave of grace.

Now he was content to sit under Roger's teaching and let God deal with him as he would.

This morning, Roger asked the people to turn in their Bibles to the first chapter of 2 Corinthians. He read aloud, "'Praise be to the God and Father of our Lord Jesus Christ, the Father of compassion and the God of all comfort, who comforts us in all our troubles, so that we can comfort those in any trouble with the comfort we ourselves have received from God.'"

Ron had reached over then and taken her hand. She heard him whisper, "Amen."

Now, strolling along the pier, amidst the hustle of tourists and bustle of commerce, Ron took her hand again. They walked until they reached a place where they could gaze down at the blue-green water. It swirled and broke around the pilings. White foam churned then dissipated as it melted back into the sea.

Dallas realized then that in the very place where her spirit had been torn by Ron's betrayal, a healing had already occurred. This broken place had carried a scar, but it was stronger now and more resilient. That was God's way, she supposed. He didn't spare the scars, he transformed them. They melted into him, and that's how he made all things new.

"Let's go down there," Dallas said.

"Where?"

"The water. Let's take our shoes off and get wet."

Ron smiled at her. His eyes danced in the sunlight that flickered off the ocean. Then he put his arm around her shoulder and, in silent communion, they walked back along the pier to the stairs that led down to the beach.

THE WHOLE TRUTH

JAMES SCOTT BELL

BESTSELLING AUTHOR OF NO LEGAL GROUNDS

Read an excerpt from James Scott Bell's
The Whole Truth

ONE

"Mr. Conroy?"

Steve heard his name. Like someone calling from the front of a cavern with him deep inside. Inside, where his thoughts were pinging off the walls like a scared drunk's haphazard gunshots.

"Yes, Your Honor?"

"I said you may cross-examine." Nasty voice. Judge O'Hara, ex-prosecutor, ex-cop, did not like screwups in his courtroom. Especially if they themselves were ex-prosecutors now prowling the defense side of the aisle. O'Hara glared at Steve from the bench, his imperious eyebrows seeming to frame the Great Seal of the State of California on the wall behind him.

"Excuse me, Your Honor." Steve Conroy stood up, feeling the heat from all the eyes in the courtroom.

The eyes of Judge O'Hara, of course.

Everyone on the jury.

His client.

And his client's extended family, which seemed like the entire population of Guadalajara, all packed into Division 115 of the Van Nuys courthouse.

Officer Charles Siebel was on the stand. The one who'd claimed that Steve's client, an ex-felon, was packing. An ex-felon with a gun could land in the slam for up to three years, depending on priors. Which his client had a boatload of. The one hope Carlos Mendez had of getting his sorry can back on the street, free of the law's embrace, lay in Steve's ability to knock the credibility out of a dedicated veteran of the Los Angeles Police Department.

And doing it with no sleep. Steve had fought the cold sweats all night. Which always made the morning after an adventure in mental gymnastics. His brain would fire off an unending stream of random and contradictory thoughts. He'd have to practically grunt to keep focus. The chemical consequence of recovery.

"Excuse me, Your Honor," Steve said, grabbing for his yellow pages of notes. He trucked the pages to the podium and buttoned his suit coat. It fell open. He buttoned it again. It fell open again. A yellow sheet slipped from the podium. Steve grabbed it in mid-descent, like a Venus flytrap snatching its prey, and slapped it back on the podium in front of him.

He saw a couple of jurors smiling at the show.

Steve cleared his throat. "According to your report, Officer Siebel, you saw my client standing on the corner of Sepulveda and Vanowen, is that correct?"

"Yes." Clipped and authoritative, like the prosecutors trained them to be.

"You were in your vehicle, is that right?"

"Yes."

"Alone?"

"Yes."

"Driving which way?"

"North."

"On what street?"

Officer Siebel and Judge O'Hara sighed at the same time.

Just like a comedy team. The whole courtroom was one big sit-com, Steve playing the incompetent sidekick.

"Sepulveda," Siebel said.

"At what time?"

"Is this cross-examination or skeet shooting?" Judge O'Hara snapped.

Steve clenched his teeth. O'Hara liked to inject himself into the thick of things, showboating for the jury. For some reason, he'd been doing it to Steve throughout the trial.

"If I may, Your Honor, I'm laying a foundation," Steve said.

"Sounds like you're just letting the witness repeat direct testimony."

Why thank you, Judge. I had no idea. How helpful you are! The DA didn't even have to object!

"I'll try it this way," Steve said, turning back to the witness. "Officer Siebel, you were driving north on Sepulveda at 10:32 p.m., correct?"

"That's what happened."

"It's in your report, isn't it?"

"Of course."

Steve went to counsel table and picked up a copy of the police report. As he did, Carlos Mendez, in his jailhouse blues, gave him the look, the one that said, *I hope you know what you're doing.*

Ah yes, the confident client. When was the last time he'd had one of those?

Steve held up the report. "The lighting conditions are not mentioned in your report, are they?"

"I didn't see any need, I was able to see—"

"I'd like an answer to the question I asked, sir."

The deputy DA, Moira Hanson, stood. "Objection. The witness should be allowed to answer."

Steve looked at the DDA, who was about his age, thirty. That's where the correspondence ended. She was short and blond. He was an even six feet with hair as dark as the marks against him. She was new to the office. He hadn't met her when he was prosecuting for the county of Los Angeles.

"Your Honor," he said, "the answer was clearly nonresponsive. As you pointed out so eloquently, this is cross-examination."

O'Hara was not impressed. "Thank you very much for the endorsement, Mr. Conroy. Now if you'll let me rule? Ask your question again, and I direct the witness to answer only the question asked."

A minor victory, Steve knew, but in this trial any bone was welcome.

"Are there any lighting conditions in your report?" Steve asked.

"No," Siebel said.

"You are aware that the corner you mention has dark patches, aren't you?"

"Dark patches?"

"What scientists refer to as illumination absences?"

Officer Siebel squinted at Steve.

"You do know what I'm talking about, surely," Steve said.

Moira Hanson objected again. "No foundation, Your Honor."

"Sustained. In plain English, Mr. Conroy."

That was fine with Steve. Because he'd just made up the term *illumination absences*. All he wanted was the jury to think he had Bill Nye the Science Guy on the defense team. These days, juries were under the spell of the *CSI* effect. They all thought forensic evidence was abundant and could clinch any case in an hour. Prosecutors hated that, because most cases weren't so cut, dried, preserved, and plattered. Steve intended to plant the idea that science was against the DA.

"*Illumination absences* refers to measurable dark spots. There are all sorts of dark spots on that corner, Officer Siebel, where you can't see a thing, right?"

"I don't know what you're talking about. I could see clearly."

Steve turned to the judge. "Why don't we take the jury down there tonight, Your Honor, and we can—"

"Approach the bench," O'Hara ordered. "With the reporter."

Putting on a sheepish look, Steve joined Hanson in front of the judge.

"You know better than to make a motion in front of the jury," O'Hara said.

"He knows, but does it anyway," Hanson added. She was like the smarty in school who dumps extra on the kids who get sent to the principal's office.

"What?" Steve said. "It was just a request."

"I know what you're doing," O'Hara said.

"Representing my client?"

"If this is representation, I'm Britney Spears. You're taking shortcuts. Well, you're not going to get away with it. Not here. And you don't want to tempt me. Another disciplinary strike and you're out."

That was true. Steve had been out of rehab for a year after dealing with a coke addiction and losing his job with the DA's office. Now that he was trying to establish a private practice, no easy task, he did not need the State Bar on his back again. They wouldn't be so forgiving this time.

"And what's that load about this illumination thing?" O'Hara asked. "You better have a foundation for asking that."

"I can find a scientist to back it up."

"You can find a scientist to back up anything," Hanson said.

"I won't allow it," O'Hara said. "I think you're just whistling in the dark, so to speak."

"Representing my client, Your Honor."

"Call me Britney. Go on. But watch every step you take, sir."

Steve didn't have to. He'd gotten what he could out of the witness. All he needed was one juror to think that maybe this officer didn't see what he thought he saw. One juror to hang the thing, and then maybe Moira Hanson would call her boss and say it's not worth a retrial. Let the guy walk.

Sure. And Santa Claus sips Cuba Libres at the North Pole.

TWO

Steve's cross of Officer Siebel was the last order of business on a hot August Friday. Monday they'd all come back for closing arguments, giving Steve a whole weekend to come up with some verbal gold. Which he knew he had to spin to get Carlos Mendez a fair shake.

It would also give him time, he hoped, to get some sleep.

Steve pointed his Ark toward his Canoga Park office. The Ark was what he called his vintage Cadillac, and by vintage he meant *has seen better days*. It dated from the Reagan administration and had been overhauled and repainted and taped together many times over. Steve scored it at a police auction five years earlier. The main advantage was it was big. He could sleep in it if he needed to. Even back then, as he was sucking blow up his snout like a Hoover, Steve suspected he might be homeless someday.

Hadn't happened yet. And with the help of the State Bar's Lawyer Assistance Program, maybe it wouldn't. The LAP was supposed to help lawyers with substance-abuse problems. Steve had managed to keep the monkey off his back for a year. Not that he wasn't close to falling, especially on those nights when he lay in bed staring at the ceiling.

Steve took Sherman Way into Canoga Park, an LA burg in the west end of the San Fernando Valley. It was a venerable town that had hit its stride in 1955, when Rocketdyne, a division of North American Aviation, made its home there. The aerospace industry brought a boomlet of people to the area, and American dreams were born and realized. Rocketdyne engines were used to help put men on the moon in 1969, and sent NASA space shuttles on their appointed rounds.

At its peak during the space race with the Soviets, Rocketdyne employed twenty-two thousand people, and Canoga Park was a great place to live, shop, and open a business. But the realities of economy and urban decline were as inevitable and poisonous as wild oleander.

The aerospace industry dried up. The blocks of apartments that once housed Rocketdyne line workers became homes for Latino immigrants. The Rocketdyne building itself, a dinosaur of 1950s architecture, was used sparingly now, surrounded by fast-food restaurants and big-box electronics stores.

But Canoga Park was going through a rebirth of sorts, with its famous shopping mall on Topanga undergoing a major refurbish. High-end boutiques and a Nordstrom were cornerstones of the new place. Things were looking up, economically speaking.

Steve wanted to see it as a hopeful metaphor of his own career. Once promising, then a descent into the absolute Dumpster, now ready for a comeback. If he could just land a well-heeled client or two. Maybe a big white-collar CEO type. Right. They always came to the small-time solo operator like him.

The building that housed Steve's office came into view. A two-story corner job, it wasn't on the best part of the main drag. Across the street was a notorious strip mall that drew a lot of Steve's future clients—young thugs. They'd hang out at night in front of the coin laundry, under the red glow of the Chinese restaurant sign. *Pick Up or Dine In*, the sign said. Steve thought they should add a line—*Hang Out*. Because that's all people did over there—mostly unemployed, mostly Latino.

Mostly tired, Steve turned into the outdoor parking lot of his office building.

And almost ran over a chair. What was that all about? True, this wasn't the toniest address in town, but they didn't need junk all over the place. Maybe some of the homeless had—

Steve recognized the chair. One of his own. A secretarial chair with rollers that was rarely used, the main reason being he had no secretary.

At the far end of the lot was a collection of more furniture. Piled up in the corner of the gray cinderblock wall. And all of it from his office.

The jerk had evicted him.

Trembling with rage, Steve braked the Ark, jumped out, and stared at his desk, chairs, credenza, filing cabinets, bookcases. It wasn't everything, but enough for his Serbian landlord to make his point.

He saw himself grabbing a tire iron from the Ark's trunk and breaking some of the building's windows. Street justice. Maybe smash a door or two. Then he saw the tatters of his reputation and called Ashley.

His soon-to-be ex-wife—they had a month left on the mandatory wait—was the only one who might help him. She'd been there in the past. But he also knew that the thin thread that held them together was close to snapping.

"What's wrong, Steve?" That was the first thing out of her mouth.

"Why do you always assume something's wrong?"

"You only call when something's wrong."

"Not so."

"Then what is it?"

"Something's wrong," Steve said.

"Not funny."

"Not trying to be. He evicted me."

"Your apartment?"

"Office."

"Why?"

"Non-payment of rent, of course. But he didn't have to do it this way. I mean, the stuff is all over the parking lot."

"Steve, I'm sorry."

"I was wondering if I could borrow a little."

The pause on the other end was heavy, like a water-soaked blanket.

"Ashley?"

"I just can't."

"Why not?"

"You know why not."

"Oh what, you're going to bring up that enablement stuff?"

"It's not *stuff*. It's for your own good. The counselor even—"

"Don't bring up the counselor, please. I don't exactly have feelings for the guy who is the reason you filed."

"I filed because it was the only thing left for me. For us."

"I'm clean, Ashley. Over a year."

"I'm glad."

"Glad enough to stop this thing and try again?"

Another pause, heavier than the first.

"Ashley?"

"It's not going to happen, Steve. The sooner you accept that, the better it's going to be all around."

"Can't we at least just talk and—"

"No. Is there anything else? I've got a client I have to see."

The finality in her voice was like a hook, deep in fish guts, being ripped out. It almost took Steve's breath away.

He saw a young woman emerge from the back of the office building. She appeared to be looking for someone. He turned his back on her.

"I'm sitting here with half my office out on the street!" Steve said. "I need to get a trailer, get this stuff moved, get some money so I can convince the guy to let me back in. I'm maxed out on the cards, nothing in the bank. Nothing. I haven't even been paid by my client yet, and I'm almost through with the trial."

"Steve—"

"I'm a mess, Ashley, and you're the only one I ever had in my whole life who could put up with me. Can't we just—"

"*We're* a mess," she said. "We're not good for each other."

"I'm just asking"—he looked behind and saw the woman staring at him. She was early twenties, wore her copper-colored hair tightly back. Her black glasses and gray suit gave off a definite professional air. So why was she looking at him?—"for a loan, basically. And one dinner together. Just to talk. No pressure—"

"I can't do it, Steve. I can't forget what it was like. I tried that once and it bit me."

The time he stole a hundred dollars from her purse for a fix. He remembered that clearly. Bad, real bad. "Please—"

"Don't call me again, Steve. We've managed to settle amicably, and I want to keep it that way."

"Ashley, don't—"

She clicked off. Steve dropped his hands to his sides and bowed his head. Eyes closed, he tried to make his brain find a file marked *It'll Be Okay*. But it was gone. Snatched and tossed into the fire pit of lost hopes.

The woman in the parking lot said, "You're not Steve Conroy, are you?"

ABOUT THE AUTHOR

JAMES SCOTT BELL is the bestselling author of *Breach of Promise*, *Sins of the Fathers*, *Deadlock*, and several other thrillers. He is a winner of the Christy Award for Excellence, a fiction columnist for *Writer's Digest* magazine, and an adjunct professor of writing at Pepperdine University. He lives with his wife, Cindy, in Los Angeles.

Visit his website at www.jamesscottbell.com.

Deadlock

James Scott Bell

She is a Supreme Court Justice. She is an atheist. And she is about to encounter the God of the truth and justice she has sworn to uphold.

For years, Millicent Hollander has been the consistent swing vote on abortion and other hot-button issues. Now she's poised to make history as the first female Chief Justice of the United States Supreme Court. But something is about to happen that no one has counted on, least of all Hollander: a near-death experience that will thrust her on a journey toward God.

Skeptically, fighting every inch of the way, Hollander finds herself dragged toward belief in something she has never believed in—while others in Washington are watching her every step. Too much is at stake to let a Christian occupy the country's highest judicial office. Even as Hollander grapples with the interplay between faith and the demands of her position, and as she finds answers through her growing friendship with Pastor Jack Holden, a hidden web of lies, manipulation, and underworld connections is being woven around her. It could control her. It could destroy her reputation. Unless God intervenes, it could take her out of the picture permanently.

Softcover: 0310243882

Pick up a copy today at your favorite bookstore!

■ ZONDERVAN®
.com

Breach of Promise

James Scott Bell

How far will a father go to get back his only
daughter? And how will he survive in a legal
system that crushes those who can't afford
to fight back?

Mark Gillen has the storybook life other
men dream of, complete with a beautiful
wife and an adoring five-year-old daughter.

Then his wife announces she's leaving him. And taking their
daughter with her.

The other man is a famous film director with unlimited funds and
the keys to stardom and wealth for Paula. How can Mark begin to
compete? But the most bitter blow comes when he is kept from
seeing his daughter because of false charges . . . and a legal system
ill-suited for finding the truth.

Forged in the darkest valley Mark has ever walked through, his
faith in God may ultimately cost him everything in the eyes of the
family law system. But it is the one thing that can keep him sane—
and give him the strength to fight against all odds for what matters
most.

Softcover: 0310243874

Pick up a copy today at your favorite bookstore!

Sins of the Fathers

James Scott Bell

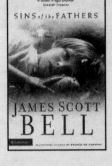

A parent's worst nightmare.
A lawyer's biggest challenge.
A young boy's life on the line.

The unimaginable has happened. A thir-
teen-year-old boy has fired a rifle into a
baseball game, killing several of the kids on
the field. Parents are devastated. The townspeople are horrified.

When public opinion swells to an enraged cry for justice, an ambitious deputy district attorney sees his opportunity—a sensational trial
that will catapult him into the D.A.'s office in the upcoming election.
There's just one obstacle: the boy's defense attorney, Lindy Field.

To all appearances, the case is a slam-dunk. Convict the killer,
make him pay. But it's not that simple. Lindy's young client is unwill-
ing—or unable—to help Lindy defend him. And as the case progresses,
it becomes clear that someone doesn't want the truth revealed.

As Lindy delves into the haunted world of her client's torment,
she finds a spiritual darkness that dredges up her own troubled past.
And when dangerous forces close in around her, Lindy must fight
for answers not only in the justice system, but in the very depths of
her soul.

Softcover: 0310253306

Pick up a copy today at your favorite bookstore!

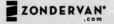
.com

Three ways to keep up on your favorite
Zondervan books and authors

Sign up for our *Fiction E-Newsletter*. Every month you'll receive sample excerpts from our books, sneak peeks at upcoming books, and chances to win free books autographed by the author.

You can also sign up for our *Breakfast Club*. Every morning in your email, you'll receive a five-minute snippet from a fiction or nonfiction book. A new book will be featured each week, and by the end of the week you will have sampled two to three chapters of the book.

Zondervan *Author Tracker* is the best way to be notified whenever your favorite Zondervan authors write new books, go on tour, or want to tell you about what's happening in their lives.

Visit *www.zondervan.com* and sign up today!

ZONDERVAN®

ZONDERVAN.com/
AUTHORTRACKER
follow your favorite authors